IN THUNDER
FORGED

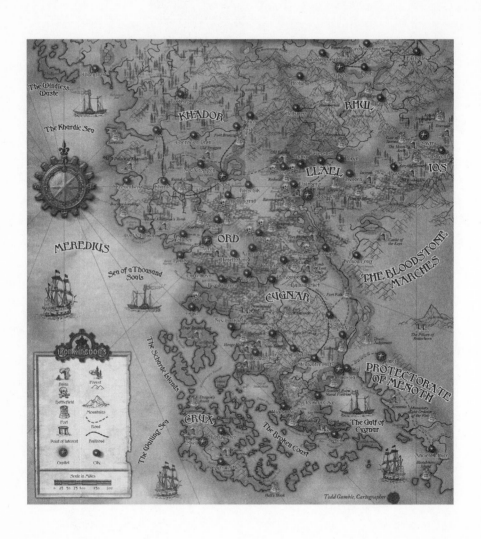

IRON KINGDOMS
CHRONICLES

IN THUNDER FORGED

THE FALL OF LLAEL: BOOK ONE

ARI MARMELL

an imprint of Prometheus Books
Amherst, NY

PRIVATEER

PRESS®

Published 2013 by Pyr®, an imprint of Prometheus Books

Matthew D. Wilson – Creator (Warmachine)

Jason Soles – Continuity Editor (Warmachine)

Warmachine Map by Todd Gamble © Privateer Press, Inc.

Cover illustration by Jon Sullivan and cover design by Nicole Sommer-Lecht

© Privateer Press, Inc.

Inquiries should be addressed to

Pyr

59 John Glenn Drive

Amherst, New York 14228–2119

VOICE: 716–691–0133 • FAX: 716–691–0137

WWW.PYRSF.COM

17 16 15 14 13   5 4 3 2 1

Library of Congress Cataloging-in-Publication Data

Marmell, Ari.

In Thunder Forged : Iron Kingdoms Chronicles : the Fall of Llael Book One / by Ari Marmell.

pages cm. — (Fall of Llael ; Book One)

ISBN 978-1-61614-773-0 (pbk.) • ISBN 978-1-61614-774-7 (ebook)

1. Imaginary wars and battles—Fiction. 2. Fantasy fiction. I. Title. II. Title: Iron Kingdoms Chronicles.

PS3613.A7666I5 2013

813'.6—dc23

2013002218

Printed in the United States of America

For George, mostly because she hasn't had one in a while; and for Colin, for saving me a metric buttload (equal to 0.85 of an Imperial buttload) of research.

FIRST REPORT

Glaceus 4th, 605 AR
Leryn, Llael

The casual observer might never even have known the nation was at war.

The sun had fallen off the world's edge more than an hour ago, and still the streets were, if not bustling, certainly a far cry from abandoned. Men and women scurried about their business, wrapped in gaudy coats and vibrant gowns against winter's insidious caress. Most were human, but the occasional fabric-swaddled figure, too short for the Ryn ethnic majority but too broad of shoulder for errant children, suggested a late-night dwarf. They tromped across a carpet of fresh snow, their finery gleaming in the radiance of wrought iron streetlamps. Some of those flickered with gas-fed flame, others with an alchemical luminescence far steadier yet somehow less comforting.

Each citizen nodded, curtsied, waved, or exchanged brief witticisms with the next, all dependent on the passerby's social status—or at least, the social status implied by the quality and cleanliness of his attire. Voices swirled overhead, blown by the winds, kicked into flurries almost choral in their harmonies. One might have overheard discussion of the Lord Regent Glabryn's latest scandals, the squabbling amongst the Council of Nobles, the winner of last week's derby, or the recent performance of Oswinne Muir's newest opus, *An Orgoth Goes a'Courting*.

One would *not* have heard mention of the expanding western front, of the shadow of Khador slowly darkening the face of Llael. One would have seen nobody acknowledge the brittle edge to jests, the tremor in the laughter, or the occasional reverberating *clang* from beyond the outer walls, the ponderous step of a patrolling warjack.

No one spoke of the war. No one acknowledged their fears.

It would have been gauche.

One particular couple, elbows intertwined, shuffled quickly, seemingly eager to catch the misty plumes they exhaled with every breath. He was regal, buttoned up tight in high-collared greatcoat atop an emerald vest, his iron-gray hair swept back in a style that not only *acknowledged* the receding hair-line, but haughtily dared anyone to comment on it.

She was wrapped in brilliant scarlet and gleaming gold, a beacon as radiant as any of the streetlamps. A fox-fur stole was her only concession to the nighttime chill. Hair the hue of a lion's pelt fell in perfectly curled ringlets around a face that was *just* too round to be called classically "patrician."

She was also, at best, half the gentleman's age. That, along with the fact that she gazed at him adoringly with eyes like dark-brewed ale when she wasn't busy laughing at his witticisms, might have gone a long way toward explaining his obvious fervor to reach their destination.

They drifted past several structures, each boasting a magnificent façade of stately columns and arched windows—all deliberate modern echoes of the architecture of centuries past. And then they arrived, ducking through one deep doorway to stand in a hall of lush carpeting and glowing chandeliers. Some herbal treatment of the fixtures—or, perhaps, of the pipes, or the gas itself?—imbued the burning fumes with a vaguely floral aroma.

The gentleman beamed, even puffing his chest out, at the dazzled coo wafting from his companion's lips. "This is just a taste," he offered. "The actual amenities are even more impressive. My suite occupies a full half of the fifth floor."

"I can hardly wait to see it," she said in a breathy tone. His own breath caught in his throat, as he wondered if her offhand comment might suggest what he hoped it did. Placing his free hand on the slender arm resting in the crook of his elbow, he led her toward, and then up, the sweeping stairs.

"Goodman Tolamos," she began right around the third floor.

"Please, please. 'Lyrran,' dear Garland, by all means."

"Lyrran," she corrected, paying for his given name with another heart-stopping smile. "I don't think I quite understand . . . This place is marvelous, but why keep an apartment? Surely a man of your success and your means could afford a home—an estate!—of your own?"

"I could," Lyrran admitted. They'd reached the fourth floor, now, and he struggled to hold up his end of the conversation *and* continue walking without sucking in ragged gasps between. *Not as young as you used to be, old fool.*

Then, with another glance at Garland's upturned face, *And you're going to need your strength . . .*

"I could," he repeated after what he hoped was a discreet wheeze. "But I often spend late nights in my workshop, and I'm no great admirer of the dormitories the Crucible makes available. I decided that living within a few minutes' walk of Thunderhead was worth the inconvenience of dwelling in a building I don't own."

Of course, had I known then that the only deluxe suite available was on the fifth bloody floor . . . !

They stepped from the landing, Lyrran again leading, and stopped at a massive door of hardwood, intricately inlaid with abstract leaf patterns.

"Just a moment, my dear."

Lyrran tugged a small chain, setting off the faintest tinkling beyond. The butler—a tall, thin, dark-haired fellow who more or less resembled every other butler the world over—had barely opened the door before his master was whispering instructions. The manservant glanced over at the woman, back at his employer. Then, with neither expression nor gesture, he squeezed past them and headed, at a stately saunter, toward the staircase.

"He keeps a small private chamber on an upper floor," Lyrran explained. "And my other servants rarely work this late. We should be able to converse undisturbed."

"Oh, my. Goodman Tolamos, do you feel that's entirely proper?"

"I . . . Ah, I . . ."

"Your man is discreet, at least?"

"Of course!" Lyrran hoped he didn't sound as relieved as he felt.

"Well, that's all right then, isn't it?" Garland breezed past him with a faint giggle. "Wine?" she asked.

"My dear, please! I'm your host, you should allow me to—"

"Nonsense! Sit, rest. I'll be just a moment." Then, her voice slightly more distant, "Um, perhaps two moments, then. My, this is a big place . . ."

Lyrran briefly wondered if the entire magical evening had been a setup so he might be robbed—then shrugged, shut the door, and lowered himself carefully into an old leather chair. He was in no position to stop her if she *were* a thief; too tired to chase her, and though he carried a double-barreled holdout in his vest, he couldn't *imagine* shooting the woman . . .

Still, he breathed a silent lungful of relief what she reappeared, a wine goblet in each hand. "No trouble finding anything?" he asked, half-amused, half-chiding.

"Oh, no! Your home is laid out so sensibly, I felt like I knew where to look for everything!"

Lyrran smiled and accepted the libation. "To Llael," he offered, raising his goblet—the closest he meant to come, tonight, to acknowledging the war.

"To Llael."

Hmm. The gentleman suppressed a scowl as the wine washed over his tongue. *She may have found everything, but she doesn't remotely know how to choose a proper vintage! This has almost gone bad . . .*

"But then," Garland was saying as she daintily wiped at her own lips with a kerchief, "I suppose you'd *have* to be meticulously organized, working with all those awful tinctures and powders and whatnot. I don't imagine you'd want to grab the wrong one of *those*!"

"No," Lyrran agreed with a chuckle. "You *really* wouldn't."

"For instance," Garland continued, "can you imagine if I'd chosen the wrong powder to mix in your wine? Or just dropped in a pinch too many? Why, you could be dying right now, instead of just growing sleepy. That would be a tragedy, wouldn't it?"

"I . . . What?" Why was his tongue suddenly so thick, as though it wore its own winter coat? He blinked, and now not only were there two Garlands, but they—and the room around them—ran like a wet watercolor.

"Now, then," Garland said, "we haven't a great deal of time, have we?" Hiking up her skirts so she could sit, she settled in Lyrran's lap. The old alchemist knew he should be excited by that—would have been, only a few moments before—but he was having trouble remembering *why*.

"So," she continued, tapping a finger almost playfully against his lips and peering into his blinking, unfocused eyes. "Before you're off on your little snooze and forget that this entire evening ever happened, let's discuss Thunderhead Fortress. And the Golden Crucible.

"And, if you happen to have made the fellow's acquaintance, a gentleman by the name of Idran di Meryse . . ."

***

This time, Garland stepped alone into the light flurries, her stole wrapped tight about her chest and shoulders. She'd never have admitted it aloud, but she was grateful that the morrecaine salts had proven so efficacious. A small minority of people proved resistant to the stuff, and Lyrran Tolamos was a nice enough man. She'd have found it unpleasant to extract his knowledge the hard way.

All was well, though, or at least as well as could be hoped. The alchemist lay at home, bound and snoring rather than whimpering and bleeding, and Garland was out in the cold, prepared to break into the single most fortified structure in this heavily fortified city.

Again she smiled or waved or nodded to those she passed, though it had grown late enough that pedestrians were scarce. The night drifted in silence, save for those same mechanical footsteps occasionally ringing in the distance, or the crack of small ice floes along the banks of the Oldwick.

Garland checked the sky, even though she knew she'd find no guidance there. Between the bulk of Mount Borgio, blocking out a broad slice of the heavens, and the lowering clouds obscuring the rest, she was more likely to spot a lurking ghost than any star.

She knew her way; no hesitation showed in her stride. Still, for all she'd studied Leryn's streets, she *was* a newcomer here. She'd have preferred the stars to confirm her course.

Then the gusting breeze thickened, not merely with the stinging cold, but the biting, eye-watering stink of the Rynyr Red and the sharp tang of spent blasting powder. Garland couldn't help but smirk. *Where even the stars and the heavens fail, trust in the absolute worst stench you can imagine.*

Garland rounded a final corner and stared into what might almost have been another world.

The bulk of Leryn—indeed, much of Llael entire—was designed for form as devoutly as function. Sharp spires, magnificent archways and flying buttresses, columns of marble and walls of rounded brick, festooned with wreaths and snapping banners, all meant to draw the eye as much as to repel the weather. Llaelese architecture was, for the most part, not merely a science but an art.

Then there was Thunderhead Fortress.

A fat, drab toad, the citadel squatted in the center of the rock garden that was Leryn. Blockish, ugly, short, heavy, and standing out like a troll in an elven finishing school, Thunderhead boasted a façade that not even an architect could love.

It was also the heart of Leryn's military power and, quite arguably, of scientific advancement throughout all of Western Immoren.

And would be guarded accordingly.

Nearer the fortress, the snow darkened from off-white to ugly gray, painted, polluted, and plagued by the thick fumes of the installation's many smokestacks. The faint crunching under Garland's feet transformed into a discomfiting squelch. Steadily, casually, she strode past Thunderhead Fortress, waving cheerfully to soldiers marching atop the wall or standing post in the recessed gateways.

A few nodded back. Most made no reply at all. But all watched with professional vigilance until she'd passed them by.

As she'd heard, then. The Crucible Guard were not to be taken lightly.

Officially, these men and women were a security force loyal to the Golden Crucible, protecting the alchemists and their works, at home or abroad. *Unofficially*, albeit quite openly, they were Leryn's private army. When Khador had advanced beyond Llael's borders, when their hidden operatives assassinated most of the local mages—including a few of the nation's already scarce warcasters—the Crucible Guard became one of the final hopes of the nation entire.

On the one hand, then, she needn't deal with very many of them; not when the bulk of their forces were deployed across the city or at the front, their explosive elixirs and expertly engineered firearms scattering the enemy like toys, their alchemical tinctures bringing relief to the wounded. On the other, those who *did* remain, standing sentinel for the heart of the Golden Crucible, were far more formidable than the average watchman.

She saw rifles and other long guns above, heavy armor and seemingly heavier pistols below; and those were only the *visible* accoutrements. Morrow alone knew how many hidden blades they might have stashed, or what sorts of herbs and elixirs might keep them swift and alert after long hours of vigil. No, these Crucible Guard were prepared to repel a small army, let alone a single intruder.

Then again, armies are a bit rubbish at sneaking, *aren't they?*

Several streets from the fortress, Garland ducked into a narrow throughway. In defiance of the cold, she unlaced her bodice and stepped out of her gown. The flimsy silken blouse thus exposed was to be expected; the trousers of lightweight, rust-brown canvas rather less so.

Next she delved into the heap of fabric that had, a moment before, been the skirts of her gown. From one of several large pockets sewn within, she drew tunic, gloves, and soft boots of that same canvas, and slipped them on. From a second, she removed two tiny ceramic vials. Finally, she wadded the skirt into a rough bundle and turned the fox-fur stole inside out to reveal a coarse woven backing. After checking to make certain she knew which vial was which— wouldn't do at all to get *those* confused!—she settled down, hunched in the shadows of the alley.

Now it was just a matter of waiting. Hopefully not for *too* long; it was bloody *freezing* out here!

***

Caje hated the midnight delivery.

Yeah, yeah, he understood *why* it was necessary. Thunderhead was the greatest producer of blasting powder in Western Immoren, and now Llael was at war, that portion of the operation ran day and night. At any hour of the clock, wagons of refined powder trundled out, other wagons of red powder, black powder, and various components clattered in. All absolutely necessary.

He understood all that. He really did.

But why the hell am I *always the guy stuck making it?*

The frosty conditions and long hours must have weighed on the young driver even worse than usual tonight. He'd halted, briefly, to let Dondy and Nosli catch their breath, shake the snow from their manes and tails and dappled coats—and had fallen asleep, Morrow help him!

It had only been for a few minutes—he could tell by the powdery accumulation on the seat beside him, and on the canvas tarp covering the wagon-load of unprocessed Rynyr Red powder—but that was a few minutes too long. He could lose his position if the Crucible found out; hell, he might even face charges! The malodorous mineral, once refined, was a vital component of blasting powder—which technically made every delivery, no matter how routine and mundane, a military matter. If anyone had caught him, if the backstreets weren't so empty this late at night . . .

"Yah!" A quick snap of the reins, followed by two longsuffering equine snorts from Dondy and Nosli, and the wagon resumed rattling and clumping over snow-dusted pavers.

At the portcullis of alchemically-hardened iron, he was met by two men in ornate armor and armed with locharns—brutal pole-arms with a long slashing blade at one end, a heavy bludgeon on the other. The armor's gothic inlays, and the brightly-dyed fabric that concealed the mail at the joints, might have fooled some into believing it—and the guards—purely ceremonial.

Ceremonial. Right. Caje knew a *whole* lot better.

"Factory delivery," he announced, hoping they'd take the heaviness in his words for boredom rather than lingering traces of sleep. As always, the guards studied him unflinchingly from broad-visored helms and demanded a sequence of pass-phrases, all of which he dutifully offered.

"Cargo?" This from the leftmost sentinel, casually stepping forward.

"Rynyr Red, unprocessed."

The guardsman flipped back the canvas to expose the coarse grit, shifting heaps of powder, and unbroken crystalline chunks. Caje felt his eyes begin to water and his stomach churn with the rotten odor; the damn stuff made more traditional red powders positively *appetizing*!

The armsman grunted something that might or might not have been related to an actual word, let the tarp fall, and waved at his partner. The second soldier, in turn, called to someone beyond the gate.

A hiss of steam, the clatter of well-oiled chain, and the heavy bars retracted into the stone above.

Caje drove through the heavy shadow of the barbican. A few quick turns along pebbled pathways, another exchanged pass phrase or two, and he finally halted his vehicle inside a large open structure, part stable and part warehouse.

Dondy and Nosli he dealt with immediately, unhitching the roans from their traces and rubbing them down with a gentle yet efficient touch. Then, lips pressed together in bitter distaste, he glared at the wagon full of red powder, the small wooden compartment into which he was supposed to empty that powder, and the heavy spades that he had gradually come to despise as tools of Thamar, the Dark Twin, herself.

"Bugger this!" he declared emphatically—presumably to the horses, since the guards outside certainly weren't likely to hear him. "I'm getting me something to drink first." And with a final poisonous sneer at the shovels, he stomped from the storehouse to do precisely that.

***

The heap of unprocessed powder shifted beneath the tarp, bulging in tiny dunes. Garland crawled, gasping and gagging, from beneath the canvas. She lowered herself to the floor—that is, tumbled headfirst from the back of the wagon, much to the puzzlement of two tired horses—and barely had the strength to drag herself of sight behind the wheels. She yanked a hood of fox fur from her head, and then bent every iota of strength and training toward *not* choking out her lungs or vomiting everything she'd eaten in the past week.

Her tools had done their jobs admirably enough. The canvas bodysuit kept the astringent grit from irritating her skin; the tiny puff of sleeping gas had put the driver out long enough for her to bury herself in his cargo; and the thick reagent with which she'd drenched the inside of her stole, before pulling it over her head, had served well enough as a filter that she'd been able to breathe.

Sort of.

She was lucky, *damn* lucky, that the driver had wandered off before unloading. Her plan had been to knock him out again if he'd discovered her, but in her current state, she wasn't certain that she could best an irate gopher two falls out of three.

Finally, once she'd wrangled her rebellious stomach and lungs back under control, she slid from underneath the wagon, reached back into the powder, and extracted the bundle that had once been a fancy gown. Again she ducked under the cart and unrolled her prize. The fabric was damaged beyond repair, but it had done what it had to: It had protected the goodies still stashed throughout several internal pockets.

Garland took a moment, thanking Morrow that full, layered skirts were the current fashion. One could practically fit an entire household in the bloody things, if one had the skill to attach the inner pockets and didn't mind walking a little funny.

From within she produced more tightly folded cloth, this time in drab brown. A simple smock and leggings, it was just the sort of thing one might see on any menial servant. She peeled the canvas from her body, careful not to smear any of the clinging powder on herself, and slithered into her third outfit of the evening. Lastly, she withdrew a pouch, which she clipped to her waist, and a pair of leather bracers—each loaded with a few useful surprises—that slid on beneath her sleeves.

The ruined canvas and savaged skirts found their final resting place a few inches beneath the dirt floor, where the constant passage of wagons had turned up enough earth that nobody would notice signs of a shallow excavation. Finally, Garland was just another servant, running some late-night errand through the grounds of Thunderhead.

It took only a moment to orient herself, thanks to the knowledge she'd gleaned from her drugged alchemist admirer. The central keep, a ponderous block of stone, made for an effective polestar. She wished briefly that her objective actually lay within that primary structure—the military museum occupying much of the lower levels was supposed to be among the most complete in all five Iron Kingdoms.

Ah, well. *Stick to business, love.*

Within the outer ramparts was a campus of additional buildings, huddling like nervous children around the skirts of the inner keep. Most were, like the fortress itself, squat, ugly things: stone constructions of little aesthetic value, rarely more than two stories in height.

Made sense, she supposed. While some were mere warehouses, or dormitories for the use of on-site apprentices and those alchemists involved in late-running experiments, others contained personal laboratories and workstations, along with umpteen storage chambers for all manner of volatile powders and sensitive reagents.

When almost any accident, then, could lead to fire, explosion, or fiery explosion, buildings of any real height—and thus vulnerable to collapse—would prove an unwise choice indeed.

The pebble-paved walkways between those buildings, which had been built at need and not according to any preplanned design, were as twisted and random as any maze. And while the buildings weren't *identical*, they were not only remarkably similar in overall build, but unlabeled to boot. A stranger could, unguided, spend *days* wandering aimlessly without stumbling across the precise structure she wanted.

As it was, thanks to Lyrran's slurred directions, it only took about two hours.

She encountered a smattering of other servants and laborers on her way, most fully intent on their own errands. She passed by wandering guards as well, half of whom ignored her, half of whom demanded pass phrases proving her right to be there. Fortunately, while they'd never have gotten her through the main gate, Lyrran's codes held up within the walls. By the time she reached her destination—tired, shivering, reeking of the chemical smoke drifting constantly across the campus—she'd regained her full confidence that she could pull this off.

Through the heavy door (locked—but thanks to a few quick prods with the tools she kept in her pouch, not for long); along a hallway of drably institutional beige and gray, lined with nigh identical chambers; up a single flight of stairs; and there it was. Third door on the left.

The personal workroom of senior alchemist and vile betrayer, one Idran di Meryse.

This door, too, was firmly locked. It was also, Garland realized as her first lockpick was snapped in half by something that chimed within the casing, mechanically warded against tampering.

With a soft sigh—she'd hoped to leave no hard evidence of her presence—she produced another ceramic vial from her pouch. Twisting her face away until her neck protested with a loud pop, she poured the contents over the lock.

Then, once the potent acid had done its job and there *was* no lock anymore, she pushed the door open and slipped inside.

If she'd been asked to sketch her idea of an alchemist's laboratory, she'd have produced a close rendition of what lay before her now. A forge sat in the far corner of the lengthy chamber, ready to melt metals, burn herbs, and what have you. Between it and her huddled several slab-like tables. Some held beakers and alembics, some racks of tubes and jars of colorful powders, some a wide array of tools whose uses Garland could only begin to guess. Quills and paper lay scattered all over, for the jotting down of notes no matter where they might manifest; a variety of burns and stains across every available surface suggested that some reagents had not reacted as anticipated.

The obvious spots—drawers, cabinets, the stacks of notes, even the books on a small shelf along the leftmost wall—she searched almost unwillingly. No chance di Meryse would actually keep her prize anywhere so obvious, but she had to be thorough, had to be certain.

That done, she scoured the room for more creative hiding places. She looked under the tables, between the cushions and the frames of various stools, even under the charcoal in the forge. Finally, built into the rear of the bookcase, a sliding panel revealed a hidden compartment.

But not what she'd hoped to find within.

A single envelope, wax-sealed and addressed only with a large G, sat within the hollow. Teeth grinding, she removed it and cracked it open.

Lady Garland,

Really, what do you take me for? After our discussions took such an unpleasant turn, why would you believe that I would leave the formulae anywhere you might think to look? I do hope you did not unduly harm anyone while effecting your illegal entry.

Rest assured, the documentation is quite safe—from harm, from discovery, and from you. It is not on me, and I shall be going nowhere near it, so even if we should cross paths, do not think to follow me.

You know my price, and you can imagine how eager certain other parties would be to acquire such a prize. May I humbly suggest, then, that you cease wasting time you do not have, and instead set about gathering some funds?

Sincerely yours,

I.

PS: I have made arrangements, if anything should happen to me, to send the documents to the aforementioned other parties. Just in case you were contemplating expressing your displeasure upon my person.

PPS: Whatever bargain we eventually make, you owe me an additional one-hundred-and-twenty goldheads for the lock.

Garland whiled away several long minutes swearing in a manner not merely unladylike, but terribly unprofessional. All the work, the risk, the sheer misery of infiltrating Thunderhead . . . Just so the bastard could taunt her. *Again.*

It had been wise of the alchemist, she admitted grudgingly, to safeguard himself against retaliation. Had the option remained open, she very well *might* have arranged for a suitably painful "accident."

Garland cracked open the door, making certain the hallway remained empty, and ventured out. It was a struggle, holding herself to a casual pace; she needed to be outside the fortress walls before anyone noticed the melted lock. With every step, new profanities resounded in her head, even if she now refrained from giving them voice.

She had a *lot* of thinking to do—but it required no thought at all to recognize that she, the mission, and quite possibly her country were in very serious trouble.

***

Even *more* trouble, she learned some short while later, than she'd initially thought.

Exiting Thunderhead had proved far simpler than entering. The Crucible Guard weren't particularly concerned with people *leaving* the installation, and while sending a servant outside the walls at this time of night was abnormal, it wasn't unheard of. After a perfunctory exchange, the portcullis had slid upward and she'd been ushered on her way.

Nor had anyone questioned her presence among the suites and apartments of the rich and powerful, despite her new lower-class garb, considering how many servants said rich and powerful employed.

No, it was only as she returned to the fifth floor and neared Tolamos's door that she discovered her night wasn't done going wrong.

Although it had been pulled to, the door hung loose in its frame. Splinters bristled in a starburst pattern where the bolts had been kicked free of the wood. Mangled as the latch was, Garland saw enough fresh scratches in the brass to suggest that the intruders, whoever they were, had tried to pick the thing before resorting to more direct methods.

A quick flick of both wrists, and the springs in her leather bracers replied with a joyful *snap*. A razor-edged blade now jutted several inches past her right fist, and the fingers of her left hand clenched the smooth handle of a dusky, snub-nosed pistol.

Silent as a snake on silk, she swept from room to room, alert for even the slightest hint of an *intention* of movement.

She found none. Whoever they were, they'd come and gone, leaving a wake of devastation that might have been the envy of a twelve-pound cannonball. Drawers and cabinets hung open, their contents tumbling in miniature avalanches across heavily trampled carpet. Furniture had been smashed apart, paintings torn from walls, shelves tipped over. Wines, inks, and colognes formed abstract patterns, their combined odors a miasma that might have been stomach-turning had Garland not recently experienced far worse.

The more portable valuables she'd noted her first time here—gold furnishings, jewelry, some fancy clothes—were conspicuously absent. All in all, it looked very much like a burglary.

To Garland, it looked *too much* like a burglary.

The damage was a touch too deliberate, too extensive. Beyond even that, the idea that some random crime would occur in *just* this suite on *just* this night was too ludicrous to seriously consider.

No burglary, this, but something costumed as one.

Garland crossed back across the suite, bits of wood and glass crunching beneath her. Only now, certain that no enemy lurked in wait, did she slide her weapons back into their sheaths and look in on the old alchemist.

"Oh, damn . . ."

Lyrran Tolamos hadn't enjoyed a pleasant end. Deep bruises and shallow gashes mottled his flesh. Dried blood traced a rough map from the corners of his lips, his slack jaw displayed multiple missing teeth, and even a cursory examination revealed a variety of broken bones.

Again, a beating that *could* have occurred in the course of a robbery—but hadn't. Garland could only hope that the lingering effects of her drug had dulled the pain and the fear of his last moments.

She hadn't particularly known the man; hell, she'd been prepared to force some information out of him herself, if need be! Still, she couldn't quite suppress a swell of guilt.

"If I brought this on you," she whispered to the broken body, "I'm so sorry."

What had they wanted from him? Information on the Golden Crucible? On Garland's own activities? Had they gotten what they were after? How long had they been watching him—or *her*? How badly might her mission, her identity, have been compromised?

The only question Garland *didn't* ask herself was "Who?" Of *that* answer, she had a disturbingly good idea. Swift, brutal, and impossibly well-informed . . .

Khadoran intelligence. Leryn's been infiltrated by Khadoran bloody intelligence!

Section Three, most probably; this seemed a bit far from the Khadoran border to fall under the purview of the more domestically-focused Prizak Chancellery. No, she couldn't be positive, but it seemed probable—and it was certainly the worst-case scenario. If Section Three *were* onto her, if they had even the slightest inkling of her mission, she couldn't put it off any longer. Garland had really wanted to complete the assignment on her own. But now?

Now it was time to scream for help and, for the sake of king and country, pray to Morrow that she hadn't left it too late.

Glaceus 7th, 605 AR
Several leagues south of Clocker's Cove, Cygnar

The vanguard of the pirate flotilla swarmed over the open shore.

Longboats, steel crenellations bolted to the hull to offer the crew protected fields of fire, sliced through choppy surf to fetch up on the sands. Each disgorged over a dozen men. Cutlasses and war-axes, most mundane, a few vibrating in time with some internal mechanism, occupied many fists. Heavy pistols, blunderbusses, and the occasional harpoon gun filled the rest. Boots and the tails of a few greatcoats carved patterns in wet sand, and the cries of bloody-minded men drowned out the crashing waves.

Farther up the beach stood one of four separate command positions, recently occupied, ready to defend this stretch of barren coastline. A contingent of soldiers—numbering fewer than two dozen—crouched behind makeshift fortifications of packed sand and iron shields, staring down the gullet of the oncoming horde. Heavy leathers, brass-hued cuirasses, and deep blue coats all sported the Cygnus—the golden swan of noble Cygnar.

"Hold . . ." This from a severe-looking, cinnamon-complexioned brunette, her officer's coat hanging open over scarred and battered armor. One hand pressed a spyglass to her right eye; the other was wrapped about the haft of a heavy carbine. "Hold . . ."

Hold they did, these men and women of the 4th Platoon, 7th Division, Second Cygnaran Army. Only the occasional creak of palms on weapons and the shifting of feet in sand belied their stoic façade.

Finally, Sergeant Benwynne Bracewell lowered the spyglass and turned. Far behind, atop the most distant and largest of the command positions, she saw the faintest flash of a green-tinted lantern.

She nodded, then, to the man beside her. "We have the lieutenant's permission. Give the go signal."

He, in turn, flipped a switch on a peculiar iron tripod, roughly half his own height. The result was a burst of steam, and a whistle so piercing it could have been heard a mile off. From both sides, she heard similar whistles of varying pitch, as the other two squads went active as well.

The beach erupted before the sound had faded.

Halfway between Bracewell's command position and the advancing pirates, a series of sand-hued canvas tarps were flung aside to waft away in the ocean breeze. From a wood-and-iron reinforced trench emerged over a hundred men, bristling with barrels of steel. Swiveling on iron posts dug deep into the ground, chain guns screamed their pent-up fury, multiple barrels blending into a single, constant note. The air before them turned to lead, and freebooters disintegrated into chunky stains.

Stationed behind the chain gun crews, long gunners cranked the cylinders on repeating rifles, picking off lone targets beyond the range of the automatic weapons, or crouched behind the fortified landing craft. Additional trenchers hefted bell-barreled scatterguns, ready to greet any foes who managed to win through the opening barrage.

Pirates dropped prone beneath the field of fire and returned salvos of their own. Despite the murderous efficiency of the chain guns, over half the initial landing party survived to take cover. Still and all, had that been the entirety of the invading force, and repelling them the Cygnarans' primary objective, the battle would have already been decided.

It wasn't.

Hundreds of yards offshore, pirate brigandines came ponderously about, turning broadside to the beach. Sails whipped and rippled while great paddle-wheels belched steam and propelled the ships against the prevailing winds. Ports clacked open, heavy guns protruded at an almost obscene slither. Thunder roared, and Cygnaran soldiers flew or fled from erupting craters.

A second wave of landing craft bounced over the whitecaps, and this time not all of them were longboats. Several broad, flat-bottomed barges crunched against the shore, becoming mobile piers, and from them marched titans of iron and smoke.

Nearly ten feet in height, they were only vaguely humanoid. From an almost spherical torso protruded a narrow waist, piston-driven legs, and spindly arms, one grasping an oversized harpoon, the other a massive scattergun. From their backs, protruding smokestacks blackened the surrounding air. An almost demonic visage, wrought in the iron of the thing's "chest," glowed with the fury of internal fires.

Nor were these the only surprises the reavers had in store. From beneath the surf crawled another metallic monstrosity, taller and heavier by far than the others. A trio of chimneys belched sickening fumes, produced by engines that drove legs capable of crushing men flat. The maw of a cannon gaped at the end of the thing's left arm, while it wielded a full-sized ship's anchor in its right fist as readily as its human compatriots swung their cutlasses.

From the soldiers in the trenches the cry arose, though surely even those farthest from the line could see for themselves. "*Warjacks!*"

"Well," Sergeant Bracewell muttered, "took them long enough." She flinched, turning her head from the shrapnel as a cannonball detonated closer to her command position than she'd have preferred.

"Isn't the navy supposed to be doing something about those?" someone asked in a voice that might have come from a pipe-smoking rock-crusher.

Bracewell shrugged at the man next to her. An older fellow, his sun-leathered face hidden behind a graying beard trimmed *just* short enough not to violate regulations, he wore an array of heavy tools on a belt around his waist, and a bandolier of pistols across his chest. Other than his eyes, protected by a pair of goggles, his face was smeared with the ambient ash and soot.

"You just stand ready to do your job, Master Sergeant," she told him. "The boys know how to do theirs."

Wendell Habbershant, chief field mechanik to Bracewell's squad, replied with a disdainful snort that, she was sure, must have proved painful in the brackish sea air. "Always assume incompetence, Sergeant. You'll be disappointed less often."

And then, a moment later, "That Mariner's getting awfully close, don't you think?" He waved idly at the largest of the enemy machines, currently advancing on the first of the Cygnaran entrenched positions.

"It is," she admitted. "I'm just waiting for—There!"

Again manmade thunder sounded over the gulf, but not from the enemy batteries. Barely visible from the command post, a steam-driven ironhull hove into view, accompanied by a small flotilla of more traditional galleons, all proudly flying the blue-and-gold. Their shells landed somewhat short of the pirate vessels—the Cygnaran ships weren't quite in range—but it certainly got their attention. The brigandine crews instantly turned their efforts, and their guns, to the new and nearer threat, abandoning their bombardment of the beach.

Benwynne took a quick breath, allowing herself—as she always did—a single instant of personal regret before battle. No warcaster, she; never had been, for all her attempts, and never would be. Whatever talent for magic ran in the blood of those rare few was utterly lacking in hers. She would never experience the mental and emotional bond between those peculiar wizards and their not-quite-living companions.

But for all that, like other so-called 'jack-marshals, she was trained well enough, practiced enough, experienced enough, to know that she could make herself understood despite the distance and the apocalyptic cacophony of the battle.

"Wolfhound . . ." Her voice rang out over the battlefield, and she knew it would be heard, and obeyed, by more than merely human ears. "Target Mariner; all other priorities secondary. Deploy!"

Again a slab of beach bulged and fell aside, but this was no array of entrenched soldiers who appeared from within the storm of grit. Behind and to the left of the advancing enemy rose a warjack all but dwarfed by the Mariner itself. Smaller even than the lighter 'jacks that had come across on the barges, it held the same hunched posture as the larger. Rather than the brass-and-iron of the pirate machine, this 'jack was matte-darkened steel. It boasted a single smokestack to the Mariner's three; a broad-bladed axe in place of the anchor; and a cannon far narrower, but far longer, than the bulky weapon carried by the heavier warjack.

Wolfhound raised that barrel and fired. An alchemically hardened shell arced over the battlefield and plunged into the Mariner's back just beneath the central stack, punching through the outer armor like it was plywood.

An enormous spent casing snapped from the breach to land with a faint *whump* beside Wolfhound's steel feet.

The larger iron beast staggered to one knee, belching smoke, fire, and fluids from its brand new orifice. With pistons roaring and gears grinding it began to rise, leveraging itself up using the anchor as a crutch, and raised its own cannon in retort.

Benwynne didn't plan on letting it engage.

"Shepherd! Bulldog! Deploy!"

Two more warjacks burst from pits in the beach, their boilers flaring from a bare simmer to a conflagration, smoke now belching skyward. Unlike Wolfhound, these were of more traditional Cygnaran design: Both displayed harsher lines and angles, chassis in blue and gold rather than dull steel, a pair of smoking chimneys and mechanical faces as sharp as a heavy plow or the cattle-catcher on a train.

Only in their armament did they differ: Bulldog sported a terrifyingly large warhammer in one hand, a double emplacement of light cannon in place of the other; Shepherd a chain gun and spiked, reinforced shield.

Raining grit, Shepherd opened up on the smaller 'jacks, some of whom were moving to reinforce the Mariner. Bulldog unloaded both barrels on the heavier warjack until the weapon's magazine ran dry, the barrage punctuated by intermittent shots from Wolfhound's long gun.

"Do you have *any* idea," Wendell asked bitterly, "how hard it is to clean sand out of those joints?"

Even as it shuddered under the new impacts, the Mariner discharged its own cannon. Wolfhound, pounding across the shoreline far more swiftly and steadily than any other 'jack could manage on the shifting terrain, easily cleared the line of fire. Swerving as it charged, the Hunter-class warjack closed the distance and burst through a rank of enemy pirates, bring its axe around in a mighty arc.

Shaking, spitting embers and ever-filthier smoke, the heavy warjack finally collapsed.

Benwynne swept her spyglass across the battlefield one last time. Wendell's cynicism notwithstanding, the other two squads fighting alongside hers had damn well *better* do their jobs, harrying the pirates from both flanks. Otherwise, this was never going to work.

"Master Sergeant, signal your team. I want Wolfhound and Bulldog reloaded. Bulldog, you're shielding Wolfhound while he resupplies, then swap out! Shepherd, I need an open path from here to the shore."

Raising her voice, shouting over the renewed roar of the chain guns—not merely Shepherd's, but the entrenched positions' as well—"Corporal Gaust! You're up!"

"Finally!" Several figures moved from the rear of Benwynne's post. "Thought you'd forgotten about us."

"Just remember your assignment, Corporal. No showboating."

"Have I *ever* lost track of an objective, Sergeant?"

"Do you mean so far this month," Wendell muttered under his breath, "or . . . ?"

"Corporal, *go.*"

Half a dozen soldiers, shoulders hunched, pounded for the shoreline at a dead sprint. The bulk of them were clad in leathers reinforced with riveted plates, armored like most other soldiers on the field, but the man who led them sported a flowing coat and tricorne hat; they almost made him resemble a pirate captain himself, save that both displayed the official navy blue fabric and golden trim.

Even as they ran, Benwynne cursed under her breath. She'd much have preferred to station them closer to the waterline, hidden like the trenchers had been. Unfortunately, they'd had no way of knowing precisely where the cleanest path to the water would appear, or when, or whether they'd have been taken out by a stray shot from the ships before it was time to move. She hated making them run the length of the field, but . . .

"All right, ladies and gentlemen! Let's give them some cover!" Hefting her carbine, Sergeant Bracewell broke from her position and opened fire, her escort following behind.

***

Atherton Gaust, corporal in the Second Cygnaran Army, scarcely felt the stinging grit in the air, the briny aura of the sea, even the shells and bullets pounding the world around him. No, as he ran, coat and untraditionally long blond hair trailing behind him, the only thing the wiry soldier felt was *eager*.

It'd been a long time since they'd thrown him a battle like this one.

Which did *not* mean, by any stretch of the imagination, that he wasn't paying attention.

"Jack, left flank!"

Like three parts of a single clockwork mechanism, a trio of the commandoes produced metal spheres from their belts, and hurled them underhand. Two of the grenades landed at the feet of the harpoon-wielding warjack; the third bounced off its shoulder and had fallen halfway to the ground when all three detonated.

Atherton didn't stop to see if the warjack was out of action. It was down, and his team was past; that's what counted.

He knew the whole race wouldn't be that easy, though.

A high-pitched whistle was their only warning. Atherton and his soldiers dived to the sand as a shell carved a crater in their path. When Atherton raised his head—absently reaching out to retrieve his hat and cram it back on his head—he spotted a cluster of pirates charging his way.

By this point, many of the enemy had won past the trenches and come too close for most of the soldiers to waste any more time reloading. Pistols and carbines, then, made way for fighting daggers, bayonets, and Caspian battleblades—heavy, cleaving swords with rounded and weighted tips. These clashed against pirate blades, accompanied by only the occasional blast of a repeating rifle or burst of a chain gun.

Atherton's own men, of course, *hadn't* discharged their weapons yet, lurking in reserve as they'd been. Five carbines fired, five freebooters dropped, but over thrice that number still stood. That his commandos could take the lot of them, Atherton didn't doubt, but they had more important uses for their time.

That and, frankly, he wanted his own piece of the action.

"Keep moving! I'll catch up."

A quick chorus of "Yes, sir!" and they scattered, each making for the waterline by a slightly different course.

Atherton stepped calmly into the path of the oncoming pirates, flipped back his coat, and drew his pistols.

Not the traditional single-shot weapons still carried by many infantrymen, these, nor the far more advanced carbines wielded by his commandos, but so-called "pepperboxes." The antiquated gun's quartet of barrels rotated via clockwork gears, allowing for four rapid shots before reloading. An effective weapon, certainly, if uncomfortably weighty and an absolute bear to reload.

Or such was true, anyway, of *normal* pepperbox pistols. But these were no more normal pistols than Atherton was a normal marksman.

The Cygnaran's lips twitched in a low mutter, and the air surrounding his weapons began to ripple with a shimmering, electric blue, highlighting the ornate knotwork of runes carved deep into every barrel. It pulsed, that aura, shifting and flickering. From precisely the right angle, at exactly the right moment, observers might have seen recognizable glyphs and runes in the blinking patterns.

"*Gunmage!*"

By the time the lead pirate had called his warning, it was already too late. Hammers fell, pistols spoke, and when the bullets flew, they carried as heavy a load of sorcery as they did of lead.

The first shot struck the man who'd shouted. Rather than punching through him, the bullet flattened against his chest, instantly bestowing an impossible inertia. The pirate hurtled backward, not markedly slower than the bullet itself had been, bowling over two of his companions with force enough to shatter half the bones in all three bodies.

The bullet from the second weapon struck with an impact more appropriate to an artillery shell, punching straight through not only its first target, but three additional pirates besides. That it actually curved to hit the final man was a detail utterly lost amidst the larger chaos.

The recoil didn't shift Atherton's guns so much as a fraction of an inch. Instead, in utter contempt for the laws of physics, that recoil pressed *sideways* into the cylinders, causing the barrels to click over without need for clockwork gears at all—gears which, in fact, were absent from these custom weapons.

It was, the lot of it, impossible. But it was what Atherton wanted, and where he commanded, firearms obeyed.

A scarred, hairy giant of a pirate appeared from outside Atherton's line of fire. He lunged, screaming, axe raised overhead in a stance more appropriate for chopping through an offending log than an offending man.

Atherton lifted one pistol in a skillful parry, turning the thick blade aside; the axe left no mark on the ensorcelled steel barrel. The second pistol he drove into his attacker's face like a punch-dagger, splitting skin and breaking bone. Whether or not that injury would have proved fatal became a moot point when the gunmage fired a shot *through* that sorely cracked and battered skull, dropping a second charging foe in the process.

Runic bullets flew and men died—pierced, broken, or tossed like canoes in a tidal wave. Finally, however, both guns had cycled their allotment of four, and only empty chambers waited for the falling hammers.

One pirate—tall, lanky, with a cruel sneer and a saw-toothed, piston-driven cutlass—survived. He offered Atherton a reeking, gap-toothed grin.

"Been countin'. Ya had yer eight, ya bastard!"

"Nine," the Cygnaran corrected him politely.

"Huh? Can't ya even count, ya—?"

Atherton flipped his right-hand pistol high, sending it spiraling into the air far above his head. In that same motion he twisted, his now empty hand flying under his coat.

By the time the pirate had torn his gaze from the tumbling pepperbox, Atherton held the grip of a standard-issue forgelock. And by the time the pirate had advanced a second running step, the gunmage had whipped that pistol forward and shot his enemy cleanly between the eyes.

The forgelock was stowed once more in its holster at the small of his back, and his hand was open and waiting, when the falling pepperbox slapped back into his palm.

"Nine," Atherton declared firmly. Then he was off, racing to rejoin his team.

***

"Shepherd's down! Shepherd's down!"

Benwynne came around, cursing, just in time to see the warjack fall beneath a barrage of scattershot from a trio of enemy 'jacks. Bits of steel lay nearby, curled like slices of warm cheese; tendrils of smoke wound skyward from spots on the blue-and-gold chassis that were most assuredly *not* meant to function as exhaust ports.

Even as the pirate machines moved in to ensure their job was done, however, Wolfhound appeared behind them. Looming like an angry god, it slammed one of the 'jacks aside with its great axe, jabbed a second in the chest with the long-cannon and blew it apart from point blank range. Pistons seized, fuels ignited, and the warjack went away from the waist up.

Wolfhound promptly kicked one of the still standing legs directly into the path of the third warjack, knocking it back a pace while the Hunter pursued the enemy it had damaged but not dropped with the axe. The shriek of rending metal and the rapid firing of pistons sent nearby soldiers of both sides running for quieter and more peaceful quarters of the battlefield.

Forgotten, then, Shepherd sprawled alone near the edges of the lapping tide.

"Habbershant!" Benwynne called out.

"On it!" Indeed, he already was, for his answering cry came from several paces nearer the shore. Growling such that only every third syllable was audible, the sergeant followed, waving several of her men to accompany her.

Most mechaniks of the Cygnaran army worked in tandem with a team of assistants, some human, some otherwise. Habbershant, however, disdained such aid, refusing to put more lives in danger. His team were all skilled mechaniks in their own rights, ready to handle tasks that didn't require his level of expertise, or emergencies he couldn't reach. But when Master Sergeant Habbershant stepped into the field of fire, he did so alone.

Benwynne had once asked him, "How do you know you won't need a part or tool you don't have on you?"

"Because," he'd answered, "if you can't tell from a glance what you're likely to need, you've no business leading a team of mechaniks."

She'd thought it braggadocio at the time, but in all their battles, she'd never seen him mistaken. Even now he skidded to Shepherd's side in a spray of grit and seawater and was instantly reaching into the first of the jagged rents with a five-pronged, asymmetrical wrench. A moment later and Wolfhound was back beside him, turning the fallen 'jack so Habbershant could more easily reach the damage.

Benwynne vaulted the trench, took over a chain gun from an exhausted crew, and prepared to shred any pirate who so much as looked askance at the mechanik while he worked.

***

By the time Atherton rejoined his team, they'd commandeered a pirate longboat and were ready to set out. The corporal paused only long enough to help them push off before clambering over the side.

"All right, boys," he told them, reloading his weapons while the others rowed, "you all know what we're looking for. I doubt they'll be kind enough to have a signed and dated 'We confess to being sponsored by Khador' letter lying about in plain sight, so look for *anything* that might constitute proof. Take that ship apart down to the waterline if you have to. If there's so much as a drop of Khadoran sweat soaked into the rigging, I want it. Got me?"

Five affirmative grunts, and then every breath was devoted to rowing.

Cannons roared across the choppy waters. Clouds of bitter smoke hung low over the various ships, angry wraiths waiting to swoop down upon the living.

The *plan* was for the Cygnaran galleons and ironhull to keep the pirates' attention, allowing the tiny longboat to reach the nearest brigandine. It appeared, however, that a particularly sharp sailor had thought to keep watch landward.

The boarding party discovered this when a single gun port dropped open and something within spat fire.

Atherton reacted so quickly he might just have outpaced his own reflection. Both pistols rose, once more crackling with a cerulean aura, and each fired off a pair of shots.

The first, striking faster and harder than any mundane bullet, obliterated the cannonball yards from the vulnerable little vessel. The other three twisted, swerved, and blasted into the shadowy chamber behind the gun port.

Atherton couldn't possibly hear the bodies falling from this distance, but he knew they had, all the same.

"Now let's just hope," he said casually, basking in the open-mouthed stares of seasoned and normally unflappable commandos, "that it was just the one gun crew that saw us coming."

Apparently, it was. Atherton cracked open his weapons to reload once more, no more guns fired—not in their direction, anyway—and the ship drew ever nearer.

***

The spent chain gun lying forgotten beside her, Benwynne hauled with a sharp cry, yanking her blade—a sword of almost saber-like design, rather than the popular and heavier battleblades—from the ribs of the latest pirate to die. As he'd been in life, his body was covetous, greedy, reluctant to give up the sharp steel, and the sergeant had been forced to plant a boot on the corpse before she had the leverage to tug it free.

All of which put her in the perfect position to watch, gawping, as a column of flame rocked the vessel Corporal Gaust had recently boarded. Chunks of the hull disintegrated, or spun off into the water. The smoke climbed fast and thick, a rather large and woefully disappointing jack-in-the-box. Ponderously but with growing speed, the brigandine began to list.

"Looks like the ship's magazine," Wendell commented, having appeared once more at the sergeant's side only Morrow-knew-when. "Guess we've either got ourselves a suicidal pirate, or Gaust's team put a shot somewhere they shouldn't."

"If he gets off that ship alive," Benwynne snarled, furious enough to turn back the tide, "I may just kill him myself. The bloody hell is he *thinking*, Master Sergeant? How useful is our proof if it's burned to cinders or sitting on the ocean floor?"

"He mightn't have had a choice," the mechanik said mildly. "Besides, there are other ships—"

"And if the only evidence of Khadoran involvement was on *that* one, Habbershant? What then?"

"Then I . . . Messenger, Sergeant."

"What?"

Wendell pointed. From far up the beach approached a single horse, hooves spraying sand as it ran, carrying a rider whose tabard sported the golden Cygnus. He reined in his mount, dropped expertly from the saddle, and moved to address Lieutenant Craddock, the officer in charge of the beachfront operation as a whole.

He, in turn, scanned the beach with his own spyglass and then pointed straight at Benwynne herself.

"Bugger." Still, the situation around her appeared largely under control. The bulk of the pirates were down, or at least hemmed into small pockets of resistance. Bulldog and the newly patched Shepherd seemed to be doing a pretty decent job of dealing with said pockets. Bulldog moved with a sharp, jolting limp, and various fluids dribbled from a cracked piston in its leg, but it appeared to be in no danger of slowing or toppling; Wendell's team ought to be able to handle repairs easily enough after the battle. Wolfhound stood, long-cannon raised skyward, perhaps dividing its focus equally between shore and sea, trying to determine where it could land a shell to do the most good.

There was, in other words, nothing that required her *immediate* attention.

"All right, Master Sergeant. Let's see what's so urgent it couldn't wait until we get home."

Her fatigued trudge and the messenger's crisp walk brought them together on an open patch of ground. Unobscured by cloud, either natural or the result of burning powder, the sunlight bounced from the sand to warm them, massaging some of the seaside winter chill from armor and tired muscles.

The messenger, a young man whose disgustingly eager features and demeanor belonged on recruitment fliers, snapped off a salute and handed Benwynne a single sheet, folded but unsealed.

"Read under orders, ma'am," he replied to her unasked question. "In case something went wrong and I had to deliver it verbally. Must be critical."

The sergeant nodded once, flipped open the paper, and then hissed through her teeth like a venting engine. "They've *got* to be joking!"

"I don't believe so, ma'am."

Benwynne handed the missive to Wendell.

"They've got to be joking," he parroted a moment later. This time, the messenger didn't seem to feel a response was required.

"Have you any idea, Private," Benwynne growled, "how important this operation could be? How meticulously we prepared for—"

"I'm just the courier, ma'am. Besides, the operation isn't being suspended. These orders are specifically for the fifth. Squads two and six are to remain here and conclude—"

"The second and sixth are good, but they're traditional army, not UE teams. We need—"

"I'm sorry, ma'am."

"Isn't anyone ever going to finish a sentence?" Wendell asked plaintively.

"I'm sorry," the messenger repeated, "but my instructions were quite clear. I was to deliver these orders immediately, and see that they were executed *immediately*. Timetable established by General Runewood personally."

It was only her own military discipline—which, if she were being honest with herself, she'd already pushed to the breaking point—that kept Benwynne from cursing aloud. Instead, drawing her shoulders up, she turned back toward Wendell.

"Think Corporal Gaust and his team could hear the steam whistle from here, Master Sergeant?"

"I can adjust the aperture to make sure, Sergeant. I don't recommend you stand nearby when it sounds, though."

"Fine. Do it. Fighting withdrawal alarm." That would be three long blasts, two shorts, under their current system of codes. "The squad's pulling out and heading home."

Where, she added silently, *general or no, archduke or no, Alain Runewood is going to bloody well explain himself!*

Glaceus 8th, 605 AR
Corvis, Cygnar

Limned in silver by cloud-filtered moonlight, the rider leaned over her charger's armored neck as though whispering secrets. "Have I mentioned," she asked, "how much I *hate* Corvis?"

Arius, named for the clergyman and national hero, twitched the chestnut ears that protruded from his heavy barding of blue plate and gold mesh, and otherwise failed to acknowledge his mistress's confession.

Lieutenant Laddermore chuckled softly. The sound echoed slightly within her helm, for all that she currently rode with visor lifted. "I thought you might have heard it already," she admitted.

Katherine Laddermore—not just "Lieutenant" but also properly "Lady," though she wasn't shy about telling people not to address her as such, thank you very much—didn't much resemble the traditional knight. Raised in the court of the Archduke Fergus Laddermore, she had the gentle face, rich chocolate locks, and bearing of a princess. Taller and broader of shoulder than average, perhaps, but hardly imposing.

Until one stood in her way, or threatened her people. Until one watched her cut down the enemy as casually as if she were trimming the roses. Until she appeared, clad not in civilian garb, but the blue-and-gold armor of the Storm Lancers, crashing down on the foe like the wrath of the gods, the lightning itself heralding her earth-shaking charge.

Although not especially bloodthirsty, she'd rather have been doing just that at the moment. Her recent assignment to Corvis—a city of winding bridges, tight streets, and viscous muddy roads, all in the midst of a river-fed marsh quite some distance from any of the active fronts—was proving rather low on her list of favorite deployments.

Nor was she the only one to feel that way.

"Tell me again why we're here, Lieutenant?" The voice drifted from behind, raised slightly to be heard over the grating chirp of distant frogs.

Katherine's grin widened, though none of the men following could possibly see it. This was the same question Blevins had asked every evening since they'd arrived four days ago. At this point, a patrol beyond the city walls wouldn't have felt complete without it. Plenty of officers might have frowned at the levity, but Katherine—again, due to her own disdain for her experiences in her father's court—preferred a more informal relationship with her subordinates.

"There's a war on, Blevins," she answered sweetly, as though it had been a genuine question—again, much as she'd done every prior evening. "You might have noticed a few *thousand* people leaving Corvis earlier this week? Those would be soldiers joining the First Army at the front. And since the *Second* Army—that would include us, in case you've fallen and hit your head again—is still mobilizing units for long-term replacements, they needed the nearest available unit to hold the fort until they arrive.

"Now, would you care to guess who that turned out to be? Or shall I stop and draw you a diagram?"

A small swell of snickers washed over her, Blevins' among them, and for that she was especially grateful. Anything to relieve the tension, in these earliest days of a reborn war . . .

She was just drawing breath to order one final sweep of the banks before starting the three-mile trek back to Corvis when a call from the rear of the formation interrupted.

"Riverboat, Lieutenant!"

Katherine hauled Arius around. "Anything suspicious?" Even with the outbreak of hostilities, both the Dragon's Tongue and the Black River were too vital as commercial waterways for traffic to cease, so a riverboat—even this late at night—wasn't automatically a danger sign. Still . . .

"Sorry, Lieutenant, make that *three* boats. Looks like a small trade flotilla. And no, nothing alarming that I can see from here . . ."

No real reason to check any further, but Katherine—a touch of informality with her people notwithstanding—preferred to err on the side of excess in the performance of her duties. "Gather up here," she told the others. "I'm going for a quick look."

Swiftly over a shallow rise, and then Arius's hooves were splashing through cold marsh, kicking up water, mud, uprooted reeds, and the occasional flattened toad. Katherine twisted a toggle on the haft of her galvanic lance, traditional weapon of her Order. Sparks crackled; cobalt coils of electricity spiraled the length of the weapon, humming and sizzling in the humid air. Not enough to be dangerous—not yet—but more than enough to illuminate her way to the banks of the Black River.

And to ensure the sailors could see her in turn.

The lead vessel was abnormally tall for a riverboat. Something to do with the distribution of cargo, maybe? Katherine didn't know enough about boats to do more than guess. Of the two smaller craft, the squat one might have more properly been called a barge, save that the deck was largely enclosed; the other was the most mundane of the lot, perhaps a crew-and-supply boat. All three propelled themselves with shallow paddlewheels astern, traveling in an uneven triangle.

She could see crew moving about on all three, though the barge held a much smaller contingent than the others.

All perfectly ordinary, other than the mild peculiarity of the late-hour travel, and any number of deadlines could justify that. So why were the hackles on Katherine's neck rising, her fingers clenching of their own accord about the haft of her lance?

"Ahoy the river!"

One of the sailors—pale, dark-haired, dressed in patched but sturdy wools, and largely indistinguishable from any of the *other* sailors—stepped to the chipped railing of the lead boat to shout back. "Evening." This was their only concession, however; the vessels showed no signs of slowing, let alone stopping.

Talkative bunch, I see. Katherine clicked her tongue at Arius, and the horse began to trot along the bank, keeping pace. The sound of mud squelching beneath his hooves was almost chipper. "Where are you bound, and with what cargo?"

"Who's asking?"

"Lieutenant Laddermore, 33rd Heavy Cavalry, Second Army."

"Uh. Just coal and a bit of raw ore heading downriver, Lieutenant. Delivery for Steelwater Coal and Steam."

Again, it all *sounded* reasonable enough . . . . "You have permits to deliver across Cygnaran borders, of course?"

The sailor coughed once. "Didn't say we was delivering to a Cygnaran port, Lieutenant."

Which meant either the Bloodstone Marshes or the gathering zealots in the Protectorate of Menoth. But before Katherine could say anything, he continued, "Still all legal."

"I'm sure it is." She frowned as Arius stumbled on the uneven swampy ground, but he righted himself swiftly enough. Had they been alone, she'd have been wildly amused at the "I meant to do that!" tilt to his head. "Would you mind heaving to, so I can come aboard and confirm?"

"I don't think so, Lieutenant. You got no right. Besides, it's *your* country who's at war. How do we know you won't just commandeer our coal?"

"Would my word suffice?"

The derisive snort was answer enough, but it no longer mattered. Because it was then that the knight finally realized what had been bothering her about these boats from the moment she'd beheld them.

These boats and, more significantly, *boatmen*.

Merchant-sailors hauling a valuable load along the Black River, in the black of night, during wartime? Of *course* they should be nervous! Anyone with half the brains of Katherine's saddle-blanket would be nervous.

Except they hadn't been. Only when she'd questioned them had their spokesman developed any sort of hitch in his voice. When they'd first floated past her, the visible crewmen had been going about their duties with absolute focus. No fearful glances out the portholes, or cast suspiciously in her direction. No pacing on deck, scrutinizing the shoreline. No quick whispers as they crossed paths.

So determined to keep themselves rigidly under control, to avoid drawing the slightest whiff of suspicion, they held themselves *too* calmly. They weren't able to drop the act enough to make it real.

"I'm afraid," Katherine said, readying herself with a single deep inhalation, "that I really must insist."

The sudden burst of acceleration she expected, but the sheer speed of it caught her by surprise. In a spray of churning foam, all three vessels lurched forward as if they'd been fired from a cannon. No normal civilian steam engine—gods, not many *military* ones!—could provide that sort of push. Even running Arius flat-out, she'd only be able to keep up for a short time, and that was assuming something unseen in the treacherous marsh didn't trip him up first.

But then, she didn't expect to *need* to keep pace for long.

Katherine had kicked her mount into a gallop even before she'd fully recovered from her shock. Just as if she charged a land-bound foe, she lowered the crackling lance, twisting slightly to aim it at the lead boat rather than straight ahead. For a moment, it almost looked laughable.

Until, with the flip of a switch, Lieutenant Laddermore called the lightning.

Generators within the haft shrieked, pitched so high they stabbed at the ears despite being nigh inaudible. The air ripped open with a thunderous burst, and the lance spat at the vessel with the fury of the storm.

The night turned white. Arcs of power raced across the hull on spidery legs of lightning, sharply reflected off the waters below. Smoke curled from the wooden paneling, and the man with whom Katherine had been shouting fell back screaming, body spasming until he disappeared from sight.

But where she'd anticipated a flaming gap in the hull, Katherine now saw only a blackened stain, smoking so faintly it was all but invisible in the darkness. Only in a few spots had the wood burned away completely, leaving cinder-rimmed holes. These exposed an inner layer of ceramics. Reinforced, or so she assumed, they would be weaker than steel but far lighter and, worse for the Storm Knight, not particularly conductive.

Katherine might not know much about boats, but this sort of craftsmanship she recognized just fine.

Dwarven craft. These were Rhulic vessels!

For perhaps a heartbeat, she hesitated. Rhul and Cygnar weren't precisely allies, but they *were* trading partners; certainly no state of hostility existed between them. The repercussions if she were wrong about this . . .

But no. The vessels flew no flag, Rhulic or otherwise, and the crew certainly were no dwarves. Whatever she'd stumbled upon, it was in no way official.

At the boats' current speed, even a heartbeat's hesitation was significant. By the time Arius had once more built to a gallop, hooves digging deep furrows into the thick mud, the flotilla had opened up a lead of several dozen yards.

Still, she might catch up long enough to slow them, at least give the rest of her team the chance to—

An array of small ports opened in the enclosed barge. From them sprayed a wide arc of a thick, glistening liquid. It sat on the surface of the water, a single undulating blob that refused to break up in the current, and spread to coat the tufts of solid ground and the patches of bog that made up this stretch of bank. From a separate porthole flew a lit brand, tracing brilliant curves through the air as it tumbled toward the sludgy concoction . . .

Katherine hauled Arius's reins and leaned right, eliciting an indignant whinny and turning the horse so sharply the weight of his barding nearly dragged him over. Even so, she was close enough to feel the flames and the gusty *whump* of rushing air. The left side of her armor grew almost hot enough to sear.

Vitriolic fire. It'd burn itself out after a few moments of almost supernatural intensity, but until then, almost no force of nature could extinguish it. No way in hell could she or her knights pursue those vessels through that raging inferno.

But then, she didn't *have* to pursue them. Not directly.

A quick gesture with her sparking lance, delivering an unspoken order to the horsemen riding up from behind, and then Katherine was charging *away* from the river as swiftly as the clinging muck would permit. The marsh rapidly grew shallower, eventually ceding the terrain to thick-packed earth, relatively dry and firm.

Arius all but screamed in delight at the solid ground beneath his hooves; Katherine didn't even need to signal for him to burst again into a full gallop. Later, the beast would tremble with exhaustion, probably require a full rubdown and some extra care, but for now he was the wind wrapped only loosely in flesh.

Paralleling the Black River, now, horse and rider pounded south, hoofbeats blending like the shots of a chain gun. Trees loomed out of the night, dark and twisted hands against black, and were gone just as suddenly. Occasionally they leaned so near that Katherine felt the tips of branches scratch and snap against her armor. Ahead, the squat walls, towering structures, and web-work of walkways that were the city of Corvis grew ever larger, ever nearer.

Only a quarter mile from the city proper, Katherine angled back toward the river. Arius slowed when his hooves left the tight-packed earth, but not so dramatically as earlier. Here, nearer the community, the patches of marshland were shallower, less eager to snatch at any who dared pass through.

They reached the water's edge, Arius doing his best impersonation of a huffing bellows, only yards ahead of the tiny flotilla. Katherine couldn't help but smirk behind her visor—now lowered for battle—at the wide, white eyes of the first crewmen to spot her.

Again she discharged a levinbolt, aimed not at the boat this time but the water directly before it. Tendrils of lightning sizzled over the surface of the Black River, some scorching the lead vessel's hull. Several score of dead fish, along with a few snakes and turtles, bobbed to the surface and floated away on the current.

As a command, it was pretty difficult to misinterpret.

Indeed, even as the rest of her knights thundered up behind her, the paddlewheels on the boat reversed, kicking up such a froth that the entire craft partially disappeared behind the curtain of spray.

But not so thoroughly that the assembled knights failed to note that something more, something odd, was occurring. The boats moved sideways relative to each other, dragging themselves across the water at peculiar angles impossible for the paddlewheels alone to achieve.

With a mechanical precision, the lead boat drew back toward the others. The barge that had extruded the vitriolic fire rotated, slid forward, turning diagonally toward the bank where Katherine stood. The second smaller boat drifted starboard until it, too, floated between the knights and the primary vessel. The result was a V-formation aimed at the attackers, with the larger boat protected in the hollow.

"How in the . . . ?"

"Some kind of chain-and-gear system, Lieutenant," answered a young, bald knight by the name of Glinn. "Caught a glimpse when the smaller boat rocked against the current. I think they're all three linked below the waterline."

Clever. Even as they watched, crewmen appeared on the two shielding vessels. Some carried breach-loading rifles, some large metal tubes and bipods that would almost certainly combine into mortars, and a few bore pumps, linked by long rubber hoses, to something within the body of the barge.

Probably more of the vitriolic fire, Katherine decided. And then she chuckled. "Firing line!" she ordered.

A rifle cracked, and a bullet ricocheted from the lieutenant's armor. She flinched only slightly, watching until her men were in position.

The knights were now arranged along the water's edge, shields and lances raised. A series of shouts and a burst of extra hustling on the part of the mortar crews suggested that the sailors knew something bad was in the works.

Oh, you've no idea . . .

"All lances, target the barge! Directly between those two men with the pumps!"

Lance-tips shifted. Armor creaked. Horses snorted. And a veritable barrage of shots erupted from the vessels as the boatmen overheard the lieutenant's shouts and fought desperately to stop what was coming.

One of those shots got lucky, and a Storm Knight toppled from his horse, clutching at his left shoulder and grunting as he met the mud with a wet slap.

Katherine's jaw clenched. *"Fire!"*

Against a single galvanic lance, or two, or even a handful, the Rhulic vessel's ceramic hull would readily have stood fast. Against roughly a dozen, it burst like a child's puzzle swept from the tabletop.

Again the night went stark white. Even with her head turned away, her eyes squeezed tight and her visor down, Katherine saw sunbursts flash across her vision.

And just as swiftly, the white turned red, and the echoes of the crackling lightning and booming thunder were drowned in the roar of a demon of raging fire.

Hunks of wood, shards of ceramic, and fragments of boatman—some violently aflame—rained over the Black River. The air thickened, scratching at the back of the throat and deep in the lungs with fingernails of ozone, charcoal, and acrid reagents. Clattering to shame a brass band falling down the stairs, several more of Katherine's knights hit the ground, knocked from their saddles by the intensity of the blast or thrown when their warhorses, for all their training, reared in terror at the conflagration. Most remained mounted, however, reins and knees holding chargers steady, and all who had fallen remained healthy enough to scramble upright.

The barge was gone. Not on fire, not floating in bits of flotsam, but *gone*. Both connected vessels, now twisted sideways and drifting toward the far bank, were aflame. The second smaller boat had borne the worst of it; it floated prow-downward, rising and falling with the rippling waves. Every exposed inch of wood snapped and popped, fueling a column of fire that overtopped the trees.

The primary vessel, farther from the blast and apparently built of sterner stuff, belched smoke from several campfire-sized conflagrations. Most of the men who'd stood topside were dead, badly cooked, or thrashing in the flaming waters.

Just as Laddermore was shouting new orders, however, the boatmen of that vessel proved that they, too, were made of pretty stern stuff. More rifles protruded from the portholes on the wheelhouse, and a hollow *thump* from an open deck hatch heralded an incoming round.

Either the mortar crew was incredibly skilled, or luck had chosen to offer them a break after what they'd just suffered. Either way, though the boats bobbed wildly, burning in a dozen spots and slowly spinning in the current, the first shell landed directly in the midst of the Storm Knights.

Between their heavy armor, their training, and the fact that they were already scattering, most of the knights and their mounts escaped with only minor splinters of shrapnel.

Two of them—one of whom was Blevins, the young jester—hit the sodden earth in twisted heaps and wouldn't rise again.

Beneath Katherine's armor burned an abrupt rage that might have rivaled the fate of the flotilla. She'd lost people before, certainly, and knew she would again; men and women for whom she was responsible, who she almost considered family as much as subordinates.

But this? Against river smugglers? In a fight that *she'd* initiated based on intuition alone, and perhaps failed to take as seriously as she should?

For Blevins and Denburrough, the other man who'd fallen, she truly *was* responsible.

Swearing behind her visor, the lieutenant scanned her fire-lit surroundings, hoping for . . .

Yes. That one would do.

Katherine blasted another bolt—the last her lance would throw until she'd given it a few moments to recharge—into the trunk of a massive tree. One of several that were already burning fiercely, the trunk cracked and began to lean, spitting splinters out over the water.

Shouting herself hoarse, certain that at least a few of her knights would hear her orders, she kicked Arius into another run and bypassed the tottering tree. Barely had she left it behind her when the thunder roared, three other bolts struck in the same spot, and the great bole toppled. Flame, water, and wood all met in a hellish sputter.

It didn't fully bridge the river. It didn't point directly at the flotilla. But if Arius was up to the challenge, if she hadn't run the faithful beast too near the brink of exhaustion, it would suffice.

Wheeling about yet again, Katherine Laddermore chose her angle and charged the Black River itself.

Flames reflected from the water, from the blue steel of her armor, veiling her in a shifting aurora of blood.

Her knees tensed in signal, and Arius leapt.

Horse and rider had worked as one for years, now, until they even thought in tandem. A horsewoman less skilled would surely have acted too soon; a charger less confident, less surefooted, would have skidded on the rocking, uneven surface, probably fracturing a leg before tumbling into either water or fire.

Not these. Arius landed firmly on the fallen bole with nary a stumble, stretched himself out in two galloping strides, and leapt once more.

The boat rocked wildly as they struck the deck, pitching one of the riflemen over the railing. Katherine's lance punched through the body of the first man in her path. He flopped along with her as Arius continued, drooping from the weapon like some truly disappointing pennant. Two bullets whizzed past, a third dug into her armor and nearly knocked her from the saddle, but the Storm Knight advanced until she stood beside the hatch from which the mortar had fired. A quick glance, to determine precisely where the weapon stood, and then she tipped the lance forward, letting it fall point first into the tube—and enfolding the mortar in the dangling limbs of the scarecrow-limp corpse.

Two men rushed her from the stern, but she'd scarcely seen them coming before Arius reared and struck with both front hooves, shattering one sailor's skull, breaking the nose and half the teeth of the other. When the warhorse dropped back to all fours, Katherine had a heavy Caspian battleblade to hand. No standard-issue tool, this, but an ancestral sword, one of the very few remnants of her past life she'd chosen to retain. Without pause she laid into everyone in reach, cleaving muscle and bone in an effortless, gory ballet.

Only twice did gunmen on the deck draw a bead on her from far enough away that she couldn't reach them before they fired, and on both those occasions levinbolts hurled from the lancers on shore ended the threat for her.

Until finally, in an image out of hell, the Storm Knight and her mount stood alone, blood-spattered, hoof-deep in gore, on the deck of a burning boat.

The current should carry her to the bank—albeit on the opposite side of the river from her people—well before the fires destroyed the vessel or cut off her escape. Still, she knew she hadn't a great deal of time. Sword in hand, in case any of the enemy remained below decks, she dropped from the saddle and made her way through the open hatch.

In the end, the only reward for her trouble was the recovery of her lance. The hold below was subdivided into several sizable rooms, but all of them stood empty—of coal or any other cargo, legitimate or otherwise. Perhaps there remained some hidden secret, a concealed hollow or some such, where the boatmen had been smuggling something they desperately didn't want her to have. She'd never know; the fire wouldn't permit any more thorough search.

She ended her night, then, sitting astride Arius on the eastern bank of the Black River, watching the last of the riverboats disintegrate into charred chunks and slip beneath the flowing waters. Two of her men were dead; over ten times that many sailors had died on the flotilla.

And Lieutenant Katherine Laddermore had nothing, nothing at all, to show for it.

She *knew* she'd been right to act. And she knew that *something* had happened here tonight, something important. Most likely, something very, very bad. But whatever it was, whatever enigma those men had been willing to run, and fight, and kill, and die for, eluded her.

Convinced that she'd lost this one, and burning with frustration that she couldn't figure out *how*, she turned Arius about and began the slow walk back to Corvis.

***

In an office on the uppermost floor of the city hall, Katherine Laddermore stood rigid as Colonel Anhearne paced before her. The helm she held in the crook of her left arm gleamed, as did the rest of her armor—save for her boots, which had been quite thoroughly soiled during her approach to the building. Nobody crossed Corvis at ground level without picking up an unwelcome cargo of sopping muck.

Not even when going to visit a superior officer, more the pity.

She'd scarcely slept the night before. Debriefing her team, transcribing the details of the encounter for delivery to High Command, drafting letters to the families of the fallen knights, and cleaning her equipment, had all kept her up unto the smallest hours of the morning. Still, she refused to reveal even a flicker of exhaustion to the visiting officer.

Colonel Anhearne was very much like the room in which they currently stood: small, sturdy, drab in appearance, but perfectly functional. One of the most trusted seconds to Commander Adept Sebastian Nemo of the First Cygnaran Army, he wasn't stationed in Corvis, wasn't directly in Katherine's chain of command, and frankly had no reason, so far as she could see, for being here at all. Surely, if she were about to face disciplinary action—and she could think of no other reason for being summoned before a visiting officer less than an hour after dawn—it should come from one of her own superiors in the Second Army.

And how in Morrow's name did he get here so quickly? We only sent the report six hours ago!

"Well, Lieutenant," Anhearne said finally, after a quick—and blatant—glance to ensure the door was shut, "this actually couldn't have happened at a better time."

Katherine blinked and focused on the man before her. "Sir?"

"Commander Nemo sends his greetings, by the way. He wanted me to ask you how the dynamic glaive performed."

This conversation was going nowhere remotely near where the Storm Knight had anticipated. "Ah, truth is, sir, it shorted out the first time I tried to activate it. Had to go back to a standard issue electro-lance. I was going to send in a report once Second Army reinforcements arrived and I wasn't quite so busy."

"Eh." The colonel waved her explanation away. "The general said he expected as much. Some problem with the conductivity of the materials. Or at least, I think that was the issue. Frankly, I didn't even recognize half the words he used, let alone know what they meant."

Katherine's lip quivered.

"Oh, at ease, Lieutenant. You're not in any real trouble here."

She allowed her shoulders to slump, if only barely (and invisibly, thanks to her armor). Colonel Anhearne leaned a hip against the desk.

"If those boats had been flying Rhul's flag, it'd be a different matter. But I read the report when I got here, and had a quick exchange of telegrams with Commander Adept Nemo and Commander Stryker. They both agree that your actions might be questionable on paper, and probably due some measure of reprimand, but they'd likely have made the same call."

Then, rather more seriously and with surprising gentleness, "Have you arranged for someone to inform the families?"

Katherine swallowed a quick lump. "Wrote the letters myself, sir."

"Good woman. I think, between the two of us, we can call that reprimand enough."

"I'd rather an alternative punishment, sir."

"Wouldn't we all? Anyway, as I said, at least the timing's fortunate. It means we can *tell* everyone you're being more formally reprimanded."

Just when I thought I was starting to get the hang of this conversation . . . "Sir, I don't entirely follow."

"You'll be leaving Corvis, Lieutenant."

"Sir, my people just—"

Anhearne raised a hand. "Not your people. Just you, along with two knights of your choice; no officers, and nobody whom you can't trust to follow orders *without question.* Assign one of your sergeants to take command in your absence. We'll be explaining your temporary absence as a punitive assignment, in reprimand for last night."

"And the truth?"

The colonel idly ran three fingers through his hair. "You probably figured that I didn't come here in response to your report?"

"I had, sir. No way you could have arrived so quickly."

"Right. On my way already, to speak with you." He passed over a letter stamped with the seal of Commander Coleman Stryker. "You can read this at your convenience, Lieutenant, but basically it states that you've been seconded to us, and you're to undertake this assignment as though Stryker himself ordered it."

"Us?"

"First Army, Second Division, 9th Brigade. Commander Adept Nemo."

"Would you mind terribly if I sat down, sir?"

"Please do."

Katherine dragged a chair—really just a stool with a tiny outcropping for back support—from the corner and thunked it down in front of the desk. It creaked alarmingly under the weight of her armor, but held.

Good old Cygnaran craftsmanship.

"Colonel," she said after a moment's contemplation, "Commander Nemo and I get along quite well—and I've enjoyed helping him field-test his creations—but I'm not First Army, and there's nothing I can do that the people under his command can't. I'm not refusing to obey, of course, I'm just wondering—?"

"Two reasons," Anhearne interrupted. "First, all of the Second Division—hell, all of the First Army—is tied up on the Llaelese front. Even those who aren't actively on the line are too vulnerable to Khadoran observation. This is a, let's say, *delicate* situation, and the general can't afford for Khador to spot any related activity.

"And second, it's precisely *because* Commander Nemo knows you. He needs someone he can trust, Lieutenant. Someone he *knows* he can trust, not just from reports and professional reputation, but personally."

Any pride Katherine might have felt at discovering how highly Nemo thought of her was swiftly tempered by the implications. "The situation's *that* delicate, sir?"

"More, really. Militarily, yes, but also politically. Put bluntly, Lieutenant, this sort of assignment isn't precisely in your wheelhouse, if you'll pardon the nautical reference after last night's incident. We'd normally assign it to someone a bit more, ah, subtle. But like I said . . . We're stretched thin, we're pretty sure you can handle it, and right now, the general's confidence and trust outweigh other concerns."

"All right," Katherine said, repressing what would have been a woefully inappropriate sigh. *I'm really not going to like this, am I?* "Let's hear it . . ."

Glaceus 8th, 605 AR
Caspia, Cygnar

"**P**ermission to speak freely, sir?"

Sergeant Bracewell, who had just asked the question every officer so loves to hear, stood at the outer curve of a massive U-shaped table. An oaken monstrosity polished first by the expert hands of carpenters, and then by years of use by a much rougher sort of person, it was one of the chamber's two most prominent features.

The other was the banner, occupying most of the rear wall and large enough to serve a heavy warjack as a winter quilt, proudly displaying the Golden Swan on the ubiquitous cerulean field.

Arrayed beside and behind the sergeant stood her various seconds. Wendell Habbershant stood at her shoulder, a few steps nearer than the corporals who commanded the individual units of Benwynne's squad: iron-haired, moonlight-pale Serena Dalton, long gunners; her near polar opposite, eight-fingered and molasses-hued Roland Cadmoore, trenchers; and, of course, Atherton Gaust.

Sitting *before* her, in the table's inner curve, was the man who'd summoned them back to Caspia—and then, beyond ordering them to prepare and provision for a long-term operation, hadn't said a word about why they'd been recalled.

General Alain Runewood, a broad-shouldered, ruddy-faced man with a widow's peak and bottlebrush moustache, both in varying salt-and-pepper shades, responded with a gruff, "Denied."

Benwynne's jaws clacking together sounded remarkably like a breach-loader snapping shut.

"Let me take a guess, Sergeant," he continued. "You'd like to ask me, just about as rudely as protocol permits, why your team was pulled from your last operation? Why we'd bother assigning a UE squad and then leave everything in the hands of traditionally trained army?"

"My people prepared for that operation for weeks, sir," Benwynne reminded him. Then, when he didn't berate her for speaking—perhaps his questions took precedence over his earlier refusal to let her speak?—she continued, "Besides, this wasn't just about stopping a pirate raid. We were supposed to determine if these were Khadoran privateers, unofficially assigned to test our southern coastal defenses—*and* to determine if the source of our intelligence on the raid was at all reliable!"

Indeed, Benwynne didn't even know from whom the warning about the raid had come; she knew only it hadn't been through the normal channels of the Cygnaran Reconnaissance Service.

"I *do* know the purpose of the mission, Sergeant," Runewood reminded her blandly. "I signed off on it."

"Then why—?"

"Permission denied, Bracewell. Remember?"

Again her mouth snapped shut. Several of her people grumbled under their breath, until she glared them into silence so the general wouldn't have to.

"The simple truth is," Runewood said, idly scratching at his moustache, "that something of rather greater urgency came up."

"More urgent than—?"

"The second and sixth squads can manage a search and interrogation. They may not have your experience, but they're not incompetent."

"Never once thought they were, sir."

"Good." Then, "Sergeants, Corporals . . . Everything you are about to hear is designated Gold-level Restricted under the Royal Secrets Proclamation. You will repeat to your soldiers *only* what they need to know to fulfill their portions of the assignment, and no more. Revelation of any of this information to anyone else is an act of high treason. Am I understood?"

"Understood, sir!" Every one of them stood a little straighter; *everything* they heard in this room was restricted, but never to that level. Not a man or woman present failed to understand the significance.

"Good," he repeated. Then, rather than speaking further, he stood, moved toward a small door near the Cygnus banner, and left the room.

"Well, *I* certainly won't be telling anyone . . ." Atherton muttered. Benwynne shushed him.

When that door opened again a moment later, it wasn't Runewood who entered. This new arrival was taller, thinner, though his age-lined face showed lingering traces of the muscular man he once had been. Like Runewood, he wore a thick moustache, but his was the stark white of summer clouds—as was the unruly mop of hair that lay flat only in a few select spots, as if it simply refused and repulsed every attempt to brush it down. Blue-tinted goggles hung from a lanyard around his neck, as though he'd simply forgotten they were there.

Most of those present had never met the man in person, but they needed neither his name, nor the golden epaulets of rank on his right shoulder, to recognize him.

Indeed, precious few soldiers of Cygnar could fail to recognize Commander Adept Sebastian Nemo of the 9th Brigade, 2nd Division, First Army—and inventor of roughly a quarter of the nation's most advanced weapons and equipment.

The second man who entered on his heels, a small and unremarkable fellow also in officer's uniform, carrying a ledger and stylus, went almost completely unremarked.

Almost. Benwynne could have sworn she saw Habbershant's forehead furrow when the (presumed) secretary appeared, but the expression faded before she could be sure.

"At ease," Nemo said before the lot of them had completed their salutes. He took the seat Runewood previously occupied; the other man sat a pace or so behind and began making notes.

"Sergeant Bracewell," the commander asked without preamble, "how long has Master Sergeant Habbershant served as Chief Mechanik for your squad?"

"Been with us a year as of last Doloven, sir."

"Mm. Master Sergeant?"

"Sir?" Habbershant asked.

"Any conflicts between you two?"

Habbershant frowned; Benwynne found herself biting her tongue. "I'm not sure I understand, sir . . ." the mechanik said.

"Conflicts. Of rank. She's never appeared threatened that you technically outrank her? Sergeant, Habbershant's never undermined or questioned your authority?"

"No, sir." It was all Benwynne trusted herself to say. She liked Habbershant; he was a good mechanik, a good soldier, a good man. She trusted him. And no, he'd never behaved any differently toward her than any of her other people did. Still, had the general come out and directly asked *Are you bothered by it at all?* she'd have been lying, if only a bit, to say no.

And given how much she trusted Wendell, it bothered her that it bothered her.

"Not at all, General," Habbershant said at almost the same moment. "Honestly, sir, I *requested* placement with a UE team. I knew it'd mean a subordinate position to a sergeant, and I'm fine with that. I just fix the 'jacks and maintain the equipment. No desire to do anything else." His beard crinkled as he grinned. "Only time I might even *try* to pull rank would be to get out of latrine duty."

That grin faded when neither his sergeant nor the commander seemed inclined to share it.

"It's, uh . . . We're not the only squad with that sort of setup, sir," he finished lamely.

"I'm aware, Master Sergeant. I'm not certain I entirely approve, but I'm aware . . . Still, if you say there's no problem, that's what counts.

"We've reserved two adjacent cars aboard the *Lady Ellena*," the commander continued, the change of tack so abrupt Benwynne felt dizzy, "as well as a cargo pallet for your warjacks. The morning after tomorrow, your squad will board the line for Bainsmarket."

The sergeant couldn't quite keep herself from blinking, and from the faint shuffling behind her, she was pretty sure her people were no less confused than she.

"From there, you'll travel upriver, disembarking just short of Merywyn. You . . . What is it, sergeant?"

Benwynne sheepishly lowered her hand and cleared her throat. "Um, sir, none of us has actually been told what's going on."

"What precisely do you think I'm doing right now, Bracewell?"

"I understand that, sir. It's just . . . We're Second Army, not—"

"Yes, yes. I *do* have some small familiarity with military structure." Nemo sighed, shook his head. "All right, sergeant. I'm not accustomed to explaining myself, but perhaps you're used to a different process.

"I have a mission that requires an Unorthodox Engagement team. I cannot, at present, draw upon any of the UE teams of the First Army. The First is already stretched woefully thin, trying to hold off the Khadoran offensive in Llael, and are potentially under the eyes of too many Khadoran spies. So I've arranged with Lord General Heltser and General Runewood to borrow you for a span."

Benwynne's cheeks stretched in an abortive frown. On paper, Unorthodox Engagement teams were just normal squads scattered throughout Cygnar's four armies. They had their stations, their standard duty assignments, the works. Unofficially, however, such squads—all of whom had received additional training and contained a broader mix of skillsets than most units—were constantly sent hither and yon to undertake whatever sorts of special operations circumstances might require.

It wasn't unheard of, then, for UE teams to find themselves operating under different battalion majors or brigade commanders than those to whom they were nominally assigned. This was, however, the first time Benwynne had ever heard of an Unorthodox Engagement team being placed under the command of an entirely different *army*.

"Your objective," Nemo was saying, "involves slipping in behind the Khadoran advance, via the Thornwood. I'll get into particulars and specific targets shortly, but in essence, you're to disrupt their forward units and positions, allowing the First additional opportunities to dig in and launch counterattacks. We'll coordinate with the CRS, of course, to ensure that you don't run afoul of any of their own operations behind enemy lines."

"And for what operation are we providing a diversion, sir?"

Nemo's expression became granite. His secretary finally looked up from the ledger, eyes wide, and Benwynne could feel the stares of her own people on her back and neck.

Internally, she blanched at her inappropriate outburst. Still, she was angry at how her squad had been treated, more than a little bewildered, and rather less concerned than normal with the niceties of protocol. Whatever doubts she felt, then, certainly made no impression on her face.

"Explain yourself, Sergeant," the commander ordered, his voice a coiling viper that hadn't yet decided whether to strike.

Benwynne sucked in a deep breath. "Commander, what you're describing is more properly a task for either the Reconnaissance Service, or a commando unit. Especially since this appears to be a fluid assignment, rather than one with any specific primary objective. That you're pulling a UE squad across the nation for this—along with its *warjacks*!—tells me that you want us to be noticed."

Nemo continued to glare, but was that just a *hint* of crinkling in the lines of his face?

"Not bad, Sergeant. You're quite right. You aren't *solely* diversionary—the objectives we'll be assigning your team are quite genuine and high priority— but yes, you are intended to keep Khador's eyes occupied in hunting for you."

For a moment, he tapped a knuckle on the edge of the table. "General Runewood explained to you the level of secrecy on this?"

"Yes, sir."

"All right. There *is* a CRS operation occurring parallel with your own; one of particular political sensitivity. Are any of you familiar with a Baron Crispin Halcourt? No? Well, suffice to say he owns a parcel of land in the Western Midlunds, and he's related, by blood or marriage, to more than a few of his . . . *southern* neighbors."

Ah. Understanding washed over Benwynne in a gentle wave. The Southern Midlunds were Cygnar's primary breadbasket. They were *also* the home of a cadre of dukes, archdukes, and barons who were less than fully committed to the relatively youthful reign of King Leto IV. Anything that might further aggravate that particular enmity, while the nation faced a war in the north, was desperately to be avoided.

"Baron Halcourt and the bulk of his household managed, with impeccable timing, to be in the midst of a sojourn in Llael—Leryn, specifically—at the time of the incursion."

This time, when several of the corporals behind her hissed or murmured, Benwynne chose not to berate them.

"For reasons of politics, business, and a breathtaking lack of wisdom, Halcourt chose not to leave when word of the invasion first reached him. Now, though Leryn hasn't yet come under attack—and won't, if we've anything to say about it—his routes back to Cygnar are cut off. He *could* escape through Rhul, if the dwarves permitted him passage, but he's not likely to ask until things reach their most desperate. The last thing he'd want is to be beholden to a foreign state, particularly an unallied one."

"So CRS is staging an extraction," Benwynne guessed. Nemo grunted an affirmative.

"But sir, surely there are UE teams assigned to the Second or Fourth Armies that are far closer to the area? They could—"

"I've my own reasons for selecting you and your people, Sergeant. You've the set of talents I require."

"It's just—"

"Sergeant . . ." If that *had* been a smile struggling to break through Nemo's regimented façade, it was certainly gone now. "Do not mistake my willingness to explain myself for permission to question your orders."

"No, sir. Sorry, sir."

"Good." The commander crooked a finger at the man behind him, who flipped the ledger back a few pages, removed a thick bundle from between two sheets, and unfolded it into a map of the Thornwood, western Llael, and southeastern Khador. "Then we'll begin with a discussion of your route to your first objective . . ."

***

Master Sergeant Wendell Habbershant shut the door behind him with an audible sigh and the faintest pop in his upper back. His eyes felt like he'd smuggled sand back from the Bay of Cygnar hidden beneath his lids, and the creases of his uniform—which had, that morning, been sharp enough to shear sheep—now looked more like they'd been trampled by waltzing warjacks. From Nemo's interminable briefing that morning, to hours spent organizing supplies for the mission, to continuing repairs and maintenance on the battle-and-sand-scarred 'jacks, Wendell had been on his feet for almost twenty hours straight. All he could think about was a hot tea, perhaps with a dash of something stronger mixed in, a few minutes with a well-packed pipe, and the warm and loving embrace of his flimsy mattress, which—

"Evening, Master Sergant."

—was currently occupied by a small-framed, dark-haired officer sitting casually at the foot of the cot.

The mechanik took a single deep breath and unclenched his fist from the dagger he kept amidst the other tools on his belt. He'd been expecting this visit from the moment he saw the man taking Nemo's notes. In the press of the day's duties, however, it had slipped his mind.

Instead of a blade, then, Wendell offered a perfunctory salute, which the other man returned even more indifferently.

"Don't seem entirely shocked to see me here, Habbershant."

"No, sir. I didn't think a Reconnaissance Service colonel was acting as secretary to Commander Nemo just for the experience."

Colonel Mathis, of the Cygnaran Reconnaissance Service, returned a tight smile. "Right you are, Master Sergeant. Scout General Rebald sends his compliments, by the way."

Habbershant scarcely even nodded an acknowledgment. "Can I take it, then, that the commander's briefing and his 'admission' this morning might not have been entirely truthful, sir?"

"Oh, it was truthful," Mathis said. "It just wasn't *complete*."

"And I assume the fact that CRS has a presence in Bracewell's squad is one of the commander's reasons for choosing us over other UE teams?"

Then, taking the colonel's raised eyebrow as confirmation, "Am I being activated, sir?" Wendell had known, from the day his superiors had assigned him to Benwynne's squad—just one of many operatives the Cygnaran Reconnaissance Service had seeded throughout Cygnar's conventional military forces—that this moment might come, but that didn't mean he *wanted* it to. He liked the squad; respected them; felt like he belonged. They wouldn't take kindly to the revelation that, while he'd never been disloyal, he *had* been serving two masters.

"We can hope not, Master Sergeant. I'm filling you in primarily as a precaution. If things go as planned, you should never need to utilize any of this information, and you'll never repeat it to anyone else, your fellow officers included.

"But if things *do* go pear-shaped, we need you in a position to pick up the pieces. You and the rest of the squad . . . Even if that means you have to relieve Sergeant Benwynne of her command and lead the team yourself."

Glaceus 9th, 605 AR
Leryn, Llael

In the battle of scents it was, thankfully, the alliance of roasting mutton and wood smoke that carried the day, though the damages inflicted by close-packed bodies and clashing high-end perfumes had certainly taken their toll.

For all its fury, it was a battle waged largely unnoticed by the chamber's occupants, as they'd witnessed the same one every few nights for the past month or more.

Overlooked by an enormous recessed window that offered a breathtaking view of Leryn's wealthier neighborhoods, the room boasted a dais on which stood the lord of the manor's own table. Here, Baron Enizzo Surros dined with his wife and sons, a few household servants who were in particular favor that evening, and—again, for roughly the past month—his most honored guest, the Baron Crispin Halcourt of Cygnar.

Already slightly inebriated—which was as inebriated as propriety would allow him to get in someone else's home—Halcourt examined his bulging, twisted reflection in the back of a spoon. Only after ensuring that his lips and oh so stylish pencil-thin blond beard were impeccably free of crumbs or dribbles did he rise, ringing for silence with that spoon against his goblet.

Conversation dwindled as several dozen men and women, mostly seated at tables across the room's lower floor, graciously offered their attention. Properly speaking, it should have been the homeowner proposing the first toast or making the first speech of the night, but Surros had hosted Halcourt for long enough that they routinely allowed one another such liberties in decorum.

"To the most honored and special guests of Lord Enizzo Surros, present this evening." He waved the glass at one of those lower tables. "Goodman

Claeddon, you and your troupe have outdone yourself. Your performance tonight was absolutely superlative. I've rarely seen its equal."

Claeddon and the members of his company stood from their seats and bowed, while the rest of the room offered a round of polite applause. This, of course, led to further toasts, and further acknowledgments, and further applause, all of which went on interminably until the servants—mostly Surros's staff, but with occasional assistance from Halcourt's retinue—arrived with the next course on steaming silver platters.

Conversation ebbed; quantities of food slowly ebbed to match; and conversation resumed. Laughter, advice and predictions offered in sage tones, gossip ranging from the whispered to the shrill . . . Just another fete among the nobility of Llael.

Except most of that discourse was just as fragile as the crystalline goblets upon the brightly patterned tablecloths. Every political discussion, every rise or fall in the price of commodities, every mention of future plans, all were stirred by unspoken fears. No matter how thoroughly everyone tried to pretend that the world around them was smooth sailing, none could truly forget the threat of war that swam, a lurking kraken, beneath the surface.

Halcourt turned from his current audience—one of his host's sons, who was either truly fascinated in the Cygnaran noble's anecdotes or had learned, growing up in Surros's court, to fake it—at the sound of a polite cough.

"Ah! Claeddon!"

Halcourt rose, then scoffed and held out a hand instead as the other began to bow, revealing a ring of dark hair around a growing bald patch. With a smile, the hatchet-faced actor clasped the baron's fist in his own.

"I wanted to thank you for your kind words, my Lord." Claeddon, who'd previously spoken only in Llaelese in deference to his host, now switched to the baron's native Cygnaran. In both languages, he displayed the rolling Ordic brogue that was, so Halcourt felt, the only flaw in his earlier performance on stage. (Not that he'd ever be so gauche as to say so, of course.) "I'm delighted you've found our production enjoyable."

"Not at all, dear fellow! I've been looking forward to seeing *An Orgoth Goes a'Courting* for some time. I'm a great admirer of Muir's work, and I was just crushed when I wasn't able to attend any of your Cygnaran tour. Truth be told, my decision to stay in Leryn during this trip was as much because you were going to be performing here as for any of my more official responsibilities.

"But tell me," the baron continued, voice falling softer and more serious, "how go the efforts to get you home? I certainly appreciate the chance to attend your, ah, unscheduled encores, but I know you were supposed be back in Ord by now."

"Going well, last I heard. They tell me Khador's agreed to permit an ambassadorial delegation to pass through the lines and come retrieve us. It's just a question of working out the details.

"What of you, my Lord? Ord has the advantage of not actually being at war with Khador, but you . . ."

Baron Halcourt managed to retain his cheerful mien, but he felt the muscles locking up beneath his friendly expression. "There's risk, certainly. But I stand with my Llaelese friends, and I've no doubt their armies and Cygnar's can stop Khador before they draw anywhere near Leryn."

He couldn't tell if Claeddon believed a word of it, or was just skilled enough an actor to fake it, but he rather suspected the latter. Frankly, the drivel was starting to taste pretty wretched on his own tongue, too.

"If you'll pardon me," Halcourt finished, managing to maintain only a modicum of courtesy as his anger flared, "I need to speak with one of my people." Scarcely acknowledging the actor's reply, he descended the dais, wended his way between servers and around knots of conversation, looking for the woman on whom that anger was well and truly focused.

***

She saw him coming from across the room, and forced herself not to roll her eyes or to slip away. Neither would have been "proper."

And Dignity, at least in public, needed to stay all about *proper*.

So instead she adjusted her bracelets and smoothed the skirts of her gown, an ornate monstrosity in deepest blue and golden trim—patriotic, yes, but chosen mostly because it nicely set off the tawny curls currently heaped atop her head in one of the latest ludicrous styles.

"Underhurst!"

Ah. When was the last time he'd called her by her family name? *His Lordship is* truly *steamed.*

She met his approach with a shallow curtsy. "How can I be of service, Lord Halcourt?"

His hand closed tight about her forearm—not abusively so, for the baron was at least a good enough man that he rarely mistreated his staff, but close.

"You can tell me," he hissed, the words grunting as they squeezed between his teeth, "what in Morrow's name I was thinking when I let you talk me into this!"

Right. This again.

"My lord, the political and mercantile prospects are worth the risk! When the people of Llael see how you, out of all Cygnar's nobility, *personally* stood by them—to say nothing of the opportunities opening up as other businesses flee the nation—you're certain to—"

"Be dead or rotting in a frozen Khadoran dungeon!" he finished for her. "I've heard it from you a few times before, woman. It's *not* as convincing as it once was."

"My Lord, the front is nowhere near—"

"Not *yet* it isn't! But our 'glorious armies' haven't done bugger all to slow their advance, have they?" His voice remained low enough that none in the noisy chamber would overhear the substance of their talk. Still, that he was publicly berating the woman who, though relatively new, had been among the most trusted of his entourage, would have been impossible to miss.

And of course, as a recent but influential addition to the baron's staff, she'd already been marked as the enemy by most of Halcourt's other servants. *They're going to be on me like a pack of jackals.*

"You told me," he continued, "that a symbolic gesture would be enough. That there'd still be time to get out. You said *nothing* about being cut off from home by Khadoran lines!"

"I . . . I can only apologize, Lord Halcourt. I misjudged how long it would take to establish certain connections—"

"And will those apologies wing us home, Underhurst? Or shield us from the enemy like Morrow's own hand?"

Apparently they won't even enable me to finish a sentence . . .

He had her pressed against the wall, now. In almost any other setting, it would have been a blatant threat of violence.

Of course, in any other setting, he might have been surprised by the consequences of said threat.

"Your primary duty from now on," he growled, "is to keep everything nonessential packed and ready to depart at a moment's notice. If the opportunity comes to get the hell out of here, I don't intend to be caught waiting. That means not just my belongings, but the staff's."

"I'm neither a valet nor a maid. Surely that's more Anessa's job, or—"

"So long as you work for me, you're what I assign you to be. *Clearly* hiring you as scheduler and political advisor didn't work out. And don't think I won't be having words with Lord Wesbarton about recommending you, either! Do well enough with this, and maybe you'll still have *some* position in my household when we get home!"

Halcourt spun dramatically on his heel, very nearly colliding with a young servant carrying a soup tureen, and swept back toward the dais and the remains of his meal.

Dignity watched him go, her expression blank as a mirror in the dark— yes, she was holding back a few choice reactions, but most assuredly *not* the ones the nearby diners were expecting—and then exited the chamber, neck stiff and head high.

She waited until she'd moved down the hall, lushly adorned with tapestries and portraits, and up a sweeping flight of stairs, before allowing herself to burst out laughing.

It felt good; she'd had precious little to laugh about in recent days. Unfortunately, it didn't last long before the heavier implications set in. If Baron Halcourt wouldn't be coming to her for advice any longer, if he expected to see her engaged in regular labor, she'd have a much harder time arranging—

The tromp of footsteps and the swish of skirts provided her just enough warning to compose herself before three of the baron's household, including the aforementioned Anessa, marched into view. She and the other two, one man and one woman, stared at Dignity with a malevolent glee before hurrying up the stairs to vanish into the Lower Guest Hall.

No doubt they've already been told of my new duties, and have gone to unpack absolutely everything in their rooms.

Shaking her head until her mountainous heap of hair threatened to come unpinned, Dignity continued on her own way. Rather than stopping on the second floor, she continued toward the Upper Guest Hall, where the baron and his closest advisors—or, in her own case, *formerly* closest advisors—bedded down. Might as well get started, at least with Halcourt's own chamber. She chafed inwardly at the wasted time, but as there was hardly anything to be done about it . . .

"Lady, ah, Underhurst?"

One foot on the topmost step, Dignity turned back. One flight beneath her stood a young servant—the same, she realized, with whom Halcourt had nearly collided a few minutes ago.

"Yes?"

"Apologies for disturbing you, but the baron requested I fetch you at once. He needs you back in the dining hall."

"That's . . . peculiar. Did he say why?"

"I'm afraid not. He intimated it was urgent, though."

"I see . . ."

Except she didn't. Halcourt had nearly reached the dais before she'd departed. Even assuming the baron had, by some quirk of fate, changed his mind about sending her away, he would have had to turn around, passing a chamber full of other servants—including several members of his *own* staff—to ask this specific gentleman to fetch her.

An almost electrical tingle danced along the tips of her fingers.

"By all means," she said, voice chipper. "Lead the way."

The young man had barely turned his back when she dove down the steps at him.

He was fast, too fast for a serving boy; he *almost* managed to spin again in time to intercept her.

Almost.

Dignity reached out as she slipped between her target and the banister. The inside of her elbow closed around his throat as her other hand snaked up to fasten across the back of his head.

Anyone with the proper training could have broken that hold before passing out—if she hadn't settled on a lower step than he. Yanking him backward off his feet, supporting his weight from below, Dignity had the man completely off balance. The grip choking his world into darkness was also the only thing holding him upright.

She held him long seconds after his body sagged limply in her arms, to be absolutely certain he wasn't feigning. Then, shifting her grip to his shoulders, she dragged the unconscious body back up the stairs. A quick moment to tie his wrists and ankles with his own belt and coat, and then she nudged him casually into the nearest third-floor broom closet.

Obviously, something was happening up here that he hadn't wanted anyone interrupting. Well, *probably* obviously. *If I've somehow misjudged this whole mess, I'm going to have a bloody lot of explaining to do . . .*

But no. Even as she slid the closet door shut, only then releasing the handle to avoid the telltale *click*, she heard it. Not a step, scarcely even a whisper of movement; fabric against fabric. Nothing remotely suspicious or out of place, except that everyone with legitimate business on this floor was still down in the dining hall.

Well, that and, once again, the fact that someone had just attempted to keep her from this hallway.

Dignity's fingers closed around a bracelet—a heavy thing of ornately engraved gold that didn't *quite* form a full ring, leaving a half-inch gap on the inside of her arm. A quick twist and the "jewelry" snapped open on a hidden hinge directly opposite the missing segment. Now held in her right hand, the bauble formed two metallic limbs jutting out like horns sprouting from her fist. A second tap with her middle finger against that concealed joint, and two stiletto-like points, scarcely more than an inch long, snapped from those prongs.

Silently, as if the carpet had become nothing more than cloud, she drifted toward the nearest chamber: neither hers nor the baron's, but belonging to the captain of Halcourt's household guard. The door was shut tight, but Dignity was certain that the ghost of a sound had come from there.

Peeping through the keyhole, she could tell that the room was lit, a fire crackling merrily in the hearth, but that in itself wasn't suspicious. At this time of year, quite a number of people kept a small fire burning, or at least smoldering, so they wouldn't return to a chilly chamber.

With almost exaggerated care, she reached for a gaudier, more flimsy bracelet on her right wrist. From it she plucked a small crystal. A quick examination, to ensure she'd chosen the proper size, and then she carefully pressed it into the keyhole.

Clever as it was, the prism couldn't offer her a *clear* view of the chamber. She saw only an array of shapes, fuzzy and oddly hued; almost an abstract image of shadow and depth.

It was enough, however, to tell her someone was in the room, roughly beside the chest of drawers, and that said someone was *probably* alone.

Dignity pressed softly on the latch, just enough to ensure that the door wasn't locked—and hurled it open.

The intruder, clad in tunic and trousers of mottled blues and uneven edges, perfect for blending into nighttime shadows, fired off a wrist-mounted crossbow. The bolt came nowhere near Dignity, who had dropped into a forward tumble at her first step into the room.

She came up into a crouch beside the bed, then kicked off both floor and frame in a sideways leap. The intruder—who was, she could tell now, a dark haired, square-chinned man she'd never seen before—had produced a length of barbed chain from Morrow-knew-where. It whistled as it spun, slashing through the space Dignity *would* have occupied had she stood directly from her summersault.

Her opponent pivoted, the momentum of his first missed attack carrying him directly into a second. Dignity threw a high kick as a stop-thrust to the man's wrist. She felt flesh and muscle flatten against bone, and though the joint didn't break, his hand spasmed in pain. The chain hurtled from his grip to slam into the bricks over the fireplace. It clung there, barbs stuck into flaking mortar.

She turned that kick into a lunge, leaning over her foot as it came down and thrusting her two-pronged punch-blade at the intruder's midsection. Her stroke went wild, knocked aside by the man's unwounded forearm—an arm that then went rigid in a swift grab. Dignity felt his fist close on her arm and start to twist, yanking her into what she knew would either be a grapple or a dislocated shoulder.

Instead of fighting it, then, she turned *with* it, jabbing her elbow hard into her enemy's gut while that arm still had some slack in which to move. It was enough to loosen his grip, but even as she pulled free, the heel of his wounded hand—apparently not so wounded as she'd hoped—caught her hard across the chin.

Dignity's head rocked back, pain drilling deep into her jaw. Somehow she was able to *smell* the blood in her mouth before she tasted it. Still, she rolled with it, and her backward stagger was no genuine stumble but a deliberate draw.

When her attacker threw a snap kick of his own, then, one that would have shattered ribs had it connected, she was ready to meet it halfway.

The lowermost of her two blades slid neatly under the man's kneecap not entirely unlike a can opener.

His scream, when it began, was a high-pitched wheeze, easily mistaken for a teakettle just starting to boil. As soon as the agony broke through his shock, however, and his lungs gathered enough air to empower it, Dignity knew it would become a deafening crescendo.

And while it *probably* wouldn't be heard floors away, in the hubbub of dinner, she wasn't about to take the risk.

She stepped over his supine, bleeding body and brought her foot down on his throat. The rising scream vanished into a moist crunch; the intruder spasmed twice, and lay still.

Dignity sighed, leaning against the chest of drawers for a moment to catch her breath, trying to massage some feeling back into her chin. She'd have liked to question the man, but his fighting style alone was enough to tell her who he probably was—and if her guess was right, she'd have been hard pressed under even the best of circumstances to make him talk.

Khadoran. Section Three.

So. They knew they had an enemy concealed within Baron Halcourt's retinue, but—judging by the room their operative had been searching—they didn't know specifically who.

Dignity peered out into the hall, double-checking that she was alone, then darted across to her own chamber. When she returned, she carried a heavy clay jar filled with a mix of silvery grit and fine white powder. This, she carefully sprinkled over the Khadoran's body.

Only enough left for one more after this. Best not drop too many more bodies.

Well, publicly . . .

Careful not to further smear the blood and other bodily excretions, she dragged the powdered corpse to the fireplace and jammed it tightly up the chimney, then meticulously wiped any excess residue from her own hands. Once the alchemical powders soaked into the skin, even the lightest flicker of flame would reduce it to so much ash in moments. A few fragments of bone and teeth might survive, but someone would have to go digging through the charcoal and embers to find them.

As far as the stains in the carpet, she soaked up what she could with rags that also found their final resting place in the hearth. The remainder would be covered soon enough, when she "accidentally" dropped a brittle decanter of wine on the spot.

Dignity Underhurst—Cygnaran Reconnaissance Service, field designation: Garland—allowed herself a single heartfelt sigh; pondered the implications of this latest Khadoran ploy; cursed the name Idran di Meryse; and wondered, not for the first time, when the bloody hell her reinforcements might deign to arrive.

Glaceus 10th, 605 AR
Somewhere in the Southern Midlunds, Cygnar

"**O**oh . . . Looks to me like she's got you, Cadmoore."

Roland Cadmoore, leader of Benwynne's trencher unit, glanced up from the game, face strobing in the flickering light-and-shadow pattern from the nearby windows. His opponent, Serena Dalton, long gunners unit, did likewise. Her eyebrows—or, more precisely, eye*brow*, though the wise didn't tease her about it—crinkled in the middle as she glowered.

"How many times," she rasped, "do we have to ask you not to comment on our game?"

Atherton Gaust casually flicked a bit of tangerine rind from under his nails and bit into the exposed fruit. A single stream of juice dribbled across his knuckles. "You're welcome to ask me as often as you like," he allowed around a mouthful of pulp.

Roland and Serena sighed in unison and returned to the game, an army favorite involving both dice and a standard deck of playing cards in combination.

For a time, the so-called "officers' quarters"—which were just the rear quarter of the second reserved car, segregated from the rest by a makeshift curtain of blankets—remained blissfully quiet, disturbed only by the *click-clack, click-clack* of the *Lady Ellena* trundling over the rails, and the occasional rattle of dice or the slap of a card. Beyond the windows, fields of winter browns, greens, and occasional whites flanked the passing train, oblivious and uncaring.

"You really want to play the nine of cups over a pair of swords?" Atherton asked a while later. His words were oh so slightly slurred, as he struggled to remove a strand of citrus fiber from between his teeth with his tongue. "You'd need to roll doubles just have a chance of—!"

"Gaust . . ." Serena warned him.

Roland, for his part, merely smiled—teeth almost blinding against the darkness of his skin—and then slapped a card from his reserve, cards he was permitted to play at any point in his turn, down beside the others.

Ten of Swords; Roland had just given himself enough of an advantage to *automatically* win the next throw of the dice, unless Serena had, and chose to sacrifice, a higher card in her hand.

"Ouch." Atherton tucked his chin back, a bit like a turtle retreating into its shell. "I don't know, Serena, maybe you should—"

"*Triumph* is not a spectator sport, Gaust!"

"That's why I'm doing more than just spectating."

"You—"

"Oh, let him butt in." The rear door, leading to the cargo pallet on which the squad's three warjacks were tightly strapped, slid shut. Wendell Habbershant pulled his goggles down around his neck and scratched at his wind-bitten beard. "I mean, it's just Gaust. It's not as though he's liable to give either of you *good* advice."

"Funny, old man."

Wendell waved three fingers at the two corporals sitting over the cards and the dice. "The audience seems to think it was."

"Shouldn't you be off lubricating a shaft or something?"

"Why, are you looking for pointers?"

And so it went for several minutes, Serena and Roland now splitting their focus equally between the game and the verbal sniping. Neither had ever entirely figured out, from the moment Wendell joined the squad, how much was friendly banter and how much genuine hostility.

It was, unusually, the younger gunmage rather than the elder mechanik who brought this particular match to an end. "Listen, Habbershant . . ." He gave the curtain a cursory inspection, as though ensuring that none of the others were eavesdropping. "What have you heard?"

"About what?" he asked, even though all four of them knew damn well.

"Come on, Master Sergeant." Atherton squeezed into the seat beside Roland, ignoring the trencher's grunt of protest, and watched the scenery go by. A copse of trees briefly broke the monotony, casting a shadow play of thrashing limbs and flapping wings across the faces of soldiers and cards both, before the terrain turned flat and largely featureless once more.

Wendell, too, sat at the table, dropping down beside Serena. Idly, he picked up one of the dice sitting alongside the deck—a cheap, uneven thing carved of old bone—and began flipping it between two fingers. With a sigh that seemed almost an industrial sound, more appropriate to the train than his own chest, he began, "I don't *know* anything, mind you. All I've got is the grapevine. But . . ."

***

"Your corporals are worried about you, Sergeant."

He'd found her precisely where he'd expected, on the tiny platform outside the rearmost car, watching the fields and the seemingly endless track pass into the unseen distance. Though speaking around the ivory pipe clenched in his teeth, he made himself both loud and clear enough to be heard over the clatter of the wheels and the whistling of the wind. Not *so* loud, however, as to render their conversation anything but private.

"Is that so?" Benwynne asked, her tone so empty they might well have used it to store ammunition. "And why would they be worried?"

"They all saw the courier hand you that letter before departure, and you've been avoiding everyone on the trip so far, except to pass along a few orders. Your people aren't stupid, Sergeant."

"No. No, they're really not."

Wendell joined her, leaning on the railing. The pair of them swayed in unison with the rocking of the train; otherwise they remained immobile, until the mechanik idly began tossing bits of orange rind out into the *Lady Ellena's* wake.

"And you told them what, Master Sergeant?"

"Nothing of consequence." *Tear. Toss. Tear. Toss.* "Just repeated a lot of what's already circulating. Rumor and guesswork. I think the prevailing theory at the moment is that your husband—whom you've kept secret from the squad—has recently disappeared with your only child—whom you've *also* kept secret from the squad—and that you're worried you'll never see him again."

Benwynne finally tore her gaze from the passing terrain. "Where the hell do they *get* these notions?"

"Morrow only knows. *I* certainly have no idea."

"Funny thing is, Master Sergeant, they're not *entirely* off-base, if you want to get metaphorical about it."

Again, the clattering wheels and the whistling wind were the only speakers for a time.

"Sergeant," Wendell began; cleared his throat. *Tear. Toss. Tear. Toss.* "I respect your privacy, and I've no standing to press."

"But . . . ?"

"But . . ." Again he coughed, then shrugged helplessly.

"But you're worried," she finished for him, "about whether I'm in shape to command."

"Well, I wouldn't have put it *quite* like—"

"I'm fine, Master Sergeant."

As that certainly sounded final enough, Wendell turned to depart. Only the rustle of paper, scarcely audible beneath the ambient roar, stopped him.

Benwynne, still leaning over the railing, reached back to offer him the letter. With equal care and even greater hesitation, he accepted.

He needed only seconds to absorb the salient details.

"Twenty-five years?!"

Benwynne nodded. "Hard labor. It's a slow death sentence."

"I'm so sorry, Ben." Wendell felt his fists clenching, forced himself to relax. The document wasn't his to destroy. "Your niece?"

"Still no idea. I'm in no position to take her in; I'm in the field twelve-and-a-half months out of the year. But we haven't any other family to speak of . . ." She shrugged, a casual gesture more appropriate to a discussion of the *Triumph* match still ongoing a few cars away.

"And Callum? Do you need any leave time to deal with—?"

"What's to deal with?" She finally faced him, and Wendell would have felt a lot more comfortable with open mourning than the implacable façade she wore. "The evidence was so overwhelming, the tribunal didn't even retire to chambers for deliberation. My brother killed almost his whole family. What would be served by taking time away from my duties now?"

Wendell couldn't decide how to answer that. *To determine for yourself that he's guilty? To find out why?*

To convince yourself it wasn't your fault?

He damn well wasn't about to say any of it. He knew Benwynne had been close with her brother growing up, that she'd practically been a parent to him in their late adolescence. And he knew, however she may have felt, that she'd hardly thank him for the implication.

What he finally settled on, then, was, "What do you need from us?"

"From *you*, discretion. From everyone? Do your jobs, and trust that I know how to do mine."

"Absolutely, Sergeant. I'm . . ." *Honored you'd trust me with this.* But no, Bracewell wouldn't appreciate that, either. "Absolutely."

She spoke one last time, just as the mechanik stepped from the platform back into the rear car. "Wendell? Thank you."

A crisp salute, far more formal than was his wont, and then Wendell slid the panel closed, locking out the loudest of the *Lady Ellena*'s exertions, leaving his commander to dance alone with her regrets.

***

"Ladies, gentlemen, honored guests, your attention, please! Lady Ellena *will be arriving in* Bainsmarket *in approximately twenty minutes. Please gather your belongings and be prepared to disembark when your car number is called."*

"Master Sergeant?"

Wendell looked up as Benwynne's holler blasted through the sounds of soldiers assembling their gear—and, in the case of Corporals Cadmoore and Dalton, sweeping the *Triumph* cards and dice back into a burlap sack. "Yes, Sergeant?"

"I want you out on the pallet. Give the 'jacks a last once-over, make sure nothing's been jarred loose and that their furnaces are stoked and running the minute we disembark."

"On it, Sergeant." One final puff, then Wendell tapped out the exhausted bowl of his pipe—drawing in irate mumble from Atherton as the ash sifted over the gunmage's boots—and headed rearward.

Clambering over the warjacks, hunting mechanical defects while the train continued to lumber on toward its destination, wasn't entirely unlike assembling a printing press, during an earthquake, while standing atop a rain barrel—but Wendell, no stranger to such things, scrambled over the steal hillocks with neither hesitation nor misstep.

A cursory examination, conducted with quick hops and scurries, revealed no obvious damage. Wendell hadn't expected otherwise—machines built for combat weren't likely to shake themselves apart over a cross-country railroad—and he didn't anticipate learning otherwise on closer inspection, either. His job was to be certain, though, not to "expect" or "anticipate." The Master Sergeant checked the sun, determining how long he had for his assessment, watched the twin columns of smoke hauling themselves skyward, linking earth and cloud like slow, blurry lightning . . .

Wendell blinked. *Two* columns of smoke?

A lunge, a leap from Bulldog's strapped and secured chest, and Wendell's fingers clasped the roof of the next car over. A bit of awkward scrambling of his boots against the wall—*I'm so* glad the others weren't here to see that!—before he finally hauled himself over the edge.

Leaning into the wind, feet spread to counter the sway, he raised a hand for shade. The first snake of haze belched from the smokestack of the *Lady Ellena*, just as it should have. The second, much farther ahead . . .

"Oh, *hell* . . ."

***

"M'lady, my duty is the safety of this train and her passengers!" The engineer, whose overall lankiness and bushy beard resembled a scarecrow wearing a bird's nest, had raised his voice so that Benwynne might hear him over the banshee scream of the engine's brakes. "No bloody way am I taking us one yard nearer Bainsmarket than I have to!"

"We don't know for sure what the problem is!" Benwynne insisted. "It might just be a random fire, but if it's not . . . Look, I'm not asking you to drive into the heart of the damn city. Just get us near enough to see what's happening, so my people can—"

"I'm sorry, Sergeant, but no chance!"

"Evacuate the civilians first," she suggested as the lumbering behemoth of iron finally shrieked to a halt. "You've got five minutes. Then take us in."

"I said no. I'm responsible for the train, not just—"

"Master Sergeant Habbershant!"

"Yes, sergeant?" This from the back of the engineer's compartment.

Benwynne gestured at the array of levers and knobs. "Can you drive this thing?"

A moment's study, then, "Well enough to get us the intervening couple of miles."

"Excellent." Once more speaking to the conductor, she continued, "You're excused with the rest of the civilians."

The man's lip stiffened under his moustache. "I'm not about to—"

"I am hereby requisitioning this vehicle for the Second Cygnaran Army, under military emergency authority. You can drive, you can disembark, or I can shoot you."

His protest transformed itself to a faint croak in mid-syllable as he realized the sergeant was dead serious. The engineer all but bolted from the train.

"Habbershant, have your men uncouple everything behind the cargo pallet." Which, unfortunately, wasn't much, but it should lighten the load a little. "Get all the civilians off the train or into those rear cars, put our people up front, and get us *moving*!"

Moments later, the foreshortened *Lady Ellena* flew along the rails, wheels sparking, engine howling in dismay. The men and women of squad five gathered on the various platforms and in the open doorways, watching the ground stream past in a liquid blur, their faces growing chapped beneath the slow mastication of winter's teeth. They stood ready to leap from the train—*preferably* once it had stopped, but if necessary, even before—and confront whatever threatened Bainsmarket. Behind them, on the open cargo car, Wendell's mechaniks stood or crouched, kept from tumbling off the platform by various makeshift harnesses. Frenziedly they stoked coal-burners and cranked generators, returning full power to the semi-dormant 'jacks.

The city was still a smudge of high walls and abstract shapes in the distance, only partly distinguishable from the larger blur of the vast Thornwood Forest beyond, when Benwynne and Wendell first got some idea of what was happening. Additional plumes of smoke, smaller and thinner than the one they'd already spotted, trailed like ducklings behind the first. Dull booms and brilliant flashes suggested detonations within Bainsmarket itself—only a few, thankfully scattered, but more than enough to disrupt the lives of every citizen.

"It's not ordnance," the mechanik muttered, confirming what Benwynne had already figured. "Doesn't sound right, and I'm not seeing any weapons fire or gathered forces outside the walls."

"Saboteurs, then," she said.

"That'd be my guess, yeah." He paused, swore, wrestled with a stubborn lever. "Khador?"

"Can't imagine who else. Too far from the coast for a Cryxian incursion, and the Protectorate would strike further east."

"How?" Atherton stood listening, not in the engine itself, but on the tiny platform linking it to the first car. "I'm not the greatest admirer of CRS, but I can't imagine they're incompetent enough to miss an entire Khadoran infiltration of—"

Benwynne and Habbershant shared not only a glance but a memory: the beach near Clocker's Cove. They never *had* proven whether that raid had been funded with Khadoran gold koitina—but here, they'd no doubt at all between them.

"Mercenaries," they said together.

"But . . ." Atherton actually seemed at a loss for words, an event that, under other circumstances, might have inspired the others to drop to their knees in paeans of thanks. "Nobody foresaw this possibility?!"

Again the two senior officers shared thought and expression, the latter a deep scowl. As the northernmost stop on the Cygnaran Market Line—and thus, a staging area for many supplies shipped to the front—Bainsmarket was an *obvious* target for sabotage. And both of them knew that His Majesty's War Council did not consist largely of idiots. There *must* have been safeguards in place. Which meant . . .

"Whoever staged this," Benwynne said darkly, "is good. Too damn good. I—"

Wendell, gone suddenly white as Commander Nemo's hair, lunged, hurling all his weight onto a brass lever. Again the brakes screamed, spitting sparks to shame a dragon. The train lurched, sending soldiers staggering, buckling as the iron grapples between cars flexed in the fierce deceleration. The *Lady Ellena* shimmied, vibrating along her entire length, and every man and woman aboard tensed at the fearsome grinding from the leftmost track, and the abrupt, ship-like listing to one side.

For long, endless seconds, as she battled both inertia and the gradual curve of her iron pathway, the most famous locomotive in Cygnar teetered on the edge of derailment.

Thanks be to Morrow and the nation's finest craftsmen, the wheels regained their precarious grip; the train righted itself rather than flopping belly-up . . .

And shuddered to a violent stop with only its foremost pair of wheels protruding over the edge of the broken rails, where an earlier explosion had severed the line for a span of two or three horse-lengths.

One hand on the wall, Benwynne hefted herself from the floor beside the instrument panel, absently wiping away the blood from an angry gash across her forehead. Her furious scowl had only begun to form, drawing new and interesting shapes in that crimson smear, when Wendell—rubbing where several of the protruding levers had jabbed him in the ribs—pointed out the windscreen.

The sergeant took one look at the ruined track, nodded her understanding, and turned toward the doorway behind her.

"All right, nap on your own time! Everyone up and out! Trenchers forward, long gunners rear, eyes to all sides! Gaust, swing wide and bring your people around from the—" She paused just long enough to orient herself and note the position of the late afternoon sun. "—northeast. Return and report if possible, but you have permission to engage if necessary.

"Bulldog, trenchers' left flank. Shepherd, right. Wolfhound, scout from the southwest, engage at discretion. Deploy!"

To the not-so-musical accompaniment of cranking gears and steel footfalls, Benwynne's squad streamed, ant-like, from the *Lady Ellena* and pressed through the clinging cold toward the walls of Bainsmarket.

***

The grasslands, hardly a jungle even at their most lush, were little more than patches of bare earth with the sporadic, crispy blades of frost-embalmed tufts. The fields lay barren, former and future rows of wheat demarcated only by spindly wooden stakes. Despite the chill and the battering gusts that sputtered in winter's sickly wheezing, no snow or sleet flounced through the air to obscure vision.

There was, in short, nowhere to hide.

Atherton's commandos hid anyway. Even he could barely pick them out, creeping on bellies and elbows like oversized millipedes, and he knew precisely where to look.

The gunmage himself, moving at a low crouch, knew that, though his talents of stealth were nothing to be derided, when compared to his men he could not have stood out more strongly if he'd been a heavy warjack.

On fire.

All he could do was seethe with envy—not that he'd ever admit it to anyone, or ever trade his own training for theirs—and hope that his own lesser skills would suffice.

And so they did. The unit reached the walls of Bainsmarket, slabs of granite that really ought to have been taller and thicker in this age of modern weaponry, without drawing a single shot or cry of alarm.

The modest height of those walls was hardly Bainsmarket's only stumble in security. A trade city, a hub of commerce, protected from the nearest hostile nation by two hundred miles of deepest, darkest forest, its urban planners had always favored accessibility over impediment. More than a dozen gates provided ingress through the ramparts, some sized for moderate foot traffic, others large enough to admit heavy carts or locomotives of the Cygnaran railroad.

And while each was *capable* of slamming shut, hunkering behind bars of steel and slabs of banded wood, they had all hung open for so long that many of Bainsmarket's native adults had never seen them closed.

Rather than slip through the gaping tunnel the *Lady Ellena* would have traversed on any normal day, Atherton chose a narrow footpath some few hundred yards northeast. It made, he figured, a far less alluring target to whoever or whatever attacked the city.

Just as he and the commandos neared the opening, a small stream of panicked citizens began pouring *out*. Most were dressed for everyday business, in vests and trousers or skirts of muted colors, and coats too light for more than a few moments in the cold. Only a few carried any sort of baggage or satchels; not an organized evacuation, then, but a haphazard crowd of fleeing townsfolk.

Atherton grabbed the shoulders of the first refugee in reach: a middle-aged fellow with a pale, sweat-shiny face and hastily misbuttoned coat. "What's happening here?" Then again, more loudly, bodily hauling the gibbering man around to see the golden Cygnus on his uniform, "What *happened?*"

"Khador!" The townsman's tone was so shrill Atherton winced, and had to stop himself from asking if the man had recently been injured in an unfortunate spot. "Khador's attacking! Artillery outside the northern walls, warjacks in the streets . . ." He broke off in a horrified sob.

The gunmage shared a sidelong glance with Hartswood, the nearest of his commandos. "Saw all this yourself, did you?" Atherton asked flatly.

"No, just the fires, but my friend's brother saw—"

"Right." Atherton released the man's shoulders as if they'd abruptly sprouted mildew. "On your way, now." Then, to his soldier, "I don't know that questioning any of the others is likely to prove substantially more helpful."

"Doesn't seem likely, sir," Hartswood agreed.

"Right," the corporal repeated. "Detail two of the boys to hang back and make sure these people all get clear safely. The rest of us, we're going in."

Hartswood relayed his orders, and then Atherton, along with four of his men, were pushing through the tide of refugees into Bainsmarket proper.

It was a more sprawling, broadly built city than those to which Atherton was accustomed—thanks, again, to its mercantile needs. The avenues stretched wide, to accommodate multiple carts; the city blocks were long on all sides, so that more storehouses and businesses might be crammed along the busiest thoroughfares. Rather than providing a sense of space and freedom, though, it all somehow combined to make Bainsmarket more claustrophobic than fortified Caspia or mud-carpeted Corvis. The sheer desperation, the obsequious need to please any and all potential customers in the naked scrabble for patronage or coin, weighed more heavily on the air than the buildings themselves.

At the moment, those streets were rivers of chaotic flesh. Citizens and visitors tried to figure out which way to flee, or even what they fled *from*. Thick smoke and rank sweat made simple breathing a test of endurance. The blue-and-gold of the city garrison appeared only sporadically throughout the crowds. Whatever happened, it'd clearly thrown the local soldiers into disarray—or worse.

As best Atherton could tell, around a dozen explosions had rocked Bainsmarket, and while none had been overwhelmingly powerful, the vast spread of the detonations had caused more panic and disruption than any single blast, no matter how potent, could have managed.

Probably the point, that.

"Sir!" This from Ledeson, a tiny man—shorter than some dwarves—who'd nonetheless proved himself a valuable soldier. "There! Forward left!"

Even if the knot of people at whom Ledeson pointed hadn't been sprinting in almost military formation, heads down and arms pumping, from the doorway of a large warehouse, Atherton would have known them for what they were. He recognized the posture, the attitude, the motions, the *breed*.

Damn mercenaries.

First things first, though. Guns-for-hire usually had some pretty specific reasons for running like that.

"Cover!" Atherton shouted.

Flame erupted from the warehouse windows, flung the door from its hinges, sprouted through weak spots in the roof like the peaks on some infernal crown. The walls contained the worst of it, though, thank Morrow for small favors. The civilians on the street, while further terrified, were no more injured than the commandos who'd dived behind the nearest shelter.

"Gentlemen," Atherton announced, brushing road dirt from his coat as he stood from behind an abandoned wagon, "I would like to have a stern word with those fellows regarding the proper treatment of public property."

Once more the commandos vanished, disappearing this time into the scattering crowd, and the gunmage calmly started down the same street the mercenaries had taken.

After that, the gunfire was more than enough indication of which way to turn.

Atherton advanced up the block, coat flaring behind. Before him, two of the mercenaries already lay dead, both stabbed from behind before they'd known they were in danger. The remaining five crouched in adjacent door-ways, exchanging fire with unseen opponents—Hartswood, Ledeson, and the others—sheltered behind similar doorways and the ever-more-shredded carcass of a dead horse.

The first mercenary saw him coming half a street away. Even from that distance, Atherton saw the man's eyes flare from gibbous to full, saw his mouth open in a shout. The sellsword's weapon, a blunt-nosed carbine, swiveled his way, the barrel a gaping, ravenous maw.

The gunmage permitted himself a smile, and kept walking.

The carbine quivered. Atherton took another step—and then seemed simply to *fold*.

Between one footfall and the next, he jackknifed to one side from the waist up, pivoting in the process. A simple move, somehow simultaneously awkward and graceful, was all it took to shift him just out of line with the barrel.

The abrupt movement, as he'd known it would, startled the mercenary into firing.

The bullet flew harmlessly by and Atherton straightened, coming out of his spin with both hands full of pepperbox. Two cerulean auras flickered, two ensorcelled bullets burst from the twinned weapons. The first blasted clean through the man who'd shot at him, the stone wall behind him, and the second shooter behind *that*, concealing the entire doorway in a cloud of powdered granite.

The second struck two doorways down, punching into the chest of one mercenary, lifting him from his feet in defiance of all physics, and slamming him with bone-crunching force into a second. Both flopped and thrashed, screaming, into the street. The gunmage fired again, putting a single mercy shot through the pair of them.

"By my count," Atherton called cheerfully, "that leaves one of you! Some friendly advice? Surrender's a solid option."

A rifle spun from behind a corner of the building, followed by a heavy pistol and a long dagger. Hands clasped firmly to the back of his head, a raggedy and unkempt thug in even more raggedy and unkempt leather armor stepped sullenly into the open.

"Wise choice," the corporal noted. He watched the scurry of activity as his commandos swooped in, searching and securing the prisoner. Only then did he approach, idly tapping the barrels of one pistol against his chin in a gesture that, for anyone but a gunmage, would have been the absolute height of foolishness. "You're not going to make me waste my time and yours with threats, are you?"

The mercenary's scowl deepened until it seemed his jaw might actually fall off and scamper away on its own, but he shook his head.

"Good. A few easy ones to start with, then."

Indeed, it was a very brief question-and-answer exchange that followed. Yes, as the fellow understood it, Khador had paid for the operation, though it had been a local who'd actually hired most of the men. Yes, their plan was to disrupt the railway and the transportation of supplies to the front. No surprises whatsoever, thus far.

Then the prisoner came around to the name of the man who'd hired them, the commander of the whole operation—and Atherton wasn't smiling anymore.

"Thamar's crotch . . ." Ledeson whispered, nursing a grazing injury to his left arm.

Atherton nodded. "About the size of it, Private." Again he hefted this pistol to his chin, whispering softly over the rune-scarred, unnatural steel. Energies crackled, hair stood on end, and for the briefest sliver of a second, it sounded as though something within the barrels whispered back.

Finally, he aimed at the sky, and fired. Like a shooting star in reverse, a faint cobalt gleam shot upward, hovered, and then hurtled away toward the southwest.

***

By the time evening began to paint Bainsmarket with its palette of shadows, Cadmoore's trencher unit had already secured the closest intersections, while Dalton's long gunners kept to the track and the massive gateway through which their train would have entered. Benwynne surveyed the city—what she could see of it, anyway—from the shadow of the barbican. She saw the rails leading away, reaching toward the horizon and the unseen railroad station before being swallowed by the intervening blocks. Only a few streets converged here, allowing for pedestrian traffic along the curtain wall and—so she supposed—providing train, track, and tunnel access to maintenance workers. As such, she wasn't faced with a large population of civilians; only a few townsfolk peeked from nearby buildings, mostly squat and heavy workshops of this sort or that, and they all obeyed when the soldiers waved for them to stay inside.

"Corporal Cadmoore!" she barked.

"Yes, Sergeant?"

"Until Gaust's commandos pop up, your people are eyes and ears. I want small groups scouting up-track and along that road, that road, and *that* road. They are *not* to advance more than a two-minute run from us, but I want them to at least try to figure out what in the name of Thamar's tits is happening in this damn city!"

"Dalton, have at least two rifles covering each team until—"

Every face turned skyward as a tiny speck, shimmering through shades so blue they'd make the sky curl away in shame, soared over the buildings and plunged to earth. So swift did it come that Benwynne hadn't even time to draw breath, nor any of her people to seek cover, before it struck the ground a yard from her feet.

Rather than any sort of detonation, however, sizzling arcs of sapphire energies danced across the dirt around the impact. Benwynne, trying to make sense of the surreal image, couldn't decide if it looked more like a dancing spider or a spectral onion.

"Gaust," she snarled at her absent corporal, "what the hell are you—?"

The lightshow faded, revealing a small concavity where the bullet had struck—and, of far greater interest, an array of cracks in the frost-dried earth.

Cracks that, impossibly, spelled out a word.

"When," Wendell grumped, appearing at Benwynne's side, "did he learn to do—"

And just like that, he fell as speechless as Benwynne. Presumably because he, too, had read the gunmage's abbreviated message.

Not a word, this, but a *name*. A name that changed everything the sergeant had planned.

Magnus.

She finally broke her silence with an enraged, almost primal hiss, and she was far from the only one to do so. It was a name with which all of her seconds, and most of her soldiers, were only too familiar.

Asheth Magnus, a high-ranking warcaster under King Vinter IV, and now, under Leto IV, Cygnar's most reviled traitor.

And its most dangerous. For Benwynne, around that name, a *lot* of puzzle pieces slipped into place.

"I suppose," she told Wendell, her voice rubbed rough across the thorns of her sprouting fury, "we know how they managed to sneak a full company of mercenaries into Bainsmarket under CRS's nose. Nobody knows our procedures and defenses better than that one-armed bastard! I'll bet he just drooled at the opportunity to aid Khador's offensive . . ."

"It also means," the mechanik noted, "that he knows exactly how and where to hit the city to most effectively cripple it. Frankly, if *he's* behind this, I'm surprised Bainsmarket hasn't already fallen entirely."

"True." Benwynne chewed her lip briefly in a very unmilitary gesture. "It can't be a full military incursion," she mused aloud. "No way he could have crossed the border without being detected. And if he had to sneak in, he'll be missing his heavy equipment. Still . . .

"The bombs we've seen so far aren't enough, Wendell. He's not done, not by a long shot." Then, more loudly, "Dalton! Cadmoore! Belay my previous orders and get over here!"

Once all four officers had gathered, a hurried discussion was enough to convince them that they *probably* had a handle on the overall gist of Magnus's plan. These first explosions would assuredly have taken out a few military installations—including the storehouses and workshops for any local 'jacks— as well as a number of more lightly guarded civilian targets. The subsequent panic and disruption of the Bainsmarket garrison would then open the door to more vital military and political objectives. The surviving local units would have been scattered, caught off-guard, easily picked apart—not for long, but Magnus wouldn't have *needed* long.

The squad had arrived before the invaders reached that stage of the operation, assuming that was, indeed, the plan. Benwynne, only moderately religious, offered a quick prayer of thanks to Morrow for their fortunate timing.

"None of which does us much good, really," Cadmoore pointed out, scowling. "We don't know where in the city he's set up, what his specific targets are—"

"We can pretty safely guess at a few of those," Wendell interrupted.

"A few. Not all. And even if we knew them all, you see enough of us to *cover* them all?"

"What are you suggesting, then, Cadmoore?"

The trencher corporal and Sergeant Benwynne actually answered simultaneously. "Draw him out."

Cadmoore flashed a tight smile at his commander and allowed her to continue.

"We need to make him see us as a threat too big to ignore," she said.

"Make him think he has pressing need to take us out *before* he moves on to more vital targets."

"And how do you suggest we do that?" Dalton asked, her voice even more gravelly and grinding than usual. "Formal invitation?"

"Actually . . ." Benwynne's whole face shifted as she broke into a half-mouthed smirk. "Cadmoore, new orders. I want your people collecting rubble. Pull down empty buildings if you have to. Start marking out some trenches *outside* the curtain wall, too. We're digging in, and I want to be able to hold this position from both directions."

"But—"

"Habbershant's mechaniks will assist with the planning and construction of makeshift fortifications. Hmm . . . Send one or two back out to the *Lady Ellena*; have them start cataloging working parts, usable scrap metal, the works. Dalton, long gunners on every bit of local high ground. That includes atop the wall, and I want some sentries watching out, not in."

Wendell and Serena both stared at the sergeant like her teeth were rusting, but Roland—who'd served with her longest—sprouted a grin to match her own.

"Only one good reason we'd be digging and fortifying the barbican," he explained to the others, chuckling, "rather than moving in and searching the streets."

Understanding finally dawned; the mechanik's and the long gunner's faces lit up like those of newly awakened warjacks.

"Is if," Serena finished, "we're merely an advance unit, securing entry for a larger force."

The smile now shared between all four, the officers turned and began barking new orders to the men and women of Bracewell's squad.

***

"Sergeant."

"Corporal." Benwynne nodded twice, first in greeting, then in dismissal to the trenchers who had escorted Atherton through the makeshift and woefully incomplete fortifications. "Nice job on ferreting out who was behind this."

The gunmage's turn, now, to nod.

Night had well and truly fallen, not that anyone could easily tell. Pockets of Bainsmarket, their own included, were so glaringly illuminated that one could, with only a modicum of eyestrain, have sat in the street and perused the front page of a broadsheet. The iron cages atop streetlamps glowed, pockets of daylight formed of gas-fed flame. Too much flame, it seemed. The system of pipes beneath the streets still worked, even after the attacks, but clearly not without faults.

Now she abruptly frowned, dragging the whole of her attention away from the construction of the rubble-made bastion and onto the newly returned corporal. "You're not the only one who made it back, I hope!"

"No, Sergeant!" This from five voices speaking as one. Benwynne turned to see Gaust's commando unit gathered some ways behind her, sporting only minor injuries among them, currently raiding the supply packs for something to eat. She'd neither seen them enter the barbican, nor heard a single call of challenge from any sentries.

"Cute, Gaust."

"I think it just comes naturally to them, Sergeant."

"Oh, of course. And you'd *never* order them to do something like that so you could have a little laugh at my expense."

Atherton clutched a melodramatic hand to his chest. "Of *course* not!" He managed to keep the insouciant leer from his lips, but it capered about clearly in his eyes. "The laugh is just a secondary benefit."

Then, when Benwynne continued not being amused, "Mostly testing the defenses, Sergeant. Hartswood should have a report for you shortly."

"Of course he should."

"Sergeant," Atherton said, all business now, "I'm sure you'll get around to telling me why we're digging in instead of advancing, but you need to know . . . We spotted more than a little bit of enemy activity while making our way back."

"We've been watching," she assured him. "They're staging in those two buildings across the way, and that third one along the tracks." She indicated them only with a flicker of her gaze, so as not to be seen pointing.

"Not just those," the corporal insisted. "I don't know how many you've spotted, but at a guess? From this angle, with these lines of sight, you've got eyes on *maybe* a third of them."

". . . Oh."

"Including a few mortar and small cannon teams. These little walls you've got Habbershant designing won't hold up long."

"Hopefully they won't have to. Corporal, when did you learn to send messages like that? And if you can reach *me* that accurately from half a district away, why not the enemy?"

The gunmage looked briefly at his boots. "Been working on that for a while, Sergeant. Didn't want to mention it until I knew it'd work. Um . . . And I can only do it because I know you, and scored the final glyphs into the runebullets in your presence. You, Habbershant, a few of the others. Won't work for anyone else."

"In other words," Benwynne said, face and voice equally flinty, "you *literally* have a collection of bullets with my name on them?"

"Uh . . . I wouldn't put it *quite* like—"

"Gaust, go find Cadmoore or Dalton to fill you in. I need to get things rolling."

"Yes, Sergeant. Hey, by the way, where are the—?"

"Now."

A perfunctory salute, a swirl of navy-blue coat, and the gunmage was gone.

Benwynne marched to the forefront of the position, peering over the improvised rampart. Her fingers twitched, itching for the spyglass, but she resisted. If the enemy caught her studying them before her own people were ready . . .

Trenchers and mechaniks scurried around her, offering reports and receiving new orders. Finally, while Benwynne wasn't entirely satisfied that all was in order, she figured she couldn't afford to wait any longer. "Master Sergeant!"

Wendell appeared, again carrying his bizarre mechanical box-on-a-tripod. Unlike its prior appearance on the beach, this time it boasted an additional tube of flimsy rubber, ending in a brass funnel.

"You won't be near as loud as the signal whistles," he reminded her, "so you'll still want to shout."

"I think shouting is something I can manage."

The mechanik coughed once, camouflaging a chuckle. Benwynne flashed a fleeting smirk in return, then raised the funnel to her lips.

"Asheth Magnus!" Her words boomed from the contraption, practically cannonballs in themselves, aimed at a target she couldn't yet distinguish. "You are wanted on multiple charges of high treason. We know you're here. Surrender yourself now, and nobody else need die here today!"

A moment, a moment more . . . And then, on a third-floor balcony halfway along the visible stretch of railroad track, a figure appeared. Now Benwynne *did* snap the spyglass open, determined to confirm what she already knew.

Yes. Broad-shouldered and worn of visage, as though he'd staved off the aging of his body by absorbing it all into his face; clad in makeshift warcaster armor, belching smoke from a pair of small stacks; left hand of flesh clutching an enormous pistol, right hand of iron clenched into a monstrous fist . . . She'd have recognized him by sight even had she not already known his name.

When the traitor called back, he used no artificial augmentation. His voice, which had once driven whole armies, required no such assistance.

"And to whom am I expected to surrender myself, precisely?" Each word was concise, distinct, and carried the weight of an incoming shell.

"Sergeant Benwynne Bracewell," she answered via the device. "31st Vanguard Company, 7th Division, Second Cygnaran Army."

"I see." Magnus shifted across the balcony, and Benwynne had to acknowledge that he knew what he was doing. At no point was he farther than a single dive from the doorway, and the cover of the edifice's heavy stone walls. "Tell me something, Sergeant Bracewell, if you would . . . How did you respond so swiftly?"

"He wasn't *expecting* a military response?" Benwynne whispered incredulously.

"Which means," Wendell said softly, "that he's got forces holding the Point Bourne line and the road to Stonebridge Castle."

Benwynne nodded, but her reply was directed once more to the enemy, rather than the man at her side. "Worried, Magnus?"

"Not terribly." They could see the shrug even from so far away. "My scouts tell me the plains are still clear. I don't know when you're expecting reinforcements to arrive, but I have every confidence I can wipe out your entire position long before they do."

"You realize he's stalling," Wendell continued.

The sergeant lowered the tube and placed a palm over the gap. "Of *course* I know that! He's moving people into position for a sudden, overwhelming strike. It's the optimal strategy."

"So shouldn't we be trying to make it *sub*optimal, then? Soon-ish?"

"Maybe you can," Benwynne challenged, speaking once more through the funnel, "but not easily. You sure you'll have enough people left afterward to do the job?"

"I think I can manage, thank you. But," the traitor continued, suddenly thoughtful, "I'm not an unreasonable man. Withdraw your squad from Bainsmarket, right now, and I'll permit you to leave unmolested."

"I think you know the answer to that," Benwynne replied. Then, with a sneer that she was certain Magnus could spot from the balcony, "But then, I suppose I ought not be surprised that you've utterly forgotten what it means to be Cygnaran."

It was impossible, of course, but she would have sworn she'd heard the traitor's teeth grinding even from here.

And then, without warning, he laughed. Long, loud, as though he'd well and truly lost control, Asheth Magnus laughed.

"You're not an advance force at all, are you, Sergeant?" he asked once he'd gotten himself under control.

Benwynne never did figure out what had given them away. Some tiny detail she'd overlooked in the way they'd fortified their position? Some idiosyncrasy involved in the fielding of larger divisions which, commanding only a single squad, she'd never learned? Or perhaps it was something far less conscious, an instinct that Magnus had honed to a bleeding edge.

Still, their deception had done its work. It had drawn him out, with the bulk of his forces.

So Benwynne simply smiled even wider. "Took you long enough."

"I don't know what you thought to accomplish," Magnus snarled, all good humor gone so swiftly it might well have been drained by a Cryxian soulhunter, "but it's over. *Ready!*"

Mercenaries in battered gear rose from behind door stoops, assembled in windows, flooded onto the streets. Mortar crews gathered behind the growing ranks, snapping weapons together with professional haste. Benwynne heard the men and women around her tensing, fingers edging toward triggers and hilts.

"Steady . . ." she ordered.

And then, as Magnus drew breath for the attack order, Benwynne's own shout, unaugmented by Wendell's device, rang over the heads of the gathered soldiers.

"Deploy!"

She only wished she could clearly see the traitor's face when the first of the warjacks appeared from concealment behind the curtain wall, striding through the railroad tunnel to appear beside the "outgunned" Cygnaran force. It was the one advantage she knew he did not—*could* not—have: His infiltration had relied on stealth and surprise, and that meant no heavy machinery.

'Jacks included.

Wolfhound stepped from the barbican, shuffled right to leave room for the others, and discharged the long cannon thrice in rapid succession. Soldiers flinched as shards and powdered stone erupted from the walls, and the entire balcony on which Magnus stood abruptly began to sag, it's main supports sliced clean through by the hardened rounds.

"Gods *damn* it, Wolfhound!" Benwynne actually felt an almost overwhelming (if also utterly useless) urge to give the warjack a good smack. It had been told to *appear* at her command, but it was supposed to await for the word to actually *engage*.

The Hunter's joints weren't equipped to shrug, but it somehow managed to convey the impression all the same.

All right, Magnus had made that building his command post; it probably *didn't have any civilians left inside . . .*

There was, of course, no longer any *need* to give the order to engage. Rifle and mortar rounds streaked from the nooks and crannies of multiple structures, pounding the squad's ragged defenses. The soldiers returned fire, but chain guns chewed mostly stone and the long gunners managed to pick off only a few sporadic targets. The drooping balcony disappeared entirely behind clouds of smoke and dust. Sparking azure bolts heralded Atherton's own contributions, and where his runebullets struck, shelter collapsed and mercenaries died—but a lone gunmage, however effective, was unlikely to turn the tide of the whole battle.

The two remaining 'jacks, though, were more than willing to pick up the slack.

As Wolfhound sought a target for its next penetrating round, Shepherd and Bulldog stormed ahead, circling around either side of the bulwark. With a coordination that came partly from Benwynne's shouted orders and partly their own experience, the massive machines fired in staggered patterns. Bulldog's twin cannon barked until the magazine was half-empty, first pock-marking and then finally obliterating the face of a nearby blacksmith's, as well as a sizable contingent of mercenaries sheltered within.

The survivors scurried from the crumbling structure directly into the path of Shepherd's and the trenchers' chain guns.

The second half of the magazine emptied as swiftly, slamming already battered stone, and the rest of Magnus's command position shattered like a glass anvil. Benwynne wondered briefly if it was too much to hope that the traitor was finally dead and buried—but she damn well knew better than believe it until she had the body at her feet.

Now out of shells, the warjack was reduced to using its massive mallet until the mechaniks could get near enough to reload. And while Shepherd's own weapon still spat and chortled, it took time for even so thick a storm of bullets to grind through solid stone. From within a third building, mortars coughed, over and over, and Benwynne winced as a chain gun crew vanished in dust and flame.

She heard the *snap-clang* of Wolfhound's breach. "Take out that mortar nest!" she shouted, though she needn't have bothered. The 'jack was already raising the cannon again, calculating the proper angle . . .

And Magnus the Traitor proved that either he still lived, or that he'd planned contingencies even against the unexpected arrival of warjacks—and also that, living or dead, he'd instilled such dread in his soldiers that near-certain suicide failed to dissuade them.

From doorway and alleyway, shadow and sewer, men charged the three warjacks. At the same moments, field guns opened up from various windows, forcing the Cygnaran defenders to duck and cover, leaving only a few in position to fire on the incoming enemy.

Benwynne raised her head over the wall and nearly choked on the ambient dust. Every mercenary racing for her 'jacks bore an armful of metal and fuses. She'd no way of telling how potent those bombs might be, but if they'd been built to take down government and military installations in Magnus's reign of terror, they had to be powerful indeed.

"Don't let them near you!"

The two more distant warjacks reacted instantly. Shepherd dropped into a crouch and sprayed bullets in almost all directions, flipping its shield horizontal in its other hand for use as a makeshift blade. Bulldog began smashing anything that drew too close, not only with its hammer but the barrels of its spent cannon.

But Wolfhound . . . Wolfhound continued to aim, adjusting the angle of its weapon a degree this way, a degree that . . .

The long cannon spat twice, and the mortar team ceased firing—or doing much of anything else. But that, apparently, hadn't been the 'jack's only calculation.

One of the enormous shell casings sprang from the weapon's breach, tumbled end over end, and landed with perfect aim on the forehead of an incoming bomber. Bruised and burned, the man recoiled, and the warjack simply swept him aside with the long gun's barrel.

Just as Wolfhound had seemed to shrug earlier, so Benwynne could have sworn she felt something vaguely akin to a smug chortle from the willful machine. Hardly even looking, it spun its axe and turned the rest of the charging enemy into oozing debris.

But while the Hunter readily dispatched the threat, and Shepherd's combination of automatic fire and shield had accomplished the same, Bulldog proved less fortunate. Bodies fell apart beneath the mallet, bones cracked with the impact of the cannon, but one of the more lightfooted mercenaries had avoided both. The charge latched against the back of the warjack's thigh with a metallic ring that Benwynne somehow heard over the gunfire and mayhem.

Bulldog dropped its hammer and reached awkwardly back with a grasping hand . . . The sergeant opened her mouth to shout some order or other . . .

And then all she could do was look away, eyes squeezed tight, as the night—already artificially brightened—dissipated beneath the dawning of a false sun.

Glaceus 15th, 605 AR
Bainsmarket, Cygnar

From here, it looked as though one of the gods had stepped through Bainsmarket, leaving a careless imprint of devastation on his way to some other appointment.

From the southeast corner of the city garrison, a watchtower—one of several—stretched high, crenellations spread, a granite flower blossoming skyward. Slumped against the stone of the merlon between two of those stubby, rocky fingers, with barely enough strength left to keep pipe between teeth, Wendell Habbershant peered over the wreckage without really absorbing much of it. What had been a temple to Morrow was now a jagged blot of rubble on the city's face; and buried beneath it, the cemetery in which so many of Bainsmarket's soldiers were interred. The twice-damned bloody traitor had certainly known how to cause the defenders the worst distraction, and the worst pain.

Steamjacks, bulkier and more squared than their combat-ready counterparts, clomped this way and that, spewing smoke, hauling enormous loads of rubble. Men and women—mostly citizens, but quite a few troops from neighboring installations and a number of Benwynne's people as well—scurried throughout the wreckage, digging, hefting, seeking. No real hope of any further survivors, not five days in, but the cleanup and the search for corpses would continue for some while. Would continue here and in roughly a dozen spots just like it, gaping wounds in Bainsmarket's fair flesh. It wasn't nearly as bad as it might have been—the fifth squad's intervention had forestalled the worst of the traitor's operation, so recovery and return to normal would be a matter of days, rather than weeks or months—but it was bad enough, for all that.

Habbershant saw none of it. The gusts swept through the crenellations, cut through his coat and the extra warmth of his beard, but he did not feel them. The sun blinked in and out, almost rhythmically, through an ever-shifting drapery of cloud, but he never noticed.

Wendell saw only the rising and falling glow of his pipe, and within each pulse of orange, the last moments of battle now almost a week gone by.

Embers flared, and . . .

Wendell staggered upright, muscles working out of habit more than any conscious intent, to peer over the ramshackle—and now badly holed—bulwark of rubble. Whole swathes of street were soot-blackened and choked with debris. Buildings, already undermined and pounded by the firefight, had folded in on themselves, heaped like a giant's discarded laundry. Body parts, to say nothing of smears and gobbets that might *have been body parts, lay strewn over the tracks, plastered to the sides of any nearby walls still standing . . .*

Pungent smoke puffed from the bowl, a tiny dust-devil swirling before Wendell's eyes . . .

He watched as Benwynne rose—bloody-faced and cinder-stained, but not severely injured, thank Morrow!—scrambled over the wall and dropped into the midst of a chain gun crew now consisting entirely of shrapnel-riddled corpses. Shouting something he couldn't begin to make out, she opened fire on the surviving enemy forces . . .

Leaves crackled and curled, the orange luminescence faded to a negligible glow . . .

Shepherd fired a last burst into the nearest occupied structure, continuing until its chain gun spun nothing but empty barrels. Hefting its shield, it barreled through the weakened stone, smashing mercenaries with aegis and spent firearm alike. Wolfhound literally *vaulted the makeshift bastion, knocking additional stone tumbling down both sides. Axe raised high, it plunged after Shepherd, and the sounds of slaughter redoubled.*

Wendell began to chew on the pipe stem. His breathing hastened, the ebb and flow of the embers grew to a more rapid pulse . . .

". . . half-score men, Master Sergeant. And twice that many who need days of medical attention."

"Gods, Benwynne . . ."

"I expect to lose people once we actually engage, Wendell, but in Bainsmarket . . . ?"

Snapping leaves, swirling smoke . . .

"... *just nothing I can do. If I had weeks to spare and a fully functioning work-shop, I might salvage enough pieces to save some coin on building a brand* new *Charger chassis, but that's it. The cortex is cracked. I'm sorry, Sergeant. Bulldog's gone.*"

The pipe blurred behind a sheen of unshed tears. It was stupid—more than stupid, *disrespectful*—to grieve more over a machine than over the tren-chers Cadmoore had lost, but . . .

"... *no trace of the bastard. Nothing!*"

"*There's a lot of rubble left to dig through!*" *Gaust protested.* "*He could be buried somewhere down there, under all that stone and furniture! We might have gotten him!*"

"*No.*" *The sergeant's tone was flat, hard as stone.* "*Maybe he was injured, maybe he just felt the battle wasn't worth the risk. He's not here because he decided to with-draw, not because we came anywhere* near *'getting him.'*"

"*Ben . . .*" *Gods, he wanted to give her, Gaust, the others some* hope. "*Anything's possible. He could* be dead *. . . Finally . . .*"

"*Do you honestly believe that, Master Sergeant?*"

And all he could do was sigh . . .

Groaning, his joints creaking, Wendell straightened and leaned back, popping his spine and shoulders. He thought he'd known exhaustion, thought he'd felt it after any number of battles, prepping for any number of missions.

He'd had no idea.

Technically, he should be heading back out there, return to overseeing the work crews, but he just didn't have it in him. He felt as though, if he were to topple over the parapet this instant, he might well lack the energy to complete his fall to the bottom.

No more, not today. He emptied his spent pipe against the merlon, leaving a small stain of ash and soot between the crenellations, already begin-ning to disperse in the breeze. Time to head downstairs—even the thought of the steps filled him with something approaching existential dread—call on the benefits of rank, and requisition himself at *least* six straight hours of sleep.

A stranger, clad in thick wools and scuffed leathers, carrying a satchel on one shoulder and wearing the brass horse-head pin of the Pan-Midlunds Courier Association, met him roughly halfway down the staircase.

"Master Sergeant Habbershant?"

"Not now." Wendell made to push past him, but the messenger skillfully shifted just far enough to prevent it.

"You're a hard man to locate, Master Sergeant."

"I said *not now*." The mechanik reached out, scooted the courier over by the shoulders, and resumed his descent. "It's going to have to wait until tomorrow. Or else talk to Sergeant Bracewell. I am officially unavailable for—"

"Master Sergeant? *Contingency*."

"*Gods damn it!!*"

Both men stood for a few heartbeats, equally shocked by Wendell's exhausted outburst. Feeling the weight of every one of his years, and a reserve regiment besides, he squeezed his eyes so tightly shut his entire visage crinkled into a parchment-like topography of wrinkles and crags.

"All right. What's happened, and what does the CRS want from me?"

"We'd better find somewhere more comfortable—and private—to speak, Master Sergeant. This might take some explaining."

***

Cadmoore, Dalton, and, of course, Bracewell looked immaculate. Uniforms crisp, eyes alert, no hair out of place. Though it lacked some hours yet until dawn, though all three bore an exhaustion and grief so heavy their shoulders threatened to buckle under the strain, they maintained themselves, in all visible ways, as professional soldiers ought.

Corporal Gaust had, contrarily, made an effort that couldn't even *aspire* to "half-assed." His coat and pants were rumpled, very much as though they'd been dropped in a corner for the night. His gaze was bleary, and his hat couldn't hide the way the pillow had mashed his hair against the left side of his scalp.

And still, he wasn't the most slovenly present. Habbershant's beard was wild and spiky, his neck and cheeks unshaven, the bags under his eyes roomy enough to have packed a change of clothes. It was inexcusable at the best of times, let alone when he himself had called this small-hour assembly. Under most circumstances, he'd have been deeply ashamed to stand before the others like this.

Today, he just couldn't be bothered to care.

"All right, Master Sergeant." Benwynne leaned forward, palms pressed to the table that was the only real feature of the chamber they'd borrowed. "What in Morrow's name is so blasted urgent that it couldn't wait for a decent hour?"

Wendell opened his mouth, closed it. *Gods*, he didn't want to do this!

"Our mission's changed," he finally forced out. "We need to leave tomorrow for Fisherbrook."

Four faces stared at him all uncomprehending. He might as well have been speaking Khurzic.

"I don't know about the rest of you," Atherton said, his words contorting themselves painfully around an abrupt yawn, "but I'm way too tired for this."

"Habbershant . . ." Benwynne began.

The mechanik raised a hand, forestalling her objection. "Earlier tonight, I was approached by a man whom I took to be a Pan-Midlunds courier. Turned out that was only his cover; he identified himself, via pre-arranged code word, as being Reconnaissance Service."

That, at least, was enough to wake Atherton, and to fully capture everyone else's attention. Benwynne's whole expression darkened. "Why would they arrange for *you* to—"

"Please, Sergeant." He tried his damnedest not to wince. He'd foolishly hoped she wouldn't ask that, even though he'd known—*known*—she would. "Another moment or two."

She nodded stiffly.

"Magnus's efforts weren't confined to Bainsmarket, though this was certainly the linchpin of his operation. Apparently, he also had people sabotaging or attacking river ports, crossings, and boats up and down the Dragon's Tongue."

"He *really* meant to cut us off from the northern front, didn't he?" Serena mused.

"He also," Wendell continued, "either got luckier than he could ever have imagined, or he has intelligence sources deeper than *we* ever imagine. *Probably* the former, but . . .

"In any event, one of the riverboats his people shelled was transporting the CRS unit assigned to Baron Halcourt's extraction from Leryn."

Even as she scowled at the news, Benwynne nodded a second time. "I see. I assume our task has something to do with assisting the replacement team into position?"

"Sergeant . . ." He took another deep, steadying breath. "We *are* the replacement team."

It was a sign of just how tired they all were, that Atherton, Roland, and Serena all began speaking at once. It took only a moment for Benwynne to shout them down, but before she could articulate questions of her own, Wendell had started up once more.

"The CRS is stretched as thin as everyone else right now. The time required to assemble, brief, and prepare another team, to say nothing of getting them anywhere near to Llael, is problematic at best. When you add in the facts that our northern rail lines were all damaged in Magnus's attack, and that Khadoran forces are *already* cutting off many of the routes to Leryn . . . We were the diversion; now we're the primary, starting today."

"Slow down, Master Sergeant. In fact, halt completely. There's no bloody way."

"Sergeant Bracewell—"

"No. I still have wounded. I haven't even had the chance to *begin* requisitioning a replacement 'jack."

"Sergeant—"

"And we are *not* Reconnaissance Service!" The entire table juddered beneath her fist; Wendell couldn't help but jump. "I need to confirm these orders with Commander Nemo—or better yet, talk him into changing them."

"Because he took to you so well last time . . ." Atherton stage whispered.

Benwynne pummeled him with a glare only slightly less forceful than his own runebullets. "We are *not* the team for this! We're not spies, we're not infiltrators. We're sure as *hell* not subtle enough to enter a city unnoticed!

"To say nothing," she added, visibly calming herself, "of the political ramifications. A secret effort to extra Halcourt is one thing, but an open military presence? His Majesty would be fielding protests from nobles and generals for months!"

"I recognize all that," Wendell assured her. "So does CRS. It doesn't matter."

"There's more to this than Halcourt, Sergeant. The whole mission was a double-blind. The operation we were covering for? It's legitimate, but it's also concealing a third—an objective more important than the baron and all the political backlash that goes along with him. Accomplishing *that* mission, I'm told, is vital to state security and the war effort."

"And that would be what, precisely?"

Wendell shrugged helplessly. "I don't actually know. They didn't trust the courier with that. That's why we're going to Fisherbrook. The CRS team was supposed to meet a contact there; I've been given a general description, and the necessary code phrases to confirm identity. He'll be able to brief us on the specifics."

For a few brief eternities, Sergeant Bracewell ground her teeth, presumably chewing on the thoughts behind them. Until, finally . . .

"No. I'm sorry, Habbershant. You know that I don't distrust *you* . . ." Her tone, however, suggested a possible change forthcoming in that regard. ". . . but there are too many unknowns. This whole ludicrous, desperate scheme came to us outside the chain of command, from a messenger we don't know, given orders by Morrow alone knows—"

"Sergeant, please. We have to—"

"I told you," she snapped at him, "we don't answer to CRS, and we are not moving until I get all this sorted out!"

"Then I'm sorry, Benwynne. I truly am." He felt his throat try to close on him, hoped his voice wouldn't crack. "I'm exercising my prerogative as senior officer present and temporarily assuming command of the squad."

Atherton, all signs of sleepiness gone, lunged across the chamber almost before the mechanik had finished speaking. "You right bloody bastard!" Had the gunmage come armed, Wendell wasn't sure he'd still be breathing. As it was, only the combined efforts of Serena and Roland, both of whom made a desperate grab, kept Atherton from physically leaping the table.

And while neither of them spoke, the open fury and nascent hatred they glared his way suggested that it wouldn't take much for them to let the younger corporal go.

"Wendell . . ." Everyone froze, straining to hear their sergeant's words, softer than they'd ever. "Why are you doing this?"

God, he'd almost rather blind himself than have to see her face right now! "Because I *do* answer to CRS."

Low growls from the corporals, but Benwynne only shrugged shallowly, as though it was the answer she'd expected.

"You don't have to go along with this, Sergeant," Roland insisted. "You have authority as commander of record. You can fight this, or at least insist on official sanction. We'll stand by you."

"Or," the gunmage added darkly, "we can put Habbershant out of commission long enough for you get this straightened out."

"No," she said firmly, body going rigid. "I have my duty, you have yours, and we all know it. Get your units prepared to move out, as the Master Sergeant ordered."

"Sergeant—" Serena and Atherton said together.

"Don't interrupt me. I want everyone equipped for . . ." She stopped, spoke over her shoulder without turning. "If we're heading to Fisherbrook, I assume we're traveling by river, sir?"

"Yes. It's out of our way, but that's where the CRS team's contact is expecting to meet them, so—"

"Right. Everyone equipped for a brief river expedition. Corporal Gaust, since your commandos require the least time to prepare, you're responsible for locating us a craft that can carry the whole squad. You're authorized to pay fair wages, but if anyone tries to milk us or nobody volunteers, you're also authorized to requisition a vessel under military authority."

"Sergeant—" Atherton tried again.

"Any of the wounded who aren't battle-ready in a couple of days are to be remanded to the care of the Bainsmarket garrison. Dismissed, corporals; get to it!"

Wendell felt himself shrink, aging a decade or so, beneath the weight of their combined stares as they departed.

"Benwynne . . ."

She spun on her heel to face him, stiff as a rifle barrel. "Yes, Master Sergeant, sir!"

"I didn't want you to find out like this. I've never been disloyal to you. *Never*."

"And if CRS had ordered you to be, sir?" Then, when Wendell didn't answer instantly, "I see, sir."

"No, you don't . . . Ben, this is temporary. As soon as we're on the mission proper, all command reverts to you. As far as I'm concerned, you're *still*—"

"Will that be all, Master Sergeant, sir?"

"Please don't speak to me like you don't know me. I—"

"Because, sir, if that's all, I have a great deal of preparation to oversee to make your squad ready."

Wendell closed his eyes. "Yes, Sergeant, that'll be all."

"Thank you, Master Sergeant, sir!"

Footsteps, a slamming door. And only when he knew he was utterly alone did Wendell slump into the nearest chair and bury his face in his hands.

SECOND REPORT

Glaceus 17th, 605 AR
Leryn, Llael

By the time she and her two fellow knights arrived at the gates of Leryn, Katherine Laddermore was so haggard and travel-worn that, without her armor, she could have convinced absolutely no one that she was either a Storm Knight *or* a noblewoman of Cygnar, let alone both.

A nightmarish cycle of chaotic days and sleepless nights, drenching river foam and biting winds, along with the occasional storm of sleet, snow, or argument and recrimination, the journey had been far more trying than many pitched battles. She and her companions, Privates Sadler and Pruscott, had been forced to commandeer a civilian riverboat. Even had any military craft been available, rather than already occupied in lugging troops and supplies to the front, using one might have tipped off unwanted observers to the importance of their journey.

Esmond Cottswell—the bearded and weathered captain of *Whitewater Caress*, and the most stereotypical river boatman one could ever hope to meet—had been only too happy to provide transport for the three knights once he knew they were willing to pay fare wages rather than press his crew into service. He'd become rather less happy to learn that they weren't disembarking at Merywyn, but meant to sail the length of Llael; and he all but blew like a faulty boiler when Katherine informed him that he'd be running *Whitewater Caress* day and night, nonstop, until they reached Leryn.

She'd stood fast, weathering screaming tirades about the danger of night travel on the river; shrugging off appeals to take pity on the men, who—even working in shifts—would be half-dead from exhaustion by the end of such a journey. And Cottswell's insistence that the steam engines couldn't *take* round-the-clock operation for that long resulted only in Laddermore bringing one of her unit's mechaniks along to help maintain the equipment.

Only once she'd made it quite clear that Cottswell could either agree to these terms and be paid for his troubles, or find himself conscripted to make the run anyway, had he agreed—between vile curses and empty threats—to cast off. But neither he nor his crewmen had missed a single opportunity, during their mad rush, first up the Black River and then the Oldwick, to remind Katherine of their displeasure. Every discussion became an argument; every meal was ill-prepared; amenities became unavailable or vanished from cabins. They even, at one point, ceased checking in on the mounts stabled in the cargo hold. *That* particular protest ended the night Laddermore burst into the mess, slugged the first mate almost hard enough to break his jaw, and absconded with his own dinner to feed to the horses.

She and her knights slept in shifts, after that.

Days droned on with nothing but the pounding splash of the paddle-wheel, the whine of the engines, and the hateful shouts of the boatmen. The lieutenant found herself torn between huddling alone in her closet-sized bunk, or freezing in the soaking spray above.

It was enough to try the patience of an ascendant.

On the penultimate day of their journey, not far from where the Black made a sharp bend to became the Oldwick, it all proved worthwhile.

Knight and sailor alike had hunched below decks, or at least ducked out of sight behind the upper stretch of hull, as the world to port erupted.

Khador's incursion had reached the city of Riversmet.

Bloodred heavy warjacks, taller than two grown men together, flattened trees and pounded at the city's walls with fist and cannon, knocking great divots into the stone. Smaller, swifter, but far weaker 'jacks—some in bright, even garish, Llaelese patterns, most of Cygnar's blue and gold—flitted amongst their larger counterparts, striking, retreating, striking once more, seeking any chink in the Khadoran monstrosities' armor. One or two heavier machines rumbled from hidden posterns, ready to go head-to-head with the Khadoran 'jacks, but these were few and far between.

Flames raced across the earth, melting frost and searing what tiny lengths of brush still managed to survive the winter. Even on the river, hundreds of yards away, Katherine had cringed from the wash of heat. Bursts of smoke stained the sky, and artillery thundered from both sides, the sound so thick and heavy it somehow dampened the wind. Greylord arcanists and Cygnaran stormcallers hurled the furies of nature at one another; stilettos of lightning stabbed from on high, layers of frost crawled across men and metal alike.

Several eyes and several barrels turned to track the *Whitewater Caress* as she passed, and a few ranging shots were lobbed, almost casually, in their direction, but overall the Khadoran forces were too engaged in surrounding Riversmet to devote much attention to a passing civilian vessel.

Katherine couldn't help but think back to her own recent riverside encounter, and offered a heartfelt prayer of thanks that the enemy were less curious, or at least more thoroughly occupied, than she had been.

More than once on their upriver run, Captain Cottswell's craft had been forced to either kick in a burst of speed nearly enough to kill the engine, or scurry to shore and hide in the brush and the shadow, to avoid the attentions of Khadoran advance patrols. But this? An entire division, or more, of the Khadoran army?

Had they passed by Riversmet only a few days later—as they would have, had they kept to the captain's preferred pace—Khador would have held the terrain far more thoroughly, and the *Whitewater Caress* would assuredly have been stopped, or worse.

For the last day of the journey, Cottswell and his sailors didn't argue with the Storm Knights anymore—though they still hadn't been at all sorry to see the trio disembark. Katherine felt a swell of sympathy for her mechanik, who still had to make his way back home without a friendly soul as company.

After a quick consultation, Katherine, Sadler, and Pruscott chose to don their armor for the brief ride from the riverbank, across a hundred yards or so of well-maintained road, to Leryn's gates. Khadoran forces hadn't come so far, as of yet—at least not in any great numbers—and there were few points from which to launch an ambush. Still, after what they'd seen on their travels, none of the knights felt comfortable riding exposed, even over so short a span.

Had Katherine not been so exhausted and numbed by the journey, so irritated by the chill winds that stuck her face, slipped between the joints of her armor to breathe across still-damp underclothes, she might have realized the problem with that approach before it was too late.

Beneath clouds so low they appeared to be grazing, sleet pinging and sloshing against their own armor and their horses', their breath steaming in the air, the trio of Storm Knights finally, *finally* approached Leryn.

They were still some bowshots distant when they heard, sulking behind the ambient sounds of the weather, the brass *blat* of a trumpet or horn.

"Oh, Morrow *damn* it!"

Her two companions apparently came to the same realization at the same moment. "Well," said Pruscott, a cheerful, baby-faced sort and a third-generation knight, "it's not as though people weren't going to notice three Storm Knights wandering around the city, Lieutenant."

"No, it's not." Katherine shook her head, dislodging a few stubborn ice crystals from her visor. "Still, I wish I'd thought up some way for us to arrive unannounced. Even for us, a fanfare and formal welcome is a bit . . ."

"Unsubtle?" This from Sadler; tall, thin, hawk-nosed, and determined to prove his family's worth.

"Sure, let's go with that one." She reached out, tousling Arius's mane. "So be it, boys. Formal manners and chipper smiles. We're about to represent the Cygnus, like it or not, so let's at least make an honorable show of it."

While the citizens of Leryn might have been excited, heartened by the arrival of Storm Knights proudly garbed in full armor and livery, they weren't so overwhelmed as to turn stupid. The gates of the city remained firmly shut, rifles and artillery tracked the riders from emplacements within and atop the ludicrously thick curtain wall. A pair of brightly painted Vanguards—one of Llael's own signature warjack models—closed from either side, crescent-bladed halberds and shield-mounted cannon leveled.

"I'd hate to see how they greet visitors they *don't* like," Pruscott muttered. Katherine shushed him, though she couldn't repress a melancholy smile; it was the sort of thing the late Blevins might have said.

Behind the rightmost warjack trailed a team of pikemen and riflemen, like enormous, metal-clad, and truly disturbing ducklings. Adorned in gleaming breastplates and crested morion helms, only their choice of weaponry distinguished one sort from the other. Frost cracked beneath their tread, and only after a long moment of examination—not merely of the three knights, but also of the open ground back the way they had come—did the soldiers marginally relax.

Katherine removed her helm, holding it firmly under her left arm, and waved for her knights to do likewise. Trying to ignore the light sleet and not-so-light wind pelting her face, she rose in the stirrups.

"I am Lieutenant Katherine Laddermore, Storm Knight, Second Cygnaran Army. I offer greetings to our friends, neighbors, and allies of Llael, and humbly request passage through Leryn's gates!"

Chains clattered; steam hissed; cogs ground; and the massive, steel-banded gate swung outward. Katherine knew that Leryn was considered the most heavily fortified city in Llael—possibly in all Western Immoren, Caspia excepted—but still she was taken aback at the breadth of the curtain wall. Had she and her companions rode single file, their horses nose to tail, the first would only just be starting to exit the gateway while the third had fully entered. It ran around almost the entire city, never thinning except where it gave way to the stone of Mount Borgio—a more natural but no less imposing bulwark.

Weapons continued to track them as they passed through, the warjacks and soldiers following close behind. Beyond the barbican stretched broad avenues, running throughout the relatively modern shops, crafthouses, and the wealthy-but-not-*too*-wealthy estates of the Outer Ward. Most of those roadways finally ended at the *second* curtain wall, and though she couldn't see it from here, Katherine knew that a third loomed beyond even that; the most ancient of the three, surrounding Old Town, the heart of Leryn's wealth, history, and government.

Standing before them, cast in an almost ghostly aura by the alchemical street lamps, were another team of pikemen. Arranged in rows, they were clearly intended as an honor guard. At their head waited a tall, slightly corpulent figure whose thick, fur-lined coat couldn't begin to conceal the green and yellow courtly garb beneath, any more than his attempt at a stylish, close-trimmed beard could conceal the rounded jowls on which it sprouted.

"Lady Laddermore, welcome!" The Llaelese accent flavoring his Cygnaran was notable, but not remotely thick enough to impede understanding. He reached up, offering to help her from the saddle; she accepted, despite needing no such assistance. "I hope," he continued once both her boots touched cobblestone, "that you won't think our examination discourteous, but under the circumstances . . ."

"Under the circumstances, you'd be foolish not to take every precaution. No umbrage taken."

"Excellent, excellent! I am Minister Chalerynne. Foreign Minister di la Granzio sends his abject apologies that he couldn't greet you in person, but I fear other duties currently occupy him. If we'd only known your Ladyship was coming, we'd certainly have rearranged his schedule."

They'd begun walking as they spoke, falling into that steady, slightly formal pace common to all official proceedings across all nationalities. The pikemen marched in columns, beside and behind; the knights between them, leading Arius and the rest of the horses.

"Think nothing of it, Minister." *I didn't* want *any of this, and if I hadn't been so foolish as to arrive under full colors* . . . "I've no wish to tear the Foreign Minister from his duties, especially in days like these. For that matter, I apologize for calling *you* away from what I am certain are far more important tasks."

"Oh, not at all!" Chalerynne turned a corner, directing them onto an avenue only marginally narrower than the first. Rapt faces stared from balconies and upper windows, watching the ad hoc parade, but nobody interfered. Civilians on the street stepped quickly out of the way, taking smaller roads or standing flat in doorways until the procession had passed. "Nothing is more important than our relations with our southern neighbors—especially, as you say, during days such as these. Will you be wanting to meet with Minister di la Granzio? We can, of course, arrange such an audience, but it may require—"

"Actually," Katherine interrupted politely—a neat trick of etiquette that few non-courtiers could master—"I understand that Crispin Halcourt is guesting with one of your citizens?"

"Yes, indeed. Baron Surros."

"I'd very much appreciate it if you could take me to see him."

"Of course." Chalerynne didn't sound entirely pleased, but was clearly far too polite to refuse. Then, apparently recovering his equilibrium, "You faced little difficulty in getting here, I hope?"

So the conversation continued, Katherine offering an abridged version of their travels. She learned, with no small relief, that word of the siege at Riversmet had already reached Leryn; she would not have cared to be the bearer of that particular news. All the while, Chalerynne marched them through the streets of the Outer Ward, bringing them ever nearer the second wall.

Nearer, but not directly toward. Katherine noted the fact, then decided it wasn't a warning sign of any sort.

Not *yet*, at any rate.

Neither, however, was she prepared to let it go ignored. "Minister," she said, "I'm a stranger to Leryn, obviously, but I can't help but notice that we've passed several roads leading directly toward the wall. Don't we have to pass through New Town to reach Old Town?"

"Ah . . ." The minister signaled, halting his people, and leaned in close. "My lady, the Outer Ward and Old Town are connected by several tunnels that pass beneath New Town. It's to one of these that I'm taking you.

"I assure you," he added hastily upon seeing her face twitch, "these passageways are quite stable and spacious. Given that we can hardly see the sky anyway, for the winter weather, you'll hardly notice the difference. Except you'll be a lot warmer, of course."

"Minister," she said, hunting for the proper words, "there are—certain shared enemies of ours who may have noted our arrival. I'd be more comfortable remaining in the open, with more options available in case of ambush."

"Oh, tosh! Lady Laddermore, I assure you there are no Khadoran agents within our walls!"

Either you're a blithering imbecile, or you're laying it on a bit thick, don't you think?

"I'm afraid," he continued, "that I really must insist."

"Why?"

It was gauche to ask, and she knew it—but she also knew, now that the question was out in the open, Chalerynne had no legitimate excuse not to answer without appearing even more uncouth in return.

"My Lady, every city, even Leryn, has its . . . *unsociable* elements. In our case, the bulk of them congregate in New Town."

"You think a group of soldiers would be endangered by a few neighborhood toughs?"

"Of course not. It's simply . . . Well, it's unpleasant, my Lady. I would be lax in my duties if I subjected you to it. And, if you'll pardon me for saying so, I would hear about such a lapse at length from my own superiors."

In other words, you'd rather we not see that Leryn has just as many poor, desperate, and destitute as every other city in the world. "Of course," she acquiesced, squeezing grace and understanding into her voice like so much sausage stuffing. "I quite understand. Lead on."

She pretended not to note the sigh of relief that he pretended not to utter.

The tunnel entrance, when they reached it, was a fortification unto itself. A great stone gatehouse, manned by a team of gunners, boasted a thick portcullis with only darkness beyond. A brief conversation between Chalerynne and the guard captain presaged a series of clanks and hisses: the younger cousins of those Katherine had heard at the city gate. The portcullis rose. More impressively, a long series of shutters opened in the shadows beyond, exposing an array of gentle chemical lanterns.

Which, in turn, exposed the passage itself.

A gradual slope, scarcely worthy of the term "ramp," angled down to a tunnel broader than some highways. The floor was cobbled in stone pavers, and the ceiling lurked high enough overhead for all but the largest warjacks to pass without slouching. Columns in the classical style, half-built into the walls, buttressed the whole affair while adding an artistic flare to what was otherwise a coldly functional construction. Katherine figured they were probably carved of traditional white marble, though the alchemical lanterns cast just enough of an unnatural, ruddy hue over everything that she couldn't be certain.

As they continued—feet, hooves, and words reverberating in the confines—Katherine noted that, roughly every hundred feet, large doors provided ingress to chambers built within the walls themselves.

"Guard shacks and maintenance," Chalerynne explained. Although he elaborated no further, the knight harbored little doubt that those guards could trigger portcullises, sliding walls, or some other form of barrier—perhaps even, in the most extreme circumstances, a cave-in.

Little sense to Leryn's massive bulwarks if the enemy had a readymade and unobstructed route beneath them, after all.

Minister Chalerynne continued his performance of unthreatening small talk and polite questioning. Katherine responded instinctively, falling back on skills learned in her father's court, without paying the functionary any real mind. She knew full well he was trying to draw her out on the reasons for the knights' visit, without being so rude as to ask directly, and she'd no intention of even acknowledging his efforts, let alone answering them.

Frankly, she didn't think he'd care for her answers—whether the ones she was permitted to give, or otherwise.

The procession emerged into Old Town via a slope and gatehouse identical to the previous. The knights, their hosts, even the horses flinched as the cold draped over them, an overeager burial shroud, biting skin and scraping lungs.

Still, Katherine retained enough poise to appreciate Old Town. Roads, narrower than those of the Outer Ward but even more meticulously cobbled and cleaned, led past edifices that were the perfect offspring of the ancient and the contemporary. Pillars, statues, fountains, and bas reliefs—mostly showcasing physically flawless men and women clad in centuries-old styles—collaborated to form a façade of classicality over angles, buttresses, and load-bearing walls of modern design. Amidst such trappings, the colorful banners and vibrant outfits favored by the Llaelese people didn't look nearly so ridiculous or out of place as Katherine normally felt them. Looming through the season's hazy atmosphere, Mount Borgio formed a magnificent backdrop for this most ornate of cities.

Even the beastly fortress squatting like a tumor near Old Town's center, and the dingy taint to the smoke-impregnated snow, failed to detract from the overall impression.

Katherine made no effort to hide her reaction—a reaction that drew a proud, even patriotic smile from Minister Chalerynne. The citizens in the streets, mostly servants of the rich and noble, occasionally the rich and noble themselves, courteously stepped aside for the procession while maintaining the impression that they saw more impressive sights every day, and acknowledged the visitors only out of graciousness.

At no point, so far as the knights could see, did their host send any sort of runner or messenger ahead of them. Yet somehow, by the time they reached the estate of Baron Surros—which no longer held the same aesthetic allure for Katherine, given that it was constructed and adorned in more or less the exact same style as every other they'd passed—word of their coming had preceded them. The baron himself, or at least an older fellow in silks and furs whom she assumed was the baron, awaited them at the manor's outer gate. Accompanying him was a small army of servants, nearly as large as the honor guard of pikemen.

"Welcome to my home!" His accent was far lighter than the minister's; had they not actually been in Llael, Katherine might have had trouble placing it. "I am only too happy to see yet more of my brethren from Cygnar, and I hope you find Leryn's hospitality to be . . ."

And so on and so forth. Katherine and the other two knights stood at parade rest and weathered the fusillade of formalities for some minutes, interjecting only to introduce themselves when asked.

After which, of course, nothing would do but for Katherine—now *ruthlessly* castigating herself for arriving in full armor—to give an equally flowery, if somewhat extemporaneous, speech in reply. She never could remember, after that day, precisely what she said, though she was fairly certain she'd used the words "honored," "delighted," and "grateful" more in that one monologue than in the past two or three years combined.

Until, *finally*, the pomp and circumstance wound to a close—or at least a pause—and she was able to address the reason for their presence.

"I understand, my Lord, that Baron Halcourt and his household have been staying with you?"

"Indeed he is. If you'd be so good as to follow . . . ?"

Servants, honor guard, baron, minister, and knights all trooped along the walkway through the Surros estate, winding between a fountain here, a flower garden there . . .

Flower garden?

"Powdered reagents in the soil," Chalerynne explained in a stage whisper when she asked. "Very expensive, even when purchased directly from the Golden Crucible. They allow vegetation to thrive in weather that would otherwise be too extreme."

"And you're using this for flowers rather than, say, food crops?"

The minister shrugged. "As I said, very expensive. It's actually more cost-effective to import vegetables and grains than it would be to make widespread use."

Katherine, now put in mind of one of her many reasons for leaving Archduke Laddermore's court, brutally suppressed a scowl.

Halcourt awaited them in the grand foyer of the manor, clad in a coat of fox fur, with servants gathered behind him in a fair imitation of Surros's own welcoming party. He'd positioned himself beneath a massive gold-and-crystal chandelier, with the sweeping stairs and a grand portrait of a Surros ancestor as his backdrop. It was so exquisitely staged, Katherine almost felt obligated to applaud.

Ignoring that urge, as well as the fact that Halcourt had assuredly been watching the entire affair from the great bay window nearby, she took two more steps and dropped to one knee.

"Lieutenant Katherine Laddermore, my Lord." She indicated the other two knights, kneeling just behind her. "These are Privates Pruscott and Sadler."

"Yes, yes, rise." Then, once they'd done so, "So, will your unit be escorting us home, Lieutenant? Or have his Majesty's armies finally chosen to fortify Leryn? It's about time he . . ." Halcourt's eyes suddenly bulged. "The front hasn't moved this far *already*, has it? Last we heard, they were tied up at Riversmet . . ."

"No, my Lord. So far as I know, that's still the case. But I fear you misunderstand. We're not an advance for a larger unit. We're here on our own."

Halcourt's face stretched grotesquely, attempting to fall in chagrin and clench in fury simultaneously, but having forgotten quite how to do either. The murmurs from the Llaelese delegation sounded equally put out. They'd obviously assumed that some amount of additional relief and safety, in the form of Cygnaran soldiers and warjacks, were even now on their way.

"There's . . ." Halcourt was turning a shade of crimson more appropriate to vegetation, or perhaps some sort of tropical avian. "There's only the *three* of you?"

She chose to take no offense at the clear disdain. "I fear so, my Lord. A larger group would have been unable to slip by the Khadoran scouts."

"I see. And precisely what good are *three* Storm Knights supposed to accomplish?"

"We're here for your protection, my Lord. We're assigned to ensure your safety until circumstances permit you to return home."

"Really." It didn't even pretend to be a question. "And you're going to provide a measure of security that my own household guards, to say nothing of Baron Surros's people, can't offer?"

Katherine started to shrug, then caught herself, glad the armor hid most of the abortive gesture. "We'll do what we can, of course. His Majesty is concerned for your safety, and we were the ones available—"

"I'm sure he is." Halcourt's face had made up its mind; definitely leaning toward rage over chagrin. "Just as I'm sure you're in no way here to keep an eye on me. Is Leto worried I'll embarrass him? Or is it fear that I'll accomplish something here that he could not?"

"I wouldn't presume to speak for *his Majesty*. I can only give you my word that we were given no such assignment."

"Hmph. All right. Your father's a good man, so I'll accept your word. For now." He stepped away, mind clearly moving on to other topics. "My staff will see you settled—in the rooms provided for my household, of course," he added to his host, who merely nodded. "Give a yell if you need someone to play squire, help you in and out of your armor. And of course, the grooms will see to your mounts.

"We have a working routine here, Lieutenant. Please see that you and your men keep any disruptions to a minimum."

Katherine turned, bemused, from the baron's retreating back, to see only her knights, and Surros's staff remaining in the foyer. Chalerynne and his honor guard had departed without a word in farewell. Now that they were no longer the harbingers of Cygnaran military salvation, apparently they weren't worth much more in the way of effort.

"This assignment," she muttered from the corner of her mouth, even as she pasted on a dazzling smile for the approaching maids, "is going to be an absolute joy."

Nodding in unison, Pruscott and Sadler followed as the senior maid directed Katherine toward the stairs.

***

From the servant-crowded recesses at the rear of the foyer, Dignity gawped in undisguised horror.

This was the backup they'd sent? *This*?!

She'd been anticipating—been *counting* on—more CRS operatives. Expecting a Storm Knight to perform a discreet operation wasn't *quite* as ludicrous as assigning a Centurion-class warjack to pick flowers, but it was certainly a stop along the same line. Either something had gone very wrong (not unlikely), Nemo and Rebald were playing a much more complex and devious game than she knew (also not unlikely), or things had gotten much, *much* more desperate. Which, alas, wasn't substantially more unlikely than options one and two.

Still and all, she might turn this to her advantage. For over a week, despite her best efforts, her search for agents of Section Three had proved just as fruitless as her search for Idran di Meryse and his missing formulae. Until today, she'd run out of options.

Now, though? The clanking and ponderous Storm Knights might not be much for stealth and secrecy, but their loud and shiny armor made for some *awfully* attractive bait . . .

Even inside, there was no escaping.

The rain was a steady pounding, as constant and far more pervasive than the rumble of wheels and the screech of engines had been aboard the *Lady Ellena*. The flimsy and weather-warped walls reverberated, an entire orchestra of mismatched drums, flexing just enough to let the chill and soggy gusts inside without permitting the miasma of cheap pipe smoke and unwashed bodies to dissipate in turn. From between the chunks of thatch and the shingles, thin ribbons of accumulated rainwater, clouded with mildew and clumps of collected dirt, dribbled into rusty basins and pots spread throughout the chamber. The place would actually have been *more* comfortable had it been snowing or sleeting, rather than raining.

It wasn't a restaurant, wasn't a tavern, wasn't a store, wasn't an inn—not precisely. Rather, the establishment seemed little more than a gathering spot for the miserable laborers, teamsters, and sailors of Fisherbrook to vent their frustrations at one another. Food and drink were available—the latter in rather more substantial quantities than the former—but only because the proprietor purchased them from the town's other businesses and resold them here. To most of his customers, the convenience of one-stop consumption was worth the markup.

Lacking even a formal name, the place played at being all manner of things without quite succeeding at becoming any of them. The bulk of Fisherbrook's citizens did the same: Even had there been anything resembling opportunity to make something of themselves—which there wasn't, here, not anymore—the will to try had been stomped out of them.

In a corner of shadow and cobweb, around a table that seemed to be made up of random boards nailed together by a hyperactive inmate, slumped Benwynne, Wendell, and the three corporals. They nursed drinks that tasted mostly of rust, chewed at gummy wads that purported to be some manner of fish, and tried to internalize their loathing for the foul place in which they found themselves.

And, in many cases, for one another.

Having apparently lost the battle with it, Atherton spit a semi-chewed gobbet back onto his cracked and filthy plate. "The hell are we doing here, Sergeant?" Like the others, he was dressed not in uniform, but in ragged clothes so caked with dirt they'd likely have turned an incoming blade. In other words, like everyone else in town.

"Following orders," she told him, not for the first time. She remained focused on her own plate, where she prodded at various morsels with a bent fork as if trying to startle one into movement.

"Hmph. Never thought I'd envy the rest of the squad," the gunmage muttered.

The "rest of the squad," as he put it, were camped near the banks of the Dragon's Tongue, far enough east of Fisherbrook to avoid the townsfolk's attention. They were, no doubt, soaked to the bone, freezing, and all-around miserable.

"I'm sure Master Sergeant Habbershant would be happy to let you join them," Cadmoore rumbled irritably.

"Not asking him for bugger-all."

Habbershant scowled. "I'm right here, you know, Corporal."

"Yeah, I'd noticed."

Wendell, who'd only recently joined them at the table, opened his mouth to reply—and then his gaze happened to flicker to Atherton's hair.

"Gaust . . ."

Atherton offered only a small grunt, which might or might not indicate he'd even heard.

"Where's the ribbon?"

The gunmage slammed his drink to the table. "I told you I'm not wearing that damn thing!"

"And I told you, Corporal. It's a prearranged signal, and you're the only one here with hair long enough to—"

"Master Sergeant, did you happen to note the paddlewheel on the boat we took from Bainsmarket?"

Mouth still moving, Wendell blinked twice in confusion. Then, "Yes?"

"You saw the decorative scalloped edges along the sides of the paddles?"

"Yes . . ."

"And how that one paddle had a crack running across it, so it was jagged?"

"Yeah . . ."

"Well, I'd rather squat over that paddlewheel naked and dangle my—"

"Stow that, Corporal!" Benwynne finally looked up, ready to chew bullets. "You've been given an order by a superior officer, and I expect you to damn well obey it!" Then, more softly, "I taught you better than this."

"Yes, Sergeant." His tone was no less bitter, his anger no cooler, but Atherton reached into a pocket, withdrew an obnoxiously bright green ribbon, and used it to tie his hair into a haphazard tail.

"How long do I have to sit here like this?" he grumped.

"Until our contact shows," Wendell said. Angrily, he attacked his own food (such as it was), the whole table shimmying with the thrusts of knife and fork.

And so it went, as it had most of yesterday, as it would until something changed. Wendell spent long minutes trying to chew the fish, less because he was hungry—the rubbery stuff was enough to suppress most appetites, anyway—than because it gave him something other than Gaust's insubordination, Ben's distance, or his own guilt on which to dwell.

Of course, if the guy didn't show soon, and it turned out that he'd rushed them and usurped Benwynne's command for nothing . . .

"You look chilly."

Wendell jumped. He'd neither seen nor heard the stranger approach. "I wouldn't mind the cold so much," the man continued, "if everything wasn't so gray."

"What the hell are you—" Atherton began sourly, but the mechanik silenced him.

"I normally like gray," he said to the newcomer, "but I do wish I could see the stars."

The stranger nodded once at the countersign and pulled up a chair. He, like the rest of them, was dressed raggedly and unremarkably, though he'd added a frayed brown cloak with a hood to keep the worst of the rain—and possibly curious eyes—from his head. This close, Wendell saw narrow features and a dark, meticulously waxed goatee beneath steady blue orbs. Something about that face, and the slightest hint of an accent, sparked an ember of memory, but he couldn't quite fan it into open flame.

"You can take that silly thing off, now," the new arrival told Atherton. The gunmage, after a glance at Benwynne, hid the ribbon back in his pocket.

"You lot," the man continued, "are not precisely what I was led to expect."

"No, we're not," Wendell admitted. "You've heard of the recent attacks up and down the Dragon's Tongue?"

"Some, yes."

Lowering his voice further, though there was really little need, Wendell said, "The CRS team was caught in one of them. We're all that was available to replace them on short notice."

"I see. And you are . . . ?"

"4th Platoon, 7th Division, technically out of Caspia. Second Army Unorthodox Engagement team. I'm Master Sergeant Habbershant. This is Sergeant Bracewell, our proper field commander." If Benwynne cared that he'd indicated she was still primarily in charge, she offered no acknowledgment. "Corporals Dalton, Cadmoore, and Gaust."

"Oswinne Muir," the other said, pulling back his hood enough to offer them a clearer view without exposing himself to the room at large. "Special operative for the Ordic Crown."

Atherton chuckled. "Oswinne Muir? Like the playwright? I can't tell if that's a brilliant field designation or an asinine one."

But Wendell, Benwynne, and Serena had all recoiled with varying muffled gasps. The face alone hadn't been sufficient—the man was rarely if ever in *front* of the curtain—but combined with the name . . .

No wonder he looked familiar!

"That's . . . not a cover designation, Corporal," Benwynne whispered.

The gunmage cocked his head, bewildered, and then his jaw dropped as understanding crammed itself between his teeth and down his throat.

Oswinne only shrugged at the array of incredulous stares. "Well, it makes a fantastic cover for traveling, doesn't it? I mean, would *you* expect it?"

"Now, wait . . ." Atherton seemed to be truly struggling. "So were you an author who was recruited as a spy? Or were you already a spy who somehow got famous? Or—?"

"Are you a soldier who became a gunmage?" Oswinne retorted. "Or a gunmage who became a soldier?"

"Uh, more or less both from the start."

"There you are, then."

"Wait . . ." Benwynne tensed, ready to rise from her seat. "How did you know he was a gunmage?"

"So suspicious, Sergeant." The Ordic operative leaned back, arms crossed. "I know quite a bit about your unit already, although I didn't anticipate meeting you in person any time soon. How *did* your operation on the coast go, by the by? Uncover any proof of Khadoran involvement with the raiders?"

"*You* provided that intelligence?!"

"Well, I didn't carry the message personally, of course, but . . ." He shrugged once more.

"Last I heard," Serena said, "Ord was pretty firmly neutral in our war with Khador. Why are you working with us?"

Oswinne raised a finger, telling her to wait. He seemed somehow to glance around without actually moving, and the others realized swiftly that he was judging the volume level of the room around them.

"All right," he acquiesced finally. "Should be safe if we keep it down. It'd be easier if you spoke Ordic, but . . ."

"Some of us do," Serena told him. At the playwright's raised eyebrow, she said, "My grandmother was an immigrant. I grew up speaking some Ordic, though it's been a while."

"Ah." Then, in his own language, "Well enough, sister."

"I, however, do *not* speak Ordic," Benwynne reminded them. "And I've no intention of sitting here waiting to hear a translation later on."

"Of course," Oswinne agreed. Then he continued, more softly, "Precisely how much have you actually been told about this operation?"

"The rest of them know only about the extraction of Baron Halcourt," Wendell replied, also little above a whisper. "They're aware there's more to it, but not what. I know a bit more—not *all* of it, but enough to tell if you were to, say, accidentally omit or alter any salient details."

Several of his fellow soldiers hissed at the accusation, and the implied insult that went with it, but Oswinne only laughed. "CRS, are you? You sound like one."

"Among other things, yes." Wendell forced himself not to look at the others as he spoke; he didn't want to know what they were feeling.

"So, here it is in brief." Oswinne leaned in. "Some of you probably already know that your Commander Adept Nemo has been working, along with his people, to develop a new generation of galvanic weaponry. More potent than your Stormclad warjacks or any arms you currently possess; a stormchamber capable of holding *enormous* amounts of power, beyond anything you've seen."

Wendell, who had long heard rumors through his fellow mechaniks of classified 'jack projects with designations like "Firefly" and "Thunderhead," nodded.

"But how would *you* know about—" Roland began.

"Please, let me get there by my own route, if you would. Nemo accomplished a great deal, but one problem he was unable to crack was how to protect the mechanisms—and, where necessary, the wielders—from the increased energies. The normal protections worked into your armors and 'jacks couldn't withstand this increased level of electricity.

"So, he turned to the only alchemists more skilled in metallurgy than any under his own authority."

"The Golden Crucible," Benwynne breathed.

Oswinne thumped a hand on the table. "Precisely! Of course, Nemo had no reason to anticipate treachery, what with the close alliance between Llael and Cygnar. The Crucible has, in fact, worked on other military projects for your nation in the past. Still, he took precautions. Different alchemists worked on different aspects of the metallurgy or the alloying process, and only a few knew what the end result was meant to accomplish. The only one who knew the *whole* picture—or at least the only one who was *supposed* to—was Engman Drew."

"A former Cygnaran army alchemist," Wendell explained to the corporals, who failed to recognize the name. "Resigned his commission when the opportunity to work with the Golden Crucible came up, and I can't say I blame him, but he's still a citizen of Cygnar. And absolutely loyal," he added.

Oswinne resumed his narrative. "The alchemists succeeded. Nemo had CRS send an operative to take possession of the complete formula and process in what should have been a simple payment and exchange."

"Funny how *simple* never is," Atherton sneered.

"Yes, quite. One of the project alchemists, a man by the name of Idran di Meryse—who, up to this point, had been a valued ally and a supporter of the alliance between Cygnar and Llael, and whom Drew had recommended personally—somehow got his hands on the *entire* formula. We don't know if he tricked his compatriots into handing over their own work, or if he stole it, and frankly it doesn't matter. The bottom line is, he's holding the formula hostage. He's demanded . . . Well, an amount that would put enough of a crimp in the Cygnaran treasury to seriously impede the war effort."

"I'm . . . not sure I follow," Serena admitted. "I understand why losing the formula after so much work and expense would be a problem, but it hardly seems disastrous. Surely Commander Nemo could reconstruct it from what remains, or take a different developmental approach to—"

"If your government does not meet di Meryse's demands," Oswinne interrupted, "he intends to make as much profit as possible by forcing you to bid whatever you *can* afford.

"And allowing, as he puts it, 'other interested parties' to do the same. He named no names, but I assume we all have a fairly good notion of who he means."

The wood of the table creaked as fingers abruptly tightened into fists.

"I don't think I need to spell out for you," he continued, "what would result if Khador's military were to learn how to temper and refine their metals to guard against weapons of lightning, do I?"

No. Judging from the masks of anger and worry Wendell could see on the others' faces, and which he knew he wore on his own, no such explanation was necessary.

"The CRS operative sent to make the exchange has, of course, been tasked with locating the formula—or at bare minimum, keeping it out of Khador's hands—but she's had precious little luck as of yet. Di Meryse's clever, and he's covered his tracks well.

"Said operative," he continued, "entered Llael masquerading as one of the traveling staff for Baron Halcourt's sojourn."

Wendell actually *felt* the last pieces slot into place, no differently than when he finally connected the last piston in an engine. A political rescue mission made for a perfect cover, a perfect reason to assemble and launch a secret operation in Leryn—when extracting the operative was the *true* objective.

Extracting, and perhaps even assisting her in acquiring the formula before Khador.

Indeed, the remainder of Oswinne's briefing confirmed precisely those deductions.

"This is," he concluded, "more properly a Reconnaissance Service operation in every last particular. But, it appears that you're what's available, so we better make it work, hadn't we?"

"Which brings us back around to the small matter," Serena said, "of *your* part in all of this."

"Oh, me?" Oswinne smirked. "I'm making all of this possible.

"The Claeddon Traveling Performance Troupe, a band of Ordic actors and stagehands, was in Leryn when the offensive began. Currently, they're stuck, much like Halcourt. Since Ord is a neutral power, we've negotiated with Khador to allow a diplomatic and cultural delegation to cross their lines and retrieve our people. Since I'm rather well known across cultures, if I say so myself—"

"And he will," Atherton whispered.

"—it only made sense, as a gesture of authenticity and a show that the delegation was genuine, for me to arrange and to lead it."

"So long," Wendell said, "as Khador remains ignorant of your, ah, 'night job.'"

Oswinne grunted something markedly inarticulate for a man of his pro-fession. "At any rate," he went on, "the plan was for your CRS team to meet up with me here. We would then, in turn, join up with the cultural delegation, disguising your people among them. When we retrieved Claeddon's troupe, we would also retrieve Baron Halcourt and his staff, disguising them both as delegates and as additional performers. Some of the Cygnaran operatives would have had to stay behind, to make the numbers work, but they were more than prepared to do just that.

"We can still follow that general course, except . . ." Oswinne began idly tapping fingertips on his knee with one hand, stroking his goatee with the other. "I don't know precisely how big your squad is, Sergeant, but I'm fairly certain it's quite a bit larger than the CRS team I meant to accommodate."

"How many was that?" Benwynne asked.

"A little more than half a dozen."

"Uh . . . That'd be quite a bit smaller, yes."

"To say nothing of the warjacks," Atherton added helpfully.

"Still," the sergeant mused, "if we sent just a single unit, that might be—"

"I'm sorry," Serena interrupted, the legs of her chair thumping as she rocked forward, "but how long are we going to let Muir keep dodging the question?"

"And precisely what question am I dodging, Corporal Dalton?" he asked.

"How did you discover all this? Why are you involved? Why is your *country* involved? The risk to Ord if you're discovered—"

"Let's simply say that a nation as small as mine doesn't survive sur-rounded by larger powers without an *extensive* intelligence network, however informal. You'd be surprised what King Baird knows about you and Khador both. And what we *didn't* already know, I learned during my negotiations with Commander Nemo and Scout General Rebald. As for the rest of it . . ." Oswinne's tone and expression both became as studiously blank as the wooden planks that called themselves a table. "*If* Ord were to become involved in these matters," he said, "it might be because his Majesty, King Baird, and our generals recognize where our best interests lie. We can survive, even thrive, as

a neutral party so long as the war continues, and we can make necessary treaties with whichever side wins. Most of us would *prefer* that side to be yours,
but we're comfortable dealing with Khador if necessary.

"*But . . .* That assumes a winning faction that has just come through an
ugly, tiring conflict, and has no stomach for further conquest. Should Khador
acquire this formula, their advantage over Cygnar could prove overwhelming.
An *easy* victory for Khador—one that leaves them with sufficient strength to
make conquering Ord a dessert—doesn't suit us."

A sound that briefly put Wendell in mind of an active rock crusher
turned out to be Atherton's grinding teeth. "In other words," the gunmage
accused, "you're not interested in helping us *win*, just in helping us not lose
too quickly."

"In essence . . . Yes."

"And the pirate raid that may or may not have been funded by Khador?"
Wendell asked before Atherton could draw breath for further complaint.
"Might I guess that it also wouldn't 'suit you' for Ordic waters to become a
primary route for Khadoran warships?"

"You might indeed. Some such activity is unavoidable, but as a primary
wartime corridor? Again, not good for us. All of which is, of course, purely
hypothetical, since Ord is *not* involving itself."

Had Wendell found himself faced with as much pure skepticism as was
now flowing toward the playwright, he worried he might actually have ceased
to exist.

"Really," Benwynne observed.

"Oh, quite. As you said, Ord is entirely neutral. That's why, should
Khador discover this operation, they'll soon learn that it was arranged entirely
by myself—a well-known author who *clearly* has no formal standing in, or
connection to, the government—and several coconspirators, taking political
matters into our own hands. Already, one of the nation's best criminal forgers
lies dead and rotting in a cellar in Merin, along with enough evidence to prove
that *he* created the false documentation we'll be using to extract the baron and
his entourage. It won't be a *pleasant* sight by the time Khadoran intelligence
discovers it, but if necessary, discover it they will.

"And I, of course, if I am not already dead by that point, will likely spend the remainder of my life in a Khadoran prison."

"That seems . . . hard," Atherton said finally.

"I'd say 'necessary,'" Oswinne replied casually.

"What's *necessary*," Benwynne announced, "is for us to take a few moments to determine how we intend to go about executing this complex, multi-layered, and international plan in which Ord is not involved in any form whatsoever . . ."

***

". . . still think that *Vinter III* is your best piece, though." Atherton's voice drifted back to Wendell as the gunmage and most of the others departed, going to make whatever preparations they had to make.

"Thank you," Oswinne, striding beside him, replied. "I'm glad you appreciated—"

"Are you planning to write another? *Vinter IV?*"

"I, um, feel that might be in poor taste, considering the man's still alive in hiding somewhere. To say nothing of his attack on Corvis a few years ago . . ."

"Eh, I suppose. Still . . ."

The words faded behind the low hum of the sullen common room, followed by a brief surge in the drumming of the rain as the rickety door rattled open, clattered shut, leaving the two remaining officers alone with one another.

"Well . . ." the Master Sergeant began hesitantly.

Nothing.

"I don't think I've ever seen Serena argue a direct order before," he tried again.

Benwynne studied a small blob of long-dried candle wax, as though determined to memorize its contours. "Can't say as I blame her, sir. I wouldn't want to leave the rest of the squad either."

"She's the only officer who speaks Ordic. If our people are supposed to pass as part of Muir's retinue, it only makes sense that she command—"

"Yes, Master Sergeant. I didn't say I disagreed, sir, only that I understand."

Wendell forced a smile across his lips, a touch of levity into his words. "Too bad we couldn't find an excuse to send Gaust away, though."

If Benwynne sensed that levity, she certainly wasn't prepared to acknowledge it. "Wouldn't have made sense, sir. His talents are pretty recognizable for what they are; not really suitable for masquerading as—"

"Sergeant, how long is this going to continue?"

Benwynne finally lifted her attention from the tabletop, directing it instead at a point just over Wendell's left shoulder. "Not sure what you're talking about, Master Sergeant."

What could he say? That he'd had no choice? That he hadn't wanted to do it? That he'd never betrayed Ben or her squad and, despite his earlier hesitation, never would have, regardless of orders? None of it would mean much, not now.

Instead, then, he said, "My orders give me sufficient command discretion to decide what happens next. The squad can either return to our original mission behind the Khadoran front, or we can attempt to find some means of assisting Muir, and our people accompanying him, so long as it doesn't disrupt their efforts or their cover."

"And what have you decided, sir?"

"I've decided to cede that decision to you, Ben."

Finally he'd gotten her to look him in the eyes. "Sir?"

"You're in command, Sergeant. It's your squad."

It might have been wishful thinking on his part, but it seemed to Wendell that a sliver of the ice in Benwynne's expression—the faintest, most minuscule sliver—softened and thawed.

"Then it's no decision at all," she told him. "I'm not about to let any of my people stand alone if there's any possibility we can help them."

"I thought you'd say something like that." Now it was Wendell who idly picked at the ancient wax on the tabletop, rubbing flakes between his fingers until they fell apart. "You realize it means getting ourselves—including two 'jacks—from here to Leryn without getting killed or compromising Serena's and Muir's group?"

"And that, when everything's said and done, we might be *stuck* in Leryn, behind Khadoran lines?" she finished for him. "Yes, Master Sergeant, that had occurred to me."

"Just checking, then."

"So," she said, tilting her chair back so she could stretch out, "we'd better get to figuring out how we're going to accomplish those minor miracles, hadn't we?"

Glaceus 19th, 605 AR
Leryn, Llael

Two days.

For two days, Katherine had waited. Through banquets and parlor games, philosophical debate and prolonged analysis of fluctuating markets, she remained at Baron Halcourt's side, or at the very least within Surros Manor. Every word, every glance, every effete gesture, every haughty sneer, was a psychic bullet against which she had no effective armor. She bled memories of life in her father's court, growing ever more irritable with each new wound.

And still the CRS operative hiding in the baron's retinue had made no effort at contact.

The Storm Knight couldn't, at first, comprehend why. She and her knights weren't precisely the reinforcements the agent would have expected, but communication should still have been the first priority. Did he think Katherine untrustworthy? Suspect some manner of trap or deception? Had something happened to make contact impossible? Worries and misgivings became constant companions, no less so than the recollections of times better left behind, and Katherine found herself yearning for an enemy she could face blade to blade. She was *not* bloody suited to this sort of work!

All of which, perhaps, is why it took those two days before it occurred to her that, perhaps, the operative was waiting for the opportunity to speak with her away from the baronial households. She'd assumed that any private moment—her chambers, the library, an empty hall—would have sufficed, but just maybe . . .

Now she walked the evening streets of Old Town Leryn, ostensibly learning the lay of the land. Halcourt, she knew, couldn't care less what she was doing. Pruscott and Sadler remained with him, and honestly, she'd be surprised if he'd even have noticed her absence if she hadn't told him she was going.

Full armor, obviously, wasn't a viable option: a bit heavy for a long walk, a bit cold for dusk's sighing winds, and rather more conspicuous than a clandestine meeting called for. She wore instead a heavy, fur-trimmed coat, buttoned snugly from throat to waist, flowing open like a cape from waist to ankles. Thick woolen trousers, lined gloves, and heavy boots completed the ensemble—or rather, the *visible* portions of the ensemble. Hidden beneath the coat, steel bracers on each forearm could serve as shields in a pinch, and a breastplate of hardened leather and thin steel plates provided a modicum of protection.

Going without full armor was one thing, but Katherine was nobody's idiot. Her ancestral Caspian battleblade hanging openly at her side, and the fighting knife strapped to her right thigh, were indication enough of *that*.

By the time night had well and truly fallen, though, and the smoke-tinged snow—swirling in the air, carpeting the streets, and clinging in patches to her coat—shone gold in the streetlights, Katherine had exactly zero enthusiasm remaining. Rivulets of melted slush dripped down the inside of her boots, she was fairly certain she had ice in her eyelashes, and her breath formed a curtain of steam so thick she had difficulty seeing through it. It was time, she decided, and *past* time, to call this another bad idea and head back.

So it was precisely then that someone finally approached her.

Wrapped tight in a shabby gray cloak and hood, the figure could have been anyone, confidante or stranger, man or woman, human or . . . otherwise. Katherine faced the sounds of shuffling feet and huffing breath, and made no attempt to hide the fact that her hand dropped to the hilt of her battleblade.

"Do you suppose," the newcomer asked in a voice abraded by weather and mistreatment both, "the snows are this gray in Rorschik or Korsk?"

The Storm Knight relaxed, if only marginally. "I would imagine," she replied, now feeling a bit foolish over all this sign-countersign nonsense, "that everywhere beyond Ravensguard, the snows are more red-stained than gray."

Now that he'd come closer, enough ambient light squirmed under his hood for Katherine to make out crooked teeth, stubbly cheeks, and a weak, almost ferret-like chin. Certainly *not* anyone she'd seen amongst Halcourt's retinue. Not anyone, for that matter, who would be allowed anywhere *near* the baron's retinue, not looking like that!

"You're not precisely what I expected," she continued, her neck and shoulders tensing once more—and *not* because of the temperature.

"Jus' follow me," he rasped. "Everything'll be explained, yeah?"

Awhirl with questions and suspicions, Katherine took a single tentative step after him . . .

Before the entire decision became a moot point.

She was already down and rolling, now coated in the oily snow, before her conscious mind identified the soft *twangs* that had resounded from both sides of the seemingly empty street.

Concealable crossbows.

Her contact sprawled limp in the road, cloak turning dark and tacky in an ever-growing spread from the miniature bolt between his shoulders. Her own back ached where a second bolt had torn through her coat to skid across her hidden cuirass. Had she not already been dodging aside, had the weapon struck her full on, she'd be just as dead as he.

And she knew, with a cold lump forming in her gut, that if the crossbow aimed at the spy hadn't shot first, thus giving her an extra split second of warning, even her instinctive dive wouldn't have saved her.

Katherine lurched awkwardly to her feet, stumbling as her boots skidded across the snow-slick cobbles. Hunched, head down, she sprinted for the nearest cover: a thick bole, leafless for the season, standing in the median between two nearby side streets. Again she dived, tumbling unevenly behind the trunk as another pair of bolts plowed through the slush just behind her feet.

Panting painfully in the chill, she fetched up against the tree, back first, reached for her battleblade . . .

Only to discover, after a few futile tugs, that the heavy leather of her scabbard, chilled and dampened for the past few hours, had no intention of surrendering her sword.

Well, obviously. How else *could this day possibly have turned out?* Katherine couldn't even find it in her to curse.

One of her attackers crept into view around the bole. Heavy coat and trousers made him look like any other citizen; only the sack, complete with ragged eyeholes, yanked over his head, and the miniature crossbow in his fist, marked him as something more.

"I don't suppose you'd allow me to call for a brief pause, would you?" she asked.

Then, as the crossbow rose, the bolt somehow gleaming evilly despite the dearth of any direct light for it to reflect, Katherine hurled a handful of snow into the masked face.

It bought her only seconds, but that was all she needed. Pushing against the trunk with her left hand, she lunged, boot-knife extended. The crossbow wasn't *quite* in line to fire when her foe's throat parted beneath her blade. Blood spattered musically, steaming and freezing in rapid succession.

The swift crunch of footsteps provided brief warning. Katherine spun from the still twitching body, letting yet another bolt hiss past. She dropped into a ready stance, knife held underhand along the length of her arm . . .

To face no fewer than three more opponents, all hefting weapons rather more intimidating than a fighting knife. Even discounting the crossbows, which none of them seemed inclined to reload, they'd all produced narrow-bladed swords with close to four times the reach of Katherine's dagger.

Before they could close the distance, the Storm Knight transferred the knife to her left hand, slashed open one of the leather ties, then yanked her sword, scabbard and all, from the belt. It might not cut but, sheathed or not, the battle-blade was more than heavy enough to break bone. Hell, with Morrow's blessing, maybe the enemy's blades might shake the damn scabbard loose.

Right. Also, I would like to discover Arius, my lance, and my armor tucked away in my coat pockets.

The first of the enemy drew almost near enough to strike . . .

Something flashed from behind the wrought iron fence surrounding a nearby property. A wicked blade tumbled end over end, seemingly untouched by wind or precipitation, to sink into the ribs of the rearmost masked man.

He staggered, grunted, but remained upright. It wasn't a deep wound, not through his heavy coat, painful and distracting at worst.

Or would have been, had the knife-thrower not followed it up.

Katherine scarcely even saw her—and it *was* a "her," at least judging by the braid of tawny hair unfurled behind her like a banner of war. Even before her throwing knife had landed, she'd vaulted the iron fencing and sprinted across the muck, seemingly unslowed. Her target straightened, reaching to pull the blade from his side . . .

The newcomer spun in a vicious kick. Foot slammed into pommel, blade all but vanished into clothing and flesh, and the man was a corpse before his knees even buckled.

The second of the trio leapt at this new threat while the first charged Katherine. The knight retreated a step, then completely lost sight of her (apparent) ally in the rapid clash of blades. A brutal offensive weapon, the battleblade wasn't at its best when parrying under *optimal* circumstances, let alone weighted down by a stubborn sheath. Another step back, and another still; her opponent would not let up, her fighting style one of swift strikes from every angle, constant twisting and sidling side to side. Katherine, a Storm Knight with years of battlefield experience, knew she had only seconds before her attacker's lighter sword would invariably slip past her heavier, less agile blade.

From the smile on the assailant's face, made visible by a subtle distending of the makeshift mask, Katherine could tell that he knew the inevitable end was near as well.

Good.

The slender sword arced in from low and to the left. No way the battle-blade, though already in motion, could possibly deflect the strike.

The sleeve of Katherine's coat opened, spilling fur and fibers, as she caught the attack on the hidden bracer. Her arm went briefly numb, and she knew she'd sport a painful bruise for days, but the attack did no real harm.

She wished she could have seen the look on her enemy's face during the split second between the unanticipated parry and the full weight of the Storm Knight's sheathed weapon cracking him across the side of the head.

The figure dropped, limp as a plague-ridden earthworm. The mask slid in the fall, just enough to reveal that the coat-swaddled attacker was actually a woman, not a man as Katherine had assumed. She saw a narrow-featured axe blade of a face, the expression hard and calculating even in unconsciousness, and hair as dark as the inside of a rifle breach. Blood smeared her left cheek, and had already begun to soak through the burlap.

Katherine ran to aid the stranger who'd come to her assistance, and found it unnecessary. The woman stood casually over the body of the final ambusher, a snub-nosed holdout pistol disappearing back up her left sleeve.

Tired, aching, confused, and frustrated, the first words out of Katherine's mouth were, "So why didn't I hear a shot?"

"Spring-fired projectiles in a modified pistol," the other woman said. "No penetrating power past a few yards, but you get a dull *clunk* instead of a bang. Since we're trading questions, any particular reason you let yours *go?*"

The knight spun, jaw opening in protest—where it stayed, hanging. A bloody imprint in the heavily churned snow was the only trace of her opponent.

"That blow should have scrambled *anyone's* brains," she whispered in disbelief. "Hell, I wasn't sure she'd *survive* it!"

"Brilliant." The strange woman approached, pausing to retrieve her throwing knife. "Just what we needed."

Katherine kept shaking her head. She hadn't fought more than three or four people in her *life* with the training to roll with a strike like that. She flinched at the sudden pressure on her arm, but it was just her companion nudging her to start walking toward one of several dark side streets.

"At least," the woman said, "we've thinned them out a bit, and I don't believe our escapee got a good look at me. And, hey, we aren't stuck with disposing of the bodies. They'll take care of it for us; don't want anyone knowing they're here any more than we do."

"They?" Katherine was starting to realize that she'd lost whatever iota of control she might once have held over the situation.

"Khadoran intelligence. Section Three."

After a brief choke, "You're not joking, are you?"

"Oh, of course. I'm entirely having you on. There's no Section Three, no war, and the people who just *seemed* to be trying to kill you were actually hired mimes. I appreciate you finishing them off; saves me having to pay them."

"No need to be snotty about it."

"It's not about need so much, really, as inclination."

Katherine took a deep breath. "How about we start over? I'm Lieutenant Katherine Laddermore, Storm Knights. And you . . . I've seen you around the Surros manor, haven't I?"

"Yes. Call me Garland, at least in the field."

"Garland? And what's that when it's at home?"

The woman sized Katherine up with a series of sidelong glances. "Dignity," she said, "when in the manor or around civilians. Lieutenant, technically, but let's avoid that for now, yeah? And I don't give both names to just anyone, so keep them straight, would you? I'd really rather you not slip up and call me by the wrong name in front of the wrong people."

"I'm not an idiot—" Katherine made an exaggerated point of peering around for observers. "—Garland," she finished.

"I know that. But you're also not trained for this work. Why in Morrow's name did CRS send *you*?"

"Commander Adept Nemo sent me. I was the closest person he felt sure he could trust. You can relax; I'm only a temporary fix. There's a CRS team en route as we speak."

"Ah. Better."

Long moments, then, of gusting breezes; crunching steps; the occasional pop and sizzle of a street lamp, or the ghosts of distant conversations. They exchanged no word between them, save the occasional grunt of a direction in which to turn.

Until . . .

"Why did you wait so long?"

Garland blinked. "Excuse me?"

"Before contacting me," Katherine clarified. "We spent two days in the same house, and I'm pretty sure we could have found a *few* moments for a private chat."

"Oh, that. I needed to draw out the Khadorans."

The knight halted in her tracks; the spy traveled a few more steps before realizing she did so alone. "What?" she asked Katherine.

"I was *bait*?"

"Well, yes. I knew Section Three had operatives in Leryn, but I couldn't come up with any way to draw them out without exposing myself. But once you appeared, I figured they'd be following *you*, hoping you'd lead them to *me*."

"I could have been killed."

Garland's shrug was all the more disturbing for its blatant nonchalance. "As you could any other day on the job, I should think." She started on her way, halted when Katherine gripped her arm.

"And the man in the gray cloak, who approached me? I was told you were working alone."

"First, kindly let go. And second, yes, I was. He was some fellow I hired off the street for a few silver keeps. I believe he thought he was brokering some criminal transaction between us."

For several breaths, Katherine literally couldn't force her mouth to form intelligible words.

"Wouldn't have done me any good to draw out Section Three and then let them shoot me in the back, would it?" Garland asked. "If it makes you feel at all better, he had no wife or children depending on him."

"You . . . He . . . Leaving aside everything else, you gave a *foreign civilian* a CRS countersign! Suppose the Khadorans *hadn't* killed him?"

Garland's lack not only of response, but of *expression*, was answer enough.

"You really would have, wouldn't you?" the knight whispered.

"I would. I wouldn't have been happy about it, but I'd have done it."

"That's . . . That's . . ."

"The kind of thing that's necessary, sometimes." Garland actually smiled, a look of genuine sympathy—and for that moment alone, the knight thought she saw a glimmer of remorse in the woman's face as well, though it had come and gone to swiftly for her to be certain. "You really weren't prepared for this particular side of warfare, were you, Lieutenant?"

Katherine clenched her teeth and drew herself rigid. "Maybe you'd better tell me *exactly* what we're into, Garland. I was only given a very general briefing."

The other woman nodded, and resumed her walk back to Surros Manor, stopping every now and again to make absolutely certain they weren't followed.

Katherine strode beside her the entire way; sat before her in a private room, once they'd returned, and listened to her speak about formulae and betrayals and one bastard by the name of Idran di Meryse.

But through it all, she couldn't quite shake a shivering chill—a chill with nothing at all to do with the miserable winter outside.

Glaceus 22nd, 605 AR
Leryn, Llael

"Hasn't his Lordship already seen the show five times?"

"This is a special performance." Dignity wandered the cramped dimensions of the knight's chamber, occasionally drumming against the wall in what might have simply been a sporadic fidget—or, for all Katherine knew, a search for hidden passages. "Invitation only. Very exclusive."

"By which you mean expensive."

"If they're stuck in Leryn anyway, they might as well make a profit, right?"

Katherine grunted something noncommittal.

"Besides," Dignity continued, "they're not performing *An Orgoth* tonight. I understand they've promised a showing of *The Storm King*."

"Just how many of Muir's plays do they *know*, anyway?"

"Rough guess? All of them."

"All right, all right." Katherine stood from her mattress with a groan and flicked a lock of hair away from her eyes. "When?"

"I believe the baron plans to leave by seven. I assume you can be ready?"

"We'll manage. Sadler will join us, I think. Pruscott needs a break."

"Fine. Oh, he wants you both in full armor and regalia."

"*What?*" She'd squeaked. Katherine hated how she sounded when she squeaked. And it's not as though she were unaccustomed to standing around for hours on end, clad in steel. Still . . . "For a bloody *play*? What, has he irritated Claeddon's troupe *that* much?"

"Wouldn't surprise me if he had, but no, I think he just wants to look impressive. You, my good lieutenant, are a fashion accessory."

"Lovely. Just what I trained for." The knight dipped a hand in the brass basin atop the dresser and splashed a bit of clean—and dear Morrow, *cold*!—water on her face. "And you?"

"I'm still in the baron's disfavor. I'm to remain here and continue my chores while the bulk of the staff is at the theatre. Not entirely certain that really qualifies as punishment, but . . ."

"And what will you actually be doing? More Red-hunting?" It was a jibe, albeit a mild one. She knew that Dignity's fortunes in locating the enemy, after her one success using Laddermore as the lure, had again dropped to zero.

"In a manner of speaking."

Katherine's thin smile faded as the other woman's grew. "I see. Bait again, am I?"

"Until Section Three identify me as their enemy, their best bet is still keeping eyes on you and the baron. With a bit of luck, I'll spot them first."

"And how will you be getting in, if Halcourt expects you to remain here?"

Wordlessly, Dignity handed over an engraved invitation: golden lettering on thick, ivory paper.

"Lady Cyndra Gaynor-Rozetta?" Katherine felt the blood drain from her face. "You didn't . . . !"

"Oh, calm yourself, Laddermore! Of course not! The real Lady Gaynor-Rozetta will awaken tomorrow with a headache and fuzzy memories of a vintage that really shouldn't have put her out as hard as it did. No harm done, unless you count missing *The Storm King*. Honestly, what do you take me for?"

"I don't believe you want me to answer that," Katherine grumbled, returning the invitation.

"Perhaps not. I'll send someone up to assist you with your armor. Oh . . ." She paused, hand on the doorknob. "Do remember not to actually look for me tonight. Might seem just a tad suspicious, yeah?"

She was gone before Katherine could furnish a suitable response.

***

An elegant evening gown in pearls and silvers, topped with a stole of fox fur; braiding and piling so ornate her hair was less "style" than "knotwork";

enough makeup that an observer could have spotted her in the dark; all were tools in the completion of Dignity's transformation into a lady of Leryn's high society.

She almost needn't have bothered. The flamboyant throng awaiting entry to the Artys III Memorial Theatre included enough servants, outfitted a tad less formally than their masters, that she could have passed with far less effort. Adding insult to injury, the brightly clad and wigged doormen scarcely glanced her way at all, being far more concerned with ensuring that her invitation was genuine.

Carried by an inexorable wave of perfumed humanity (and the occasional dwarf), Dignity climbed a shallow ramp, carpeted in majestic crimson, into a lobby almost large enough to have its own weather system. Sweeping arches and octagonal pillars supported a vast ceiling garnished in bright but fading frescoes. Crystal and brass chandeliers, heavy enough to double as siege weaponry, dangled parallel to an array of circling balconies. Stairs swept around two sides of the room, providing access to those balconies—and to the theatre itself, beyond.

So packed was it with aristocrats, their entourages, and servers carrying trays of wines and finger foods, that even the manmade cavern felt positively claustrophobic.

As no amount of searching or eavesdropping was possible in these conditions, Dignity didn't bother to mingle, but instead pushed through to the theatre proper.

The winding rows of chairs were largely empty, thus far, but enough other patrons had taken their seats early that she didn't stand out too terribly. Dignity chose a spot in the general audience, far enough back that she should remain well shadowed once the house lamps were extinguished and the stage lights kindled. From here, she could observe not only the bulk of the audience, but many of the private boxes above, with only a moderate amount of neck-craning. That would be Baron Surros's box there, on the left, so . . .

Having oriented herself, Dignity settled in to wait, watching the velvet stage curtain rustle in the great chamber's occasional drafts. Odds were that she wouldn't see anything from here, that she'd have to excuse herself for a more careful search of the grounds, but better to hold off until everyone was well and truly distracted by the performance.

The gallery slowly filled, not unlike a gigantic basin—*or chamber pot*, the less charitable voices of her soul couldn't help but add—until the crowd and the noise were just as oppressive as they'd been in the lobby. They were no longer a collection of individuals; they were an *audience*, a unified and thriving organism.

Another upward glance revealed movement in Surros's box. She couldn't spot Baron Halcourt personally, but the occasional glint of steel was enough to tell her that Katherine, at least, was where she was supposed to be.

A sequence of bells chimed in quick succession; house lights dimmed with the hiss of narrowing valves; a hush rippled over the audience; and the curtain rose on the poetic chorus that opened Oswinne Muir's classic *The Storm King*.

For half an hour Dignity waited, oblivious to both her neighbors and the events unfolding on stage—though she did briefly take note when the simulated cannon fired, during the scene in which the Queen of Rain's cloud was shot down over the mysterious Isle of Ais.

All right, enough dallying. Best get to work. She allowed herself one more moment, for her eyes to recover from the flash, took one last look around as she prepared to rise . . .

And froze. *Come on! You can*not *be serious!*

Roughly halfway around the cavernous hall from the Surros family box, a pair of opera glasses glinted as they occasionally caught flickers of the stage lightning. No surprise there; roughly half the nobles in attendance used them, or similar gadgets.

This particular pair of opera glasses, though, were turned *away* from the stage. And Dignity hardly needed to check—though she did anyway, just to be certain—to know they were aimed instead at Halcourt's retinue.

It *could* be some theatre-goer, bored with the play, stealing a glance at the fully armored Storm Knights. Dignity watched for several long minutes, however, and the glasses never once wavered back to the stage.

It was sloppy. Obvious. *Amateur*. Nobody would *survive* the first year of Section Three training making mistakes like that.

Which meant either she was *supposed* to notice, and it was some manner of ruse, or else Halcourt had someone besides Section Three observing him.

Either way—trap or not, playing into their hands or not—it wasn't something Dignity could ignore. But she didn't have to be stupid about it, either.

With a fusillade of whispered apologies, she shuffled out from the aisle, stepping on only a few feet in the process, and made once more for the lobby.

Other members of the audience milled about, not only in that lobby but on the various stairs and in the winding hallways of the many-tiered gallery. Some had stolen out for a bit of conversation; others for a few puffs of a pipe, or to stretch their legs, or to visit the jakes. (Although, presumably, the latter sort weren't lingering in the halls.) Dignity paid them no heed, save the occasional polite nod when one of them happened to meet her gaze, and they showed her precisely the same diffident courtesy.

Up stairs and shallow winding ramps, beneath glittering chandeliers and alongside banisters of polished brass, until she reached the uppermost level. Here, intricate carvings of various repeating motifs—including the crown-and-stars of the Llaelese flag—swarmed across two score hardwood doors. Through these, she knew, lay the luxurious booths and private boxes of the wealthiest or most aristocratic of Leryn's wealthy aristocrats.

All right, the Surros box is number seven, and the other was almost exactly halfway opposite, so . . .

Up here, she passed fewer rogue spectators and far more servants in the nearly blindingly bright livery of the theatre. Dignity wasn't certain whether the purpose of those gaudy affairs was to make the guests look better by comparison, or to make the staff easier to locate in the dim illumination, but they'd accomplished both with, so to speak, flying colors.

Ludicrous or not, however, they could cause her problems. The men and women hefting trays of bottles weren't the issue; the larger, beefier specimens assigned to check guest chits, to assure that their most valued patrons weren't disturbed by lesser folk who had no businesses being here, were something else again.

Head held high, her pace determined and even aggressive, Dignity strode past the first pair of wandering bouncers. She wasn't attempting to enter a booth, so neither chose to stop her. But then she passed a second pair wandering the gallery, and a third, and she was running out of room. Not only would she shortly pass by her intended destination, but she must eventually reach the end of the hall; should that happen, and she start back without having entered "her" box . . . Well, even the dullest doorman would have to realize something was amiss.

She had just begun to wonder if any of the bouncers were bribable, or if she could somehow take down a pair without causing any real harm or attracting the attentions of everyone else in the hall, when fortune finally smiled at her. At just the right moment, as she approached her target door, the previous pair of servants had vanished around the passageway's gentle curve, and no others had yet appeared in their wake.

Dignity slipped inside before her luck could flip once more. She caught a glimpse of heavily cushioned chairs, several small tables with a variety of aperitifs and snacks, and a rack containing theatre programs and recent broadsheets.

For the most part, however, she remained focused on the young man in well-kept but somewhat outdated formalwear. He spun from his seat at her entrance, opera glasses falling from his open fist, his expanding chest nearly popping a button as he drew breath to shout.

From beneath her sleeve—flowing and loose, in defiance of the current fashion and in contrast to the rest of her gown—Dignity's dagger dropped into her waiting hand. Shifting its weight, calculating how best to manage the awkward throw, nearly cost her too much time. Just before the man could voice his cry, however, the weapon thumped against his throat . . .

Pommel first, rather than edge.

The breath rushed from him in a hoarse croak as he clutched at his neck, trying to catch his wind. Dignity landed at his side, having vaulted the intervening chairs, smacked his hands away, and wrapped an arm beneath his chin.

A few more seconds of thrashing was all he managed before he fell limp. He wouldn't be comfortable when he woke up, and he might speak funny for a few days, but he ought to be fine.

Dignity had paid for his silence, though: Questioning him now seemed an unlikely proposition. Instead, she laid him out across two seats and rooted through his coat pockets and pouch.

A few coins, which she left; a scribbled note that *probably* wasn't relevant, as it said something about picking up smoked venison and oregano, though it could conceivably have been a code of some sort; and . . .

Ah.

Not one but *two* private box admission chits. One, as a guest, for this particular booth; the other, a servant's chit for box twelve.

Another instant to return the dagger to its spring-loaded sheath and to palm the chit, and then Dignity returned to the hall, carefully shutting the door behind her.

This time, as she neared her new objective, a pair of the doormen *did* stop her, politely but firmly. They scarcely glanced at the chit once she'd produced it, however, and dismissed her to go on her way. An easy enough proposition, that . . . Until she reached the door itself.

So what now, genius?

She had no idea whatsoever who—or what—to expect behind this door. One person? Half a dozen? Khadoran operatives waiting to spring a trap, or some local political rival of Baron Surros spying on the man's foreign guest? Violence? Deception? Some kooky misunderstanding that Oswinne Muir couldn't have written into even his lightest comedies?

"Oh, do come in already, m'lady."

Dignity didn't even need to feel her muscles tense; she actually *heard* it happen. She'd no idea how he'd known she was here. She certainly didn't see, even for all her training, any sort of spyhole, tripwire, or other warning system.

Nor, really, did it matter, because she *did* recognize the oily pitch, the precise intonation of every syllable. Just as it no longer mattered if this was, indeed, a trap, or if she was risking exposing herself as Cygnaran Reconnaissance.

Exerting iron control just to keep from launching her blade or her spring-pistol into her hand, Dignity pushed the door open and stepped inside.

The box was accoutered very much like the previous one; similar array of chairs, small tables, expensive vintages, and so forth. The differences were, of course, in the occupants.

One sat in the back corner, as far from the door as space would permit. Distant from both the stage lights beyond the gallery and the small lamp on the central table, it sat in shadows, obscured and unidentifiable—an effect that Dignity figured was quite intentional.

The other, who had called for Dignity to enter, was the traitorous Idran di Meryse himself.

The alchemist spoke through the slightly sagging features of a man who never passed up an opportunity to indulge his appetites, yet remained relatively slender thanks solely to the gifts of a fortunate breeding. His thinning hair was slicked back, his face clean-shaven, his garb the height of style save for his choice of subtler, more muted hues. A crystal goblet, half-filled with something of an almost golden sheen, hung between his thumb and forefinger.

"Won't you have a seat? I was beginning to worry that you'd missed my invitation. Should have had more faith, obviously."

Dignity edged around the box, drawing nearer di Meryse without turning her back on the shadowed figure across from him. "Is there any particular reason I shouldn't kill you here and now?"

He frowned theatrically. "Aren't you going to ask how I knew you'd be here?"

"No. Are you going to answer *my* question?"

"We'll get to that. I think you already have a pretty good idea, though, or you'd have done it already." He waved at an empty seat.

After a quick check of the chair, which the alchemist pretended not to notice, Dignity sat.

"Are you sure you wouldn't care for a drink? The Umbrey '29 is astonishing. I promise you've never had its like."

She glared. He poured himself another glass.

"Have you ever actually seen the entirety of *The Storm King*?" He sounded genuinely curious.

"A time or two."

Di Meryse smiled. "I think Domateos's speech at the bottom of Act II is still one of the most inspiring addresses ever written. 'Let us, then, comport ourselves so that our forefathers, gazing down upon us from on high, might proudly say *It is for this alone we lived and died, that such men might stand in this place, on this day. This alone was our meaning, and we are grateful.*'

"I still shiver to hear it. I understand it's even more stirring in the original Ordic, but I never had any facility for that tongue."

"And what of *your* forefathers?" Dignity asked sweetly. "Do they look upon your acts with pride? Have you offered them meaning?"

The alchemist's smile slipped, if but a little. "I prefer to think of myself as one of those forefathers, doing my part to pave the way for generations to follow."

Dignity couldn't help but scoff aloud, and realized she wasn't the only one.

"Oh! My manners; I'm so sorry. Though I do believe you two may have met before, at least in passing. You share so many professional circles.

"This," he said, raising his drink to Dignity, "is Garland, of the Cygnaran Reconnaissance Service. Garland, meet Vorona. Section Three."

The shadowed figure leaned forward, but Dignity knew who to expect even before the flickering illumination fell over her features. And yes, there they were. The raven-black hair; the narrow face; the empty eyes.

And the hideous mottled and abraded bruise blackening her left temple.

"We *have* met," Vorona said, not currently bothering to suppress a Khadoran accent as thick as borscht. "Though we had no opportunity for introductions. I believe I got to know your friend—Laddermore, yes?— somewhat better."

"You certainly seemed to hit it off," Dignity said blandly. Vorona raised her own glass, acknowledging the point.

"Oh, good!" Di Meryse actually seemed about to applaud, until he discovered he still held a goblet in one hand. "I'm so glad that we're all able to avoid being uncivil."

"The night is young," the Khadoran pointed out. "There is still time."

"Ah . . . Yes, quite. Well, then, before the night grows decrepit, shall we to business?"

With no objection forthcoming from either party, he turned his chair around to face them and leaned back, lacing his fingers together in his lap.

"I am quite aware that you have both attempted to follow me, at various times, whenever I've appeared in public. And it has, of course, done you no good at all, because I have gone nowhere near where I've concealed the formula you're both so eager to possess. Nor do I intend to do so in the future. Nor will anyone I speak with be going near the formula. Nor will anyone *they* speak with, and so on and so forth. I have enough people working for me, and I work though sufficient channels, to make any attempt at backtracking quite impossible.

"Killing me will not only not earn you the formula, but will ensure your enemy acquires it. And yes, my people have fairly sophisticated means of determining which of you might have caused any 'unfortunate accidents.'"

The two spies exchanged a look that clearly said *He might not want to bet on that*, but neither interrupted his obviously prepared, and quite possibly rehearsed, monologue.

"Now, as it happens, neither of your governments was prepared to meet my initial asking price. I suppose I knew I was being too greedy, but I'd thought, just maybe . . .

"Well, neither of you preempted the other, so let me tell you how this is going to play out. I'm giving you exactly two weeks to make whatever arrangements you need with your superiors back home. On the eighth of Casteus, in the evening, the two of you will meet me at a designated location."

"Where—?" Dignity began.

"Oh, do be serious. I'm not giving you two weeks to set up surveillance or booby traps. I'll let you know where to meet." He reached into his coat, removed two folded papers sealed with wax, and passed one to each woman. "Each of these contains an address. Go there on the seventh, and I'll have someone waiting to tell you where the meeting is to be held. Don't bother questioning them, or following them; they'll both be hired messengers with no knowledge about any of this."

Dignity dug fingernails into her palm, irritated but unsurprised at di Meryse's intricate precautions. "Speaking to CRS could prove difficult," she said instead. "Seeing as how Khador's cut most of the lines of communication between Llael and Cygnar."

Vorona smiled and once again raised her glass in toast.

"You're clever, Garland," the alchemist said. "I'm sure you have means.

"This will be a closed bid," he went on, before she could protest. "You will not have an opportunity to hear your rival's bid. Each of you will arrive with the highest price your government is willing to pay. I expect said payment in easily portable form. Gemstones are fine, as are banknotes guaranteed by governmental seal and exchangeable at *any* holding company that does business with your home nation. Once I decide which bid to accept, I will depart. The formula will be delivered to you at the same address indicated on those papers you just received."

Vorona's forward lean was very nearly an abortive lunge, shaking the chair beneath her. "If you believe that we would permit you to depart with payment and then simply *trust* you to deliver the formula—"

"You have no choice," di Meryse said blandly. "I intend neither to have the formula on my person, nor to risk falling into your hands once you have it—or have lost the bidding. Believe me, however, I also have no intention of cheating whoever wins. I gain nothing that way save the enmity of an entire nation."

You've already got that*, you bastard*, Dignity sneered internally.

Vorona growled something unintelligible.

"I hope," he concluded, "that the non-victorious party has the grace to walk away, but honestly, I don't expect so. As I plan to be well away by that point, however, you're certainly welcome to try to kill each other if it makes you happy. Have either of you any questions? Is any of this at all unclear?"

It took everything Dignity had not to break the man's neck, stab him with something, or throw him over the balcony—possibly all three—and though her Khadoran counterpart's face remained ice, the tension in Vorona's shoulders suggested that the other woman felt the same.

Both restrained themselves, as di Meryse had known they must.

"Excellent!" Di Meryse finished his goblet in one final swallow and stood. "I hate to miss the rest of the performance—especially Domateos's speech— but I think it best if I take my leave. Do feel free to remain and enjoy the amenities; the box is paid for."

Two swift bows, one for each of them, and then he was gone. The door swung shut, leaving two of the deadliest women in Leryn sitting across the table. For some time they studied each other, Dignity openly, Vorona over the rim of her goblet, the only sounds the various lines of dialogue projected from the stage below.

"Impressive work last year in Port Vladovar," the Khadoran said finally.

"I'm sure I'd thank you," Dignity replied, "if I had the slightest idea of what you were talking about, or if CRS had any active operations in your nation, which of course we don't."

"Yes, of course. How foolish of me."

"And how many Voronas have there been in Section Three? I recall reading of 'your' exploits from as far back as the First Thornwood War. I'm fairly certain it's not due to makeup that you appear younger than a hundred-and-twenty."

"I am the third so honored with that particular designation."

Dignity tapped two fingers against her temple. "I wonder who would have been the fourth?"

The raven-haired spy raised a hand, gingerly ran her fingertips over the mottled bruise disfiguring almost half her face. "Your Lieutenant Laddermore is quite good," she admitted without overt rancor. "And fast. I should have avoided that blow from almost anyone else."

"I'll tell her you said so. She was astonished you'd dodged as much of it as you did."

Vorona bowed from the neck in false modesty. "I do as I was trained. I look forward to the opportunity for a rematch."

"Katherine's sort of rematch, or yours?" Then, when the Khadoran's lips merely twitched in reply, "I see. I'll tell her to watch her back, then."

"Much good may it do her."

Vorona sipped at her drink. Dignity idly lifted one of the sculpted glasses from the table, turning it this way and that, examining the light reflecting from its facets.

"How did you get in?" she asked, as though the question had just sprung to mind. "Forged invitation?"

"Oh, no," Vorona said. "Quite genuine. Yours?"

"The same. I left the original recipient of mine alive, though."

"As did I. It may startle you to learn, Garland, but I take no pleasure from the more violent aspects of our shared calling. I prefer to avoid unnecessary bloodshed."

"Good to know. I imagine you take a fairly liberal attitude when determining what constitutes *necessary* bloodshed, though?"

Again Vorona only smiled her acknowledgment.

"I suppose this invariably has to end with us trying to kill one another, then?"

Vorona shook her head. "Not at all. If you depart now and give up any claim on di Meryse's formula, I would be absolutely delighted to let you go."

"It's not di Meryse's formula. It's ours."

"I figured. Then yes, all paths do seem to lead toward a tombstone, or perhaps merely a shabby, shallow grave—for one or the other of us."

The tension in the box was growing dense enough to muffle the words of the actors onstage.

"Of course," Dignity pointed out, her tone still quite reasonable, "trying to kill me here, in a crowded theatre, is likely to attract attention, private box or no. And I don't believe you want the authorities undertaking any investigation that might expose your presence."

"And you, Garland, cannot afford even *that* much risk. Eliminate me, and the rest of my cadre remains to continue the mission. But you are alone, save for your newly arrived knight protector. Die trying to kill me, and your entire operation evaporates like a stagnant puddle."

Dignity slowly stood, dagger and pistol feeling like fifty pounds of searing coal beneath her sleeves. "Some other time, then?"

"Absolutely." Vorona made the same show of staying put as Dignity had of rising. "Quite soon, I would think."

A few quick steps, never entirely turning her back on the Khadoran, brought Dignity to the door. Only when she'd opened it, and placed a foot outside, did she speak once more.

"Anything you'd like me to tell Laddermore when I see her?"

"Thank you, but no, that shouldn't be necessary." One final time, Vorona raised her glass in a mocking toast. "I'm certain any message I might concoct has been delivered by now."

Dignity held herself rigid until the door clicked firmly shut, only then breaking into a mad sprint for the stairs.

***

It was her imagination—it *had* to be her imagination—but Katherine truly felt that her skin was chafed far more raw beneath her armor after a few hours at the theatre, in Halcourt's company, than after an entire *day* of parade formation. Muscles ached as they hadn't since her days as a squire in training. Sweat had soaked into the thick padding of her arming doublet, then frozen into irritating patches during the walk back to the manor.

The baron and his current favorites blathered the whole way about the performance, about its meanings and symbolism, its strengths and weaknesses as compared to Muir's other works. Now that they'd returned to the manor, ditching their formal coats and sitting down for a nightcap with Baron Surros and his people, the conversation sounded unlikely to taper off until the wee hours of the morning.

For Katherine, who found the play bombastic and overblown—especially, good Morrow's mercy, that endless bloody speech at the bottom of Act II!—participating any further in said conversation was a torture so unbearable that it could have taught the scrutators of the Menite crusade a thing or two. Thankfully, Halcourt was largely indifferent to her presence, and most of her lingering duties could reasonably wait until tomorrow. A polite goodnight to the baron, and then, Morrow willing, a good seven or eight hours wrapped in—

She stiffened as something jostled her arm; a hand, she saw, glancing down, closing tight about the steel rerebrace covering her upper arm.

"With me," Dignity hissed in her ear. "*Now.*"

As much as the urgency in her tone, it was the fact that Dignity still wore her formal gown and snow-kissed shoes—an abominable lapse in professional etiquette for a spy maintaining two different personas—that set Katherine's adrenaline pumping and a frisson of worry capering across her back.

Up two flights of stairs they hurried, Katherine easily keeping up despite her exhaustion and her armor, spurred on by a growing worry she couldn't begin to name. The third floor was silent, every member of Halcourt's retinue and every household servant either asleep or downstairs attending the pair of jabbering lords.

Katherine never did figure out how, but she managed to be both violently shocked and utterly unsurprised when her companion led her to the sleeping quarters shared by Sadler and Pruscott.

"Oh, no. Dignity . . . ?"

"I'm sorry, Katherine."

The knight found herself oddly grateful that she still wore her armor; the heavy gauntlet hid the trembling in her fingers as she opened the door.

It was all as neat and tidy, as meticulously organized, as a knight's dormitory should be. Pruscott lay on one of the paired mattresses, the sheets tugged to his chin somehow straighter than most people could arrange even on an *empty* bed. His eyes were closed, his features relaxed, even peaceful. He might have been sleeping . . .

Save for a single stiletto, inserted so neatly the wound barely bled, protruding just below the knight's left temple.

Katherine leaned over, placed one hand on Pruscott's head and bowed her own. "I've got another letter to write," she whispered.

"What do you plan to tell his Lordship?" Dignity asked her, after a respectful moment of silence.

"The truth; the parts he needs to know, anyway. We'll have to dramatically increase security on the manor."

"Just as well. They know my face now, too." Then, before Katherine could ask her to expand on that, "Halcourt travels with a contingent of household guards. They've not been doing much since we arrived; there was no need."

"Then it's time they started." She looked up from the dead man's face. "They were good, Dignity. It doesn't look like they even woke him up."

"No sign of forced entry at the door or window, either. You know this was a message, don't you?"

Katherine had already moved back to the doorway. "I didn't think the location of the wound was a coincidence, no."

"I spoke to her this evening," Dignity admitted. "I'm sorry I didn't have the chance to kill her."

"Don't be." She had to break the news to Sadler, then the baron; had to prepare missives, arrange a funeral and shipment of the body; work up new patrol schedules for the guards, shore up any obvious holes in the manor's security . . . And of course, there were the events of Dignity's evening, which she obviously needed to hear. Sleep, it seemed, was no longer on the night's schedule. "I'm really hoping for the opportunity to do it myself."

Glaceus 28th, 605 AR
Black River, Duchy of Esmynya, Llael

"**S**ergeant Bracewell! *Sergeant!*"

The door exploded open beneath the young soldier's pounding, and he stumbled into the tiny cabin that the leaders of the fifth squad had been using, cramped as bullets in a bandolier, for their sleeping quarters. Normally, Benwynne would have chewed him out for the breach in etiquette. In this case, as she'd been awakened by the first of the detonations and was already yanking on her boots, she figured the situation warranted a bit of forbearance.

"Report, Private!"

The trencher drew himself upright, tossed off a quick salute, and tried his damnedest to pretend he wasn't gasping for air after his quick sprint below decks. "Incoming artillery, Sergeant! Probably a Khadoran battery, according to Corporal Cadmoore."

Benwynne reached for her other boot. "Distance?"

"Pretty far, Sergeant. They haven't found our range yet . . ." She nodded; if the boat had taken a direct hit, she'd certainly have felt it. ". . . but the snows are heavy enough to make pinpointing their location a—"

Smoky Rose rocked as another round landed closer than any before, spraying mud and water over the cabin's porthole.

"—challenge," the private finished lamely.

Fully shod, she crossed the room in a single step, snapping open the breach in her carbine and testing the mechanism's play. Then she was past the soldier and pounding up the steps.

The air outside was a haze of falling snow and swirling smoke, glowing in the reflected glory of the unseen winter sun. Benwynne stepped from the hold and her feet promptly skidded beneath her, unable to find steady purchase in the half-frozen river water coating the planks. Behind her, *Smoky Rose*'s paddle-wheel roared, churning the froth as it lurched into reverse, hauling the boat back from the incoming fire and turning her toward the eastern bank.

Perched atop the wheelhouse, spyglass pressed to his eye for all the good it would do in this miasma, Private First Class Markham struggled to pinpoint the enemy emplacements. With his other hand he held tight to a small smokestack, occasionally letting go just long enough to brush snow from his fuzzy moustache.

He was a good man, Markham, and an excellent gunner, but Benwynne couldn't help wishing Corporal Dalton were here, rather than leagues away with Oswinne Muir's delegation. She just couldn't be sure how Dalton's temporary replacement would hold up.

A spray of frigid water lashed her face, the whip of a phantom slavedriver, and she turned her mind to far more urgent matters than wishful thinking.

"Cadmoore!"

The trencher corporal waved from his position at the railing. As best as the slick surface allowed, she jogged to his side. "Status?"

"Mostly what you see, Sergeant. Captain Jankis is trying to get us to land, so we can get the 'jacks and the fuel out of here before the Reds get our range."

"Any indication that they might know we're aboard?"

"I don't think so." He jabbed his own carbine upward, indicating the wheelhouse without aiming straight at it. "Markham reports a whole mess of half-sunken riverboats strewn along the banks ahead. I think they're shelling anything that comes upriver."

"Fantastic. Their position?"

"Northwest."

West. Good. At least the emplacement wasn't between the squad and their destination. "I assume Habbershant's already got the 'jacks fired up?"

"Below decks, ready to disembark as soon as we hit dry land."

Benwynne rubbed at the back of her neck. "There's no way we're going to get them off the boat without being seen by Khadoran spotters. If they have to learn we've got a full military detail aboard anyway, we might as well make the most of it." She *could* have shouted her commands directly, but as Habbershant—the only other 'jack marshal in the squad—currently had control, the last thing she needed to do was confuse the machines with conflicting orders.

"Get below," she told Cadmoore instead. "Tell the Master Sergeant that I want Wolfhound standing ready beneath the cargo door. As soon as we get a precise position on the enemy, he's to return fire. Right now, they think we can't hit back. If they have to dive for cover, we might have time to get out of here with our hides intact."

Roland saluted and took off, practically skating across the deck.

It all went as Benwynne predicted, and as well as she had any right to expect. Tracking the incoming shells, Wolfhound succeeded in pinpointing the battery before the enemy had put any significant holes in *Smoky Rose*. The resulting pause in the fusillade, though brief, was more than enough for the squad to abandon ship and for the craft to head back the way she'd come.

None of which made the sergeant particularly jovial about it. Lucky as they'd been to escape *Smoky Rose* unharmed, she didn't feel all that fortunate. They'd known they would have to abandon the Black River eventually, finish the journey overland, but she'd hoped to get a lot farther before it became necessary. When they'd commandeered a vessel with a military-grade engine, they'd also requisitioned two wagonloads of coal for the warjacks. Even with that extra fuel, however, trying to march the machines overland was certain to prove a laborious, complicated, and agonizingly slow process.

And that was assuming they *didn't* have to engage the enemy en route—a stroke of fortune on which Benwynne was absolutely unwilling to rely.

With Atherton's commandos scouting ahead and the two warjacks hauling the coal-laden wagons, the squad moved at a glacial pace away from the banks and into the snow-swept lowlands beyond. The thick flurries Benwynne had cursed earlier were their allies now, for no other cover would present itself for many miles.

They had covered only a few hundred yards when one of the rear guard gave a shout. Benwynne and the others turned in time to see the sky light up far behind them, flickering various shades of red before fading once more to gray. Benwynne couldn't even imagine how bright the phenomenon must have been, for it to be visible from so far away.

"Flare!" Master Sergeant Habbershant's voice carried clearly enough from farther back in the formation. "Sergeant, that was a signal flare!"

"You don't say." Benwynne exchange grim looks with her other seconds. "Nothing for it," she said firmly. "We move on, and we hope we're able to avoid anyone who was near enough to see it."

***

It seemed, for a time, that their luck might actually hold.

For hours they navigated empty plains and gently rolling hills, taking the occasional detour around random rocky outcroppings or scattered towns. Smoke poured from Wolfhound and Shepherd in ever thickening swirls, until the surrounding air smelled like a foundry and a canopy of shadow followed overhead. Benwynne cursed, and muttered, and cursed some more, and prayed the weather would hide them.

They were drawing slowly near a darker smudge in the foggy distance, most likely one of Llael's many forests of pine and yew, when Wendell struggled up to Benwynne's side, gasping in the cold.

"We need to halt for a while, Sergeant."

"Not a chance. I want to at least make the tree line before dark."

"Sergeant, the 'jacks—"

"Didn't we *just* refuel them two hours ago? They should have at least—"

That Wendell interrupted her was clear sign of his own frustration and fatigue. "It's not about coal," he insisted. "The engines need some down time for regular upkeep now and again. Cleaning soot out of the ports, tightening seals . . ." Then, at Benwynne's sour glare, "Sergeant, these things aren't made for this sort of continuous operation. You *know* that."

"Yeah." She sighed. "All right. How long?"

"If you only plan to run them another few hours before we bunk for the night, about thirty minutes should do."

"Fine. *Squad, halt!*" she called. "Cadmoore, quick perimeter. Just spread the men out, overlapping fields of fire; we shouldn't be here long enough for fortifications. Dalton—ah, Markham, I want at least one rifle with each chain gun team."

Soldiers scattered as the sergeant barked orders. In minutes, they'd arrayed themselves in concentric rings, weapons bristling in all directions. Wendell's team hovered around the languishing warjacks, ready to stoke the fires and get them back on their feet at a moment's notice.

Only Atherton and his men continued onward, scouting their route to the forest. The commandos' footsteps traced a somehow maudlin path in the snow, eventually vanishing into the haze.

"I'm not crazy about this." Wendell settled himself beside the tiny fire, one of several now coughing and spitting throughout the camp.

"I don't think any of us are exactly thrilled to be here, Master Sergeant," Roland grumped, warming his asymmetrical hands frighteningly close to the flame.

"I mean the overland travel. We've got leagues and leagues to go, some through pretty thick forest. There's going to come a point where it's too much for the 'jacks, even with cool-down intervals."

"What would you suggest?" Benwynne asked bitterly. Her normally dusky complexion was almost gray with weariness and cold, as was Cadmoore's own; the others, far paler of feature, were chapped and chafed an almost festive pink. "Leave them behind?"

"No, of course not! But—"

"Khador holds the river. So unless you've built something to fly us the rest of the way, Master Sergeant, we get to walk."

"Um . . ." Private First Class Markham, still unaccustomed to serving as a unit commander, actually half raised his hand.

"You don't need to ask permission to speak, Private."

"Right. Well, I'm just wondering . . . What about the wagons?"

"What about them?" Benwynne replied.

"Couldn't we, I don't know, spread some of the coal out among the boys' supplies and use the wagons to transport the 'jacks? Not both at once, of course, but . . ."

Everyone was staring at him, eyes so wide they were in danger of freezing over. Wendell actually slapped a hand to his forehead, dislodging tiny crystals of frost from his beard.

"I'm *such* an idiot!"

"Can we actually do that?" Benwynne asked, clearly skeptical.

"Not yet. Still too much coal to carry. But later, when we've burned through a chunk of it? Might be doable. We'll have to reinforce the wagons with local lumber, lash them together to make a large enough platform, but that should be pretty simple. Then the 'jacks can take turns playing chauffer for each other.

"Sergeant?" He aimed a finger squarely at Markham's forehead. "Promote this boy."

The long-gunner beamed.

"I just might—"

The four of them abruptly scattered, leaping to their feet, hands darting to weapons, as a sparking cobalt comet arced from the blowing flurries to bury itself at their feet.

"I need to have a word with Gaust about doing that," Benwynne hissed, once her heart stopped beating at *quite* the speed of a cycling chain gun. "He—"

She cut off yet again as cracks formed in the packed snow, forming another one-word message.

Flares.

It could have meant half a dozen things, but Benwynne chose to assume that the gunmage wouldn't have sent a warning save for the worst.

"Master Sergeant, I want the 'jacks up the *second* you think they can handle it. Corporal, Private, we're on high alert moving forward. Scouts to rear and both flanks, trenchers and rifles both."

"I'm not sure I understand," Markham admitted.

"If Gaust spotted flares like the ones we saw earlier," Roland explained grimly, "it means either the Reds have somehow caught up with us—or there's another unit waiting ahead."

***

In the end, their extra wariness and preparation did little good.

They encountered no one on their march toward the woodland; no signs of life at all, in fact, save the occasional small burrow in the snow, the flapping dive of a winter owl ready to feast on whatever made those burrows, and the rapidly fading tracks of Atherton's unit. The moan of the wind, and the answering whisper of the trees, were the evening's only voices.

The gunmage and his commandos awaited them at the forest's edge, smoothly falling into place at the vanguard of the formation. Other than to confirm Benwynne's interpretation of Atherton's message—he had, indeed, spotted crimson flashes in the clouds to the north—conversation remained as sparse in the woods as it had been on the plain.

Roughly a mile into the brush, Benwynne called a halt for the night. They could risk no fire, she'd decided, but at least the trees dramatically cut down on the gusts, and the soldiers could glean some warmth from the slowly cooling warjacks. Trenchers and commandos spread out to stand watch, long-gunners found perches in nearby boles, and at least a fifth of the squad remained awake at all times, watching in rotating shifts.

They remained tensely alert, twitching at every shifting branch, starting at every birdcall. And still nothing untoward befell them, no enemy appeared.

Dawn was little more than an abstract notion, a feeble lightening of the drab gray sky visible between the overlapping conifers. Soldiers rose from ragged sleep to a joyless breakfast of cold rations, sullenly broke camp to face another day of frigid shuffling. Wolfhound and Shepherd manhandled ('jackhandled?) the wagons around the trees, sometimes forced dozens of yards out of the way before they could find an opening large enough to accommodate them; and with each such delay, everyone else's shoulders slumped that little bit further.

They would never complain, never balk, the men and women of Cygnar's armies, but Benwynne knew their spirits were low, tugging at their heels as stubbornly as had the deep snows back in the lowlands.

The commandos ranged ahead, reported back; ranged ahead, reported back; and detected no sign of danger.

Not until it was too late to matter.

The first shots rang out, so close together that each sounded like an echo of the last. Hartswood, Atherton's second and most experienced of the commandos, died between words as he spoke to Corporal Cadmoore, his head turning to grit and fine mist. Two mechaniks dropped—only the fact that he'd been twisting back for a glance at the 'jacks saved Wendell from making it three—alongside a trio of trenchers. Even Wolfhound staggered, a well-placed bullet slipping between the armored plates on its leg to mangle portions of the knee joint.

It was a remarkable display of precision fire, nigh inhuman in the dark and cramped confines of the woods, and that alone was enough to tell Benwynne who they faced. Even as she dove for a fallen log, screaming *"Cover!"* at the top of her lungs, her mind was already shuffling through half a dozen strategies, not for attack but *escape*.

Widowmakers.

Although relatively few in number, the Khadoran sniper corps was among the most dangerous forces on the battlefield. Through endless training and brutal, methodical cruelties, they were shaped into killing machines, only slightly more human than the warjacks themselves. Only the best of the best, the absolute elite of Cygnar's long-gunners, could match their skill with the rifle.

And even had they not been lurking in ambush, had squad five been in a position to give as accurately as they got, the truth could not be denied: Markham and the other long-gunners in the squad were good, *damn* good— but almost surely not *that* good.

Already several of them were indeed, returning fire, as were many of the trenchers and Atherton himself. The Widowmakers had hidden themselves well, though, spread out amongst the branches and cloaked in shadow. Cygnaran bullets tore through leaves and branches, and possibly the occasional small mammal, but Benwynne had no doubt they'd missed all their targets. *Maybe* all but one, if blind luck was with them.

Her pessimism was confirmed when the distant rifles barked once more, and four more of her people—*her* people!—crumpled.

"Gaust!"

He was already on it. If the gunmage still couldn't pinpoint the shooters, not even enough for his runebullets to seek them out, at least he'd narrowed down the possibilities. The pepperbox barrels surged and crackled, their ensorcelled glow painting the nearby trees a spectral blue. Bullets flew in pairs, carving a crescent into the forest between the squad and the Widowmakers, and where they struck, entire trunks splintered. In a matter of seconds, a veritable wall of timber and fallen foliage shielded the squad from further attack.

Briefly.

"Move out, southeast!" Benwynne called, her orders swiftly repeated up and down the formation. "Bodies in Wolfhound's cart!" Cold as it sounded, it was all she could do for them at the moment. "Cadmoore, get a chain gun crew riding in Shepherd's. I want anyone following us to have to climb through a wall of bullets. Do try to make sure they don't ignite the coal, yeah? Atherton, send your men ahead, but you're with the rear guard; anything gets through the barrage, put holes in it until it goes away.

"Everyone else, eyes and barrels! Something moves, don't wait to see what it is. Go!"

If their pace had frustrated Benwynne earlier, it was downright torturous now; she felt like she'd seen molasses run downhill faster than the close-packed trees and the fuel-packed wagons would permit them to go. Fallen twigs and scattered leaves crunched beneath dozens of soles, the cracks and crinkles combining into the muted roar of a slowed, phantasmal fire.

It seemed that every shot the enemy fired scored a hit, but the shots were, at least, sporadic. Even Widowmakers couldn't shoot through so much foliage with any real hope of accuracy, and since any sign of movement was answered with a burst from Cadmoore's trenchers, they dared not find themselves *too* unobstructed a line of fire.

At least the squad was still partly on-course, the sergeant mused. Get far enough southeast, maybe they could circle around the enemy and resume their northeastern track . . .

Ledeson, the dwarf-short member of Gaust's commandos, materialized at her side like a half-remembered dream. And if his eyes were slightly more raw than the weather alone could explain, well, it didn't show in his posture or demeanor.

"Forest thins substantially ahead, Sergeant. Too misty to tell if it's just a large clearing or the actual tree line. Either way, we should be able to put on some speed."

And lose all our cover, too. Still, it might be the better option; Gaust and Shepherd could cover their flight pretty well, at least for a while . . .

Flight. This was hardly squad five's first withdrawal, and it likely wouldn't be their last, but still it tasted of arsenic and charcoal on her tongue. She'd lost soldiers today, not in any meaningful battle, not to an overwhelming force, but to a lurking enemy they couldn't even *see*. Just a small contingent of the Khadoran advance, scouting well ahead of the creeping front.

A part of her wanted to burn the whole bloody forest down, leaving a swathe of scorched woodland and charred Widowmakers behind, and to hell with collateral damage.

She did nothing of the sort, of course; but Morrow knew, her heart thudded and her jaw trembled with the urge to give the order.

The blurry, watercolor horizon shifted from black with gray smudges to gray with black smudges; as Ledeson had reported, the trees were thinning, and dramatically at that. No way was this a clearing; they had, indeed, reached the border of this particular sea of greenery.

Again Benwynne barked orders, this time for the company to follow the tree line north-northeast. It was, at least temporarily, the best of both options: They could move faster here than they could in the deep woods, but the boles stood nearby should they need to take cover. If she had to decide to go one way or the other further on, both options were readily at hand.

It was after roughly half a mile of such travel that Benwynne discovered she'd been outmaneuvered.

She'd truly thought it the best option. North or northwest took them into the teeth of the Widowmakers. West and south were both the absolute wrong direction for their objective. Eastward had been the logical choice.

Unfortunately, when the squad first cut east from the river, the Khadorans must have figured out that Leryn or the city of Rhydden were their most likely destinations—which meant they *knew* that the Cygnarans would keep moving east.

The squad had emerged from the woods' eastern edge—and now, mere moments later, found the enemy ready and waiting to meet them.

They poured from the trees and rose from the slush, Winter Guard soldiers in crimson and gray. Some fired bulky rifles, forcing the Cygnarans to duck and cover, while the rest charged, closing so they could bring wide-barreled, flesh-and-steel-shredding blunderbusses to bear.

Most of Benwynne's soldiers darted left, taking cover behind whatever nearby boles offered themselves. The commandos vanished; the chain gunners, having no better option and hoping to end the battle quickly, dropped to their bellies and opened fire. Atherton's bullets traced lines overhead, landing like cannonballs, battering the enemy with debris, blinding them with churning snow and soil.

It was a tight spot, but the squad had dealt with worse. Paradoxically, the attack had actually given Benwynne real hope for the first time in hours. If all they had to do was punch through a contingent of Winter Guard . . .

From within the woods echoed the deadly crack of the Widowmakers' rifles.

"Look on the bright side," Atherton told her as he appeared from nowhere, dropping flat beside her. "If they were Kossite rangers, we probably wouldn't have made it out of the forest at all."

"Oh, thank you *so* much. Get into those trees and *find those bloody snipers!*"

As quickly as he'd arrived, the gunmage was gone—*presumably* alongside his commandos, though Benwynne hadn't seen any of them in a couple of minutes.

"Chain gun crews, mind your fields! Friendly coming through!" She knew they'd never hear her over the chatter of their weapons, but the order would swiftly pass from soldier to soldier.

Then a last pair of commands—and these, she knew, *would* be heard.

Wolfhound's cannon thundered, the powerful shell punching through the gathered Winter Guard. Only a handful died, but the lot of them scattered, diving away from the incoming artillery.

For a few seconds, then, their barrage ceased.

Shepherd pounded through the lines, smoke flowing from its stack, smaller clouds of steam where its furnace-heated armor melted the accumulated frost. Alerted by Benwynne's warning, the chain guns fell silent as the warjack tromped past, then spoke in far more controlled bursts, carefully aimed to either side.

Once past the forward rank, Shepherd slowed. Dropping into as low a crouch as its chassis allowed, shield raised before its face and torso, it crept toward the enemy. Atop that shield, using it as a stand, the 'jack balanced the body of the massive chain gun that was its own right arm.

Bullets flew in veritable waves, tearing Khadorans apart, fertilizing the soil for seasons to come. And though the occasional shot caught Shepherd in an arm or leg, staggering it, most impacted harmlessly on its massive slab of a shield.

Even over the chaos, Benwynne heard Wolfhound's breach snapping shut, its cannon reloaded and ready to fire. She saw blue flashes amidst the trees, gleaming off snow and frost-coated bark, and knew that Widowmakers were starting to die. Again, she began to think that, just maybe, her squad might win through with a minimum of further losses.

And again, the gods declared that she was wrong.

It was a declaration that came with a literal tremor of the earth. Not substantial; no earthquake, this, no nearby detonation. Just enough for everyone to feel it, shaking bones, rattling teeth. Again it came, and then again, each time just that slightest bit heavier. Snow shook from leaves; coal sifted and tumbled down the carefully heaped piles in the wagons. Neither side ceased firing, yet Benwynne could have sworn that the guns grew quieter, muffled, more distant.

Perhaps because she knew from past experience, even before it appeared, what she was about to see.

It was, initially, little more than a solid block of deepest red, smeared and distorted by the dancing flurries. Smoke poured from its back like a volcanic eruption, so thick it appeared a trembling column, supporting the unseen sky. The roaring of pistons and the screaming of gears were an out-of-tune orchestra that would have sounded fully at home in a Cryxian torture chamber.

Again the earth shook, and now she could see the massive legs, ready to crush the whole world beneath its tread; the brutal spike that all but hid the grillwork face, and the gaping barrels on each shoulder; shield the size of a rowboat, lance as long as a railroad car.

A full yard taller than Shepherd and five times as heavy, it was an unbelievable sight, a manmade mountain of steel and blades and searing fire.

Benwynne couldn't imagine what a 'jack like this was doing so far from the front, in the midst of a region where no equivalent enemy could possibly appear. Perhaps Khador had stationed such units throughout Llael, in case Cygnar tried to sneak forces through. Perhaps they were hunting something or someone specific. Hell, perhaps they'd known the squad—or at least *someone*—was coming, though the sergeant could only begin to guess how. She didn't know, probably never would.

What she knew was that her people, and her two light warjacks, could never stand successfully against it.

She opened her mouth, drawing breath to shout orders, and two of the tubes bristling from the monster's shoulders flashed.

"Incoming!"

Again the soldiers scattered, again Benwynne threw herself to the snow, seeking what flimsy safety she could find. Fetching up against a drift which was, in turn, piled against a mass of dead brush, she landed on her shoulder— and so happened to be looking the right way to watch one of her best officers, and best friends, die.

It happened so slowly, with that bizarre combination of fuzziness and almost obscene clarity normally reserved for uncomfortable dreams. She saw the grenade plunge to earth, spin and skip over the ground, leaving a furrow in the carpet of slush and leaves. She saw it come to rest beside a crew of trenchers, whose mad scrambling couldn't begin to carry them to safety in time.

She saw Corporal Roland Cadmoore, with one final glance at his men who were about to die, dive onto the grenade and start to curl his body around it . . .

And then a quick flash, a geyser of steam and smoke and blood.

The soldiers who should have died stared for long, horrified heartbeats.

Then, voice joined in a singular cry, they spun their weapons toward the Khadoran warjack and opened fire. It was all but useless, a mere gesture of defiance, using small arms and a single chain gun against that wall of armor. They blasted away all the same, the act itself of greater importance than any result.

The 'jack's second grenade had landed some dozen yards further along the line, wiping out a second chain gun crew who hadn't been so fortunate—if "fortunate" was the proper term—as the first. Perhaps if they'd had time to dig in—or had the fury of the blast not suggested that these grenades were rather more potent than standard armament—the crew might have had a chance.

But not as it was.

The remaining trenchers, and Shepherd itself, turned their attentions to this newest threat, allowing the torn and battered Winter Guard to withdraw, melting into the forest whence they'd come.

The monstrosity advanced, each footstep the stomp of an angry god, and the second pair of grenade launchers coughed, followed immediately by the third.

Benwynne swore that the screams were louder than the detonations.

Sparks flew from the armored monstrosity as Markham's long-gunners joined in—to little effect, for the most part, though occasionally a particularly well aimed shot found a gap and dealt a modicum of actual damage. Ricochets and fragments from carbines and chain guns formed an aura of shrapnel around the thing as it approached, a buzzing swarm of insects far more dangerous to the squad's own people than the warjack itself. So far, it hadn't even bothered raising its shield.

Wolfhound stepped from the mass of scattered soldiers and fired. The massive shell punched into the metal mountain like a shooting star, leaving a tunnel of shredded armor in its wake. Again it fired, and again, each time peeling aside layers of reinforced steel. For the first time, the enemy apparatus staggered. A dozen ragged voices cheered as smoke began to drift from the wound.

Those cheered died as abruptly as they'd begun when the thing lunged forward, sweeping its lance in a horizontal arc, shattering Cygnaran bodies and flinging them carelessly aside.

Cannon empty, Wolfhound raised its massive axe and charged the larger 'jack. Mere feet beyond the reach of the thing's lance, however, the Hunter swerved, circling. Unable to match Wolfhound's speed, it lumbered in a tight circle, struggling to keep either lance or shield interposed.

"Shepherd!"

The other 'jack was closing even before Benwynne's command. Not quite so steady as its counterpart on the yielding terrain, still it was swifter than the Khadoran giant. Circling counter to Wolfhound's arc, Shepherd unleashed short bursts from its chain gun, pelting the enemy, slowly chipping away at its defenses.

Wolfhound veered once more, stepping inside the reach of the Khadoran's lance. Its right arm flew up and around, clasping the longer weapon between torso and the empty cannon that was the Hunter's lower arm. For just a moment, the weight dragged the larger 'jack to a halt. Wolfhound began pounding at the thing's head and chest with its axe, while Shepherd stepped in from behind, pouring bullets and slamming its shield into the giant's back, right around the quadruple smokestacks.

The crimson 'jack shuddered, staggered almost to one knee beneath an assault that might just have buckled even its own impossibly heavy plating— and then it rotated its own shield into a horizontal blade and drove it with pile driver strength into Wolfhound's torso.

Metal crumpled with a rending scream, sparks flew, and the smaller warjack stumbled, gears grinding in protest . . . And opened just enough space for the Khadoran machine to rear back and strike with its newly freed lance.

Steel tore, now, rather than folding, and the Hunter collapsed, unable to support its own weight. Wolfhound's eyes still glowed with internal flame, smoke still pumped from the metal chimney, but it could do little more than lie there and watch as the lance rose high, angled downward like the gods' own lightning . . .

It spun away at the last instant to catch Shepherd's furious charge. The two 'jacks locked together, shield hooked behind shield. Bullets poured from Shepherd's chain gun into the larger 'jack's face, until the ammunition finally ran dry. Even then, it continued its attack, jabbing with the barrels again and again, using them as a dull spear. In turn, the Khadoran—unable to bring the lance into play at such close range—punched at Shepherd with the fist wrapped around the weapon's haft. For a moment they staggered together, teetering like the mast of a sinking ship, but nobody could doubt how this would end. Already the stronger Khadoran machine was gaining control, steering Shepherd where it wanted to go, causing more damage with each punch than the Cygnaran could deliver with four or five.

Wendell and two of his mechaniks dashed from the cover of the trees, carrying shells for Wolfhound's cannon. Even if it couldn't support itself, couldn't rise, it might be able to aim from the ground—but the odds of them getting there before Shepherd was pulped into scrap looked poor at best.

Benwynne ordered her troops to take any shot they had, but only a few of the long-gunners responded. For the trenchers, the two machines grappled and spun too swiftly for them to fire without possibly hitting Shepherd. Benwynne raised her own carbine, seeking an opening, dully aware that nothing she did would make any great difference.

Something flew from the branches of a nearby tree.

Flapping in the winter haze, it looked at first to be some sort of bat, or perhaps a kite broken loose from its string. Only when portions of it began to flicker blue did Benwynne realize she was staring at Atherton, coat spread, making an apparently suicidal leap from above.

Just as he began to slow, to arc back toward earth, he fired both pistols straight down. The detonation was immense, leaving a pair of craters in the dirt. Benwynne had known the gunmage could charge his bullets, granting them the kinetic energy of artillery shells. She had *not* known he could do what came next.

Somehow, without shattering his arms or ripping the weapons from his hands, he'd allowed the recoil of those supercharged projectiles to push back against the pistols, rather than simply dissipating it as his magics normally did. As though he were a ball struck by a particularly angry child, his fall abruptly transformed into an upward arc, easily tripling the distance of his original leap.

With an impossibly graceful flip that seemed almost as surprising to him as it was to Benwynne, Atherton rotated in mid-air and landed hard in an awkward crouch behind the wrestling warjacks.

Or, more accurately and perhaps more importantly, directly behind the *Khadoran* warjack.

Terrain even marginally less forgiving might well have broken his ankle; as it was, he clearly limped as he rose and staggered two steps. When he raised his pistols, however, his arms were steady and stable as a dwarven keep.

Six shots, nigh inaudible compared to the struggles of the metal giants; six cerulean sparks, carving elegant—and sharp, utterly impossible—arcs through the winter haze; six bullets, hypercharged with all the arcane energies the gunmage could muster, plunged into the open barrels of the warjack's grenade launchers.

Even without any ordnance in the spent weapons, the effects were impressive. The machine staggered, rocked by a sequence of internal detonations, its vaunted armor now quite useless. It swiftly grew impossible to tell whether the thick and choking plumes came from the smokestacks, the grenade launchers, or various other gaps and crevices. Still it fought, but slower, weaker, less stable than before. Shepherd tore free of its grip and pounded away with its shield rather than risking further damage to the chain gun-turned-bludgeon.

Benwynne raced around the mechanical duel, skidding to a halt beside the fallen Wolfhound. Wendell and his assistants had barely managed to leverage the 'jack over far enough to access the arm-cannon's ammunition cylinder. One of the younger mechaniks was prying a shell out of the padded crate that they had dragged over when Atherton appeared, looming over his shoulder.

"One minute . . ."

Favoring his left foot and wincing with every step, he all but fell into Wendell, yanking a narrow chisel and a hammer from the older man's tool belt. Then, muttering under his breath, he knelt beside the shell, scratching and tapping at the brass casing.

"You want to speed this up?" Wendell snapped. "You hurt that thing bad, but I still don't think Shepherd can—"

"Shut *up*." Then, through gritted teeth and over the cling-clang of tools, "Sir."

Seconds stretched into infinity. The sounds of the battle grew somehow more urgent without drawing any nearer.

"There." Atherton fell back on his haunches, shoulders slumped. His breath came in ragged gasps. The shell was now shallowly etched with quick, haphazard glyphs, and shone with the same azure glow, if perhaps a bit dimmer, as the gunmage's own runebullets. "I can't do that again any time soon. Hell, I'm not even sure it worked *this* time. So make it count."

Through sheer muscle and determination, Benwynne, Wendell, and the mechaniks helped Wolfhound prop itself up on its left arm. Servos whined, hissed, threatened to give; the upper half of the 'jack trembled, even as the lower failed to so much as twitch. Yet the tenacious machine succeeded, if only through a beat or two of Benwynne's fluttering heart, in holding the cannon steady.

Magic and metal blasted through the damaged Khadoran warjack, peeling armor like the rind of ripened fruit. It spasmed one final time, spitting sparks and jets of oils, before it finally, *finally* toppled. The entire forest, or so it felt to those nearby, rocked with the impact.

And then . . . silence. Not utter or absolute; flames crackled, gun barrels creaked as they cooled, soldiers groaned in pain, wind shook hands with leaves and branches. As compared to a moment earlier, however, it was no less than the hush of the grave.

A quick examination of the Khadoran corpses offered no sign as to which of them had served as marshal for the lumbering mechanical beast. Or perhaps its controller had been among the escapees.

Either way, Benwynne supposed, it didn't matter much.

Moving almost as mechanically as the 'jacks themselves, the sergeant turned to the nearest mechanik. "Casualty reports," she ordered in a monotone. "Soon as possible."

A quick salute, and he was off, gathering what remained of the fifth squad.

"Wolfhound?" Benwynne asked.

"Can't walk." Wendell had gone beyond chewing at his lip; he seemed to be working, now, on his beard. "Can't stand. Half the pistons and actuators in his lower torso are either crushed or split."

After all the death and loss of the past hour, the notion of abandoning

Wolfhound—machine or no—was more than Benwynne could bear. "Maybe the wagon . . . ?"

The other mechanik shook her head. "We wouldn't be able to carry enough coal to keep Shepherd going. I don't think we have any—"

"Wait a minute!" The sergeant and the others actually recoiled, startled by Wendell's sudden outburst. With a spurt of energy that exhausted Benwynne just to *look* at, he sprang to his feet and ran to the fallen Khadoran warjack.

"Don't just stand there!" he called back. "Help me put it out!"

Not quite understanding, a handful of soldiers gathered around, dumping snow on the glowing embers and flickering flames that showed through the rents in the crimson armor. Even Shepherd assisted, using its shield as a great scoop.

By the time they were done, she'd puzzled out what her chief mechanik was thinking. "Can you do it?"

Wendell had scrambled atop the behemoth, peering intently into one of the wounds. "Think so. Not a great fit, not all compatible, and I don't have the tools, the facilities, or the time to make a halfway decent job of it. But I think I can get him walking, long as that's about *all* he's got to do."

Benwynne couldn't help it; she felt the tiniest smile break through her lingering resentment of his recent actions, his borderline betrayal. "Get on it then, Master Sergeant."

She turned away before he could acknowledge either her order or the expression she'd been too slow to hide. *I do* not *have the energy to examine this right now . . .*

And found she'd stepped directly into the path of the mechanik she'd sent to take stock of the squad.

The news was even grimmer than she'd feared. Not counting her surviving seconds—she clenched a fist until her fingers ached, until the seams of the glove cut into her skin, until the wave of grief for Roland had receded—squad five now constituted a grand total of seven trenchers, three mechaniks, three long-gunners, and two commandos. Or at least, two of them still lived when Atherton had last seen them, but they hadn't yet returned from the forest foray.

"Squad"? They almost qualified as a single large unit at this point.

Wendell and his people ferried pieces back and forth, cannibalizing the fallen enemy to make what repairs they could to Wolfhound. Tools banged, metal clattered, men and women cursed. Shepherd watched over them, its chain gun reloaded, the barrels sawed down a few inches to eliminate the dents, burs, and bends caused by the weapon's brief career as a bludgeon.

Benwynne watched none of it, staring instead at a veritable carpet of cloth and armor, flesh and blood. The bodies of everyone she'd lost in the past day, gathered by her remaining soldiers as a final and woefully insufficient mark of respect. Or at least the bodies of all those who'd *left* a body; half a dozen were absent, Corporal Roland Cadmoore among them. She couldn't even order them carried along anymore, delivered home for proper burial, not with so many dead and so many essential supplies still to be transported.

"Corporal Gaust?"

The gunmage appeared at her call, pistols drawn. "You should step back, Sergeant."

She almost asked *Why should I bother?* but swiftly quashed the thought. No time under these circumstances, and no room in any useful commander, for that sort of self-pity. She took several paces away, waved for everyone else to do the same.

Atherton fired, and again, until all eight barrels were empty. Each runebullet ripped trees apart at the base or tore them out by the roots, forming a makeshift cairn atop the gathered bodies. No proper burial or cremation, perhaps—the squad lacked the time for the former, expendable fuels that would burn anywhere near hot enough for the latter—but the most respectful gesture they could manage.

Several of the survivors uttered short prayers to Morrow for the souls of the deceased. Benwynne stood by impassively, aware her presence was essential yet unable to force herself to speak. It would have felt somehow dishonest.

So she waited, and listened to their prayers, and shivered with a soul-deep chill she feared might never thaw.

". . . a pyre for them?" It was Habbershant, hissing a question to Gaust at the rear of the assembly. "I've seen gunmages create all sorts of conflagrations, hotter than any wood or oil fire."

"Some of the others can. I don't work with fire."

"You don't . . ."

"I focused my studies elsewhere, Master Sergeant. Think about it; *everything* I do is a trick of inertia and momentum. It's all variations of that core principle. I don't—"

"Gentlemen!" Benwynne didn't need to turn; she *heard* the both of them jump. She knew they meant no disrespect, that this was how they dealt with their emotions. Still . . . "This is *not* the time!"

"Yes, Sergeant!"

"Sorry, Ben."

Her mood lightened finally lightened a bit, later on, as Wolfhound slowly clambered to its feet. The cacophony of rending and grinding made it sound like the warjack was chewing an orchestra, and it staggered worse than a drunken sailor on every third or fifth step, but it was up and moving.

"Can he keep up?" Benwynne asked Wendell, who was wiping grease, freezing sweat, and a smear or two of blood from his hands with a rag of indeterminate color.

"I wouldn't risk rushing him," the mechanik replied. "But given that we've got to keep to a sedate pace if Shepherd's going to manage the wagon, I think he'll do fine. It's not a long-term fix, but it should get us where we're going—long as he doesn't have to do any more fighting."

"You're still a miracle-worker, Master Sergeant."

"I . . . Thank you, Ser—"

But again she was turning away, shouting orders, getting her men and women ready to march once more. Shepherd tromped toward one of the wagons, now piled not only with coal but with weapons, ammunition, and provisions belonging to soldiers who no longer had need of them. The other wagon was nothing more than a mess of tinder and smoldering coals, obliterated by one of the Khadoran grenades.

The squad had just completed their preparations, and Benwynne was dithering over what to do about the two tardy commandos, when the problem resolved itself.

"Sergeant!" Ledeson and his partner, a quiet, muscle-bound bruiser by the name of Reighdly, materialized from the trees. "Sergeant, we're in trouble."

Of course we are.

"I'm listening, Private."

"Winter Guard, Sergeant. We're late getting back because, well, we saw the Reds retreating through the woods, and we figured someone ought to keep an eye on them."

"You should have checked in first. Still, not a bad notion. And?"

"They've regrouped, and they're coming back this way." Only then did the short fellow note the savaged metal carcass sprawled on the earth beyond his teammates.

"Private? You're going to fill up with snow if you don't close your mouth."

"Sorry, Sergeant! Is that what it looks like?"

"Used to be."

"Well, I guess the Reds figured out that their 'jack didn't squish you all like it was supposed to. They look like they mean business."

"*Move it out!*" she called over her shoulder. "Now!"

"There can't be many of them left," Atherton said. How *did* the man keep sneaking up on her like that?! "Not after Shepherd and Rol—" Everyone pretended not to notice the hitch in his voice, or the pause as he wrestled it under control. "Roland's boys got through with them."

"Not that many, sir," Ledeson agreed. "But—"

"But a lot more than there are left of *us*," Benwynne finished for him.

The commando nodded, not only his expression but somehow his entire posture grim.

"So we run."

It turned out that "running" was unduly optimistic. Exhausted soldiers, one damaged warjack, the other burdened by a load the squad could not afford to leave behind . . . Their pace could scarcely be dignified with words like "crawl" or "creep," let alone "run."

The forest blurred and faded in the mist, the snow, the fading light of evening—but not so utterly that the rear guard failed to spot the shapes moving within those leaf-cast shadows and out into the lowlands beyond.

"What now?" Private First Class Markham asked, his voice shaking. "If they're already at the tree line, there's no way we can outrun—!"

"We need to delay them," Atherton said softly.

Benwynne followed his gaze, then stiffened. "Absolutely not!"

"Sergeant, we don't have a choice."

"We almost lost Wolfhound back there, I am *not* going to sacrifice—"

"Ben . . ." Wendell put a hand on her shoulder; she just as swiftly shrugged it off, barely restraining herself from backhanding him. For all that, the glimmer of unshed tears in his eyes stopped her cold before she could speak.

"He's right, Ben, and you know it. Unless you'd rather add the rest of us to the list, instead?"

"*Shit!*"

Every face in the squad swiveled her way, twisted in shock and growing fear.

Get a grip on yourself, Bracewell! She couldn't fall apart, not now. Her people needed her.

"Shepherd?" *It's only a machine. It's only a machine . . .* "Shepherd . . ."

It cocked its head, meeting her gaze through slits of flickering coal-fire— and Morrow damn her if she wasn't sure, absolutely sure, that the 'jack understood what was being asked of it.

Shepherd made a parade-perfect pivot—it couldn't *really* have straightened its shoulders in prideful determination; that *had* to be her imagination, didn't it?—and began the long march back toward the Winter Guard, gun and shield raised high.

"We need to keep moving," Benwynne rasped. She saw Wolfhound stagger over to assume the burden of the wagon; all the while it watched Shepherd fade slowly into the haze. "Or this is all meaningless."

Slowly, painfully, exhaustedly, they moved—and every last one of them pretended not to hear, or to flinch, at the sounds of combat erupting far behind.

Casteus 2nd, 605 AR
Leryn, Llael

For the second time in less than a week, Katherine Laddermore sat in a plush, creaking chair within one of the dormitory chambers of Thunderhead Keep. Sparse but comfortable, it contained little more than an old mattress, a wardrobe leaning canted against the wall as though nothing else were holding it upright, a granite-topped table, and the set of mostly matching chairs from which Katherine had selected her current seat. Both the Golden Crucible and the chamber's occupant could readily have afforded better, very much so, but why? Why bother, for a dormitory intended to be used only sporadically, never to serve as anyone's permanent home?

And also for the second time in less than a week, the man she'd come to consult had greeted her with haunted eyes, his shoulders bent as though he not only carried the weight of the world, but was running horribly late in delivering it.

Engman Drew was balding, graying, wrinkled, squinting—the absolute archetype of the "old scholar" image, save for the lingering muscle still visible where neck and forearms protruded from his tunic. It was, he'd remarked to the knight last time she'd been here, the result of habits leftover from his military days, not any deliberate effort to stay in shape.

At the moment, the Cygnaran-born alchemist was disappearing into the open wardrobe, hunched and digging through a haphazard stack of clothes.

"Ah! Here we go."

Shaking away a wrinkled sock, he dumped a thick folder of papers onto the table. "Didn't want anyone finding it, did I?" he asked in response to his visitor's raised eyebrow. "Not a lot of places here to hide anything . . ."

"I suppose not, no." Idly she shuffled the sheaf of papers, but it might as well have been written in code, in another language, upside down, by a blind man, for all the sense she could make of it.

"Lady Ladd—that is, Lieutenant Laddermore . . ." Engman began. His hands twitched across the table, as though he were writing something with an invisible quill. "You know that even I never saw the whole formula, right? Or even *most* of it? Any remotely competent alchemist will figure out this is a forgery without *too* much effort, and a *good* one should tumble to it in a matter of minutes . . ."

Katherine's smile was a mélange of genuine amusement and frustrated impatience—more the former than the latter, she hoped. "I know, Master Drew. You've explained that to us. Nobody expects otherwise."

"It's just, I'm not sure—"

"It doesn't have to fool anyone long," she reassured him—as she'd done the last time she was here, when she'd first commissioned the fake. "Odds are, we'll never have a use for it anyway. We just felt . . ." by which she meant *Dignity* had felt, and Katherine had no reason to gainsay her, "it was the sort of thing that might prove handy. Better to have and not need, and all that, right?"

"Yes, yes, of course." He seemed determined to study the rough carpet, the tabletop, the room—anything but her face.

Apparently, not all *his military habits lingered . . .* She shoved the documents in the satchel sitting beside her, slung the trap over her shoulder. "Master Drew? How did di Meryse acquire *your* portion of the formula?"

She'd meant to draw him out, as well as assuaging her own curiosity, but if anything, his posture sagged further still. "I'd wondered about that at first," he said miserably, "when I heard things had gone tits up. And then I remembered.

"It was a few weeks before all this started. I'd arrived at my laboratory one morning, and found the lock on my door . . ." He paused. "Many of us augment our security, you see. Mechanical devices in the keyhole to snap tools or sound alarms. False locks, or—"

"Yes, I understand," she interrupted, not wishing to be rude, but wishing to sit through a lengthy recitation of the safeguards of paranoid alchemists even less.

"Right. Well, that day, my own lock seemed stiff. It ground a bit when I opened up. I suspected tampering, of course—even the best lock can be bypassed—but nothing was missing. Far as I could tell at the time, nothing had even been *moved*. I figured the mechanism had just started to break down; happens even to the best craftsmanship. But now . . ."

Katherine nodded. "You think di Meryse broke in and copied your work?"

"Not by hand; he wouldn't have had the time, and he certainly couldn't have left everything so pristine. But remember, Lieutenant, we're all alchemists here. Spread the right treatment on thick enough paper stock, lay it over another document, and it recreates the patterns of the ink. Near perfect duplication, wouldn't have taken more than a couple of minutes per page."

"Something *else* I didn't catch in time."

"Drew!" He actually snapped upright, almost like a longbow, when Katherine slammed the satchel to the table.

"Master Drew," she said more gently, "this is not your fault. None of this."

"I recommended Idran for the project. I trusted him—"

"So did everyone else here. So did Commander Adept Nemo. He'd always *been* trustworthy."

"Until now."

"Right. Until now. Nobody saw it coming. No way *you* should have."

The alchemist didn't appear entirely convinced. "But—"

"Your country is at war, remember? If you fall apart, you're no use to us— and we *are* going to need you. So *straighten up and get back to it!*"

He was not only standing but halfway through a salute before his brain apparently caught up with his body and reminded him that he hadn't been army in over a decade. For the first time since she'd met him, Engman Drew actually smiled. "Yes, Sir!"

Katherine laughed, clapped him once on the shoulder, and departed.

It only weighed a few pounds, that satchel full of documents, and they weren't even genuine. Still, the knowledge of what they represented, and what was at stake, added enough weight to the strap to make her stumble. She was certain that only her armor kept it from digging into her skin.

Yes, full armor. Katherine and Dignity knew they were watched, knew there was no way for the knight—or anyone else whom they could trust—to travel to Thunderhead in secret. This way, at least, she was fully protected, and just *maybe* Section Three would assume her visit to be diplomatic or ceremonial, rather than related to their ongoing competition.

Right. And maybe they'll mistake me for Queen Ayn, and I can just order them to surrender.

Marching guards, harried servants, and only the occasional alchemist crossed her path on the way to the front gate. Some ignored her, despite the less-than-inconspicuous armor. Some offered neighborly greetings. Others glared in simmering resentment, perhaps worried that her presence put them in danger, perhaps angry at the reminder of the war. Katherine returned the greetings, made no acknowledgment of the others, and continued along the pebble-paved citadel walkways. The past few days had seen little snowfall, which made these paths, and the city roads, somewhat easier to travel. On the other hand, it meant there was no white to cover the polluted, rot-gray sludge that had accumulated earlier and never melted. It was worst near the fortress, but Katherine couldn't help feel that all of Leryn looked vaguely leprous.

Beyond the front gate waited two of Halcourt's household soldiers, whose names she honestly couldn't recall. Both men appeared familiar enough with the blades and pistols they carried, but likely had never actually made use of them in anything deadlier than a formal duel or a drunken scrap. She honestly wasn't certain that having them at her back was preferable to finding a solid wall—the wall might not warn her of danger, but it also wouldn't catch her with a wild backswing—but these were the new rules, now that the Reds had made their intentions clear. *Nobody* went out alone.

Well, nobody but Dignity on her bloody secret forays, of course.

With them, huddled together for warmth—which made them smarter than the two baronial guardsmen, frankly—were a trio of saddled horses. Arius snorted and stomped at her approach, which in turn set the other two mounts to nervous whickering.

"Ah, ignore them," she told the warhorse, running a palm across his neck. "They just don't understand your enthusiasm."

"Ready to head back, Lieutenant?" one of the men asked, bored and clearly only half-present.

Apparently they don't, either. "I am." Despite the weight of the armor, Katherine hauled herself into the saddle with a dancer's grace. "Do try to keep at least *somewhat* alert, would you? This isn't a game just because none of *your* people have died yet."

So casual was her tone, it took the two men a few seconds to truly process what she'd said. Both then snapped to attention—more formally and properly than Drew had done, though perhaps lacking his conviction—shouted a unified "Yes, Lieutenant!" and clambered into their own saddles.

I guess they aren't entirely *useless, then.* A flick of the reins, and Arius pranced out into the main thoroughfare, as swift and apparently carefree as the afternoon traffic would permit.

Actually, rather *more* swift and carefree than the traffic permitted, narrowly missing a pocket of civilians and one slowly trundling wagon, until Katherine leaned over beside his left ear and whispered, "You stop that!"

She tried not to smile at the confounded expression the two armsmen shared, and obviously *thought* they were hiding from her.

Katherine's passing provoked the same array of reactions from pedestrians on the street as it had from the personnel of Thunderhead, and she reacted—or chose not to react—in precisely the same way. The navy blue steel grew cold, even through her arming clothes beneath, but she allowed no trace of discomfort to mar either her face or her bearing. Here, more so even than at home, she would show the world only a true Storm Knight.

Later, Katherine would wonder if she'd gotten too wrapped up in the showmanship; if she'd gotten too lax, made the same mistake against which she'd warned her escort. Odds were, probably not. Odds were, she'd honestly missed it, and nothing she might have done differently would have changed anything.

But she'd never know for certain.

"Sniper! Left flank high!"

The first shot followed the guard's cry as though deliberately punctuating the warning. Katherine swung her shield high, but had the bullet been aimed her way it would already have struck, and she knew it. Instead, she could only curse as the baronial guard who'd spotted the danger that she'd missed, who'd tried to warn them, died in a spray of blood and skull fragments.

It made sense, in a way. Storm Knight plate, stronger than any other armor of the same weight, could often turn even a high-powered bullet. Better to eliminate a softer objective with the first shots.

But it should *have been me, damn it!*

While her mind reeled, her body acted. Already she had raised her galvanic lance, triggered the charging cycle, and blasted a line of lightning back through the window whence the shot had come. It was a small, low-powered bolt—in part because the weapon was still powering up, in part because she wasn't looking to obliterate the entire room or any innocents potentially nearby—but still it was enough to blow out the entire window frame and several chunks of brick to either side. The street grew thick with screams and sizzles, smoke and ozone, and citizens scattering in so many different directions that Katherine felt they might actually have discovered some *new* ones.

Lance tucked tight under her arm, she dropped from Arius's saddle. A quick click of the tongue, and he trotted away, seeking his own cover until he heard her call. Katherine continued laying down flickers of lightning, less in hopes of actually searing the enemy than to ensure the sniper kept his head down until the field was clear of noncombatants. At this point, she couldn't even *see* the target window any longer, so obscured was the wall by brick powder and swirling smoke.

Eventually, however, after a minute or two that felt like a *month* or two, the road was clear of anyone save the knight and the remaining guard, both of whom had taken shelter behind a half-height garden wall. Katherine allowed her sizzling barrage to end, the obscuring smoke to clear.

The window was completely gone. A jagged maw gaped in the bricks, more than twice the size the sash itself had been, surrounded by a corona of searing and soot. Crouched as they were, the sharp angle made examination of the room beyond all but impossible, but Katherine couldn't imagine it remained anything but a blackened hollow.

"You ever use one of these?" she demanded of the surviving armsman.

"I, uh . . ."

"Quit gawping and answer the question, soldier!"

"No, Lieutenant, I have not!"

She passed the lance over despite his answer, grabbing the man's pistol in exchange. "Trigger is this stud here, inside the guard. Treat it like a rifle; at this range, the difference in time to target shouldn't matter. Don't fire unless you have a clear shot; I don't have time to give you a primer on recharging right now."

With that she was up, vaulting the wall and sprinting for the building. Somewhere within, assuming he wasn't dead, lurked at least one ambusher, and Katherine was looking forward to a long conversation. She ducked into the alcove beside the doorway, double-checked that the pistol was loaded and its powder dry—and that her sword was loose enough in its scabbard for a quick draw, despite the cold. *That* wasn't a mistake she intended ever to make again.

Two deep breaths to steady herself, and Katherine kicked the door open, instantly rolling out of sight to the other side of the frame.

Sure enough, a shot cracked through the open space, one that would've taken her clean in the chest had she remained in the doorway. She refrained from returning fire—no sense in wasting her one shot—and risked the most abbreviated glance around the doorframe.

The shot had come, not from the stairs leading up, as she'd anticipated, but from the end of a long hall. Carpeted in once-but-no-longer-lush shag, lit by a staggered sequence of gas lanterns, the passageway led straight through the building to a . . .

Backdoor. Bloody . . .

It hung slightly open, she could see even from here, and vibrated on its hinges.

It was to be a chase, then, was it? Fine. Katherine was a lot faster in her armor than most folk suspected, and with the guard watching over the horses and the avenue, no chance the assassin would double back and—

The Storm Knight had dashed to within a pace or two of that rear entrance when she jerked to such an abrupt halt that she actually pulled up several carpet tacks.

A *single* sniper for a party of three, one of whom, at least, was no easy target? An attack in broad daylight, in front of scores of civilians? What the hell were Vorona and Section Three playing at?

And why here? The route between Surros Manor and Thunderhead wasn't especially long, but it provided plenty of opportunities for ambush. Why here, then, so near the fortress—and, if they chose to involve themselves, the Crucible's soldiers therein?

Because, you sorry excuse for a Cygnaran soldier, they've either laid a trap, which they're just waiting for you to stampede into headlong . . .

Or they're trying to keep you away from the manor.

She burst back through the front door like a cannonball, splitting the heavy wood where her armored shoulder slammed it aside. Already Arius was bounding her way, summoned by her ear-piercing whistle. Bewildered as a first-time drunk, the other man rose from cover and ran for his own mount, spurred on by the obvious urgency in Katherine's reappearance.

"Back to the baron!" she called as she passed him, yanking her lance from his startled grip. From yards ahead she tossed back his pistol, which he successfully caught only through a maddened display of frantic grabbing and juggling. "Now!"

Arius galloped through the streets of Leryn, head down, emulating the lightning that so often danced at his rider's fingertips. Civilians jumped aside, shouting and screaming; a time or two, the doughty steed actually leapt *over* an obstacle, inanimate or otherwise, that didn't clear his path quickly enough.

And still, as a rooster-tail of mucky snow spread across her wake, Katherine wondered if she'd already delayed too long, if even Arius could bring her home in time to do any good.

***

Dignity slipped along the hallway in a low crouch, spring-pistol and fighting knife all but quivering in anticipation within their hidden sheaths. The staccato beat of an ongoing firefight stomped, an uncouth and unwanted guest, throughout the many corners of the manor. The terrified screams, hollered commands, and despairing sobs carried less well, creating a mechanical background hum.

Was Halcourt dead? Surros? Sadler? How big was the siege? *Why* was the siege?

Well, that last wasn't hard to figure out; it was why Dignity hadn't gone running to protect the baron as soon as she heard the opening salvo.

It was almost assuredly what the enemy *wanted* her to do.

Instead, she'd forced herself to remain patient, to wait . . .

Until, finally, she'd heard enough to take a pretty good stab (so to speak) at where the closest of the intruders might lurk.

At the end of the passageway, near where it intersected the manor's main hall, one last door provided ingress to one last bedchamber. The simple lock slowed her not at all, and Dignity was quickly inside and across the room. There, a pair of casement windows, latticed in diamond patterns of wrought iron, overlooked a narrow slope of roof—and, of more immediate import, a potentially crippling twenty-five foot plunge to the manicured lawn below.

Kicking off her shoes, she pulled a pair of floppy, soft-soled boots from her belt sash, where she'd jammed them moments earlier. No sooner had she slipped them on than she carefully pushed open the window, wincing at the faint creak she was powerless to prevent, and scrambled out onto the thin and heart-stoppingly precarious ribbon of slanted wood.

The cold swarmed her, an army of invisible ants prickling at her skin. For all the ways it could be worse—the wind might be stronger, the attack might have come at night, the roof might be covered in frost—it was still enough of a distraction that Dignity found herself clinging to the iron window frame, briefly unwilling to relinquish her grip.

Oh so carefully, she lowered herself to the shingles, muscles aching with the awkward effort. She released the window only when she felt the toes of both feet and the fingers of her left hand secure purchase on the many wooden edges, when the angle of her own body matched that of the roof. Now sidling sideways, pressed so tightly to the shingles that her blouse, skirt, and hair all threatened to snag, she gradually worked her way toward the main body of the house.

Twice, a conspiracy of shallow grip and numbed fingers nearly sent her tumbling to earth, and twice only a last-second scramble and years of training kept her aloft.

Who the bloody hell builds a roof this sharply sloped, anyway, gods damn it?!

Finally she reached the broader (and shallower, thank Morrow!) roof of the main body of the manor. Here, the slope was gentle enough for her to walk upright, so long as she watched her step. It took only another minute or so before she worked around a chimney, around a gradual corner, and to the edge of a large alcove. Within, a recessed window overlooked the great dining hall; one of several, positioned all around the magnificent chamber. During the day, they ensured that sunlight fell within, regardless of the time, and the enormous windows provided a touch of elegance at any hour.

They also provided a perfect sniper's nest if anyone felt inclined to pick off the diners below.

The gunfire slackened, coming only sporadically now—which could mean any one of a half a dozen things, some positive, some disastrous—but still frequent enough for Dignity to be certain she'd heard right and guessed right. One of the shooters was, indeed, ensconced in this alcove.

Silent as a ghost's whisper, even with the awkward footing, she crept nearer the niche. A flex of the wrist dropped her pistol into her hand. With a bit of luck, the sniper would be so focused on the room below that he'd be dead before he knew she was coming.

Dignity reached the edge of the shadowed recess, twisted sharply around the corner, gun raised . . .

A heavy forgelock discharged from within, aimed not into the house but directly at her!

Instincts honed for years on the grindstone of constant peril had her hurling herself aside, going with the momentum of her initial lunge. The shot was deafening, disorienting; her head rang like a cracked church bell, the breath went out of her as she slammed into the niche's opposite wall. Only gradually did she become certain that the bullet had actually missed.

Two of them. Bloody godsdamned burning hell, *two* of them lurked in that single alcove. And while one was indeed hunched behind a rifle, chambering a new round intended for the room below, the other had clearly been watching for just such an attack from the rooftop.

Doubtless she'd been right in her earlier assessment: The entire point of this attack wasn't to kill the baron, but to lure *her* out into the open. And, presumably, to kill her so the Khadorans had no competition for their bid with di Meryse.

Dignity rebounded from the wall, pistol belching its familiar muffled *whump*. The man who'd shot at her staggered back, groaning, hands closing on his suddenly blood-drenched gut.

She was on him, fighting through her own dizziness and disorientation, blade in hand. Even injured, he was able to throw out a hand in self-defense; *unable*, however, to do so fast enough to matter. Skin split, more blood sprayed, and at least he no longer needed to worry about the belly wound.

Now the sniper was on his feet. Leaving the long gun—an awkward weapon in the confines of the alcove—where it lay, he drew a blade and pistol combination not unlike Dignity's own.

She dove, allowing her own pistol to fall away, launching a scissor-kick at her enemy's ankles. The startled Khadoran's shot passed harmlessly over her head, but he had presence enough to bound aside—an awkward-looking hop, but one that carried him beyond her kick.

Dignity spun with the missed attack, hoping to come up beside him in a surprise lunge, but either she was slower than she realized or he'd anticipated the move. She was up only on one knee when he tackled her, slamming them both down to lie with their heads in the now empty window frame.

Before she even realized it, Dignity was pinned. Her right leg was held fast, his ankle locked over hers. His other knee rested on her left thigh, an agonizing pressure digging deep into muscle and flesh, sending spasms through the entire limb. His knife was almost at her throat, held at bay only by her own blade—but she couldn't get any real leverage with that arm, awkwardly pressed by the weight of both his hands on the crossed knives. Only her right hand remained free, but while she struck at his arm and shoulder, over and over, again she lacked the leverage for a meaningful blow.

The Khadoran was stronger, heavier. Given even a moment to figure out his peculiar leg-lock, she knew she could slip out of it, but he didn't appear inclined to allow her that moment. The blades trembled, inched closer, and Dignity knew her arm was about to give.

Giving up the useless pounding, she let her free hand thrash about the edge of the alcove. *Come on, come on, I know it's here, come on . . . !*

Her fingers closed on the stock of the Khadoran rifle.

Her opponent sneered. The length of the barrel, the size of the recess, and the awkward grip meant that Dignity had no means of turning the weapon around to fire at the man atop her—and the both of them knew it.

Instead, she dragged the weapon closer, smacking the butt into the Khadoran's elbow. It elicited a pained grunt, but no more.

Then Dignity shifted her grip along the stock and pulled the trigger.

The weapon's fierce recoil, easily absorbed against the shoulder of a trained shooter, proved rather harder to ignore against the nerve just below the elbow. Her opponent fell back with a cry, his arm gone momentarily limp. Dignity coiled her legs, wincing, teeth gritted against the throbbing in her thigh, and kicked up with both feet.

It *almost* wasn't enough. He tumbled backward, hit the roof, so nearly caught himself . . .

And plunged over the eaves.

Dignity half-staggered, half-crawled to the edge, nearly toppling over a time or two herself. She needn't have rushed. The Khadoran operative had landed head first; no chance whatsoever that *he'd* trouble her again.

She hauled herself to her feet and limped back to the shattered window, peering down at the dining room. The bulk of Surros's guests and staff huddled in a makeshift fortification, the raised dais shielding them on one side, over-turned tables on the other three. *Probably the first time the bloody ostentatious hardwood actually served any good purpose.* Several of the guards occasionally rose from cover to take a shot at the recessed windows, but the conflict had mostly become a standoff, each side waiting for the other to expose itself. Dignity couldn't make out individuals huddled behind the barriers; couldn't tell if Halcourt were living or dead. She *could* make out an array of corpses scattered throughout the chamber, servants and guards who'd fallen to the initial assault or died running for cover.

More than half of them were women with hair of various brown shades—women who, when viewed from a distance, could have easily been mistaken for Dignity herself. The snipers had apparently targeted them first, even in favor of armed guards.

It wasn't remotely the first time in Dignity's career that someone set out to kill her, but the heartless, methodical brutality coiled itself around her spine, squeezing like a ravenous constrictor.

She considered putting a few shots into the window across the room, but even if she could pick out a target within the shaded niche, the man with the bullets was currently beyond reach. Instead, she dropped to one knee and, after retrieving her fallen pistol, made a quick search of the other dead body. The blood was already tacky, congealing swiftly in the cold.

The baggy black outfit made sense for the attack, but would draw more than a little attention during a getaway. Dignity ripped the coat open already certain she'd find *some* sort of disguise or uniform beneath; her only question was *what*.

Brazen bastards, aren't they?

No armor, of course; the breastplates, greaves, and such would be stashed elsewhere. But she recognized the *rest* of the uniform well enough. Anyone who'd spent more than a day or two in Leryn knew the black and gold of the Crucible Guard.

Bold, but a savvy choice. It would take time for reports of gunfire to make their way across Old Town, longer for the Guard to mobilize, but they'd arrive here *eventually*. At that point, another five or ten soldiers dashing about on various vital assignments wouldn't draw a glance, be it first, second, or otherwise.

Dignity found herself at something of a loss; her duty to protect Baron Halcourt smacked headlong into her greater mission. She could make her way around the entire manor, hoping to catch each and every Section Three pair by surprise, but the odds didn't exactly favor success. She knew, now, that she was the target of this operation; her death here could cost Cygnar the entire war. So what—?

She almost cheered aloud at the sudden rumble of hoofbeats and the shouting of a familiar voice.

Quickly as she could without breaking her neck, Dignity shimmied down the bricks and sprinted for the manor's opposite side. There, indeed, was Lieutenant Laddermore, along with one of the baronial guards. (One? Hadn't there been two?) At the moment, the Storm Knight had dropped from her horse to kneel beside a corpse—one of several strewn across the lawn, murdered long minutes before.

"Laddermore!"

The lieutenant had her lance raised and ready to fire before she realized who had called to her. "Dignity! What the hell—?"

"Khadoran snipers. Recessed windows around the dining hall. Too well ensconced for returning fire, but a few blasts from your lance should end this tolerably well."

"I . . . Wait, what—?"

"No time. Just do it. Protect the baron." And with that she was running again, this time away from the manor proper, ignoring the knight's harried questions.

Carriage house. Has to be.

The small outbuilding, at the very edge of the Surros property, was the only logical spot—close enough for a quick regroup before the Khadorans retreated, sufficiently out of the way that nobody was likely to stumble upon their escape plan.

Indeed, casually shoved under a couple of saddles, Dignity found the expected bits of light armor, the right make and hue to complete the Crucible Guard disguises. She also found the corpses of several stablehands and a valet, shoved into Surros's own carriage; more servants whose only crime had been to stand in Vorona's way.

Lightning screamed its rage, followed by the first cry of thunder. Laddermore; good. One way or another, this would end soon. Dignity considered cutting the straps or otherwise sabotaging the armor, leaving Vorona's people without their disguises—and then realized she had a better option.

Dignity carefully shut the carriage house door, leaving no trace that she'd been inside. Then, stopping only to grab some boots, a long coat, and a hat from various bodies on the lawn, she dashed through the front gate and out into the street. All she need do now was find a convenient hiding spot, and wait for the Crucible Guard to make their inevitable appearance.

***

". . . ready to leave in an hour! You hear me? *One hour!* Why are you still standing here? Where the hell is Underhurst?! *Ow!* Careful, damn you!"

Katherine stood at attention in the wreck of the dining room, listening to Baron Halcourt shriek his orders while one of Leryn's finest physicians cleaned and stitched the bullet wound in his arm. His Lordship was more than a little intoxicated—he'd refused more potent anesthetics than hard liquor, but made up the difference in volume—but drunk or not, Katherine worried that he wouldn't readily be talked out of his decision.

"My Lord . . ." She approached him as cautiously as she would have unexploded ordinance. Shards of glass, mangled bullet fragments, and splinters of hardwood crunched beneath her steps, occasionally throwing her off her stride when a chunk refused to give. Around her, an endless array of servants carried large pieces of rubble from the room or swept smaller bits into wooden bins. Others scurried in the alcoves above or balanced precariously on vertiginous ladders, washing and repairing the frames in preparation for the installation of new panes.

They had, at least, waited for the bodies to be removed before starting work on the rest of the cleaning.

Neither the baronial armsmen nor the Crucible Guard were to be seen in the dining room-turned-war zone. The injured had been taken to their chambers to recuperate; everyone else patrolled the grounds, fingers twitching on triggers, working themselves into a frenzied state of paranoia. It was an even bet whether the first casualty would come from one of the household guards accidentally shooting someone, or from one of the barons' tempers finally flaring beyond rational thought.

"My Lord," she began again once she was close enough to command his attention without screaming, "I believe you ought to reconsider."

"Reconsider? *Reconsider?!* They tried to kill me, Lieutenant! They sent gunmen *into my home*—"

Baron Surros's home. But somehow, this didn't seem the right time to correct him.

"—to assassinate me! What part of that should inspire me to *reconsider* leaving?!"

It would have been easier, of course, if she could mention the real reason—the *military* reason—that she and Dignity, at least, needed to remain.

Then again, judging by the wild look in his eyes and the alcohol on his breath, maybe it wouldn't have been.

"My Lord, leaving aside the fact that it's getting on toward nightfall—"

"Who the hell cares about the *time*?" The bottle flew, shattering on Katherine's breastplate in a spray of glass and spirits. "What kind of idiot reasoning is *that*? Someone—*Ow!*" He looked prepared to bite the nose off the physician who worked on him. "I said *be careful!* Someone fetch me another bottle."

"Leaving aside the hour," she bulled on, trying not to squint against the fumes now rising off her armor, "if they want you dead, surely they have people awaiting you outside Leryn's walls?"

Halcourt blinked stupidly and grimaced as though he'd bitten into something hairier than it should have been.

"Even if you reach the border alive," she pressed, "there's no guarantee the dwarves would permit you to pass. And if they *do*, you can be certain there will be a hefty price tag—monetarily, politically, or both—attached to it. *And* you'd still have the long trek through Rhul back to Cygnaran territory, during which any number of Khadoran operatives might be able to reach you."

Halcourt began to rock like an anxious child, drawing a fierce scowl from the physician, who had to drop his needle lest the stitches rip themselves open. "I don't . . . I don't know. Where's Underhurst?" Apparently, he'd forgotten that Dignity wasn't one of his chief advisors any longer. "I need to talk to—"

"Um . . . Apologies, my Lord." Knight and baron both turned toward one of Surros's valets, a sweating young man who couldn't keep from glancing at the patterns of dried blood on the floor.

"I'm sorry to interrupt," he continued, spindling the hem of his vest in his fingers, "but there's a gentleman here to see you."

"Tell your master," Halcourt ordered with a dismissive wave.

"My Lord, he specifically requested *you*."

The baron surged to his feet, once more pulling the needle from the physician's reach just as the man had been grasping for it. It hung from Halcourt's arm, his own drunken wobble setting it swaying like a pendulum. "Do I damn well *look* like I'm *entertaining right now?*"

Katherine couldn't begin to guess if it was the rage, the volume, or the reeking breath that drove the servant back two paces.

"Actually, it appears that the entertainment has already ended."

The new speaker was tall, wrapped in a gray cloak, and spoke with a moderate Ordic brogue.

"He, ah, let himself in," the valet explained. Every ounce of Katherine's self-control went toward not smacking either him, or herself, in the forehead and shouting *What do you not understand about security?*

"Who the hell are you?" Halcourt grumbled.

The fellow lowered his hood, revealing a goatee that had probably once been meticulously styled, now made ratty by the rigors of travel. "My name is Oswinne Muir. Yes, really. You can close your mouth now, my Lord."

"You—but . . . You . . ."

Katherine wasn't at all drunk, but those mirrored her own questions pretty well.

"I'm here in the company of, among others, Corporal Serena Dalton, Second Cygnaran Army. I'm sorry we didn't come to you sooner, but we've spent the last two days playing games of ceremony and diplomacy with Ministers di la Granzio and Chalerynne. Beastly amount of paperwork, too. Point is, my lord, we're here, in part at least, for you.

"Is there perhaps somewhere we can sit where the chairs are actually still, well, chairs? And can someone get his Lordship some food and a strong tea? We have a *great* deal to talk about."

Casteus 3rd, 605 AR
Leryn, Llael

The eastern sky was only just brightening, a nebulous aurora illuminating the swaddling clouds as dawn mixed colors across its palette for the coming day. Only the most steadfast of Leryn's early risers had thus far braved the morning chill. They were little more than bundles of ambulatory furs and fabrics as they shuffled along empty streets that stank of recently extinguished gas lanterns.

Along one particular thoroughfare, maintaining as rapid a pace as surreptitiousness would permit, strode Dignity and her groggy companion. Ahead of them loomed one of the many gates of the innermost wall, the line of demarcation between the wealth and respectability of Old Town and the poverty of its neighboring district.

"Would you *please* slow down!" Engman Drew gasped at her. The old alchemist's coat was rumpled, his trousers tucked into one boot but not the other, his hair still flat against one side of his head. If he gave the impression of a man dragged from his bed the instant that the Thunderhead Fortress guards began to admit morning visitors, there was a damn good reason for it.

"This *is* slow!" Dignity—Garland, as Drew knew her—hissed back. "You told me you could keep up!"

"I *can* keep up," he protested, all wounded dignity. Well, all wounded dignity and heaving, panting breaths. "It's just . . . this stuff you asked me to bring . . . It's awfully volatile . . ."

"Either keep up or hand over the satchel."

The alchemist clutched the heavy bag more tightly to his chest, scowled, and redoubled his efforts.

Passing into New Town required no effort at all; Dignity wasn't sure the two sleepy sentinels at the gate even noticed their passage. The authorities weren't really concerned with keeping people *out* of New Town; they just didn't want "undesirables" crossing freely in the other direction.

The difference between the districts wasn't so much "night and day" as "spring and autumn." While not that much smaller than those in Old Town, the various structures were in markedly poorer repair. Flaking whitewash, cracked brick, decaying wood, shifting foundations, holed roofs, boarded windows—a good-quality home or business in New Town was one that suffered only one or two such problems, rather than the whole collection. Where the streets were cobbled, the pavers were dirty and chipped, pounded deep into the dirt. In other spots, the roads weren't cobbled at all, either because they never had been, or because the pavers had long since been stolen for use elsewhere. Only every fourth or fifth corner boasted a lamppost; only every fourth or fifth lamppost still worked. At least most of those were still connected to the gas lines, though a few had been replaced with simple oil- or even wood-burning vessels.

It all stank rather less than one might have expected—the sewer systems of Leryn were among Western Immoren's best, and keeping the network flowing meant maintaining the *entire* system, including those portions servicing New Town—but otherwise, the district was indeed the epitome of the worst most major cities had to offer.

It also included, just a few blocks from the dividing wall, the hidden lair of the Section Three infiltrators.

Finding them had taken all the skill Dignity possessed—and yet, in the end, had also proven far more straightforward that she would ever have anticipated. As she'd known they would, Vorona and her people fled the scene dressed as Crucible Guard, losing themselves in the chaos while soldiers, fire brigade, and a vast crowd of morbid spectators thronged the avenues outside the Surros estate.

Swathed in the coat and hat she'd snagged from the dead servants, and utilizing every surveillance technique the CRS taught, Dignity had pursued. She ducked into doorways; attached herself to larger groups of pedestrians;

changed clothes, ditching the coat for a chilly block or two here, the hat for a few streets there; traveled a short distance on the rooftops, when the buildings huddled close enough to make that possible.

They'd led her, first, to the back of a small pottery and ceramics shop— the sort that produced gaudy, decorative gewgaws of substantial cost and no genuine utility whatsoever. The rear door waited for them, unlocked; Dignity could only imagine that the owner had either been bribed or murdered—or possibly both.

The store was clearly a rally point, not an actual headquarters, and the Khadorans spent only a few minutes inside. Now dressed in inconspicuous civilian clothes, they slipped out, alone or in pairs, over the span of half an hour. Once Dignity was certain that Vorona herself was *not* waiting to go last—she was, in fact, half of the second pair to depart—she lurked atop a nearby roof until the final operative, by her count, took to the street.

His outfit allowed him to blend with the rest of the evening crowd, and he'd been at least as watchful now as before he ditched his disguise, but though she came awfully near discovery a time or two, Dignity managed to follow. It was then that she'd discovered Vorona's lair was a house in New Town—a house whose proper owners were almost certainly dead and either stashed in the cellar or buried in the yard. Throughout the evening and through the night she'd watched, crouched beside the crumbling chimney of an even more dilapidated domicile across the way. A couple of times, one or two of her quarry departed, but always returned a few moments later. Not another ral-lying point, then, or temporary shelter. This was the real deal.

Half an hour before dawn, she'd bolted for Thunderhead, determined to see Drew the moment the gate guards would admit her—and that, after a brief and rather volatile discussion, had led them both back here, the alche-mist weighted down with a few surprises he was *not* happy carrying.

He didn't speak again until they huddled behind the same house on which Dignity had earlier perched. The streets were beginning to flow, now; a few more minutes, and they'd qualify as crowded. *Too* crowded for what Dignity had in mind.

"Garland . . . Are you sure about this?"

"You wanted to help undo some of the damage, Drew. This is how."

"It's just . . . People could get hurt."

"That's rather the point, actually."

"The *wrong* people," he said with a glare.

"Not if you got the ratios right. Besides, sometimes there's no help for it."

Still the alchemist looked unsure, twisting the satchel around in circles. At least, he did so until Dignity lunged forward, faster than a goosed serpent, and snatched it from his grip.

"Hey! I—"

"Go home, Drew."

"No . . . No, I should see this—"

"You're a well-known alchemist. I suggest you not be anywhere near the spot where the authorities start to gather."

"I—"

"*Go.*"

Constantly looking back over his shoulder—Dignity was absolutely stunned he didn't run into something—he went.

Around her, the house's shadow slowly leaned beneath a swiftly brightening sky.

This is taking too long . . .

With dangerous haste, she unpacked the three jars from the satchel. The lids opened with a trio of metallic clacks. *Pour third jar into the first, shake* very carefully *to mix; pour combined powders into the second jar, shake* even more carefully . . .

The result was a blotchy, rust-hued powder with various flecks of sickly yellow. A small length of fabric, ripped from the hem of her skirt and closed in the jar's lid, made for a nicely decorative fuse; the whole affair, now perhaps the most dangerous jar in Leryn, she slipped back into the satchel.

More torn cloth, this time wrapped around her nose and mouth; it was too light out, now, to risk going barefaced. And then she charged.

Did the Section Three operatives spot her on her way? Quite possibly—they'd have to be fools not to keep watch on the surrounding streets—but she gave them no time to act. She crossed the distance in a matter of heartbeats, scrambled up the side of the house almost as swiftly, putting even the local arachnids to shame.

To the chimney, then. Dignity yanked open the satchel, pulled a flint-striker from an inside pocket, then dropped the whole flaming package down the flue.

And then there was nothing to do but fall prone, brace herself for the impact, and let herself roll from the roof.

It was, thankfully, less than two full stories from the edge of the sloping eaves. Still, the ground hauled back and slugged her with the punch of a small god—at the same instant the house was slammed beneath the heel of a large one.

The blast tore through the structure's inner walls to pound against the outer. Boarded windows blew out in a volcano of burning splinters and noxious gasses. Smaller jets of fume squirted from between the bricks, finding new paths through layers of powder that might, at some point in the past, have been mortar. The air grew thick, acrid, searing her eyes and the back of her throat.

Even though she knew the house had contained the brunt of it, she struggled to her feet and staggered away, wheezing and limping. A quick scan of her surroundings, to be sure that all eyes were drawn to the conflagration and not to her, and then she ducked behind the house across the street yet again. Returning to the roof was far more of a challenge; she couldn't seem to catch her breath, and her right ankle refused to take her weight. Finally, however, she hauled herself over the eaves and flopped over on her back, sucking greedy chestfuls of air.

Between the blast itself, the scorching flame, and the incapacitating gas of which she'd gotten only the faintest whiff, the odds of Section Three survivors were less than slim. Still, Dignity spent the following hours, until the sun had reached its noontime peak and slid halfway to the farther horizon, lying flat on that roof. Everything hurt, her lips and tongue felt like old bone, and her stomach rumbled louder than a foundry. And still she waited, watching the fire brigade and the Crucible Guard—both of whom were clearly having a really unpleasant couple of days—dousing and then searching the wreckage; watching as crowds gathered, eager for news, as spreading rumors both whispered and shouted attributed the blast to some oncoming Khadoran offensive.

Only when they'd begun to haul charbroiled bodies from the rubble, and still no survivors had made any attempt to slip away, did Dignity decide the job was done and it was time to slip away herself.

***

The throng of emergency personnel around the burning house wasn't nearly so sizable as it might have been had the blast occurred in Old Town or the Outer Ward, but it'd been big enough. The crowd around Surros Manor, even though it was now almost a full day since the firefight, was larger still.

The walk back had taken Dignity far longer than it should, not just because of her injuries but because she still insisted on checking behind her, on taking unnecessary turns, and on all the other standard precautions against being tailed—just in case.

The city's mood had become one of nervous suspense and half-suppressed panic. The idea that the explosion heralded a Khadoran attack seemed to have taken root and flowered swiftly in the citizens' war-fertilized imaginations. This despite the fact that nobody had the slightest notion why Khador would choose a residential neighborhood in the poorest part of town to begin said assault. The people moved at a hurried pace, trying to rush without *looking* like they rushed, craning their necks every which way as though expecting a crimson warjack looming around every corner. She'd spent much of the walk laughing—internally, of course—at the foolishness of civilians the world over, regardless of nationality.

As she'd neared the manor, she'd begun cooking up a plausible story, something about her being injured in the attack and then passing out somewhere in the trees at the edge of the estate. It'd be a bit of a stretch to explain a full day's absence that way, but she was pretty sure she could sell—

That was when she'd spotted the crowd still milling about the manor. An official presence was to be expected, certainly, but this seemed like an awful lot of people, this long after the incident.

And then she'd drawn near enough to spot the armor and uniforms sported by many of the lingerers. The black and gold of the Crucible Guard was, again, to be expected. The navy and gold of Cygnaran military was *not*.

All Dignity could think, as she broke into a staggered run, was *This better not mean that I'm not getting my CRS team!*

***

Nightfall. Sheets of cloud swept by overhead, carried on blustery winds, flashing the occasional star or sliver of moon before shyly wrapping up tight once more. Such brazen displays always seemed perfectly framed in one of the windows, allowing those gathered in the sitting room—one of several in the manor's many halls—to gaze at the sky while they tried to wrap their heads around everything they'd learned.

In the cushioned, high-backed chairs sat Oswinne Muir, Dignity Underhurst, Corporal Wendell Habbershant, and Lieutenant Katherine Laddermore. On smaller stools, dragged in for the occasion, perched Corporals Serena Dalton and Atherton Gaust. Serena's eyes were rimmed in red, her regulation hair less neat than was her custom. If Dignity understood properly, she'd only last night learned of the deaths of over half her squad, including at least one close friend. Pacing the far wall, the roaring hearth constantly throwing her shadow over the rest of them in almost mechanical intervals, was the squad leader, Sergeant Benwynne Bracewell.

Even before she'd heard anything of their journeys, Dignity had known something was eating at Bracewell. She'd seen that look before, in the eyes of other officers. So far, she'd seen the sergeant's grim façade crack only once, when she'd been introduced to Laddermore.

"It's an honor to work with you, Lieutenant. You're something of a legend in the Second Army."

The knight had clasped her hand tight. "For me as well, Sergeant."

Bracewell had seemed a tad puzzled by that. "You've heard of me?"

"No." Katherine smiled at her. "We wear the same colors and serve the same king. That's honor enough."

Dignity, who'd forgotten how pompously career veterans could speak to one another, had forced herself not to gag.

Hours dragged by while Dignity waited to address them all, to find out just what in Morrow's name was going on. First she'd had to sit through the baron's tirade over her absence, moderated only a little by her hastily concocted story. Then she'd had to wait while Halcourt and Surros exchanged pleasantries not only with the Cygnaran guests, but the playwright Muir, and Minister Chalerynne, who had escorted the haggard squad from the gates.

Now, finally, they were gathered around a tray of brandy, the bare bones of their tales exchanged, and Dignity couldn't help but feel that perhaps she'd inhaled more gas during the explosion than she'd initially believed.

"How much did you tell his Lordship, exactly?" Habbershant asked when Muir finished speaking.

"Just enough. He knows we plan to smuggle him and his entourage out along with the players and the rest of the Ordic delegation. I explained to him that your Reconnaissance Service helped set it up. I did *not*, obviously, say anything about the real mission, nor enlighten him regarding my own affiliation with King Baird."

Dignity shook her head and seriously considered violating her "no heavy spirits while on a mission" policy. "I still can't believe it," she muttered, rubbing at her temples. "How did we not know about that?"

"A few of your superiors did." Muir somehow managed to combine a casual shrug and a sip of his drink into a single elegant gesture. "Truth be told, I'm not overjoyed that the lot of you know it *now*. No lack of trust, you understand, but we may not always be on the same side of things as we are today. Had there been any way around it . . ."

"This whole mission falls under the Royal Secrets Proclamation," Benwynne said from beside one of the room's many oaken bookcases. "We'd be committing treason just to tell anyone about you."

"As you say." The playwright didn't look entirely mollified, but he offered a friendly smile all the same.

"The Khadorans aren't stupid," Katherine noted. "If Halcourt and his people vanish from Leryn the same time your delegation leaves, don't you think they'll put it together?"

"We've thought of that. Several of my people are remaining behind at the manor. They'll dress in Cygnaran styles or the occasional household armsman uniform, just enough to create the impression the guests are still present. They'll disappear a week or so *after* we do."

"And they can get home all right?"

Muir nodded. "I should think so. Khador's looking for military units, not lone civilian travelers or—"

"Perhaps one of you can explain," the sergeant interrupted, her mind clearly on other matters, "just how the bloody Reds knew where to ambush us?! They can't possibly have known we were coming!"

"Not you personally, no," Dignity said. "But once Section Three learned that we had operatives in Leryn, working to buy the formula, it wouldn't be unreasonable to assume that Cygnar would be sending someone to support me. After that, it was just a matter of watching the obvious routes and arranging swift communications—such as those flares you mentioned." Then, although nobody could possibly blame her for it, "I'm sorry, Sergeant."

Benwynne grunted something that might have been, at best, the primitive ancestor of a word.

"And a godsdamned heavy warjack?" That from the gunmage, Atherton. "Those things move about as fast as grass growing uphill. How'd *it* get there?"

Laddermore cleared her throat. "At a guess, the same way they got so many clandestine operatives into Leryn, and who knows how many other cities. They've had plenty of time to arrange their pieces, Corporal; it's not as though the invasion came as a surprise to *them*."

"The Llael/Khador border is guarded," Muir explained further, "but it's hardly airtight. As long as they were prepared to move slowly, in small groups, they could have scattered advance forces throughout Llael weeks or even months before launching their offensive."

"Fantastic," Benwynne spat bitterly. "Now we all know how we got here, and why over half of us *didn't*. Brilliant."

Everyone suddenly seemed intent on memorizing the patterns in the fire or the colors of the many books.

"The question," she continued with a little less bile, "is what happens *now*."

"Our meet with di Meryse is in five days," Dignity said, idly rubbing a thumb across the upholstery. "Master Muir—"

"Oh, Oswinne, please."

"Oswinne. Can you and yours be ready by then?"

The playwright nodded. "Sooner, actually, but five days is good. It's an appropriate amount of time for a cultural delegation like mine to gather its people and prepare for the return trip."

Katherine coughed and raised her hand to cover it, in a gesture Dignity had come to recognize as the stifling of an inappropriate laugh. "I'm sure," the knight said, lips twitching, "that I don't wish to be nearby when you tell Baron Halcourt he's stuck here for almost another week."

Dignity, too, had to suppress a chuckle. Benwynne, on the other hand, didn't appear especially amused. "So, what? We do nothing until then? Did I lose half my people getting here just to sit around before trying to survive the trip back?"

"Not at all." Dignity rose and began to pace, forcing herself not to fall into precisely the same rhythm as the sergeant. "I *think* we've taken the enemy out of the competition," she said, "and I *think* we can trust di Meryse to honor his agreements, but we're not going to assume either. Your men aren't barracking here, are they, Sergeant?"

Benwynne cocked her head at the apparent non sequitur. "No, Minister Chalerynne has arranged for us take an entire floor at one of the local hostels."

"*Most* of us, anyway," Wendell grumbled. Apparently, he was still irked that the squad's warjack—Wolfhound?—was being stored and repaired over in an Outer Ward facility.

"But I imagine," Dignity pressed, "that you'll be spending a great deal of time here, though?"

"His Lordship was, ah, most insistent that we contribute to his security, yes."

"All right." Dignity ran the idea over in her mind, examined it in the light of the fire. "I want you to keep, oh, five or six of your people *out* of sentry rotation, Sergeant. In fact, don't let them appear publicly in uniform, and find them some other place to stay. I can supply the coin from operation funds, if necessary."

She had everyone's attention, at least. "What have you got in mind?" Katherine asked.

"I suddenly find myself allied with a number of people whose faces di Meryse and his underlings *haven't* seen." Her grin had turned absolutely feral. "I think, with Sergeant Bracewell's kind permission, I'm going to teach them the lay of the city and see just how well we can make use of that anonymity."

Casteus 8th, 605 AR
Leryn, Llael

I'm missing something . . .

Located smack dab in one of the Outer Ward's most industrialized quarters, the factory had been waiting for them, the loading doors unlocked. Ostensibly shut down for renovation and upgrades, it instead looked as though it had been utterly forgotten. Massive mechanized looms huddled under coatings of grime, shuttles dangled loosely over strands of decomposing fibers. Moth-eaten sheets hung from drapers, lackadaisically flapping in the faint cross-drafts like indolent phantoms, wafting dusty, free-floating sneezes throughout the chamber.

I'm missing something . . .

Dignity had hoped to track down the formula and make di Meryse choke on his arrogance, without this meeting ever taking place. Twice the alchemist had appeared at this or that public event. Twice had members of the newly arrived squad, men and women whose faces he couldn't possibly know, tried to follow first di Meryse himself, and then his various contacts. And twice, they'd come up empty. The man was just *that* cautious.

Still, for all she'd tried to avoid it, she knew this was the right place. She'd confirmed the address three times with the messenger, an unshaven, unwashed, but clearly sober fellow who'd delivered her the information both memorized and in a wax-sealed envelope. Although the windows were tightly shuttered against what little daylight managed to crawl its way through the shroud of weather, the chambers within were dimly lit. Roughly one in four of the factory's gas lamps burned with a low, bluish flame.

Muir and select members of the squad were even now making their way toward the border, the soldiers and the baron's entourage disguised and hidden among the Ordic actors, stagehands, and cultural delegates. A handful of others, along with Master Sergeant Habbershant and Corporal Dalton, held position on nearby streets, hidden but ready to act at the first sign of trouble.

At her side, Sergeant Bracewell, Katherine Laddermore, Corporal Gaust, yet *more* of the sergeant's people, and the young knight Sadler, spread out amongst the various warpers and spinners, ducking around whole cobwebs of fiber, alert for any ambush or deception. For the past five days, Dignity had kept careful watch on her surroundings, hunting any trace of an enemy presence, and hadn't caught so much as a sidelong glare.

I'm missing something, godsdamn it!

"Ah! There you are, my dear Garland! I feared you might be running late."

A trio of lamps flared on the observation balcony above, burning equal quantities of gas and melodrama. There, where factory managers might have overseen the workers in days past, stood Idran di Meryse. He was clad in deep colors and white ruffles, as formal as his garb at the opera had been. His teeth gleamed an almost unnatural hue.

Smug bastard hasn't even bothered to bring any guards with him.

"Wouldn't dream of keeping you waiting," Dignity called back with a blatantly artificial sweetness.

"So I see. I see, too, that you've brought guests. I'd *heard* you had a few friends arrive in town recently. As I understand it, Minister Chalerynne was fit to be tied. He seems to be taking it rather personally that Leryn's receiving so many dignitaries who can't be bothered to inform him they're coming."

"How traumatizing for him," Atherton muttered. "You know, I could shoot—"

"Don't even think about it!" Benwynne hissed.

"I do hope," the traitorous alchemist continued, "that your companions aren't here to stir up any trouble. I quite thought we had a friendly little arrangement. Besides, the formula—"

"Isn't here, yes, I know." Dignity ran a fingertip across the nearest loom, then idly scraped away the dust clinging to her skin with her thumbnail. "Nobody's here to cause trouble, di Meryse. Unless you are, of course."

"My dear, I would never even consider it."

"Fantastic." Dignity reached into a satchel at her side and removed a thick stack of papers. "Bank notes, as you requested." She shoved them back into the leather bag, fastened it shut, and dropped the whole thing at her feet. "Cygnar's bid. Also the winning bid."

Di Meryse chuckled. "While I admire your confidence, Garland, perhaps we ought to wait for our other guests?"

"I fear your other guests are unable to attend," Dignity said with a broad smirk. "They had a more, ah, pressing engagement."

For the first time, the alchemist's expression slipped. "I'm not entirely certain I can just take your word for that."

"Oh, take my word for it. I delivered the invitation to Vorona myself. You might even have heard something about it? A few days ago, in New Town?"

"Ah." His own smile returned, but his fingers looked as though either they, or the banister they clutched, were about to split. "You understand that my people still have channels of communication with Khador? If you try to cheat me or do me harm, they can still deliver—"

"Would you please just take your blood money and make your delivery so we can be done with this already?"

"Fine. Toss up the bag, so I can be certain—"

"A moment, if you'd be so kind."

The voice came from everywhere and nowhere, echoing from the darkest corners of the factory. The acoustics made it all but impossible to pin down; the reverberations somehow making each individual syllable more distinct, rather than less. Benwynne and the soldiers spread out, hands closing on weapons that, as of yet, lacked any clear target.

While she might not have been able to *locate* the source of that voice, however, Dignity had no trouble whatsoever *identifying* it.

Bloody hell . . .

"I have to confess to being a tad disappointed," Dignity said to the room at large. "I really went to a lot of trouble to blow you up. I suppose you just left your companions to burn while you found some escape?"

"Much as I would like to taunt you with how I foiled your amateurish attempt on my life, no." Even through the thick Khadoran accent, the fury simmering

beneath Vorona's words was unmistakable. *"The simple truth is, I'd left the house not long before you showed up. I wasn't there when your bomb went off."*

It was all Dignity could do not to curse her bad luck aloud. She'd been away from the place for less than an hour, fetching Drew and his reagents. For Vorona to have just *happened* to leave in that single window . . .

"I suppose I'll have to be a bit more precise next time, then."

"One of us will."

Atherton was swiftly scanning the chamber, peering intently into the shadows, one finger caressing the hilt of a pepperbox.

"Don't," Dignity whispered.

"But I might be able to—"

"Do you have a clear shot? Do you know even roughly where she is? Then don't reveal what you can do on a long shot."

The gunmage grumbled, but nodded.

"Well," di Meryse said, clearly struggling to regain control of the situation, "since you're here, would you care to come join us and deliver your bid?"

"No, I don't believe so."

She kept *moving*, Morrow damn her! Dignity still couldn't get a handle on where she might be. Gods' sake, the place wasn't even *that* big, was it?

"Would you *care,"* the disembodied voice continued, *"to take a guess as to where I was that morning, Garland?"*

"Not especially."

"Ladies, please!" The alchemist was all but pleading around tightly clenched teeth. "If we could just—"

"I was meeting with our other *operatives in Leryn. The ones not part of my team. The ones who've been here for* months, *making themselves nothing more than part of the crowds and scenery.*

"The ones, Goodman di Meryse, who have been watching you and your 'cut-outs' for the past week, and who delivered your formula to me not two hours ago."

"Ha!" Di Meryse put a palm to his chest. "You wound me, if you think I'm fool enough to . . ."

"Truth or not," Katherine hissed as the alchemist pontificated, "why is she *explaining* all this?"

The hair rose on the back of Dignity's neck, and she drew breath to cry out . . .

"*If it weren't true,*" Vorona asked, "*could I afford to do* this*?*"

The chamber ignited.

***

Katherine felt the air slam across her body, hard as any solid impact. The wall of heat followed a split second after, but she was already down, her head pounding as though Arius had clambered inside and gone for a quick gallop. She felt something sticky pooling along her cheek, in the hollow of her jaw, matting strands of her hair to her skin, and only then realized that she was bleeding from her left ear.

She made it up to one knee before someone grabbed the world and gave it a good spin. She'd have sworn the floor was no longer solid but consisted instead of rising and cresting waves; that the ceiling and the walls were engaged in a maddened waltz, constantly trading partners. She tried to stand, fell; rose again, collapsed back to that same knee.

Her sword—her father's sword, her *ancestors'* sword—no longer hung at her waist, ripped away only gods knew when. Even in her disorientation, her agony, she found enough attention, however briefly, to mourn.

The flames raged around her, greedily sucking up old strands of fiber, chewing rather more slowly on the wood of the looms and drapers. A second concussion shook the factory—was it smaller and more localized than the first, or was that an illusion created by her damaged hearing?—and she felt a rush of outside air, a brief touch of winter's cold before it was wiped away by the conflagration.

Raising a hand to shield her face from the heat and swirling embers, Katherine tried to take stock, to find any of her companions. Straight ahead, another curtain of fire rose as though deliberately seeking to obscure her view, but not before she saw it.

Saw, and even in her disorientation, understood.

The far wall, and the balcony on which di Meryse had stood, were soot-blackened and slowly starting to ignite, but otherwise undamaged.

The charges had been placed to ensure minimal damage to that side of the room.

Katherine tried to call out to anyone still near enough to hear, choked on a lungful of smoke—and then something hurtled from the dancing fires to slam her, sprawling, across the floor.

***

The barest instant before the detonation, Benwynne came to the same realization that had struck Dignity a half second too late. She launched herself to one side, scraping a strip of skin from her hand as she slid beneath some rickety piece of equipment or other. Chunks of wood, some of which were already burning, rained over her meager shelter before the initial blast had faded. She blinked against the rolling heat, tears coursing down her cheek.

Something fell to the floor behind her with a very un-wooden slap. A quick glance revealed Atherton, bleeding from an ugly gash across his forehead, trying to beat out a small lick of flame on the hem of his coat.

"Gaust! *Corporal Gaust!*" Then, when she understood there was no way to shout above the roaring of the fire and the likely ringing in his ears, she grabbed the nearest hunk of debris—what appeared to be a foot pedal blown from another of the machines—and hurled it at him. She saw, rather than heard, his sudden yelp.

"What?" She didn't hear that, either, but it wasn't hard to figure out.

"Make us a way out!"

He just looked at her, puzzled. Again she shouted, and again he didn't hear.

"Way. Out," she mouthed at him, exaggerating every flex of her lips. Then, for good measure, she raised two fingers and thumb in the form of a gun and "fired" over his shoulder.

Atherton took a moment to take in the burning wall, and drew. Benwynne saw the crackle of unnatural blue in the air before she turned away and covered her head with both arms.

***

"What the *hell?*!"

From a nearby rooftop, where she and her rifle had a clean line of sight to the factory, Serena Dalton watched the windows blow out, the walls buckle, the flames lick and sputter through every crack and crevice. Her neck and cheeks stung in the rapidly alternating currents of hot and cold. "Get down there!" She waved both arms, very nearly jumping up and down, making certain she had the attention of her long-gunners on other buildings before the billowing smoke cut them off. *"Get down there!"*

Her surge of fear was equally as potent as the blast had been; she couldn't lose any *more* of the squad, not so soon! Still, Serena was a lifelong soldier. She slung the rifle over her shoulder by its strap, rather than simply dropping it and running, took the stairs at a swift but careful clip. Wouldn't do anyone any good if she turned an ankle en route.

She shoved through a knot of huddled civilians, sheltering in the foyer and yammering fearfully about the explosion, then through the rickety front door. It was like walking to a furnace, and Serena flinched before forcing herself out into the street. Something sloshed beneath her boots. The street was soaked, filthy rivulets running across the cobblestones in all manner of abstract patterns, and it took her a moment to realize she was seeing melting runoff from the old, polluted snow.

Two splashing strides toward the burning factory, before a hand on her shoulder yanked her to a halt. She'd already spun, fists rising, before she recognized Wendell's haggard face.

"With me," he ordered, already starting to turn away.

"Are you bloody joking?! Our people need—!"

"Di Meryse escaped the fire!" he snarled at her. "If we don't get after him now, we'll lose him!"

"But our people—"

"You know how vital this is!"

Serena straightened, whether bristling at his tone or pulled taught between conflicting urges even she couldn't rightly say. "Are you pulling rank again, *Master Sergeant?*"

"Will I have to?"

She was saved the necessity of an answer—one that might have gone either way until the moment it escaped her lips—by a second, smaller detonation. The north wall of the edifice blew outward, crumbling to so much debris. For less than the blink of an eye, cerulean sparks flashed throughout the new gout of smoke and flame.

"There! They're getting out. Now *move*, or this whole affair could be for shit!"

Scowling, but no longer arguing, Serena took off after the mechanik, desperate to keep the rogue alchemist in sight.

***

"D . . . Dignity?" *Gods, I sound awful . . .*

"Don't try to talk yet. I've almost got you out."

Katherine felt like she was *peeling* her eyes open, wondered how much was just in her head and how much was congealing blood. The twin gleams of the conflagration and the evening sun were a dagger through her forehead; and her wince against *that* pain, in turn, launched a new surge of agony through her bad ear. The ground felt as though it were sliding beneath her, and it was only as she bumped jarringly over a small heap of broken brick that she realized it actually *was*. Someone—Dignity?—was dragging her from the burning building by her shoulders.

"What . . ." She coughed, felt something break loose from the back of her throat, and tried again. "What hit me?"

"I did, actually." Despite the agony, Katherine forced herself to focus. The tawny-haired spy was indeed the one leaning over her, tugging her through a massive hole in the wall and out onto the damp road beyond. She probably ought to be freezing; at least the fire was good for *something*.

"I'm sorry about that," Dignity continued. "But it was either me, or a burning crossbeam from above. I figured I was probably a *little* bit softer."

Katherine made herself grin, though the sensation of dried blood cracking and flaking from her cheek was disturbing. "I wouldn't be so certain of that. Thank you, though."

Another tug, and they were clear of the factory—or clear enough, at least, that Katherine's next breath was more air than soot. "A few of Bracewell's people have gone for horses. They'll get you mounted and make sure you don't break your neck before you've caught up with Muir and the baron. They shouldn't be more than a couple miles outside the city by now."

"No!" The knight clutched almost desperately at Dignity's arm. "No, I'm seeing this through. I can still—"

"Katherine . . ." Dignity gently pulled out of her grip, then wrapped her own hands around hers. "Di Meryse made it out alive. A few of Bracewell's people went after him. Bracewell and the gunmage followed *them*. Only reason I'm not doing the same is that they were already gone by the time anyone told me what was happening, and as soon as I have any idea where they went . . ."

"Could you honestly keep up? Can you even *stand* up?"

Katherine's answer lodged in her throat, refusing to rise any higher.

"Catch up with Halcourt. Go home. We'll finish this for you."

"I'm sorry . . ."

"Don't be stupid. You've done Cygnar proud."

Again Katherine's grip abruptly tightened; she scarcely noted Dignity's wince. "The blast . . ."

"What about it?"

"The east wall? The balcony? They were barely singed. The charges were set *not* to touch them."

"Are you—"

"Yes, I'm sure. Seen enough bombs in my time."

Dignity's gaze grew vague for a moment. "You clever bitch . . ."

"Excuse me?!" Katherine demanded.

"Not you. Vorona. Take care of yourself, Lieutenant."

"Wait . . ."

But Dignity was already gone, snapping questions at anyone who would listen, and all Katherine could do now was curse her injuries and wait for the soldiers to come and help her up.

***

"That one." Serena craned her head toward one particular house, a large but not overly luxurious affair on an avenue full to bursting with others very much like it. Constructed for the moderately successful and newly rich of the Outer Ward, they lacked the ornate gardens, classical statuary, and vast unnecessary wings of Old Town manors, while still boasting enough space and amenities to comfortably house any four New Town families. "He ducked in there, around the back."

"Are you . . . ?" Wendell hunched forward, hands resting on his knees, oblivious to the mutters of several coat-wrapped pedestrians who had to swerve around him. "Are you certain?"

"I've kept my eyesight better than you have. My stamina, too, apparently."

"We're neither as young as we used to be," he grumped at her.

"Maybe not," Serena mused, "but it looks like I'm closer."

The mechanik's glare could have fired up the engine of a dormant 'jack entirely on its own. Serena couldn't help but snicker, though she grew serious again quickly enough.

"Do we go in?" she asked.

Wendell wiped the sweat from his brow before it could begin to freeze in the evening chill. His hand came away dusted in snow, and only then did he notice the gentle flurries, dancing in the breeze, which had begun to fall sometime during their pursuit.

"We don't actually know what happened back there. We need more information. We'll go around, see what we can see."

In back, the yard *was* divided into garden plots, though of course little actually bloomed this time of year. A simple wooden fence demarcated this property from the next, and a single stone fountain stood beside it, lightly frozen over.

What attracted the soldiers' attention, however, was the back door, currently standing ajar.

Wendell withdrew a heavy pistol from amongst the tools on his belt, while Serena—after a quick peek inside to judge the width of the hallway—produced a long fighting knife, foregoing the rifle that hung from her shoulder.

"Cover me," she whispered, then slipped in through the open door, Wendell two steps behind.

They found themselves in a small foyer, an open coatroom to one side and a clear view of the sitting room beyond. Like the house and its surrounds, the furniture was comfortable without crossing into ostentatious. A faint layer of dust and even fainter stale odor suggested the place hadn't seen much use or cleaning in weeks, but the faint imprint of shoes in the thick shag carpet could only have come from a far more recent visitor.

Serena slipped in, crouching, while Wendell swept every corner with his pistol, but no enemy lurked within the room. The both of them did, however, hear a faint shuffling from a chamber off to the left. Creeping in unison, they positioned themselves on either side of the doorway and peeked around the jamb.

Beyond was a cozy library, the younger cousin of the one in Surros Manor. The bookshelves were less tightly packed, the fireplace smaller, the thickly upholstered chairs fewer in number, but it conveyed almost precisely the same atmosphere.

Or would have, under normal circumstances.

Idran di Meryse—alchemist, extortionist, perhaps the greatest threat to Cygnar in recent memory, for all that most Cygnarans didn't know it—lay sprawled on the carpet, marinating in his own blood. His throat gaped in an obscene leer, muscle fibers and a sliver of trachea protruding in a withered, awful bouquet. Beside him, also soaking in the gory bath, was a large tome, its pages hollowed out to create a storage niche.

And crouched beyond him, collecting sheets of paper from where they appeared to have fallen—perhaps during a brief and clearly one-sided struggle—was a severe, narrow-faced woman with black hair, an equally black long coat, and the last fading remnants of a grotesque bruise on her face.

Serena and Wendell both jerked back from the doorway. Neither one needed a word to know that this couldn't possibly be good, to take a pretty good guess at what they were seeing. Wendell raised three fingers; Serena nodded sharply.

Two fingers . . .

One.

Again she lunged through the door first, knife raised, skirting quickly around the puddle of gore. He followed after, ready to fire, boots hitting the carpet with an unnerving wet *splurt*.

Other than the alchemist's slowly cooling corpse, the two of them were alone in the library.

Seconds. They'd taken their eyes off the room for mere *seconds*! How—?

Even afterward, the mechanik couldn't begin to guess where she'd concealed herself. She was just suddenly *there*, blade flashing. The impact sent Wendell staggering back into the sitting room, bleeding from an ugly gash on his chest; only the thin plates of armor worked into his coat had prevented a mortal wound. His pistol skated across the floor to vanish under one of the chairs.

"Not as silent as you think you are," she purred in her thick Khadoran accent. And then she was diving *over* him, tumbling back to her feet on the far side of the room, as Serena appeared behind her, slashing with her own blade. Not yet able to regain his feet, Wendell rolled from between them and fetched up against the legs of a small table.

Serena sidestepped, slinging the rifle from over her shoulder into her free hand, at the same instant the Khadoran—*Vorona*, Wendell assumed, based on Dignity's description—charged. No way the older woman could have her weapon up and aimed before the spy closed . . .

But Serena, while not the close-range fighter Vorona was, was no fool. Rather than raising the rifle to her shoulder to fire, she drove it *down*, using it as a club to strike at the other woman's knee.

Vorona hissed at the pain, though she avoided enough of it that the injury didn't appear crippling. Then, as fast as Wendell had ever seen, even in his youngest days of CRS training, she lashed out with her free hand, grabbed the rifle, and twisted it like a baton.

The weapon discharged, eliciting a rain of powder from the ceiling above. Serena stumbled, yanked off-balance by the shoulder strap, now twisted around her wrist and forearm. Vorona's good knee rose, cracking hard against the extended elbow. Serena locked up, her entire body shuddering with the shock.

And Wendell, just now staggering to his feet, could do absolutely nothing as Vorona's blade punched up under Serena's jaw, stopping only when the tip lodged against the inside of her skull.

Serena's face twisted—in confusion, it seemed to Wendell, more than pain—then went slack. Vorona had Serena's own blade in her fist, to replace the one currently wedged in the long gunner's head, before the body fell.

Wendell was sure he shouted *something*, though he never could remember what.

"I am sorry about your friend," Vorona told him, though from her tone she might have been apologizing for taking the last sandwich. "If you'd simply let me go on my way, none of this would—"

Snarling, Wendell drew his own service blade, very similar to Serena's own. For the first time, Vorona actually looked surprised.

"Really, old man?"

"You're not leaving this house."

"So be it."

She came on like a tornado, swift and relentless. Drawing on everything he'd ever learned, Wendell snapped a kick into her already injured knee. Vorona staggered, and he was on her. Metal shrieked as his blade grated against hers, and they both knew that she'd only barely raised the parry in time.

Wendell also knew, though, that he could keep this up for only seconds before she got her bearings.

He lifted a foot from the carpet, feigning another kick, and then leaned in across her arm, catching it in a joint lock, forcing it back, shoving her further off balance . . .

Vorona jerked aside, slipping from his grip, though she jarred the flat of her blade against him, knocking it from her grasp, in the process. Unwilling to let her put any distance between them, he slashed awkwardly, grinned as he felt fabric and flesh part.

They both straightened, facing one another across perhaps two yards of the sitting room. Blood poured from the gash he'd just put in her thigh; nowhere near the artery, more the pity, but certainly painful enough—especially considering it was the leg already injured.

"You're no mechanik," she accused, as though he'd somehow personally misled her.

"Sure I am. I'm *also* Reconnaissance."

"Of course. I should have recognized the technique." Grunting, she pressed a hand to the open wound. "Perhaps we should—"

Gods, she was fast! She made a hurling motion, spraying a cupped palmful of her own blood at Wendell's face. Instincts as old as the human race had him twisting aside, blinking to protect his eyes, before he even knew what it was she'd thrown.

She was already on him before he recovered. Her first strike shivered the bones in his wrist, numbing his arm and sending his blade across the room, perhaps to go in search of his pistol. Her second caught him in the gut, doubling him over, driving the air from his lungs.

Had her leg not been injured, weak, the knee that followed up would probably have shattered his jaw, cost him teeth. As it was, he felt something give inside his nose. The world vanished briefly behind a shower of sparks.

As they began to fade, his vision to clear, he found himself staring up at the ceiling. He knew he had to get up, to move, to do *something*, or he was dead—but his body utterly refused to translate that knowledge into action.

And why were the flashes and speckles growing *worse* rather than fading? So bright were the streaks of blue flashing before him that he almost had to squint to avoid . . .

Blue? *Oh.*

That wasn't the pounding of blood in his ears and agony in his head, at least not *all* of it. He finally identified the gunfire, the blasts as whole sections of wall simply went away. He heard a few growled syllables that might have been Khadoran profanity, heard the patter of footsteps, saw the hem of a navy blue coat flap in and out of sight.

Wendell's heart almost stopped when he felt hands on his shoulder, until he realized they were gently helping him sit, recognized the face looming above as Ben's.

"Careful, Master Sergeant," she said softly. "Careful . . ."

He started to speak—and then screamed, instead, as Benwynne reached out and did *something* to his nose. Wendell hovered on the very edge of passing out, and the Sergeant went blurry behind a sheen of tears.

"It's set," she explained simply.

"But is it still *attached*?!" he demanded breathlessly. Then, struggling to bring himself under control, "Ben, she's got the formula . . ."

"I figured. We're after her, almost the whole squad. She's got nowhere to hide."

"Serena?" He knew it was stupid, knew he sounded like a plaintive child even as he asked, but he couldn't help it.

"She's gone, Wendell."

His chin sagged to his chest, renewed grief threatening to overwhelm him; he released it in one long breath. Later, there would be time for mourning. Later . . .

"How did you find us?"

"Gaust and I were following you, a few streets back, while you trailed that Khadoran bitch. We lost you here, though; didn't see you duck into this house.

"Gaust sent word to the others. We figured if we could gather everyone, we could make a more thorough search. We'd still be out there waiting if we hadn't heard Serena's rifle."

The rifle that had gone off only as Vorona yanked it from Serena's hand. Serena never actually had a shot . . .

He didn't say it. It wasn't something Benwynne needed to hear.

"Help me up, please, Sergeant."

"Wendell, you should probably rest a little—"

"Please."

It wasn't *too* hard to stand, not with her aid, and he only stumbled once before finding his balance. A nod of thanks, and then he *very carefully* crouched beside the nearest chair, fingers stretched to retrieve his knife and pistol.

"Wendell, there's not a street for blocks in any direction that doesn't have at least one of us watching it. She's not going far."

"Still," he said, knees and calves trembling as he straightened, "I want to be there to see it."

He didn't add *If you're right*. He didn't have to; he knew she heard it regardless.

***

Atherton dashed down the center of the avenue. Between the thickening flurries and his own breath, everything before him blurred, shifted. He felt like he passed through infinite layers of gauzy curtains, perhaps, or cobwebs.

Still, the gas lights of the Outer Ward burned bright at almost every intersection, and the sun still peeked over the city wall to the west, if only by the narrowest sliver. It wasn't much, but at least so far, it allowed him—or, if not always Atherton, then *someone*—to keep their enemy in sight.

Oh, she'd tried every trick to lose them. Slipping into knots of late evening pedestrians; pushing through a shop over here that was still open, a private house there with its doors unlocked. At one point, she'd ducked out of view long enough to scramble up a drain pipe, and the Cygnarans might well have lost her then—save that Atherton had been wise enough to station Ledeson on the rooftops, running parallel to their pursuit. Now, the diminutive commando sprinted beside him, keeping up tirelessly, and one of the others had assumed roof duty. At every crossroad, Atherton glanced right or left, and every time he spotted rushing figures against the falling snow: More of what was left of the squad, on neighboring streets, ensuring Vorona had no easy means of escape.

She was headed *somewhere*, though, not just fleeing at random; her choices were too methodical, her path too unswervingly northwest. With her pursuers so close, it certainly wasn't a safehouse or hidey hole, so where . . . ?

It was Dignity, who had appeared at Atherton's side at some point over the last three blocks, breathing as easily as if this sort of sprint were an everyday affair, who pieced it together first. "She's heading for the gate!"

"What's she going to do, fight her way through an entire guardhouse? Talk about desperate . . ." The gunmage trailed off at Dignity's pinched expression. "You don't think . . ." He struggled to catch his breath. "Don't think she's planning to fight through a whole team of guards, do you?"

"I think that Vorona's had two weeks to develop an exit strategy. She may not have anticipated pursuit, but she bloody well has a plan of *some* sort!"

As if in deliberate confirmation of that guess, Vorona yanked a device, bulkier than a heavy pistol, from a large satchel at her side. Without slowing, she aimed it straight up and fired; even through the flurries and low-hanging clouds, the sky lit up like Morrow's own candle.

"That can't be good," Dignity muttered.

Atherton shouted something impolite and fingered the butt of a pepperbox. Again he strongly considered taking the shot, and again reluctantly decided he couldn't afford to. Even his runebullets weren't *completely* unerring. Vorona's speed, agility, and borderline supernatural ability to know when an attack was coming had already allowed her to avoid two of them, and while the streets were far from crowded—and growing even less so, as Cygnaran soldiers stormed across the district—there remained sufficient civilians that collateral damage was a real concern if he missed.

He'd never have admitted it aloud—*certainly* not to Dignity!—but Atherton couldn't help but feel a grudging admiration for the Khadoran operative. He'd seen the ugly wound on her leg, and the occasional constellation of red specks in the gray snow that proved it wasn't getting any better. And still she'd maintained her lead, ran with no obvious hitch in her stride. It was the sort of unyielding iron will Atherton had read about in the pulps, but never thought to see, and felt sure he'd never possess himself.

The massive curtain wall hove into view, rising between and then over the rows of buildings. The wall—and then the gatehouse, its iron-banded gates and shadowed barbican forming one of the many maws that could either provide ingress to Leryn or chew an intruder to pieces, depending upon its mood. Lanterns blazed on either side of the manmade tunnel and within the windows of the structure itself, clearly outlining a dozen sentinels, pikemen and riflemen both, stationed beside the passage or atop the wall. Most had turned their gazes inward, perhaps attracted by Vorona's flare.

Atherton grinned, a horrible rictus thanks to his growing exhaustion. "Seems she's planning to fight her way out after—"

From somewhere out in the cloaking flurries of snow, perhaps as far as the scattered trees that grew no closer than several hundred yards from the wall, came a salvo of rifle fire.

At that range, in the inclement weather and growing whiteout, even the champions amongst the Widowmakers couldn't have aimed those shots with any accuracy. And indeed, they appeared to be shooting wild: Bullets smacked into the curtain wall, disintegrating into powder and scrap, doing no harm whatsoever.

The guards, however, reacted to the unexpected attack exactly as soldiers do: They dove for cover. For an instant, they could see nothing at all; for an instant more, they were too busy scanning the snowy nothingness for any sign of the oncoming enemy.

And that was time enough for Vorona to sweep through the barbican and make a mad dash into the concealing haze.

Had any of the sentinels actually *tried* to take her down, they could have landed several shots before she vanished. They were, however, too busy looking for the source of—and occasionally ducking—the haphazard incoming fire.

Once Atherton, Dignity, and the others poured into the gatehouse, in pursuit of the woman they'd scarcely even noticed, it might have occurred to the guards that they'd been had. By then, there was precious little they could do about it, though.

Atherton thought he could just *barely* make out figures moving in the distance, beyond the many veils of winter, from which those shots were coming. He drew both pistols, fired a pair of runebullets that sent whole showers of earth and snow erupting upward where they struck, and whoever was shooting at them wisely stopped.

The snow wasn't falling so rapidly that they lost Vorona's tracks—though they could probably have followed her anyway. The spy was making a beeline, never varying from one specific heading. A heading that would take her straight to . . .

The Oldwick River hove into view. The flow was largely unimpeded, though a few small chunks of ice bobbed near the banks. Atherton could see Vorona again, albeit as nothing more than a nebulous silhouette.

Prow beached on the nearest bank was a large paddleboat. Even had Vorona not been racing directly for it, Atherton would have known it to be no innocent traveler. Few merchants had traveled this stretch of river for days or even weeks, and few would likely do so for days or weeks to come.

With Khador squatting over the waterway at Riversmet, where the Oldwick became the Black, there wasn't much of anywhere to *go*.

A large door in the wheelhouse flew open, and Vorona . . .

Vorona flopped to the snowy earth, arms covering her head.

"Down!" He saw Dignity shout the warning, though he couldn't actually *hear* it over his own identical cry. And then he, too, was frantically diving, barely skating beneath a withering barrage of gunfire.

Raising his head as high as he dared, peering between frost below and hot lead above, Atherton watched as figure after figure poured from the wheelhouse. It was almost ludicrous, something out of a clown show; clearly the structure contained a passage to the hold below.

So, okay . . . Winter Guard soldiers, already a dozen and counting, their blunderbusses spitting swarms of lead shot. That was bad.

Apparently, the Khadorans were not content with standing on deck and defending their vessel. No, the soldiers poured out onto the slushy banks, axes or sabers in the fists of those who had already discharged their guns, advancing in a staggered charge toward the woefully outnumbered Cygnarans. That was worse.

And misfortune wasn't done with them yet. Hulking figures of red-tinted steel clunked and clattered from the hold and took to the banks, following their swifter Winter Guard comrades. Smoke and steam poured from grated tubing on their backs; enormous and unwieldy pole axes, shield-mounted cannon, or motorized chain-bladed swords, too large for any normal man to carry, were their tools.

Khador sent a godsdamn Man-O-War unit!

Cygnar, like most nations of Immoren, regularly utilized two separate classes of warjack: the heavy 'jacks, ponderous but inexorable juggernauts of brutal weaponry; and the light models, such as Wolfhound or Shepherd, less fearsome but far swifter and more maneuverable.

Khador's military mechaniks produced some of the most fearsome and overwhelming of the former variety, but had shown precisely zero interest in the latter. Instead, where other armies fielded light warjacks, Khador deployed the Man-O-War soldiers: zealous troops, highly trained, wrapped in steam-powered armor that granted inhuman strength and resilience. A single Man-O-War could potentially take on a small squad of normally equipped soldiers. In teams, they could give even warjacks something to worry about.

Here, now, in addition to the contingent of Winter Guard, there were four of them.

"Fall back!" Atherton ordered, scrambling to his hands and knees.

"No!" Dignity looked ready to either spit nails or chew them, Atherton wasn't sure. "Damn it, she's *right there!*"

"You know your enemies; I know mine." He was backpedaling toward the walls of Leryn, glancing frequently over his shoulder to ensure that his people—Dignity included—obeyed. "We fall back or we die."

The others had turned to run, leaving only the two of them making a slower retreat, hunched low to avoid the sporadic shots that still came their way from the advancing force.

"Gaust, we *can't* let her get away. That formula—"

"I said we retreat." A spark seemed to flash in Atherton's eye. No, it didn't just *seem* to, it *did*; a single sizzle of cobalt blue, echoed by a far larger array around the barrels of his guns. "I never said we let them get away."

Atherton raised both pistols toward the distant sky and fired, round after round, emptying all six remaining barrels. Runebullets streaked across the clouds and plunged unerringly into their target—not Vorona, not the Man-O-War soldiers, but the riverboat itself.

The first two landed with the force of artillery, blasting open a huge swath of the deck. The other four plunged through that newly made gap . . .

To strike within feet of the boiler.

Nobody was shooting at Dignity or Atherton anymore. The Winter Guard, the Section Three spy, even the normally overconfident Man-O-War troopers, were too busy running—or, in the case of the latter, shuffling as swiftly as their weighty armored contraptions would permit—from the bank.

The agent and the gunmage had just reached Leryn's gate when the boiler blew and the riverboat burst in a nova of twisted iron fragments and splintery wooden shrapnel. Small ice floes near the vessel ceased to exist entirely, and two or three riverside trees split across the trunk and toppled.

"As I said," Atherton noted smugly, "they're not going anywhere."

It looked for a moment like Dignity was carefully weighing the ups and downs of smacking him. "Not by river, they're not. Unless your magics are a lot more impressive than I've been told, though, their *feet* still work."

"As do ours. And the sergeant's. And Wolfhound's. We've more than enough time to catch them up, and they'll never know what hit them."

***

Of course, despite Atherton's blithe certainty, it wasn't to prove so easy.

". . . can't possibly hold *us* responsible for any of this—"

"Can't? *Can't?* Sergeant, you're absolutely responsible! If you and your people hadn't elected to bring your war to Leryn—"

"*Our* war? It's *your* city crawling with Section Three! Your bloody nation is the one being invaded! If your Prime Minister shares your opinion, I'm quite sure his Majesty would be delighted to discuss a withdrawal . . ."

Emerging from the barbican back into the light, Dignity and Atherton found Sergeant Bracewell and Minister Chalerynne toe-to-toe, red-faced and hollering, apparently having left diplomacy far behind. Beside the former stood a pair of the soldiers Atherton had ordered back to the city, having stepped up to support their commanding officer. Assembled behind the latter, half a dozen Crucible Guards leaned on pikes and peered through narrow visors. Neither group of warriors seemed particularly on edge or eager for violence, but their mere presence testified to the vehemence of the argument.

"Uh, Sergeant?" Atherton sounded as unsure as Dignity had ever heard him. "I'm sorry to interrupt, but—"

"Not at all, Corporal. We were done." Benwynne stepped away, her first stride more of a stomp. Dignity almost expected her heel to carve a divot from the nearest paver. She didn't order the others to fall in behind her; the order was pretty implicit as it was.

"Sergeant!" Chalerynne's shriek rose higher than a whistling teapot. "Don't you *dare* just walk away from me!"

"Minister, trust me," Benwynne called back, neither turning to face him nor slowing in the slightest. "Walking away is *exactly* what you want me to be doing right now."

Dignity, who *did* glance back over her shoulder, saw the gawp of utter disbelief on Chalerynne's face even through the snow and thickening dark of night. Under other circumstances, it would have been hysterical.

For half a block they marched in silence, before Benwynne's frustration boiled over. "Morrow piss on all politicians!"

"Sergeant?" Atherton asked.

"Bastard doesn't give one damn what's actually happening in his city. He just wants to blame someone for the damages and chaos and security breaches, so none of the shit spatters back on *him*. Why couldn't we have dealt with Minister di la Granzio? At least he's supposed to have a working brain . . ."

She turned down a side street, leading the small procession toward a squat structure of markedly lower quality than its neighbors. The earthy tang of straw and manure announced it as a public stable well before Dignity spotted the sun-bleached equine silhouette painted above the door.

The spy assumed they were here because it was the nearest place that provided both shelter from the elements and relative privacy. Benwynne *could* have chosen it for some other reason, but Dignity decided that now wasn't the time to ask.

The establishment wasn't heavily occupied. All but three stalls stood empty; the trio of horses cast apathetic glowers at the newcomers before tossing their manes in dismissal and returning to the far more urgent tasks of transforming the heaps of hay in front of them into far less appetizing heaps behind them.

The rest of the soldiers who had accompanied Atherton and Dignity during their pursuit were already here. They'd dragged a few stools, saddles, and hay bales into a vague circle, and most were now seated, having claimed the most comfortable of the makeshift chairs.

At the sight of an old, worn saddle sitting atop a half-height wall between stalls, Dignity couldn't help but wonder if Katherine was all right, had caught up with Muir's delegation.

"So," Benwynne began. "I see neither Vorona nor the formula. What the hell happened out there?"

Dignity remained mostly silent, letting Atherton provide a concise report of the pursuit, chiming in only occasionally when he skipped a detail or two she felt might be important.

Benwynne slowly lowered herself to sit atop one of the hay bales and gazed into nothing, seemingly hypnotized by a flicking horsetail.

"Corporal, Privates . . . Go find everyone else. I want the whole squad here. Yesterday!"

"Where—?"

"Most of them should be at di Meryse's place, between there and the gate, or at the workshop where we've been storing Wolfhound."

"And if anyone isn't?" Atherton asked.

"Then you bloody well *look for them!*"

Even the horses jumped. Atherton and the others shot to their feet, saluted, and streamed toward the door.

"And fill them in on route!" Benwynne called after them. "I don't want to sit through that report three more times."

Dignity wondered, for a few minutes, if the sergeant had forgotten she was there, or had expected her to depart with the others, when Benwynne finally spoke once more.

"I'm tired, Garland."

"You . . . What?"

"I used to love serving, but this army's taken *everything* from me—my life, so many friends, now my family and even my faith—and it never ends. I'm just . . . tired."

"I—"

"What the hell was Vorona's plan?" It sounded like she wasn't even *aware* she'd just been speaking on something else entirely. "What was with that performance at the textile factory?"

"It . . . Um." Dignity actually had to fight the urge to shake her head and blink a few times, trying to keep up. "My best guess? Trying to kill us was just a bonus. The audience for the show was di Meryse."

Benwynne blinked, then *hmphed* in understanding. "She was lying about having the formula."

"I think so. Just claiming that these 'secret allies' of hers—who may or may not even exist—had thwarted all di Meryse's efforts . . . No way he'd believe that. But make it look like she was trying to kill him, like she didn't need him anymore? *That* sold it."

"It was still a pretty big risk, wasn't it?" The sergeant stood and drifted over to the nearest horse, absently stroking its neck. "What if he *hadn't* gone straight to his hiding place?"

Dignity shrugged. "I suppose it was her only shot. There were a lot of us, but just her; she must have figured we weren't going to let her walk away if she won the bidding."

"No. No, we weren't."

"Di Meryse was a clever bastard, but he wasn't trained. He thought she had the formula, and panicked—went to make sure she was telling the truth, or to try to figure out how she'd managed it, or maybe it's just where he felt safest. You or I would have known better, but . . ."

"You think she's heading for Riversmet?" Benwynne asked.

"Positive. The besiegers are the nearest Khadoran force of any size. At the very least, she's passing *through* it; her attempt to use the river proves that much."

"You know we've already lost, right?" Still Benwynne remained focused on the horse, refusing to look Dignity's way.

"What are you talking about? Gaust—"

"Gaust kept them from taking the river, yes. Forced them to travel overland. So we're supposed to chase them down, is that it?"

"I figured that was the—"

"If we go for speed, we have to move without Wolfhound. We can't run him more than about five hours or so. But without him, there's no chance that what's left of my squad can stand against those Man-O-War bastards—certainly not with a dozen Winter Guard backing them up.

"If we *do* take the 'jack? That armor may be slow, but they're already ahead of us. They might avoid us long enough for Wolfhound to run down. And if we *do* catch up? The M.o.W.s can hold us off at least a short time, even *with* Wolfhound, while the others make a run for it. And without those armored bastards, they can move a *lot* faster.

"So you tell me, Garland, option one or option two? I'm a soldier, so I'm not about to quit, and I'm ready to attempt the impossible. Which way do we want to fail?"

Dignity couldn't remember how to form words, how to make her mouth actually function.

"Actually . . ."

Both women turned toward the doorway. There, silhouetted against the street lamps beyond, stood one of the trenchers Benwynne had dispatched to fetch the squad. With him were several other soldiers.

Including, at the front of the pack, Master Sergeant Habbershant.

"If we don't have our hearts set on losing *quite* yet," he went on, "I think I may have an option three . . ."

Casteus 10th, 605 AR
Between Leryn and Riversmet, Llael

The boat didn't even have a name.

Loumbard, the squat, surly tradesman who captained it, had never bothered to come up with one. So far as he, his crew, and his customers were concerned, it was just "Loumbard's boat."

Even beyond being nameless, Loumbard's boat had little to distinguish it. It was worn and rickety without crossing the line into dilapidated; large enough to accommodate most reasonable cargo without reaching gargantuan; powerful enough without boasting a particularly intricate steam engine or fancy paddlewheel.

There had been, in fact, one and only one factor to recommend the craft over any of the others. When Benwynne, Wendell, and the bulk of squad five had stormed up to Leryn's docks, demanding that someone carry them and their warjack down the Oldwick River, coming as near to Riversmet as possible without drawing Khadoran artillery down on their heads, Loumbard had been the only captain who had both agreed to their terms, and been ready to ship out immediately.

Well, almost immediately. Chalerynne's petulance, and the diplomatic paperwork associated with it, had cost them additional hours they couldn't spare.

Nor had their transport come cheaply. The bank notes Benwynne turned over to Loumbard—drawn from the same accounts that had provided the payment for di Meryse, funds secretly arranged weeks before by Cygnar's government—could have purchased the boat outright, with change expected.

Given the risks they were asking the crew to take, however, to say nothing of the urgency, the sergeant hadn't argued.

It was a solid plan; no reason it should fail. Traveling under steam and on the currents of the Oldwick, they should be many hours and many leagues ahead of Vorona and her team, just waiting for the signal to deploy. Knowing what *should* be, however, wasn't remotely the same as knowing what *was*.

Now, Benwynne stood on deck, leaning out over a banister that groaned various complaints about holding her weight. Ignoring the crew shifting and scuttling behind her, she stared into the flashing lights painting the sky to the south and west, trying to summon up that signal by sheer force of will.

Or, barring that, sheer force of burning, frustrated impatience.

"You've been awfully quiet the past day or two."

She couldn't even be bothered to look at the figure who'd appeared at the rail beside her. "Seems to me we've had this conversation before, Master Sergeant. I don't know that I care to repeat it."

Wendell apparently chose to ignore the less-than-subtle hint to drop it. He tugged his coat a bit tighter over his shoulders—to protect against the cold, or against the words to come? "You need to stop flagellating yourself over all this, Ben."

Now she *did* turn his way, and it was all she could do not to land a right hook to his chin. "Oh, *do* I, Master Sergeant? And which part should I be most proud of, then? Losing most of my people on the way here? Letting Vorona get away? Or just my own *idiocy*, in needing you to suggest we use a riverboat to get ahead of her?"

"You've lost soldiers before. It's never hit you like—"

"Not over half the squad on *one damn mission!*"

Wendell, too, straightened, took a step until they were almost nose to nose. "You want to take a swing at me, Sergeant? You go right ahead, if that'll snap you out of this!"

"Snap—?!"

"Yes, we've lost a lot! Yes, it's a new experience for you, and Morrow knows how it must feel! It's torn me ragged, and *I'm* not in command."

"At the moment," Benwynne interjected, bitter as rotting horseradish.

"And if you feel the need to punish yourself, or resign, or jump off a bridge, or whatever, I can't stop you. But you do it *after we get home!* Godsdamn it, Ben, the squad *needs* you! Best way to convince them this is hopeless is to let them see that *you* think it's hopeless! So *keep it together!*"

What sounded, initially, like the boat running up on the rocks was, she realized, the popping of her clenched knuckles. "I shouldn't need you to tell me that," she admitted.

"You've never suffered like this," he conceded. "Of course it's going to weigh on you. But you can't afford to bend under it, Ben. *We* can't afford for you to bend."

She leaned out over the water once more. "I'll keep it in mind, Master Sergeant." Then, as though it tasted off and she was spitting it out before it sickened her, "Thank you."

"Ben," he said hesitantly, "about Bainsmarket . . . Uh, right." Wendell actually retreated a step beneath her glare. "Not the best time. Later will do." He didn't *quite* run back to the hatch, but it neither did he quite *not* run.

Benwynne returned to examining the distant conflagration—shots and detonations from the siege of Riversmet, *almost* as violent as those within her own soul—and waited intently for Gaust's signal.

***

"Bloody godsdamn *snow!*" Atherton cursed. Or at least, that's what Atherton *meant* to curse. He wasn't sure how much of it was intelligible, given how violently his teeth chattered. "We're royally buggered here, aren't we?"

"I told you, *relax!*" The vehemence in Dignity's voice was quite strong enough to make relaxing pretty much impossible. "We'll pick the trail back up. We know where they're going."

"So you said an hour ago."

For a day and a half, the two of them—along with Ledeson and a couple more of Bracewell's soldiers—had tracked Vorona and her escorts through the blanket of powder covering Leryn's soil. They slept only a few hours at a stretch, lest the enemy get too far ahead. They struggled to maintain the proper distance, neither falling back nor drawing close enough to attract attention. They remained constantly alert for ambush or any attempt to double back.

It was enough to put even the iron-nerved spy on edge. So when flurries thickened into curtains, and gusts into the gale of a genuine blizzard; when the weather leeched not only heat but color from their skin even through jackets and coats; when the surface of white before them filled itself in, obliterating the footprints . . . tempers had frayed down to their last dangling threads.

"I told you we should have stuck closer to them!" Atherton reminded her, not even remotely for the first time.

"And I told you to *shut up* already! Seems we're both bound for disappointment."

Morrow alone knew how things might have deteriorated after that, had Ledeson not appeared abruptly before them, parting the snowy curtain like an actor ready for his final bow. "Storm's clearing up ahead," he reported.

"There!" Dignity crowed, her tone and her sneer as unprofessional as Atherton had ever seen them. "See?"

"Any sign of the enemy?" The gunmage asked.

"No, sir. Not a trace."

"There," he said to the spy. "See?" Then, before she could explode, "Now what do we do?"

"Now we go find them."

"Just like that, then?"

"Just like that."

As Dignity had said, they knew where Vorona was headed. Once they'd cleared the fringes of the storm and passed into an ever-lightening morass of haze, a few minutes of scouting were sufficient to recover the trail. The tracks appeared at the edges of the storm, as though the Khadorans had fallen along with the snow itself, several dozen yards to the north.

And led them straight to the ashen remains of a tiny hamlet, some few hundred yards beyond that.

It wasn't the first they'd come across; probably wouldn't be the last. Like the warjacks they resembled, the Man-O-War suits couldn't function long without coal. And for the Khadorans, here in the open lands between Leryn and Riversmet, there was really only one way to acquire it.

Atherton had given up trying to count the dead after the second such raid.

"You were right," he admitted, trying both to be graceful and to distract them all from the newest scene of carnage. "Good show."

Except Dignity wasn't even looking at the tiny ravaged village. So why the hell did her forehead crease, her lips turn downward?

"Something wrong?" he asked.

Her response was a low mutter, barely heard.

"What was that?"

"The tracks are wrong." She knelt, leaving divots in the quilt of white, for a closer examination.

Atherton examined them, then Dignity; back to the tracks, and back to his companion once more. "I don't follow."

"I can't put my finger on it," she admitted, rising and brushing slush and powder from her knees. "But something's off. We need to hurry."

So they did, passing through and amongst sporadic trees—far too wide-spread to constitute a forest, but rather occasional features of an otherwise barren winter vista—until Dignity stiffened, fists and jaws clenching tight enough to crush granite.

"They've split up," she hissed in response to Atherton's questioning glance.

"What?!"

"The soldiers' tracks are shallower than the Man-O-Wars'."

"Of *course* they are! You know how heavy those—?"

"I mean more than they *should* be, you blithering idiot! They're older, had more time to fill in!

"Plus, they're farther apart—moving at a faster pace. They've gone ahead, left the Man-O-War contingent to follow."

"So what the hell do we do?"

"Send the signal."

"The Reds might hear—"

"Just *do* it!"

Atherton grunted, drew, and fired. A flat *crack* sounded over the land-scape, refusing to echo in the emptiness. The shot flew high, far higher than it had any right, and soared northward in a gentle arc.

"Now get a move on," Dignity ordered, breaking into a run, "and hope to all the gods that we can catch them before they reach Riversmet."

***

"Suggestions?"

Dignity scowled, shivering. "Working on it."

The Cygnarans lay in a snowdrift, staring over the lip at the Man-O-War quartet. Though they were scarcely more than reddish shapes in the mist, still they projected a sense of menace, of *weight*; somehow more real than the fuzzy world around them.

They progressed at a leisurely pace, even as compared to their normal lumbering. Even without being able to see their heads move within the helms, or the helms rotate atop the armored trunks, neither Atherton nor Dignity could doubt that they scanned in all directions, serving as rear guard for their comrades who had gone on ahead.

"We can't attack," Ledeson chimed in from behind, as if they'd even have considered such a thing. "They'd slaughter us."

"Right," Atherton said with a grim smile. "They outnumber us four to five."

"Cute," Dignity said, "but not helpful."

"Look," the gunmage continued, "the idea of leaving an enemy at my back makes me painfully clench all sorts of things, but all we really have to do is get past them, right? They're slow enough that we can keep ahead of them, at least long enough to do whatever needs doing with Vorona and the Winter Guard."

"Right, but if we try circling around, we may lose—"

"Just be ready to move," he repeated.

"What?"

"*Quietly.*"

"What?!"

Atherton drew both pepperbox pistols, and had to swallow a braying guffaw as Dignity's eyes bulged until they threatened to pop like soap bubbles. "Are you *insane?*" she demanded. "You'll draw them right to—"

The tail end of her protest suffocated and died, buried beneath twin blasts. Her hands twitched toward her waist, seemingly of their own accord, and Atherton wondered briefly whether her first shot would be trained on the enemy, or on a target substantially closer.

Perhaps it was fortunate for him, then, that she never had cause to make that choice. The armored soldiers started at the sound of the gunshots, halting and peering about for an enemy they couldn't see. As Atherton had hoped, the flat sound of the open plain, combined with the muffling weight of their massive steel helmets, made it impossible to determine with any certainty from where the shots had come.

An instant later, the bullets—tiny warhorses, ridden and steered by the gunmage's sorceries—slammed into one of the red-armored warriors from the *opposite direction*.

All four reacted as swiftly as their metal suits would allow, turning their backs on Atherton's actual position. Two immediately advanced, axes held high, while the other pair lobbed grenades from massive launchers, utterly obliterating an inoffensive pine.

"Go!" he hissed.

Ledeson had already vanished. The other soldiers and Dignity followed with a bit less skill—although, in the spy's case, only a *tiny* bit less—and then Atherton brought up the rear, watching for any sign that the enemy had seen through his trick.

He himself turned out to be the least stealthy of the lot, and still they'd crossed beyond the Man-O-War squad and out of sight while the enemy hunted desperately for a nonexistent target.

"That wasn't bad," Dignity admitted, once they'd stopped for breath around the base of another lonely tree, a half mile on.

"I try," Atherton said, quickly reloading the empty barrels. "They're *eventually* going to find our tracks, though, unless that storm meanders this way. And if they're carrying any more of those damn flares, they can signal that someone's gotten past them. We need to catch Vorona up before then."

"There's another reason we need to hurry, sir," Ledeson added.

He couldn't have timed his pronouncement better. In perfect punctuation, a blast of artillery sounded from far to the west, nowhere near—but near *enough*.

They—and Vorona—were finally approaching the siege of Riversmet.

***

The thunder roared, sharp, constant, the fury of weapons rather than weather. The unseen sky grew bright, reflecting the all-consuming glory of lightning and fire. Almost too viscous to breathe, the air was smoke, ozone, spent powder . . .

Blood. Enough blood, he was sure, to melt away the winter snows and fertilize an early spring.

Initially, Atherton could see none of it, and that was somehow worse. Every eddy in the flurries was an onrushing Khadoran soldier; every shadow housed a towering crimson warjack. And every scream, carried to them by the shifting winds, was the voice of his own soul, crying out in exhausted terror.

And then, as they reached the perfect vantage atop the crown of a modest hill, the fading haze drifted apart in what seemed a conscious, deliberate show of melodrama.

And the gunmage had to change his mind: Seeing was worse.

Thick gray air cast a feverish, dreamlike pall over the entire vista. The pockmarked walls of Riversmet—perhaps nothing special when compared to Leryn's own, but imposing all the same—seemed unreal, more painted stage prop than genuine city. An array of multi-hued seas ebbed and flowed, beating against those walls or against one another, and Atherton found it difficult to convince himself that these were thousands of men and women in armor and uniforms, blending into abstract blots.

Throughout and between those seas, towering above the tumultuous surface, were giants of cerulean and gold, titans of crimson and steel. The smaller, swifter Cygnaran 'jacks bounded around their larger counterparts, seeking to overcome strength with speed and strategy. From such a distance, they were mere toys, marionettes; Atherton caught himself hunting for strings.

It was fake, all of it, a cheap façade over the face of the world. All of it but the fire. The explosions, the conflagrations that scorched the sky, the smoke that threatened to strangle the sun—those he could never imagine to be unreal.

A dull pain blossomed in Atherton's side, drawing an unwilling hiss from between his lips. "What the *hell*?!"

"Pay attention." Dignity, who had just elbowed him in the ribs, pointed across the expanse of drifts and rolling hills, shorter than the one on which they stood. "We have trouble."

Roughly a third of the way between the Cygnarans and the outermost fringes of the siege, Vorona and her Winter Guard comrades plunged ahead as fast as the clinging slush allowed.

Beyond, spreading from the battle's edges like a growing infection, rolled a contingent of Khador's so-called assault kommandos. That they were splitting off from the main forces, risking discovery by the Cygnaran units scattered around the perimeter, and heading *this way* . . . They could only have been dispatched to meet up with Vorona and her prize.

"If they link up before we can reach them . . ." Atherton warned. Dignity was already moving ahead, Ledeson and the others on her heels, but the gunmage hesitated. There might just be a quicker way . . .

The Llaelese defenders had plenty of Cygnaran allies within Riversmet itself, but multiple divisions of King Leto's army had also approached from the south, pinching many of the Khadoran forces between themselves and the bastion. Tactically, it was an overwhelming position—or it would have been, had the Khadorans not outnumbered and outgunned the Cygnarans multiple times over. As things stood now, despite the Cygnarans' strategic advantage, it was anyone's guess how this particular battle might turn out—or when Khadoran reinforcements might appear over the horizon.

What it all meant for Atherton personally, however, was that a Cygnaran unit of infantry and long-gunners held position relatively nearby, on the battle's fringe.

And that the oncoming kommandos were attempting, with all stealth, to circle *around* that unit in order to reach Vorona. They *could* have tried to fight their way through, probably even made it, but not without tipping off their enemy that this tiny band of Winter Guard was somehow significant.

Atherton raised a pistol, aimed at the *Cygnarans*, and fired.

Again the bullet flew unnaturally far, struck with unnatural force. It impacted behind the rearmost soldiers, showering them with earth. It did them no real damage, but it absolutely got their attention.

From his vantage point, the gunmage saw the kommandos freeze, holding position just out of the Cygnarans' sights, crouched behind trees or drifts of snow. Now that the Cygnarans were actively searching that way, however, it could only be a matter of moments before the Khadorans were discovered.

This particular unit would not be coming to Vorona's aid any time soon.

Dignity gawped back at Atherton in various states of disbelief—though the spy was also clearly struggling to keep from snickering. The corporal, however, kept his attentions firmly fixed on Vorona's team, who had quickened their pace yet again.

"Something wrong?" Only when Dignity asked did Atherton realize he'd been mumbling aloud.

"Don't interrupt. Even for me, this takes some calculation." Still, only seconds later, he stopped to reload the single empty barrel. "All right. Go."

"'Go'? Go *where*?"

The gunmage was abruptly grateful that the chapping on his wind-battered cheeks effectively hid his blush. He only then realized that he hadn't actually *explained* the plan he'd just concocted.

"Are you sure?" she asked him, once he'd sheepishly done so. "You'll be on your own until we can—"

"Go, before they're too far ahead or some other unit comes out to reinforce them."

Dignity, Ledeson, and the others faded away, forgotten memories in the haze, and Atherton began to mutter once more. "One-hundred . . . ninety-nine . . . ninety-eight . . ."

They flew by so quickly. Had the others gotten into position? Should he give them some extra . . . ?

"Seventy-three . . . seventy-two . . ."

No. They'd all heard the plan; he'd do them no favors by altering it now.

"Forty-eight . . . forty-seven . . ."

Vorona and the other Khadorans had now passed the halfway point between his position and the outermost reaches of the siege—and, potentially, escape into Khadoran ranks.

"Fifteen . . . fourteen . . ."

Angles, arcane formulae, and velocities ran through his head. Arcs, graphs, trajectories, all inked themselves over the world, drawn across his vision in lines of cobalt blue. As though planning to shoot the clouds themselves from their flight, he aimed both pistols skyward.

"Three . . . two . . .

"One."

The gunmage emptied the barrels two by two. Between each pair of shots, he lowered the guns a few degrees; reshaped the magic in the runebullets, shifting the balance of unnatural inertia from distance to impact, so that each would fly shorter, hit harder.

He knew that not only his targets, but also the Reds at the rear of the battle raging around Riversmet, might well hear the shots. But a few additional pistol rounds, from such a distance? What possible harm could those do?

All eight of Atherton's runebullets, their angles and speeds perfectly meshed, landed amidst the Winter Guard escort only fractions of a second apart; and though the power in each varied, even the weakest was a cannon shell unto itself.

Atherton saw it all, heard it all—the blasts, the screams, the raining dirt—and smiled.

A smile that died as swiftly as Atherton's own targets had, at the coming of a *new* series of sounds. Thumps. Clangs. Hisses. The heavy, plodding footsteps of heavy, plodding creatures.

From *behind*.

His fists full of empty pistol, Atherton slowly turned, the hem of his coat slicing a shallow crescent into the snow.

Four soulless visors in four crimson suits of steam-powered armor glared over a bristling array of axes and chain-blades.

That these were almost assuredly not the *same* Man-O-War troops he'd won past earlier, unless the snowdrifts had slowed the powerful armor far less than it had the Cygnarans, did little to improve the situation.

Godsdamn it, not now! *Not here! I've got so much more ahead of me . . . I'm supposed to do so much more than this . . .*

"Gentlemen." He hoped, prayed, his voice sounded as insouciant as he intended, that the faint tremor was wholly in his mind.

"Drop the weapons, Cygnaran. Now." The accent was thicker than the armor plating, and Atherton wasn't even certain from which Man-O-War it had come, but he understood it all the same.

"Of course."

Two pepperbox pistols tumbled to the snow . . .

Four pairs of eyes, hidden behind visors, flickered to follow . . .

Atherton dove into a forward roll, leaving a peculiar trench in the white slush. The Man-O-War soldiers started; all had weapons raised, yes, but all had expected him to run. That he would *close* some of the distance, one man against four soldiers in Man-O-War armor, was enough to stun them, however briefly.

The gunmage came up running. In his right fist he clenched the forgelock he carried at his back—a powerful weapon, yes, but not against armor like this.

The two axe-wielders raised their shields, each of which sported a miniature cannon in its center. The other two, with the chain-swords and grenade launchers, refrained from firing on him; at this range, their ordnance was all but suicidal.

Atherton passed them to one side, so that the nearest shield cannon-wielder blocked any shot the other might take. For a second, he faced not four opponents, but only one.

The forgelock fired first, if only just, but "just" was enough. Guided by an unnatural skill and even less natural sorceries, the bullet hurtled down the center of the cannon's barrel. The shell within erupted, taking shield, cannon, and arm along with it. Blood and steam spewed, a grotesquely beautiful geyser, and the steel figure toppled.

Glaring defiantly at the other three faceless soldiers, Atherton tossed the forgelock—its own barrel mangled by the runebullet it was never designed to accommodate—aside.

Not even bothering with cannon, now, the remaining axeman advanced on him, the other two following a step behind.

"I'll expect you to tell people all about how I did that," the gunmage informed them. This time he *knew* his voice shook; he could only hope they didn't notice. "It's the least you can do."

Axe-blade rose; chain-swords roared.

Atherton shut his eyes . . .

***

Winter Guard infantry lay scattered, limp and broken toys with which the gods were well and truly done playing. Gaust's bombardment had been brutal, raining death first in the midst of the formation, then broadening to both sides, so that even those soldiers with the reflexes to dodge one incoming volley had hurled themselves into the path of the next. Half a dozen or more, dead already; most of the remainder injured, or at least dazed, hurled prone by the blasts or by their attempts to *escape* the blasts.

One man, older and more grizzled than the rest, rose shakily, took three stumbling steps toward Vorona, hand outstretched either to help her stand or to take possession of her satchel. Either way, the opportunity passed him by.

Not unlike a snowman un-melting, Ledeson rose from the white-carpeted earth. A shadow of a nightmare, the commando had closed undetected in the seconds following the deadly torrent. His trench knife danced across the Khadoran officer's throat, singing a gleeful soprano as it grated on bone.

Ledeson caught the dead man's blunderbuss and blasted another of the groggy Winter Guardsmen off his feet. Six or seven yards away, a trio of Khadorans had taken what feeble cover they could, lying prone in a shallow depression. From there, they exchanged fire with the other Cygnaran soldiers who, lacking Ledeson's stealth, had attacked from farther back.

The Winter Guard still held the benefit of numbers, but only marginally, and the chaos and confusion of the Cygnaran strike more than countered that advantage. Bridges of bullets linked the warring sides, and two more Khadorans fell, their furs bleeding until they looked freshly hunted and skinned. Distracted, deafened by the firefight, they never noticed Ledeson moving behind them, carbine in one hand, blood-smeared blade in the other . . .

Vorona, clearly, wasn't about to wait around to see how it all worked out, especially not with reinforcements almost in sight. She rose from her crouch, one hand steadying the satchel hanging from her shoulder . . .

"Hello again, Vorona."

"Garland."

Her voice remained steady as ever, but Dignity was gratified to note the faintest widening of the enemy's eyes, the brief tic in her cheek.

"Care to drop the bag and leave?" Dignity asked, gesturing with the pistol in her right fist. "I'm willing to extend the offer. Once."

The Khadoran laughed. "Do you think me so stupid as to still have the documents on me? Knowing that I would be your first target, were you to somehow catch up?"

Both women flinched at the ear-splitting clap of a grenade detonating somewhere uncomfortably close—the Cygnaran unit had at last located the Khadoran kommandos, and reacted accordingly—but neither took her eyes off the other.

"You wouldn't trust anyone else, certainly no mere *soldier*, with the formula," Dignity said. "And you never *expected* us to catch up."

Again Dignity read her answer in Vorona's expressions, indistinct as they might be.

"You're hurt. You're exhausted. Drop the bag and go."

Vorona's shoulders slumped. "All right. You win." She closed her fingers around the flap of the satchel, flexed her shoulder so that the loose strap slipped down her arm . . .

And hurled it underhand, like an inverted trebuchet, at Dignity's head.

Or rather, where Dignity's head had been. She was ducking aside before the bag left Vorona's grasp, anticipating just such a maneuver. Still, the hurtling lump of canvas briefly obscured her view, and by the time it cleared, Vorona, too, had her finger on the trigger of a pistol.

Each operative spun while she fired, sliding sideways, plunging into awkward crouches to clear the other's line of fire. The two guns bellowed with a single voice, the two bullets penetrated empty air rather than flesh and blood.

What Dignity did *not* expect was for her opponent's spent forgelock to come hurtling her way immediately after. She swayed aside, easily evading the clumsy missile, but by then Vorona was already on her—*Gods, how did she move so fast with that leg?!*—her blade flashing.

Dignity, too, became a whirlwind of thrashing limbs, parrying the knife with her own empty pistol. Here she landed a kick, there an open-hand blow, but never with any significant impact; the Khadoran simply rolled with those few strikes she couldn't avoid.

She felt Vorona's left hand closing on her forearm in what was surely meant to be a painful, perhaps even bone-breaking joint lock. She yanked herself desperately aside . . .

Directly into a high crescent kick.

The world spun; Dignity was certain that only the clinging snow kept her from being hurled into the overcast skies. Three separate Voronas confronted her, sliding around and overlapping, discourteously refusing to settle down.

And that, too, had been with the injured leg! She could only assume that she'd be down, possibly unconscious, had Vorona been at her peak.

Dignity rolled backward, ignoring the added vertigo as best she could, swallowing her rising gorge.

Vorona kept pace with a single stride, launching another kick meant to catch Dignity off-balance. Again she struck with her wounded leg; presumably she felt it wouldn't support her weight if she kicked with the other.

Dignity threw out an arm to absorb the blow that might well have cracked ribs. She swore she felt the humerus *flex*, and her whole body tried to lock up in shock—but the bone held, and Dignity refused to freeze.

Instead she twisted into the kick and brought her other fist down on the injured thigh.

The Khadoran fell back, screaming. Blood roiled from the reopened gash, and the whole limb trembled. It required neither Dignity's training nor experience to know that leg was about to give out entirely.

263

Still the woman refused to fall. Still she held the knife steady in her hand.

And while Dignity's own vision was clearing, the vertigo fading, the ground still trembled. It only gradually dawned on her, to her growing horror, that each tremor was accompanied by a crushing *boom*.

Warjacks; warjacks resembling a mountain of steel sprouting from the soil, far nearer than the fringes of the siege. Around them swarmed soldiers, in far greater numbers than the previous team. A second unit of reinforcements had come to retrieve Vorona, and Dignity was out of time.

Vorona sneered and, as best her injury would permit, leapt for the fallen satchel and the prize within.

Dignity dove the other way, and came up clutching a fallen Winter Guard's blunderbuss.

The weapon roared. Vorona tumbled aside as best she could and vanished, rolling behind a snowdrift. An ugly, uneven smear of blood marked her wake.

Was she alive? Dead? Dignity desperately needed to know, but the mighty 'jacks were raising arm-mounted cannon, the soldiers their blunt-nosed rifles. She even heard the baying of some vicious, ravenous beast from the forefront of the oncoming enemy.

Fighting every burning desire in her roiling soul, she sprinted instead to the satchel. Snagging it without slowing, she slung it over her shoulder and ran, a tide of gray furs and bloodred steel rising rapidly behind.

***

"Unidentified approach, Sergeant!"

It was far, far from the first time they'd heard that call. After making way to display for them the tumult and carnage of the ongoing siege, to show off the rolling multicolored throngs, winter had clamped its fists around them yet again. The flurries were light, but still thick enough to hide behind, and where the snow remained sheer, the less tangible haze was more than happy to fill in the gaps.

This was, in fact, the *third* such warning raised by the scouts. The first time, it had been a Cygnaran squad, pulling out to regroup and reequip. After a few moments of questioning to ensure that the uniforms weren't faked or stolen, they'd allowed squad five to continue on their way, assuming they belonged to some local division other than their own.

On the second occasion, things hadn't been so simple. Khadoran blood and scraps of uniform still clung to everyone's boots.

Benwynne snapped the carbine to her shoulder, ready to take aim the instant she saw a target. Around her, the few surviving long-gunners did the same, while the trenchers crouched low over rifles or the last pair of surviving chain guns. From behind, she heard grinding as Wolfhound raised axe and cannon.

"Check your sightlines!" Benwynne snapped in reminder. She knew her people were exhausted beyond reason; knew it, because she felt the same. But they couldn't afford the mistakes exhaustion so often heralded. "Remember, it could be—"

"Garland!" The call came from Private Markham, positioned near Wendell and the 'jack. "Hold fire!"

Damn, the kid's got good eyes! It took Benwynne another few seconds to be certain, but he was absolutely right. Running like the legions of Cryx were on her heels and their dragon-god circling above, the spy burst from the thickening flurries. When she slid to a halt beside Benwynne, her gasps were ragged and uneven. The satchel swinging from her shoulder nearly pulled her over at the sudden stop.

"Is that . . . ?"

The winded spy could only nod. The sergeant felt something slimy uncoil from around her soul and slither away.

"Peeked . . . on my way . . . just to be sure . . ." Garland wheezed. "It's in . . ."

Again the forward scouts warned of an approach, again the squad braced, and again it proved unnecessary. Ledeson staggered into view, looking only marginally less exhausted than the spy.

"Are you all that made it?" Benwynne asked softly.

"Renwick took a bullet before we killed most of the Winter Guardsmen." Though bent and leaning on his knees, Ledeson raised his gaze to meet hers. "The last Red blew himself up with a grenade. Took Sterling and Shaw with him."

Damn it! Damn, damn, damn . . . "And Gaust?"

"We . . . don't know, Sergeant."

"Morrow's name . . ." *How many more of us is this going to take?!*

"Sergeant Bracewell," Garland said, having finally caught her breath, "I'm sorry, but we have to mourn later. There's a heavy squad just minutes behind me."

Instantly, Benwynne was all business. "Nature and number?"

"I elected not to hang around and count. But multiple units of assault troops, at least one of which has a bloody drooling war-dog on a chain.

"And two heavy 'jacks bringing up the rear." Garland shook her head. "It'll take those longer to reach us, but the others can swarm us under, or at least delay us for the big guns to—"

"Go."

"What?"

"Head northeast," the sergeant ordered. *Where's this coming from? Who the hell's talking? These aren't my words, are they?*

But they were. Benwynne knew what was coming, knew what had to be done—even if she couldn't admit it, yet, to herself.

"You'll find a steamboat, captained by a man called Loumbard. Ledeson and . . ." She studied her people, finally settling on the young long-gunner. "Markham. You two are on escort duty."

"Sergeant—" Markham began, at the same time as Ledeson's "With all due respect—"

"I'm *not asking*!"

Both men saluted and took position beside Garland.

"Markham, Loumbard knows you. Have him take you a few miles upstream at full steam. That should buy you whatever time we can't."

Garland's shoulders tensed; Benwynne could see it even through the coat. "What do you mean, 'that we can't'?"

"Once you disembark," she continued, ignoring the question, "you ought to be far enough from the front to cut south and then back around to Merywyn. Getting a boat home from there shouldn't be difficult."

"Sergeant—"

"You can't ask us to—"

"I'm not—"

"You know what's at stake here." Her smile looked palpably artificial. It had to—she felt like she was stretching muscles she'd forgotten she had—but she forced it all the same. "It's been an honor serving with you. Now *go.*"

Never had she seen three healthy adults move so stiffly, shuffle so reluctantly from sight, scarcely noting where they stepped because they were too busy looking back the way they'd come.

But they went, and if any tears were shed, the trio did Benwynne and the others the courtesy of concealing them until distance and weather swallowed them up.

"You *all* know what's at stake here," she repeated, this time to the tattered, sorry remains of what had so recently been one of Cygnar's foremost Unorthodox Engagement Teams. "Garland *has* to get those documents back home. We can*not* let the enemy catch her up.

"I'm sorry this falls to us, but we're going to make the Reds a lot sorrier. I know you'll make his Majesty, and all Cygnar, proud of you. As you've already made me.

"Hop to it!"

Snow fountained as trenchers dug shallow holes—poor cover indeed, but better than none—and jammed chain gun tripods deep into the slush. Wendell's mechaniks swarmed around Wolfhound, ensuring its joints flexed smoothly, its cannon was clear. At random distances, in random directions, they scattered heavy shells, ensuring the 'jack and its support crew would have immediate access to ammunition.

Benwynne, as well as the remaining long-gunners, sought cover of their own. Most dropped to their bellies behind shallow bulges in the snow or the terrain beneath; several, the sergeant included, crouched in the lee of the sporadic evergreens.

"Ben . . ."

She recognized the voice; hell, she recognized the crunch of his steps. "You probably ought to find a more secure position, Master Sergeant. I don't think this tree is broad enough to shelter the both of us."

"We need to talk."

In the distance, only lightly obscured by the freshly accumulating haze, the world began to bleed. Benwynne knew what she was seeing, long before the crimson smear resolved itself into individual troops.

"This really isn't the time," she pointed out.

"I don't know that we'll have another. Ben, please. I need you to hear this. What happened in Bainsmarket and Fisherbrook—"

"Don't." Benwynne's palms were sweating, the lining of her gloves soaked despite the cold. *So damn many of them . . .*

And behind those, beyond the crimson bloom of the oncoming soldiers, loomed larger shapes. Not yet near enough to be clearly seen, not nearly so fast as the charging men, but unmistakable. Had the earth been dry and clear, she might already feel the footsteps; though she knew it was impossible, she swore she smelt the choking smoke of their furnaces.

"Don't," she said again, finally facing him—as much so she wouldn't have to watch the oncoming storm, as for his sake. "Duty can be a . . . demanding liege. I understand. I really do."

Wendell's beard crinkled, but his smile was the saddest, Benwynne thought, that she'd ever seen. "But you don't forgive."

It was absolutely not a question.

"Master Ser—Wendell . . . I haven't had *time*. And it . . ." The Khadorans were near enough, now, to distinguish their cries, and the feral baying of the war-hound, from the background chaos of the larger battle beyond. Perhaps, though the slate-hued daylight made it hard to be sure, even to see their breath on the air. Behind them, the scarlet-steel giants grew ever more solid, stepping from some half-forgotten nightmare into the waking world. "It doesn't seem that I'm likely to, now."

Her voice cracked, there at the end. The mechanik began to turn away.

"Wendell . . ." Before she could talk herself out of it, she reached out. "For what it's worth, I think . . . I would have tried."

His hand clasped hers: an anchor, a reminder of everything she fought for. His smile was no longer sad.

Sergeant Benwynne Bracewell hefted her carbine, called out her final orders, and opened fire.

AFTER-ACTION REPORT

Trineus 2nd, 605 AR
Corvis, Cygnar

"**. . . d**elighted you made it back safely . . ."

Dignity stood at attention, focused on the Golden Cygnus hanging behind the commander adept's shoulder. She scarcely saw him at all, or the desk at which he sat.

". . . remarkable service for your nation, and possibly saved the entire war effort . . ."

She didn't want to be here. She was exhausted, utterly wiped out from the frenzied and often terrifying race for home.

". . . owes you a great debt . . ."

She'd already made her report to the CRS via Colonel Mathis, who'd been waiting on Corvis's docks when she stepped off the boat, limp and battered. She'd told him everything, leaving out not one detail. She'd turned over the documents without delay or preamble. (The genuine ones, at any rate. The fakes . . . One never knew when something like that might come in handy, did one?) Everything since then had been repetition or ceremony, even when Commander Nemo himself had arrived to congratulate her.

(Well, to take possession of the formula, no doubt; congratulating her was, at best, a secondary priority.)

Now, all she wanted was the chance to sleep for about three weeks, a hot meal that rivaled her own body in weight, and—just maybe—a few last answers.

The officer and inventor seemed, finally, to recognize that his speechifying was falling on deaf, or at least unappreciative, ears. "What's on your mind, Lieutenant?"

Dignity finally forced herself to pay attention. "Sir, nobody's told me how anything worked out." Then, at the befuddlement that tweaked his moustache, "I don't mean the documents. I mean the others."

"Ah."

"Baron Halcourt? Lieutenant Laddermore? Did they make it out?"

Nemo nodded. "Indeed they did. Our Ordic friend was as good as his word. Laddermore is, in fact, on her way to Corvis as we speak. And it's actually *Captain* Laddermore now. Or it will be, once she arrives and we can make it formal."

That, at least, was *some* of the load off her shoulders. "Glad to hear it, sir. She's more than earned it." Any relief she felt, however, didn't last long. "And Bracewell's squad, sir? Any word at all?"

"Most of our lines of communication to the region were severed when Riversmet fell. No, we haven't heard anything.

"But, Underhurst . . . I think you know as well as I do that we'd have heard nothing anyway."

Dignity felt a sudden, powerful need to study the threadbare carpet at the foot of the desk.

"You're here because of their bravery," he reminded her. "Khador didn't acquire the formula—our greatest weapons haven't been rendered useless—because of their sacrifice."

"Somehow, it doesn't feel like enough, sir."

When Nemo answered, the formal, iron-spined, overbearing officer spoke as gently as she'd ever heard him. "It never does, Underhurst. It truly never does."

Trineus 9th, 605 AR
Rorschik, Khador

"Is this necessary?"

"Not at all," the stooped, thickly bearded physician replied. "If you wish for the pain to return, that is entirely your prerogative."

Vorona's snarl would have crowned her the alpha of any wolf pack, but she took the mug of bitter muck and choked it down. All her protestations aside, she eagerly awaited the concoction's numbing effects. Some days, it was all that made her leg or her ribs bearable.

The journey from Llael to Khador had passed in a fever dream of agony and infection—the most horrific experience in her life, made marginally more tolerable by the fact that she could remember only a fraction of it.

The first few days, once she'd finally reached a surgery with the necessary physicians and equipment to tend her injuries, were almost as bad. Not only was survival a hit-or-miss proposition, but it might well have been the *less* attractive option.

It was weeks, now, since her leg had been sewn up, the many pellets of shot dug from her flesh. The surgeons told her, again and again, how astonishing her progress had been. Vorona, herself, felt no surprise at all; of *course* she was stronger than this. She had a ways to go, yet, but she knew—she *knew*—she would manage it, and more.

She had to. For Khador, too much was at stake for her to fail.

Only when she'd awakened and proved so resilient, when her recovery had progressed a good ways, had anyone bothered to inform her of all that had transpired. Garland's recovery of the documents was a canker on her soul, but that wasn't the worst of it.

No, her ever burning, searing hatred was reserved for one Oswinne Muir, and the nation of Ord.

Everyone believed that the Cygnaran baron had somehow escaped Leryn almost a week after Vorona was injured, a week after the playwright had led his "cultural delegation" across the fields of battle and back home. But Vorona, Vorona knew better. She'd been in Leryn; had eyes throughout the city; spent long days watching Surros Manor.

And there was *no. Godsdamn. Way!* that Halcourt and his household of imbeciles had come up with a viable escape plan and snuck from the city unaided. Nor was it remotely likely that Cygnar had succeeded in inserting yet another team of operatives into Leryn so soon.

Which meant the baron and his sycophants had departed earlier than the evidence suggested. And so far as Vorona could see, that allowed for only a single possibility.

The pain held at bay by her fury as much as by the elixir, she forced herself up, stepped carefully across the room to stand beside a hardwood table. Atop it, a basin of water, a bowl of fruit, and various toiletries. She leaned on the wood, and fumed.

So, Ord conspired with the enemy while hiding behind their neutrality? That worthless, rodent of a nation, crouched—as it should be—at Khador's feet? Oh, they would learn the price of deception, would come to envy *the fate of Llael!*

Not yet, no. Vorona knew the ways of politics, of diplomacy. Her theories alone wouldn't convince the high command to move, nor was she prepared to risk an international incident on a hunch, no matter how certain.

But she *could* turn Section Three—and perhaps the Prizak Chancellery, if she spoke convincingly enough—to uncovering the truth. And then, when she had her proof . . .

"Doctor Dvoynev, kindly fetch my coat. I believe I'm up to paying Kommandant Kosorokov a visit. We have much to speak of."

"Oh, certainly."

The voice was far too close behind her, and very definitely *not* the doctor's.

Even wounded, slowed by the drug, Vorona lashed back with a high elbow that should have crushed cartilage, cracked bone. Instead, she felt a hand slap against her arm, deflecting the attack—at the same instant a lance of fire pierced her side.

She felt herself spasm, the air flood from her lungs in a silent scream, her bladder release. Her head rebounded from the table's edge as she fell, and she recognized a peculiar sensation—a strange pressure in the midst of the pain—as a length of steel *sliding out* of her right kidney.

Flopping very much like a trout smacked from its upstream leap by a hungry grizzly, she flipped herself over to stare into the face of her murderer.

"That . . ." She could no longer tell if she was actually speaking, or if her lips moved in silence. "That's not . . ."

"Not possible?" The man placed the knife that had killed her beside the corpse that had once been Doctor Dvoynev. She recognized the blade that had slain the doctor as one of her own.

Probably hid a pouch of Cygnaran gold swans somewhere on the body, just for good measure. It's what she'd have done . . .

Her assassin carefully wiped the blood from his hand and then stroked his neatly trimmed goatee. "I shouldn't be here? This place is too secure?" He *tsk*ed his tongue a few times. "Did you imagine his Majesty recruited me solely for my intricate storytelling and witty dialogue? Getting in wasn't that difficult. Getting out ought to be child's play."

"Oof. 'Child's play'? Such a cliché. I really need to come up with a more original line when I file the report on all this."

"Why are . . . in Khador . . . ?"

He knelt, inches out of reach—just in case she had one last strike left in her. "We're not at war, remember? One of my troupes is performing *An Orgoth Goes a'Courting* over in Volningrad. I figured I'd make a brief detour to scenic Rorschik. Should be back before anyone knows I'm not just snoring off a wild night in a private room somewhere."

Now he did hunch inward, his face so near her own. "Sounds like I almost waited too long to come calling. Did you really think we wouldn't suspect *your* suspicions? That we could afford to let you live with them?"

"You . . . You can't hide . . . hide what you've done from us . . . forever."

"My dear Vorona . . ." said Oswinne Muir, "I think you'll find that we can. Or rather, I suppose, you won't. Dead, and all that."

Something wet gurgled in her throat as she tried to retort, and then, blessedly, the pain began to fade.

Alas, the heat of her rage, and the light of the world around her, went with it.

Date unknown
Location unknown

Mold clung to the walls in sheets, accumulated in rivulets between the bricks. The room itself was sick, the mucus ever-flowing. The straw that was the chamber's carpet sagged in spots, drenched by those horrific droplets; poked and stabbed in others, dried and stiffened by the perpetual cold.

He wore rags, and they did nothing to keep the chill from his skin. His only illumination was a single lamp burning beyond the tiny window in the iron-banded door, and it was never enough for his light-starved vision. Filth, the room's and his own both, coated him in layers. The grime actually kept him warmer than the rags did.

How long had he been here? Where *was* here? He'd no way of knowing, and he doubted the guards would tell him even if he were to give them the satisfaction of asking. Weeks might have passed in his pain-drenched fugue; more weeks, perhaps even months, since he came out of it. And in all that time, he had seen nothing but the walls of the cell, no one but the guards who occasionally brought him murky water and gristly gruel. They hadn't even bothered to interrogate him yet.

And why should they rush? What was the hurry? He looked to his left wrist, chafing beneath the manacle that bound him to the wall. He looked to his right wrist—or rather, where it should have been. Old, encrusted bandages marked off the length of his arm, sheered away midpoint between wrist and elbow by the roaring chain-sword of a Khadoran Man-O-War. His hip throbbed, where he had caught the edge of a brutal battle-axe. Clearly, he was going nowhere. Clearly, he was no threat.

They were right, of course. He *was* no threat. Not today. Not now.

But maybe, just maybe, tomorrow. Or the next day. Or the next.

They had taken his freedom. They had taken his hand.

They hadn't taken away who he *was*.

The guards carried guns. And one day, he would remind them that where he commanded, guns obeyed.

Through the pain, through the hunger, through the filth, through the despair, Atherton Gaust stared at the door to his cell, and grinned.

THE IRON KINGDOMS

CYGNAR

The Kingdom of Cygnar has no lack of gold, iron, timber, food, gems, rock quarries, or any other resource coveted by a modern nation. It is a state boasting many great minds, which have pushed advances in alchemy and mechanika to new heights, giving the nation a technological edge over its neighbors. Its warjacks boast inventive armaments that harness the power of electricity, and they bow to the will of their warcasters, who are trained at one of the two finest military academies in all the Iron Kingdoms.

From the time of the Corvis Treaties, Cygnar has bordered each of the kingdoms those treaties created: Ord to the northwest, Khador on the far side of the Thornwood Forest, and Llael to the northeast. The Bloodstone Marches made up its eastern border until the Cygnaran Civil War, which gave rise to the Protectorate of Menoth. Khador's invasion of Llael has put Cygnar on the offensive, as it struggles to help its northern ally stave off the Khadoran juggernaut. The loss of the Thornwood and the Black River would separate Llael from Cygnar and diminish hopes for the smaller kingdom to regain its autonomy.

Cygnar endured political upheaval in recent times when Leto Raelthorne, "the Younger," ousted his tyrannical brother King Vinter IV, "the Elder." The deposed king managed to escape before being put on trial for his crimes. Nearly a decade later, he reappeared from the Bloodstone Marches with strange allies from the far reaches of eastern Immoren. Since his return, the former king has created constant peril on Cygnar's eastern border, even attempting to seize Corvis in 603 AR. While it has never been easy to wear the Cygnaran crown, King Leto has borne more burdens than most sovereigns have to bear, yet there persists a growing divide within the nation between those who support their king and those who are discontented by the privations of interminable warfare . . . and beginning to conspire to arrange for a different sovereign to occupy the throne.

KHADOR

The people of Khador are tough, irascible, weathered, and proud. They learned well from the ancient days, when man endured through strength of mind and body, and see no reason to court folly and weakness now. The north keeps deep and ancient customs derived from a time when tribal horselords roamed its vast forests and mountains and ruled the Khardic Empire supported by priests of the ancient god Menoth.

To better understand these hard-hearted northerners, consider that much of Khador is frozen five months out of the year. Strong winds snap trees in half, and sudden snows sweep in so fast that entire wagon trains can vanish in mere seconds. Only a harsh people could hope to survive in such harsh environs. Khador's military personifies this strength, with huge warjacks thundering along next to indomitable men and women armed to the teeth with axes and guns. Over the last century enlightened leaders have done much to modernize the Khadoran military, and while its mechaniks prefer simplicity and rugged design over needless complication, their engineering and mechanika have nonetheless become very nearly the equal of Cygnar's, and the soldiers themselves are often superior.

Morrowans form the majority in Khador, as they do in Cygnar, Llael, and Ord, but not an overwhelming one, as the Menite faith is stronger in the north than anywhere outside the Protectorate. Regardless of personal faith, Khadorans love their sovereign above all. They are a patriotic people who have always chafed at the compromises made in the Corvis Treaties, for they lionize the days of the old Khardic Empire and seek every opportunity to restore its glory. Every so often, as is currently the case, a new sovereign ascends the throne and declares the time ripe to reclaim lands that are rightfully

Khadoran. Even the Kossite and Skirov tribes no longer care to remember that they once stood as independent kingdoms. Now all Khadorans long for the rebirth of their empire and are willing to put aside personal comforts—or even sacrifice their lives, if necessary—to achieve this goal.

PROTECTORATE
OF MENOTH

For years historians and politicians both have pretended the Protectorate of Menoth was not a nation of its own because the agreements that ended the Cygnaran Civil War left it technically beholden to Cygnar's crown. Over time those obligations proved to be a farce, and now it is clear the Protectorate stands as the youngest of the Iron Kingdoms, with prospects for long-term survival that seem more promising with each passing year.

Caspia was divided in the aftermath of the Cygnaran Civil War. The larger, western portion of the city remained part of Cygnar, while the eastern portion across the Black River became Sul, capital of the Protectorate. This placed bitter enemies in close proximity, with only towering walls and a rushing river between their heavily armed garrisons. The rest of the Protectorate stretches east and southeast into an arid and resource-poor region adjacent to the dangerous Bloodstone Marches.

Sul-Menites practice a strict form of worship and believe their only chance of evading endless torment in the afterlife is obedience to the True Law. Priests and scrutators instill a terror of the clergy in the population, teaching the people to obey without question and to expect the lash for expressing the slightest doubt. Perhaps because of these harsh measures, the Menite faith has been in slow decline for many centuries, steadily losing ground to the (moderately) more benevolent message of the Church of Morrow.

The recent appearance of the so-called "Harbinger of Menoth" has provided the spark the Menites have long sought to revitalize their faith. This young woman emerged from an obscure town on the fringes of the Protectorate and displayed clear signs of miraculous contact with the divine, including the fact that her feet refuse to touch the unclean earth. It is said she sometimes communes directly with Menoth, and can even speak his words. Witnessing her visage has prompted thousands of foreigner Menites to immediately convert to her cause, pull up their roots, and relocate to the Protectorate.

CRYX

The Scharde Islands lurk in the pirate-infested waters past the Broken Coast of western Cygnar. The largest isle hosts the capital of the nightmare empire of Cryx. The island's jagged, foreboding coastline hints at the realm's true nature—a land even more grim and treacherous than it appears. Its vicious forests and mountains are home to blighted trollkin, twisted men, and various warped half-breeds. These peoples may resemble races of the mainland, but the cruel culture of the island and the necromantic energies pervading the kingdom have transformed them into something malicious and vile.

The inhabitants of this land live under the shadow of their ruler, Lord Toruk the Dragonfather—the first dragon. Those who obey his governing lich lords and the priests of his cult deem him a god. Toruk is the source of the malignance that radiates from this island as a palpable energy, the blight that affects every plant and animal in his kingdom. A master of undeath, he has gifted his chosen vassals with unnatural immortality as the undead, which walk alongside the living in the bleak cities of his empire.

The Dragonfather has dominated his territory for sixteen centuries, and his privateers terrorize the western coasts of Cygnar and Ord by preying on shipping routes and pillaging lightly defended villages for their resources and inhabitants alike. Entire communities have vanished after Cryxian raids, the inhabitants seized and presumably added to the undead armies. Although Toruk seems content to rule his remote island realm, the mainland nations fear the day he decides to expand his borders, and it seems likely this day has come to pass. Those at the higher echelons of other nations have discovered that Cryxian bases exist hidden within their own borders, underground or amid the trackless wilds, and from these places of power Toruk is starting to extend his reach. The true goals of these forces are still not well understood, and the movements Cryxian military units often defy ordinary notions of strategy and tactics.

LLAEL

Llael's primary geographical advantage turned out to be its greatest weakness: sharing its borders with four kingdoms with few natural barriers to inhibit trade—or the movement of armies. This served to line the pockets of certain entrepreneurial nobles and merchants, who exploited the shipping along the Black River flowing from Rhul to the Gulf of Cygnar. Llael's merchants were centrally located to serve as middlemen for a variety of lucrative mercantile organizations, while its gentle valleys and lush farmlands offered few barriers to slow the advance of the soldiers who marched to seize them starting at the end of 604 AR.

It may be an overreliance on Cygnaran soldiers and mercenaries led to a certain denial among the Llaelese people about their vulnerability. Llael earned its early fame during the Rebellion against the Orgoth for being the birthplace of blasting powder, and long boasted many of the finest pistoleers and alchemists in western Immoren. Unfortunately, these talents were directed more to commercial gain and less to bolstering the kingdom's rotting defenses and inadequate military. Instead, its people spent their time in appreciation of the finer things in life, from expensive locally produced wines to great books written in their native tongue, works of art, music, and architecture, all sponsored by bickering nobles competing to control the trade that was the nation's lifeblood.

Corruption from within hastened the Khadoran invasion and occupation of the small country. Llael's last king died decades before, and his heirs all fell prey to murderous conspiracies by those seeking to exploit the chaos. The nobles who came after allowed Llael's small army to languish, relying increasingly on foreign aid and unreliable sell-swords. The nation's renowned pistoleers became duelists and assassins for hire rather than protectors of its borders. The Llaelese people now suffer the consequences of this neglect, as they're forced to contend with the fallout of full-scale military invasion.

ORD

The western kingdom of Ord is a land with deep history and its own rich culture, but one that lacks the natural resources of most truly great kingdoms, being a moody realm of foggy bogs, wet marshes, and backbreaking hilly farmland. Land-owning castellans maintain themselves on herds of cattle and horses, aloof from the masses struggling to put food on the table. The Ordic people are tough and not easily discomfited, though. They find diversion in song, gambling, and ale rather than dwelling on life's inequities.

Most of Ord's people descend from the old kingdom of Tordor, famed for its powerful warships, and the lure of the sea is still strong among those who dwell here. Ord's coastal cities are a sailor's paradise, and the nation boasts the best human mariners ever to live; the Ordic Royal Navy is counted a peer among those of western Immoren's greater powers. The Ordic army is also highly respected despite its smaller size and outmoded weaponry as compared to the northern and southern powers. Its soldiers are deemed as tough as trollkin and have courage to spare, but the poverty of Ord is reflected in its reliance on simpler gear and its heavy use of defensive tactics, such as fixed cannon emplacements and using knowledge of the difficult local terrain against any aggressors. Ord's clever sovereign, King Baird II, has taken measures to improve Ord's lot and spent the nation's meager treasury to bolster both navy and army with certain advances, but remaining neutral in the larger wars is still deemed vital to the nation's survival.

Staying neutral has other advantages, as Ord's merchant houses benefit considerably from trade brought through the region between parties who might not otherwise be willing to interact. Certain Ordic towns and hamlets have become favored haunts of mercenaries and sell-swords of all varieties.

Similarly, refugees from war-torn lands often flee to Ord, bringing with them their talents and knowledge. For a nation lacking in natural wealth, the exchange of information has become an industry unto itself.

RHUL

Compared to the dynamic kingdoms of men, the dwarven Rhulfolk are a bastion of order and reason. Their society has persisted without major upheaval for over a thousand years, and the history of Rhul traces back longer than any other established civilization in the known world. Even their armed disputes are more like duels than wars, being organized and adjudicated by the dwarven parliament, known among their own kind as the Moot. The traditional leaders of the Moot are the Stone Lords, aged and respected dwarves who can trace their bloodline all the way back to the thirteen Great Fathers—divine progenitors of the dwarven race. The other members of the Moot are representatives from the Hundred Houses, the most powerful of the landed clans. It is this group that is responsible for forging the laws of dwarven society, using an incredibly lengthy set of procedural rules dwarves call the Codex.

Across all the known lands Rhulfolk are renowned for their fine craftsmanship and their prowess as engineers and builders. Any child knows the quality of dwarven metalwork and stonecraft, and the stout folk's skill at mining and love of building is matched only by their ingenuity in mechanikal engineering. Yet equally prized by non-dwarves is the famed Rhulic skill in battle. While their society is eminently stable, mastery at arms and warfare is a craft undertaken with the same serious attention as any other. Every dwarf clan boasts its own great warriors, and many of these seek to earn distinction, profit, and a sharpening of their skills in the (many) wars that take place outside their borders.

To wit, entire dwarven conclaves beholden to Rhulic law exist in several of the human kingdoms, and these communities are deemed invaluable sources of skilled labor, quality crafted goods, and reliable sell-swords. It is widely understood that these mercenaries are ultimately still devoted and loyal to Rhul, and that they would immediately return to their homeland should it ever need defended from outsider aggression.

THE MORROWAN CALENDAR

Dwarven astronomers developed the first known calendar, based on their observation of the relative interplay between the planet (Caen), its three moons, and the stars in the sky. The race of men adopted it after the rise of the Morrowan faith, but installed their own naming convention. The calendar consists of thirteen months of twenty-eight days each, with seven days to each week, and one intercalated day—called "the Longest Night"—every three years.

Month Number	Morrowan Name	Rhulic Name	Equatorial Period
1	Glaceus	Dovern	Early/mid-winter
2	Casteus	Uldern	Mid-winter
3	Trineus	Dolern	Mid-/late winter
4	Tempen	Ormul	Late winter/early spring
5	Cinten	Odul	Mid-spring
6	Rowen	Gordul	Mid-/late spring
7	Solesh	Lodar	Late spring/early summer
8	Octesh	Durgar	Mid-summer
9	Katesh	Odomar	Mid-summer
10	Goloven	Godesh	Late summer/early autumn
11	Doloven	Sigmon	Mid-autumn
12	Khadoven	Rordon	Mid-autumn
13	Ashtoven	Jhoron	Late autumn/early winter

ABOUT THE AUTHOR

ARI MARMELL would love to tell you all about the various esoteric jobs he held and the wacky adventures he had on the way to becoming an author, since that's what other authors seem to do in these sections. Unfortunately, he doesn't actually have any, as the most exciting thing about his professional life, besides his novel writing, is the work he's done for *Dungeons & Dragons* and other role-playing games. His published fiction includes the Widdershins Adventures YA fantasy series, along with *The Goblin Corps*, from Pyr Books; as well as multiple books from other major publishers, including the Corvis Rebaine duology and the official computer game tie-in novel *Darksiders: The Abomination Vault*.

Ari currently lives in an apartment that's almost as cluttered as his subconscious, which he shares (the apartment, not the subconscious, though sometimes it seems like it) with George—his wife—and two cats who really need some form of volume control installed. You can find Ari online at http://www.mouseferatu.com and on Twitter @mouseferatu.